D1614388

ANY FOOL CAN BE
A COUNTRY LOVER

Any Fool Can Be A Country Lover

JAMES ROBERTSON

Illustrations by Larry

BOOK CLUB ASSOCIATES LONDON

This omnibus edition published 1986 by
Book Club Associates
by arrangement with Pelham Books Ltd

Printed and bound in Great Britain by
Mackays of Chatham Ltd

CONTENTS

Any Fool Can Be A Country Lover

Chapter One

THE GAMES of love have always been among the most popular pastimes of the human race. Down the centuries every possible aspect has been explored, discussed, observed, tried and perfected on countless occasions.

In the countryside, games started young. Even at the village primary school, the sexes were separate and different from their first day when little girls played house and little boys showed each other how to castrate piglets. By the age of eleven the advanced little boys were already torn between birds' egg collecting with their contemporaries and shy dalliance with the willing pre-liberated little girls. By their early teens the river bank was sighing and sobbing on the warm summer nights when the owls hooted and the fish plopped and unwary tender flesh all too often brushed against the darkened nettles.

When it rained, the world of the lovers closed in a little. The church porch was a favoured location; so too was the shelter on the common which housed the war memorial tablet. It was partitioned off into four sections sharing the same centre and each with one side open, so that four different couples could find out how far the girl was prepared to go and whether the boy was capable of taking her there. With the rain pattering down on the shingle roof to drown the cries and groans, the names on the tablet could look down at yet another generation of local youth, courting as did they themselves with no living witnesses save the bland-faced, incurious Charity Webber's sheep.

For adults, particularly married adults, it was more difficult. Middle-aged matrons were not as keen to besport themselves in the hayloft as they might once have been and the sophistication of a motel room was beyond both the pocket and the imagination of all but a tiny minority. But they made do. Snow brought out the gossips like truffle hounds: more than one couple had been found out as a result of incautious gumboot tracks leading to a remote barn from opposite directions. Caravans, many of which lurked in the corners of fields where they were part of the summer infrastructure geared to the goal of fleecing the tourists, took on their main role as popular winter trysting grounds.

This was the game of love. Occasionally, or even not so occasionally, the participants believed the game was real. Women, when they reached a certain age, often succumbed. They looked at their approaching middle years and their dull, farting husbands and rebelled. Some found careers; some found God; some found the books of Erica Jong and feminism; but many found themselves a lover. The onset of a grand passion could have catastrophic effects on the stability of the small society of the parish. Down the generations, virtually everyone had come to be related to everyone else and, if one marriage became mixed up with another, particularly if either should unscramble itself, the consequences could reverberate for years, reshuffling families and friends until all were ultimately forced to come to terms with added layers of complication on their kinship.

A certain expertise had developed among many of the local men in detecting those women who lifted their heads above the parapets of their marriage to sniff the air. It was Kelvin, a widower who had farmed in a Cro-Magnon way on the edge of the village for forty-five years, who first observed the onset of the symptoms in Mandy. It was very acute of him as most people had never noticed a tender feeling inside her and they would put any moodiness down to dyspepsia rather than to the yearning angst which preceded love. He told everyone about it in the pub.

'Mandy is a bit down in the mouth,' he announced after he had taken a long draught of beer and smacked the glass down on the counter. 'She was talking to the vicar after the service on Sunday.'

'Perhaps she was apologizing for not going to his services every week,' suggested Bill, another elderly farmer. He was rumoured to be bald but he never took his hat off so that one could see. He kept it on because that was where he kept his money. 'He must have had a nasty shock seeing you there.'

'I told him I only went because I wanted a look at that bloke who paid £180,000 for Redworthy Farm. He looked a right stupid idiot too. But Mandy was doing a lot of praying and she's not the sort to do much praying if she's in her right mind. Cursing – she'd do a lot of that, but not praying.'

'That's true,' reflected Bill. 'Now you mention it, I met her down by the river the other day reading a book. I asked her what it was and she gave me a real funny look and said that it was poetry.'

'Aha! You know what that means!' exclaimed Kelvin. 'Poetry! You know what women go and do when they start reading poetry! I thought it might be something like that when I saw her praying.'

There was silence round the bar as everyone considered the implications. 'Poor Keith!' remarked the commander, a man who had been on the receiving end of his own form of cuckoldry when his wife had decided to stop doing most of the work on their market garden and gone to Greenham Common.

'I should think Keith would be delighted,' replied Bill. 'It might give him a bit of peace if his wife concentrated on someone else.'

'That's quite true. But who the hell is there for her to concentrate on? There's the rub.' Malcolm Jarrett was an English teacher and was clever.

The drinkers uneasily let their mental files on the male population of the community riffle through in their heads. All the freely available males were too old, too drunk or too smelly. Moreover, Mandy had such a horrendous local reputation as a harridan that not even they would dare go near her. She was not bad-looking in a Thatcherite sort of way and would probably suit beautifully someone who had a

11

penchant for nannies in jackboots, but that was a sexual quirk that seemed to be unrepresented in the village.

'I'll have a chat to her when she's next in and see if I can pick up any information on what she's about,' volunteered Kelvin. The others looked at him with respect. Close encounters with Mandy were often dangerously unpleasant experiences as she had a general contempt for men, together with a tongue that could have polished diamonds. Granted, Kelvin would be in the enviable position of having original and authoritative gossip about her with which he could titillate the market by releasing it in dribs and drabs, but the price could be very high. The conversation moved on to the well-explored subject of the price paid by the idiot from upcountry for Redworthy.

Kelvin and Mandy coincided in the pub a couple of days later. The bar was as crowded as usual, with the regulars at one end. Mandy, who had been seen moodily pacing the common earlier in the day wearing a nylon fur coat and white gloves, ordered a cherry brandy and went to sit by herself in front of the fire which grizzled sullenly in the inglenook.

Kelvin topped up his pint as a precaution against being forced to buy Mandy one when his own ran out, received winks of encouragement from his peers and went over to fossick for information. Mandy looked up at him with eyes tragic with mascara. 'You're looking very nice this evening, Mandy,' he said with heavy gallantry. She was wearing sky-blue slacks and white high-heeled shoes.

'How very, very sweet of you to say so, Kelvin.' She managed to squeeze a tear and Kelvin watched with interest to see whether it would have the nerve to take the plunge and plough its way through her make-up. Its courage failed. 'Not many people seem to say nice things to me these days.' The tear was frozen by the onset of a speculative gleam generated in the eye behind it. Kelvin put as sympathetic a look as possible on his face. He was confident that his manifold drawbacks would soon kill the speculation. Even so, he thought it wise to waggle his grey false teeth warningly.

Mandy suppressed a tiny shudder and turned her gaze back to the fire.

'Tell me about it,' he breathed.

Normally such an encouragement from a source like Kelvin would silence even an insurance salesman, but Mandy was not in a normal frame of mind and she pulled a lace handkerchief from the sleeve of her cardigan to dab gently at her eyes. She then pulled out a compact, to inspect herself for damage. All was still secure. She looked round at Kelvin who had seized the moment to sit down beside her and light himself one of her king-size cigarettes. He gave an incredulous cough as the menthol hit the back of his throat and pitched the cigarette into the ashes of the fire.

'You're a kind, sensitive man,' said Mandy.

'I can't bear to see an unhappy woman,' replied Kelvin with simple insincerity. 'It'll help if you tell me about it.' The other drinkers were sitting silently by the bar, their ears twitching as they strove to hear the conversation by the fire.

Kelvin looked over, gave them a wink and moved even closer to Mandy. 'Is it Keith?' he whispered hoarsely.

'He doesn't understand me,' quavered Mandy.

'Is that right? How do you know?'

'He never talks to me when we're alone together, even when I tell him to.'

Kelvin clicked his tongue sympathetically. 'That must be terrible for you.'

'Yes. I need to know that I'm loved and I don't think Keith loves me any more.'

'I know Keith has a tremendous respect for you.'

'What the hell's the good of respect?' demanded Mandy with some force. 'I want to feel like a woman.'

'Perhaps Keith feels intimidated,' suggested Kelvin, knowing full well that Keith, like every other man in the village, had to suppress the urge to squeal with fright if Mandy so much as glanced at him.

Mandy looked thoughtful. 'Do you really think so? Intimidated. I didn't think of that. Do you think that Keith might really love me?'

The last thing that Kelvin wanted was that Mandy should start looking for fulfilment of her needs in her husband again. That would be extremely boring. 'You should know. How long is it that you've been married? Twenty years?'

'Twenty-two.'

'That's a long time. A very long time. A very, very long time. Any marriage must lose its sparkle after a quarter of a century.'

'How true!' murmured Mandy.

'You're an attractive woman, Mandy. It's a right shame if you're not appreciated.'

'You're really sweet, Kelvin,' murmured the unappreciated one. She placed an affectionate hand on his knobbly knee.

'If I was a younger man, Mandy . . .' Kelvin sighed a great theatrical sigh and drained his glass.

'Would you like another drink, Kelvin?'

'Oh, Mandy!' Unconsciously she had found the route to Kelvin's heart and, for a frightening few seconds, he teetered

14

on the edge of an emotional abyss before the imperative to fill his glass with free beer drove him to his feet and to the end of the bar away from the little group of regulars, ignoring their curious glances. He stood there, a shaken man, as Helga, whose mature Nordic beauty had launched a thousand extra barrels of beer in the year or two she had owned the pub, topped up his pint as he tapped his horny finger-nail nervously on the counter. Helga took her time about it. Kelvin liked a full pint, and if there was any trace of foam he would claim loudly that he was being cheated. Kelvin edged his way across to the others who opened to allow him into their midst.

'Have you thought of anyone?' he whispered hoarsely. Life had been going on while Kelvin had been by the fire and it took the others some time to catch up with what he was thinking.

Malcolm Jarrett got there first. 'Anyone for Mandy? It is like that, is it?'

'Yes,' whispered Kelvin.

'No,' said Malcolm.

'For Christ's sake. I need a name.'

'What's the hurry?'

'I'm beginning to fancy her. She's buying me this drink.'

To the credit of the others, Kelvin's urgency and the situation he was in did not drive them to mirth. There, but for the Grace of God, might go any of them. 'I don't see how having a name is going to help you out. But how about one of the men from the commune?' suggested Malcolm.

Kelvin's face cleared. 'Of course! That fellow Howard Something-or-other who quit the place last month! I haven't seen him with a girl for a fortnight. He'd be perfect.' He collected his drink and returned to Mandy. She smiled up as he approached. Kelvin sat down beside her and hummed a few bars of *Land of Hope and Glory* to show that he was at ease and that what was to follow was merely casual conversation. 'By the way, Mandy, I was talking to that fellow Howard—'

'Who's Howard?' Mandy demanded.

'You know. That man who left the commune the other day. He's moved in with that other ex-communard who goes

15

around in rabbit-skin waistcoats and does gardening. Dick – that's the other fellow.'

'No, I don't know him. What about him?'

'You must know him,' laboured Kelvin. 'He's that tall, handsome chap. The one with the light-coloured hair and the blue eyes. In his thirties. Anyway, he was asking me about you.'

'Asking about me?' Mandy incredulously put her hand on the shelf above her bosom. 'What did he want to know about me?'

'Just wanted to know who you were and a bit about you. He said that he would like to get to know you.'

'Did you tell him what I was like?' asked Mandy sharply.

Kelvin was very reassuring. 'Heavens, no! I said you were very nice. He's well-spoken too.'

'Mmm,' said Mandy thoughtfully. There was silence for half a minute or so. Kelvin stirred restively. He was unsure whether he needed to do any more selling. 'Blond hair, you said? And is he sensitive?'

Kelvin relaxed. 'Straight out of the commune. As sensitive as hairs on a stinging nettle.' Kelvin's metaphors could be bucolic but Mandy was oblivious. Her eyes were on the smoking fire, lost in a reverie that would have sold millions of copies if written between the covers of a Mills and Boon. Kelvin rose to his feet and tiptoed silently away.

The matter was only half-resolved. Mandy may have been pointed at Howard, but Howard needed to be pointed at Mandy before the men of the village could feel safe. There was not likely to be any trouble with Howard. He still had to redevelop his critical faculty after half a life spent immersed in blind faith in fashionable alternative philosophies. Any interest from Mandy would be grasped by him with the same delight he might show at a major pools win or a prettily shaped cloud.

Keith presented more of a problem. Kelvin and his cronies knew, through experience, that Mandy's delicate condition could lead to trouble, however they tried to avert it. All they could do was try to channel her in a direction in which she would do as little harm to anyone else as possible. But was it ethical not to consult Keith upon the subject? Some thought his heart would not grieve over what his eye did not see. Others that, as the husband, he had a right to know. There was also the problem of Napoleon, their teenage son. Did they owe any responsibility to him? Dennis, a middle-aged gentleman who also farmed, won the day.

'Napoleon? Why should we have to consider him? I saw him combing his hair in the post office the other day. Imagine it! Combing one's hair in public. I certainly don't think we need to worry about a youth like that! As far as Keith is concerned, I don't see any need to hide the good news. With a dragon like Mandy as a lifemate, he deserves to be told that he's due to have a break.'

'Right then, Dennis,' said Bill briskly. 'You can tell him the good news yourself and Kelvin can tell Howard.'

'I didn't mean that I should have to tell him,' objected Dennis. 'But I suppose somebody has to.'

All the various strands came together the following Saturday night. On Saturday nights the pub throbbed. There was dancing in a large room at the back to the sounds of Jason Loosemire and the Harvestmen with the emphasis on the Country rather than the Western. This brought in large droves of people from the surrounding towns and villages who, by 9pm, no longer minded that the music was appalling. There were other Saturday attractions. The skittle alley was usually the venue of a match against a rival pub which often brought along its darts team as well. Even the lounge bar had a traffic warden who came out to play olde tyme favourites on an organ. The only peace was to be found in the public bar where the barrier of scowling locals fixed strangers with beady, contemptuous eyes should they venture in from the fleshpots of pleasure in other parts of the establishment and usually managed to drive them out again. If a look failed, then Jimmy, the pub's most antiquated patron, would regurgitate a great gob of phlegm and hawk it ponderously and splashily on

17

to the toecap of his boot. Few stayed for long after that experience, and if they did they were probably the sort of company that the villagers liked to keep.

Mandy liked olde tyme organ music and so she and Keith were in the lounge bar, listening to the traffic warden. Howard gravitated to where the music was loudest and was to be found with his ear to the speaker through which Jason Loosemire's attempt at a Kentucky accent came whining, greatly amplified. The operation moved smoothly into action once it was discovered that all the protagonists were present and their various locations had been noted. First to peel himself from the bar was Dennis. He drained his pint and braced himself to move to the lounge and the sounds of *Danny Boy*.

Mandy was sitting near the organ with a faraway look in her eye. She had recently taken to using a long cigarette holder and Keith kept a good few feet from her in case of accidents, so Dennis had no trouble in hooking him away in order to talk. Keith was somewhat surprised to be hauled to his feet and dragged through the crush of olde tyme music lovers to a corner near the silent jukebox, but he did not query Dennis's right to do so. He had been conditioned by years of life with Mandy. Keith looked deeply down-trodden. He bared his teeth beneath his scrubby black moustache in a cringing grin.

'Hullo, Dennis.'

Dennis had not really thought about it before, but he had very limited experience in ways to tell a husband that his wife is probably going to have an affair and that it was something to rejoice about. He fumbled around for inspiration.

'Er ... ah ... hmph.' The fact that Keith was not a gentleman made it more difficult – not that Dennis had anything against him because of this, but it meant that they did not share the same language and attitudes. 'It's about the old girl. Would you mind frightfully if she . . . er . . . bolted?'

'Bolted? Old girl?' Keith was understandably puzzled.

'You know – Mandy.'

'What about her? She's over there.'

Dennis tried again. 'Er . . . have you noticed anything odd about her behaviour recently?'

Keith looked over at her. She was waving her holder dreamily to *Davy Crockett* coming from the increasingly flustered organist who was now competing with Jason Loosemire's imitation of Dolly Parton through the cob wall. 'No, I don't think so. She's looking for a lover, though. Do you mean that?'

'Er . . . yes, I suppose I do.' Dennis regarded Keith with astonishment. It was as if Mother Theresa had suddenly revealed a secret life as a mafia hit woman.

Keith continued without noticing Dennis's surprise. 'The problem is finding someone to take her on. It's been that way for years. It was dreadful in Reading. That's why we came here. There were all these parties and things and I got on all right, but Mandy was always left out. It was a real shame.'

'Heavens!' Dennis was having the same sort of feelings as must have been experienced by all those beautiful princesses of old immediately after they had kissed their frog. 'Are you saying that you and Mandy used to go to . . . er . . . *those* sort of parties?'

'Sure we did. But nobody would ever pick up my car keys. I had a Morris then and there was a big "M" on the key ring and everyone knew it was ours and so none of our friends – the men, that is – would ever pick it up. It was rather embarrassing to go home with someone else, knowing that Mandy was by herself.'

'You amaze me, Keith,' said Dennis faintly.

'No, really, it was difficult. Can you imagine leaving your wife behind in that situation? I used to feel so sorry for her. Anyway, eventually she couldn't stand it any longer and we moved down here. And it's just the same down here, really.'

'What?' exclaimed Dennis. 'You don't mean that there are parties like that round here?' Astonishment turned to injured vanity. 'I've never been asked to one.'

'No, I haven't found any parties. I wouldn't feel right about going to one anyway, after Reading. I'm just talking about . . . er . . . other friends.'

'Do you mean you've got a mistress?'

'Well . . . yes . . . I suppose you could call them that.'

'*Them?!*' echoed Dennis faintly.

The customers in the lounge broke into a spontaneous *King of the Wild Frontier* to accompany the climactic notes of the organ.

Dennis waited until the applause died down. 'You'd quite like it if Mandy found a "friend", then?'

'It would be wonderful', said Keith, turning and searching Dennis's face eagerly. 'It would get her off my back. Do you mean you fancy her?'

'Good God, no!'

Keith's face fell. 'Oh. Well, if you'll excuse me, he's playing *Sally* next. I must get back to her.' He scuttled through the crush back to his wife and Dennis slowly retraced his steps to the public bar.

It was an oasis of silence amid the jollifications taking place in the rest of the building. The problem of Mandy had given the patrons something different to concentrate upon and all were awaiting Dennis's report. A dozen pairs of eyes raked across his face as he entered. There was a dreadful possibility that Keith might have disapproved of the Plan and then they may have been forced to cancel it. Dennis did not look downhearted, nor did he look pleased. He just looked slightly stunned, which was uninformative. He went behind the bar to help himself to a large whisky. On Saturdays, the regulars were left to fend for themselves while Helga dispensed to the more profitable customers in other parts of the pub.

'Well?' demanded Malcolm. 'How did you get on?'

'Fine,' replied Dennis, sinking his scotch in one practised gulp before filling up once more. 'There'll be no problems with Keith. Quite the contrary. Kelvin might as well get on with it and have a word with Howard.'

'Not before you tell me exactly what happened. Did you actually tell Keith what was going on?'

'Not in so many words—'

'What the hell's the good of that?' shouted Kelvin. 'We

20

wanted to be quite sure what he felt about it. I mean he's the sort of bloke who'd string himself up in his barn if you so much as gave him a bollocking.' Kelvin paused. 'Except he hasn't got a barn, of course.' He paused again. 'He could always use someone else's, mark you.'

'I don't think there's much chance of that happening,' said Dennis.

'He's not stupid, you know. He's quite capable of working out that he could always use someone else's barn when he realizes he hasn't got one himself.'

'No. I mean he's not going to be too upset.'

'So you say. But if he should go and do something daft, I don't want it to be on my conscience.' Dennis could not help smiling, while a couple of others laughed outright. Kelvin looked puzzled. 'What did I say that was so funny?'

'I'm sorry,' Dennis apologized. 'It was just the idea of you having a conscience.' He walked round to the customer side of the bar. 'Honestly, there's no need to worry about Keith. He said they had to move down here because he was having lots of affairs and Mandy was jealous because she couldn't get fixed up.' There were incredulous looks from everyone. 'It's true. It really is. He also says that he's been . . . er . . . at it since he came down here – with more than one lady, too.'

'Don't be ridiculous!' scoffed Kelvin. 'He's been spinning you a yarn. Ladies, indeed!'

'It's difficult to believe, I know,' acknowledged Dennis. 'But I'm sure he was telling the truth. After all, it's so damn unlikely, he couldn't have made it up.'

There was a silence broken eventually by Malcolm. 'Women!' he said uneasily. 'I wonder who they might have been?'

'Or still are,' said Dennis, knocking back his second drink. 'Think on that!'

'It's astonishing,' said Bill. 'Who would have thought that Keith would be such a dark horse?' Bill was a bachelor and could afford to take a detached view of the affair or affairs.

'That's part of the trouble,' replied Malcolm, bring urban sophistication to bear. 'It's the ones you least suspect who do

21

it. A fellow like Frank Mattock who's all hairy chest and suntan are just talk and people like Keith are all action.' The question that was in everyone's mind was with whom he could be having his action.

The commander had been holding his peace until now. His Elfrieda was hardly the most desirable of women; on the other hand, nor was Keith the most desirable of men. The combination had the commander feverishly trying to work out whether he might be wearing a pair of horns. He dropped a 'hmm' into the silence. Everyone looked at him hopefully to discover whether he was about to contribute anything useful. 'I was wondering whether this might not change things a bit.'

'In what way?' asked Malcolm eagerly. He was feeling rather vulnerable since his was a modern, liberated relationship in which each partner respected each other's privacy and had their own friends. He trusted Stephanie, of course, and Keith was surely too much of a nonentity to be a threat, but there were no other wives who bounced round the lanes in running shorts and tee-shirt which displayed their charms to any passer-by.

'Well, I'm not sure that it would necessarily be a good idea to give Keith any more freedom. If what he says is true and if we get Mandy out of his hair, who knows what he might get up to next?'

'What do you mean?' asked Kelvin.

'If he can be as active as he appears to be with a wife who can make a lion whimper with a single glance, he might be round the parish like a bloody stoat if she gave him the nod. No woman would be safe. Not even your Prudence, Kelvin.'

'I bet my Prudence would be safe,' said Kelvin.

The commander was forced to agree. 'Well, no woman under eighty would be safe, except for Prudence.' The said lady, Kelvin's middle-aged daughter, did all the farming for her father. The last time she had been heard to utter in public had been a couple of months previously when she had thrown a 50-kilo bag of fertilizer at a hunt follower who failed to close a gate on the way through the farm. She had just missed him and broken her favourite dungfork. Then she had cursed.

Everyone considered the possibilities of Keith stoating round the village. The commander certainly had a point.

'I wonder how he does it?' mused Dennis. There was a faint note of yearning in his voice.

'Perhaps he understands women,' suggested Malcolm.

'I knew a fellow in the navy who said he understood women,' said the commander. 'Poor chap got his throat cut in a whorehouse in Marseilles.'

Kelvin brought the company back to the nub of the matter. 'If we do nothing about Mandy because you lot are scared of Keith, then she's going to be rampaging round the village looking for a fancy man – and if that happens, God help us all. I know what I'm going to do and that's go and tell Howard that Mandy fancies him.' He heaved himself off his barstool, deftly lifted Bill's almost untouched pint without its owner noticing and moved hurriedly towards the door. Nobody made a move to stop him, not even Malcolm.

Mandy was determined to wring every possible ounce of romance out of her experience. As the prime consumer of bodice-ripping fiction from the mobile library, she had very clear ideas about how things ought to progress. They should not be hurried. The First Encounter was on Monday morning. Howard had come in on his bicycle to cash a Social Security cheque. Mandy, who must have peeking through her curtains, saw him cross the bridge into the village and she hurried up to the post office after him, bearing a letter. It was as well for the community information network that Maud, who ran the establishment, was an imaginative and dedicated gossip – as a cousin three times over to Kelvin, it was in her genes.

Howard had collected his money and was engrossed in a pamphlet about the importance of opening a National Savings account by the time that the panting Mandy crashed through the door. She strutted up to the counter to buy her stamp, waggling her hips at him. Howard did not appear to notice. All was grist to Howard's undiscriminating mental mill and his concentration on the prognosis for £5 a month over five years was total. Mandy turned and dropped her letter at his feet. It was not enough so, her lips tightened, she kicked him sharply on the ankle. The average man would have looked at Mandy to see why he was being kicked, but Howard looked down at his ankle to see what had disturbed it. His butterfly mind was easily distracted by the letter, lying by his foot.

'Hey! Somebody's dropped a letter.' He looked up at Mandy. He recognized her, which was quite an achievement. 'You're Mandy, right?'

Mandy fluttered her eyelashes. Her best feature was her vivid blue eyes which she framed in sets of stick-on lashes that could have been used to whitewash a ceiling. As they flapped, they stirred tiny clouds of powder and mascara which swirled and eddied round her cheeks. 'La, sir,' she said.

Howard was not a reader of romantic fiction and failed to recognize a Cartland come-on when he heard it. 'You'd better pick up your letter.'

Mandy looked at him critically. It was obviously his job to pick up the letter. No romantic hero would expect her to do it. But she had to make allowances for ignorance and the fact that he had spent many years being brainwashed by a

succession of gurus in a succession of communes. If Howard would follow a louse-infested, half-naked Indian fakir, it certainly was not beyond her capabilities to make him follow her and he looked as if he would be worth the effort – tall and slim with a delicious little bottom. The clincher was that he was interested in her. 'You pick up the letter,' she ordered.

This course of action had not occurred to Howard, but he greeted it with his customary enthusiasm. 'Hey! Yes. That's a good idea. I never thought of that!' He smiled happily.

'Well, do it then,' said Mandy patiently. She was beginning to learn.

'Gosh, yes. I'll pick it up.' He bent down, took the letter and studied it. It was addressed to Littlewoods. With a remarkable demonstration of initiative, he noted the fact that it was stamped, turned it over and checked that it was sealed before slipping it through the slot into the postbox. He turned proudly back to Mandy. 'There!'

Maud, who was watching with open interest, nearly burst into applause. Her choked cheer earned her an icy look before Mandy, her eyelashes clapping like the wings of a pheasant at take-off, flashed him a beaming smile of thanks. She had had an excellent dentist and so her smile was quite impressive. 'You are so very, very kind.'

'Hey! That's nice: "You're very kind." Oh yeah.' Howard had a short memory span. 'You're Mandy, aren't you? Kelvin was telling me about you. I think that's really nice. I really like your eyelashes. They're really thick.'

'Oh, thank you very much,' Mandy managed to summon a blush almost as deep as Hermione Grimshaw's in *Master of Darrowby*. It was not too difficult as this was more the sort of thing she was after.

'Where did you buy them?'

Chapter Two

IT IS WELL known that the course of true love never did run smooth. The evening after Mandy and Howard had commenced their liaison, the pub was disturbed when Howard came in with an alternative girl on his arm. A communard, or even an ex-communard like Howard, could be put in the middle of the Sahara Desert for half an hour and he would emerge with a short girl with no conversation and large breasts, clothed from head to toe in cast-offs from an Oxfam shop. Nobody quite knew where these females came from. There had been a festival at the commune a few years back where stalls sold candles, jewellery made from horseshoe nails, and various kinds of food that equated lack of hygiene with wholeness, while guitarists and troubadours dirged away or turned laboured cartwheels to amuse the public. Then the lanes round the village were filled with these young women. They could be found on roadside verges sitting in crosslegged meditation with a corona of dun-coloured clothing round them or in tight and intimate embrace with their scrawny, bearded male counterparts.

The girl with Howard was typical of the breed: a bush of straight brown hair through which a nose could be seen and a great shapeless bundle of clothing that covered any contours she might have had. Howard led her to one of the rough oak tables that were against the wall and sat her down before coming towards the bar to order drinks. With the eyes of the pub on her, she pulled out a tobacco tin, expertly rolled herself a cigarette which she lit, and then stared at the wall in front of her. The pub followed her gaze, but there was only a rather mean set of antlers on the wall with a plaque which told that the stag that had worn them had been accounted for at Horney Bottom in 1925. The pub then turned back to Howard as he waited by the bar. It frowned at him and he bared his teeth in a smile.

'What do you think you're up to?' demanded Kelvin.

Howard had had a hard day. Lots of attention and lots of things being expected of him. 'What do you mean?'

'Well, you were going out with Mandy yesterday and you've got a different woman now. You can't do that sort of thing round here. It's not like it is upcountry, you know.'

Howard wrinkled his brow. 'Mandy was my karma yesterday. She might well be it tomorrow. But today's today.'

Once Kelvin had worked out his meaning, he drew in his breath sharply. 'That's immoral.'

'Yeah,' replied Howard happily. 'Isn't it great?'

Kelvin did not know what the world was coming to and so he shook his head sadly and turned deliberately back to his pint.

Malcolm then tried to make Howard understand the implications of his actions. 'Did you know Mandy was due in this evening?' he asked innocently.

Howard turned to him, his face lighting up. 'Is she? Good. I'm sure she'd like to meet Sweetbriar.'

Malcolm did not even flinch. 'I wouldn't be so sure about that,' he said drily.

'Don't waste your breath,' remarked Kelvin. 'That bugger won't have the faintest idea of what you're talking about.' Kelvin knew his man. Howard had forgotten about the concepts like jealousy which make us human. He looked puzzled, shrugged and took his drinks back to Sweetbriar.

'What time do you think Mandy and Keith will be in?' asked the commander.

Kelvin looked up at the old station clock that hung on the wall above the bar. He did not wear a watch. 'It's Tuesday, so they'll be here in ten minutes.'

'Oh dear,' moaned the commander. 'I'm not sure that I'm looking forward to that.' An outsider might have considered that an over-reaction, but there were no outsiders present and all knew Mandy. However, the cohesion of the mob gave everyone the moral strength to wait until the pub door opened to allow Mandy's and Keith's entry.

Mandy was first, her loose sheepskin jacket filling the doorway. She swept in, her handbag dangling over her arm, and looked slowly round the room as she waited for Keith to escort her to the bar. Her eyes reached the eyrie that was Sweetbriar's hair and saw Howard's head behind it. Theirs were the only two heads in the pub that had not automatically swivelled to see who was coming in. Mandy turned pale. Her hand flew to her throat, the handbag on her arm clouting the back of the head of Mr Loosemire, the local postman and peeping tom, who was enjoying a quiet drink with his wife. His cry of pain – Mandy's bag was loaded with bottles of scent and heavy-duty deodorant – penetrated through the concentrated attention between Howard and Sweetbriar and they looked over. Howard recognized, smiled and pulled Sweetbriar to her feet to bring her over.

'Hey there, Mandy!'

'Judas!' Mandy hissed. 'Are you so faithless that you cannot remain true for a day?'

'What's that?' demanded the puzzled Howard. He shrugged uncomprehendingly. 'Anyway, I thought you might like to meet a friend of mine. This is Sweetbriar. I have been telling her about you.'

'Keith!'

Keith had been engaged in hanging up his coat on the line of pegs beside the door. Years of conditioning made him drop his coat to the floor at the first consonant of the call and, by the time that her mouth was closing behind the last spat lisp, he was by her side. 'Yes, dear?'

'This . . . this libertine has insulted me. Do something about it.'

Howard and Keith looked at each other in dismay. The first did not know what he had done wrong and the second did not know what he was supposed to do about it. 'Er . . .' faltered Keith.

Mandy had been enjoying being the heroine of a romantic novel all day. She had been through the Encounter and the Dawning Realization. The Quarrel was not due until after the Declaration, while Betrayal was a chapter she had never liked anyway. She brushed Keith aside and brought down her stiletto heel hard on Howard's toe. Poor Howard was wearing trainers as usual, but he had a defender to hand.

From beneath the eyrie emerged an eagle. 'You bloody old cow!' yelled Sweetbriar. 'You did that deliberately!' She was carrying a glass of lager which she emptied down Mandy's front.

Violence was very rare in the pub, so there was consternation round the room as Mandy, breathing heavily, removed her soggy coat and handed it to Keith before advancing on Sweetbriar. Howard and Keith clutched each other in alarm while there was a scrape of barstools as the regulars drew back for fear of flying beer or glasses.

It was the commander's luck to have chosen to visit the lavatory shortly before Mandy and Keith arrived. His route back to the bar led directly between the two protagonists. Since he was there already and nobody else showed much inclination to become involved, he thought he might try to maintain the peace. With his back to Mandy, he waved his arms, shooing Sweetbriar back towards her table. He met with little resistance. She was beginning to realize that she was in danger of being consumed by a primeval force rather more tangible than ley lines or planetary influences. 'Get her out of here!' shouted the commander over his shoulder at Keith. Keith chose to misunderstand. He abandoned Howard, side-stepped neatly round the commander and put his arm round Sweetbriar. The cool efficiency with which his hand casually thrust its way into her clothing to establish that there really was a breast in there somewhere was quickly noted by the pub as the first tangible evidence that he might be the lounge lizard Dennis claimed him to be, but Mandy was still the prime focus of attention. The commander turned fearfully back towards her, his shoulders hunched ready to ward off any blow. He was right to be worried. Mandy was standing looking at him with her lips slightly ajar, a dazed look in her eyes. 'Commander! You were wonderful! You saved me!'

'What?'

'You came to my rescue when I might have been hurt. Commander! Oh, Commander!' Mandy gazed at him, her eyes shining.

There was a hiss of indrawn breath from the barstools and the commander suddenly understood. 'Oh God! No! I didn't, really I didn't. It was Keith. Look, over there! See? Keith is still protecting you. Aren't you, Keith?' But Keith was concentrating on charming Sweetbriar. The commander turned desperately to Kelvin for confirmation. 'He is, isn't he, Kelvin?'

Kelvin considered. His love of seeing someone else in trouble warred with his feeling that some troubles should not be wished on a dog. Regretfully he spoke. 'That's right, Mandy. It's Keith who's protecting you all right.'

'That's true,' agreed Bill, a man more generous of spirit, and Malcolm grunted concurrence as well.

But they might well have saved their breath. Mandy's plot had changed. A Gallant Knight had come to her rescue. The commander was doomed.

Mandy smiled with the smile that Andromeda must have used when she saw Perseus wearing his winged sandals, flapping across the sea towards the rock to which she was chained. 'You were wonderful, Commander. It's just like you to be so modest. Elfrieda is a lucky girl to have you as her husband. She's away this week, isn't she?'

'Shit!' said the commander, as he tore himself from Mandy's adoring gaze and staggered out through the door of the pub and into the night, his eyes bleak with the fearful knowledge of the future.

Mandy called after him, 'Good night. I'll pop in to thank you tomorrow morning!'

Chapter Three

MANDY'S INFATUATION with the commander was to prove
the first harbinger of a disturbed autumn and winter. The
second was Ivor's decision to hold a village day. He was
chairman of the parish council, a man of considerable power
whose chief interest lay in commentating through loudspeakers
at events like gymkhanas and point-to-points. Unfortunately
the tide of progress had caught up with him and his chosen
field was now cluttered by smooth-talking youths with the
glamorous crowd-attracting qualification of playing records
on the local radio station. If he could not persuade the
organizers of such events to come to him, he would create his
own and was open to ideas.

Somebody suggested an exhibition of village history.
Somebody else suggested dancing on the common, even
though it would be October. Ideas snowballed, only to melt
away when it was realized that someone would have to take
responsibility for translating them into practice. However, the
village day had the wholehearted support of the entire
community so long as nobody was expected to provide any
practical assistance in making it happen. Everyone congratulated everyone else on such an exciting idea and then forgot
about it, secure in the knowledge that it would come to
nothing.

Three people ensured that the carnival did not die: Ivor,
who wanted to loudspeak; Lindy, the district nurse; and Dick.
The last named, like Howard, was a graduate from the
commune, although he had had a couple of years away from it
to clear the cobwebs from his brain. He earned a precarious

living as a professional countryman from an old farmhouse into which he had recently moved. He rented it from the owner, last twig on the tree of a family that had farmed there since 1620, who now ran a kosher delicatessen in Toronto. He caught and ate rabbits and deer, feasted on blackberries, mushrooms and nettles and sold things made from fur and bits of wood to tourists. He dressed like Bilbo Baggins in a brown tweed suit and moleskin waistcoat, made from real moles, which disturbed the squire since the suit, once his favourite, had been given by his wife to a jumble sale without his knowledge.

Dick did not often come into the pub because he never had much ready cash and because he both brewed and grew his own intoxicants. When he did come in, he remained in character, so tended to sit by the fire nursing a glass of beer and saying very little but looking wise. It impressed visitors but the effect was always spoiled if he spoke when Black instead of West Country issued from his mouth. On this occasion he came right to the bar and spoke. 'Who's organizing the historical exhibition?'

'What historical exhibition?' inquired Mandy. She was waiting for the commander, but the commander did not now come to the pub in the evenings unless he could see the television flickering behind Mandy's lace curtains.

'The one that's going to be part of the village day.'

'Oh that! Why do you want to know?'

'Because I've got something that ought to go in.'

'What?' asked Malcolm.

'A turtle. I found it in my garden.'

'Ah, yes! Of course.' Malcolm was reluctant to follow the conversation further for fear of it entering the uncharted waters of communard lunacy, so he carefully lit a cigarette, leaving it to someone else to pick up the baton.

Kelvin obliged. 'What has the history of the village got to do with a turtle? And what the hell's it doing in your garden? I haven't heard of many of them round here.'

'That's true,' agreed Bill. 'I've only seen them in the sea. On television, that is. I suppose you might have them coming

33

up the river.' He turned to Keith whose cottage virtually fronted on the river. 'Have you seen many turtles about?'

'I can't say that I have. But it could easily be a tortoise. They look like turtles and it could be an escaped pet.'

Dick laughed. 'It's a fossil turtle, not a live one.'

Kelvin turned to Bill. 'Fossil?' he asked under his breath.

'Turned to stone. Like those dinosaur bones.'

'I thought it might make an interesting exhibit to show that strange creatures used to live in the area,' continued Dick.

'They still do,' said Kelvin caustically.

'Where did you come across this fossil turtle?' asked Malcolm.

'It was rather odd. I was planting comfrey and found it just below the surface of the soil. It's more than two feet long and very heavy. You can see the markings on the shell quite clearly.'

'Why were you planting comfrey?' asked Kelvin.

'Comfrey? It's a vulnery.'

Kelvin looked at Malcolm, but he shrugged. 'What's a vulnery?'

'You put it on wounds.'

'Oh,' said Kelvin. 'Why don't you use sticking plaster?'

'Comfrey heals bones as well.'

'Splints,' contributed Kelvin wisely. 'Splints is the best thing for broken bones. When I broke my arm – it must be twenty years ago now – I had to put on a splint for a couple of months. Nobody mentioned anything about comfrey. It's not a proper medecine anyway. It's a plant.'

'That's what antibiotics were, plants,' said Malcolm.

'Don't be stupid. They're pills. You don't see pill plants growing in the hedges.'

'But penicillin is the mould on top of jam. Fleming first discovered it growing on a culture dish in Paddington Hospital.'

Kelvin's scorn was unassailable. 'It was probably soot from the Cornish Express. That went into Paddington. Pills are white anyway and mould is black.'

'About my turtle fossil—' interrupted Dick.

'I don't believe it can be a turtle fossil,' said Ivor. 'You just don't get fossils lying about in flower beds. They are in quarries and coal mines.'

'True,' agreed Dick. 'But some previous inhabitant of the farm might have found it somewhere and brought it back home.'

'Your house was lived in by Percy Bladderwort and his father and grandfather before him. Those Bladderworts were so thick they wouldn't bring home a nugget of gold, let alone a dirty great stone tortoise.'

'Why don't we go down and look at it?' suggested Malcolm. 'I would quite like to see it.'

'Why don't you?' invited Dick.

'If you go down that lane of yours in anything less than a four-wheel drive, you could be there forever,' said Kelvin scathingly.

'What have you been doing coming down my lane?' asked Dick.

'I wooed Chastity Bladderwort forty years ago and that lane was pretty bad then, and it was no better when I went to Percy Bladderwort's wake. That old fool owed me a fiver for a bag of potatoes when he died. I've got better things to do than look at dead tortoises.'

'Well, I'd like to see it,' said Malcolm. 'Can I buy you a drink?'

'Thank you. I'll have a glass of water.'

It was probably the first time that such a sentence had been uttered within those walls since John Wesley may or may not have had lunch there in 1759 or 1765. Certainly the stunned silence in the room was broken by a sudden gust of wind down the chimney which could only have been the ghosts of generations of villagers who had cheerfully puked cider out on the verges of the lanes on the way home of a night.

Kelvin shuddered. 'Why?'

'I've got Sweetbriar staying with me and she recommended tincture of campion for my feet and I can't have any alcohol for an hour after taking it.'

'What's wrong with your feet?'

'An ingrowing toenail.'

'And you'd turn down a free drink because of an ingrowing toenail? You stupid Jessie!'

In the end, Lindy was appointed to organize the historical exhibition. As district nurse, she toured the countryside all day visiting the sick, the lame, the old and the slightly mad – just about everyone, in fact. So it was reckoned that she knew where possible exhibits might lie. Her first duty was to go down to inspect the turtle. Mandy came along too so that she could inspect Sweetbriar. Mandy would have gone by herself but she preferred to risk Lindy's car down the lane to the cottage rather than her own. She was giving a home for a fortnight to a Yorkshire terrier belonging to her hairdresser who had gone to Corfu for a late holiday and suspected that the animal might be car-sick – another reason for preferring Lindy's car.

The lane was everything Kelvin had promised. Centuries of rain and generations of cattle had worn it well below the level of the adjoining fields and the ash, oak and beech on each hedgebank had joined to create a tunnel whose floor was littered with water-filled potholes that were home to whirligig beetles, water boatmen and the occasional stickleback. It took ten minutes to drive the few hundred yards to Dick's house and once Mandy found herself unceremoniously ejected from the car to sound a pothole on the surface of which Lindy thought she saw the spreading rings left by a trout rise.

Their route crept round the side of a crumbling stone barn and they drew up on a small open space ringed by unkempt trees and bushes. On one side was the house, its windows almost invisible under a thick coat of ivy. Lindy looked at it uneasily. 'It must be dying for a good scratch.'

'It looks damned unhygienic,' sniffed Mandy. 'Probably full of rats.'

Mandy attached a thin chain leash to the dog's collar and they walked to the door. The ivy lapped at its edges as Lindy hammered on the knocker. The oak plank door creaked open on rusty strap hinges to reveal a large dank hall, its wooden walls covered in flaking grey paint. The two women looked at each other nervously, but the terrier trotted ahead and lifted its leg against a line of scuffed and muddy gumboots by the wall. Mandy tugged on the chain and it hopped back, spraying the stone-flagged floor. She looked at it with distaste. 'Dirty little brute.'

'Come in!' shouted a voice from the interior of the house. 'I'll be with you in a second. I'm just skinning a hare.'

They stepped inside, looking at the half-dozen doors that led off the hall and wondering which concealed Dick or Sweetbriar. The hall was dominated by an immense print of one of Landseer's more Rambo-like stags. Trapped behind the glass were the desiccated corpses of several tortoiseshell butterflies. On another wall there was Dick's famous collection of antlers. In his initial revolt against the ethics of the commune, he had gone through a Daniel Boone phase, but he was in the process of reverting to organic environmentalism. Among the antlers was an Ordnance Survey map of the district crisscrossed by black felt-tip pen lines. 'What are those lines?' asked Mandy coming over to join Lindy.

'They're ley lines, I think,' replied the nurse.

'I knew it. He's really just a communard!'

The door behind them suddenly opened to show Howard framed in the doorway, wearing his jeans but displaying his sinewy torso. He was, of course, delighted to see them.

'Hey, great to see you, Mandy. Hey, it's really nice.'

Mandy's nostrils flared. She had switched to the commander but she had not told Howard. He was supposed to be still pining for the love of her and was due to have his heart broken when Mandy got round to telling him that she loved another. 'Howard! What are you doing here?'

'Staying with Sweetbriar—' A look of concern crossed his face. 'Are you feeling all right?'

Mandy had leaned back against the wall and put her hand to her breast, a look of pain on her face.

Howard went over to her and grasped her hand. 'Is it heartburn? Very painful, heartburn.'

Mandy snatched her hand away. 'How could you? You . . . you rake!'

Howard backed bewilderedly into the room from which he had emerged. 'Hey, that's a bit heavy. What's the matter?'

Mandy, breathing heavily, followed him through the door.

'Faithless bastard!' she hissed.

'Wuff!' agreed the dog, having no choice but to follow since the lead was round her wrist.

It was a bedroom, the floor littered with discarded clothes and the air blue with the smoke from a cluster of joss-sticks that were stuck in a vase on a pine chest of drawers. Sweetbriar was crosslegged on the bed examining a plastic daffodil on the blanket in front of her.

'Oh!' cried Mandy in horror, her hand flying to her throat. The dog, which had been sniffing the atmosphere in disgust, let out a gurgle as its collar tightened against its throat. 'You betrayed me, you seducer!'

Howard appealed to Lindy who was cautiously looking round the edge of the door. 'Lindy! Help me!'

'That's right! Bring another woman into it! Aren't two enough for you? If that ridiculous child can be called a woman!' Mandy had been expecting Sweetbriar to react with guilt and shame but, when she did not react at all, she went over to look at her. 'What's wrong with her?' she asked as Sweetbriar continued her scrutiny of the daffodil.

'She's meditating,' replied Howard.

Mandy stepped back from the bed. 'No!' she cried. 'You've drugged her! You degenerate!'

Lindy was standing in the doorway. 'For heaven's sake, Mandy. Stop being so overdramatic.'

Mandy stepped back another pace and struck a pose. There was a shriek of anguish from Howard. 'My jacket! You're standing on my buckskin jacket!'

'Sod your jacket!' replied Mandy, grinding it into the floor with the stiletto heel of her red boot. Howard bent down and tugged sharply at his jacket. There was a crack as Mandy's heel broke off the boot. The room froze; even Sweetbriar cocked a wary eye away from her daffodil.

'You bastard! Look what you've gone and done!'

38

Mandy had always been verbally violent but the power of love made her translate words into action for the second time within a few days. Howard retreated towards the window, managing to avoid a wild haymaker from her left hand. She limped towards him and delivered the follow-through. This came from her right hand which was attached to the dog's leash.

The animal was lifted off its feet, hurtled through the air just above Howard's head and crashed through the window, taking with it two panes and the wooden batten that supported them.

'Shit!' said Mandy, momentarily distracted from Howard. The latter seized the opportunity to grab his shirt and scuttle round her out of the bedroom. There was the sound of the front door of the house opening and he could be seen running up the lane, tucking his shirt into his trousers. His progress was slow as he had been forced to leave his shoes and socks behind. Mandy, Lindy and Sweetbriar went over to the window to watch him go. 'Swine!' exclaimed Mandy with considerable venom, peering through the ivy at his disappearing figure.

'What *is* going on here?' said Dick from behind them.

'There's been a bit of a disagreement between Mandy and Howard,' explained Lindy.

'Why is my window broken?'

'Mandy swung her dog through it,' contributed Sweetbriar. 'It made quite a crash.'

'I know. I heard it. And where is it?'

'Where's what?' asked Lindy.

'The dog.'

One end of the leash was still wound round Mandy's wrist. Everyone looked at it and followed the chain which disappeared out of the window. 'Damn!' said Mandy, hauling in her line. The head of the dog appeared above the window sill.

'Oh! Poor little thing. Be careful!' said Sweetbriar as it rolled its eyes at those inside the room. They were bulging slightly which was not surprising as it was hanging from its collar several feet above the ground. Sweetbriar rushed forward and picked it up, cradling it in her arms. 'It's bleeding!' she exclaimed.

'I'm not surprised,' said Lindy. 'You'd be likely to be cut about a bit if you had been flung through a window. Let me have a look at it.'

The dog had realized that it was safe within the protection of Sweetbriar's bosom and had relaxed enough to begin shivering as Lindy touched it. 'Where's it bleeding?'

'I felt blood on my front,' replied Sweetbriar.

Lindy ruffled through the dog's fur and then looked at Sweetbriar's shirt. 'It's all right. I don't think it's been cut.' The dog was looking as pathetic as only a Yorkshire terrier can. 'Mandy, that was really a dreadful thing to do.'

'I was provoked,' replied Mandy sullenly. 'The dog's OK. Aren't you, Flossie?'

Flossie was quite happy where she was and cowered deeper into her valley of safety. Sweetbriar peered down through her hair. 'Are you sure the poor little thing's all right? I could have sworn I felt blood.'

'It was probably urine,' said Lindy briefly. 'It's peed down your shirt.'

Sweetbriar opened her arms. The dog did not fall straight down as Mandy had some tension on its collar from the leash. It fell in an arc against Mandy's leg and promptly sank its teeth into her ankle. A defensive compensation for being tiny was that it had teeth like hypodermic needles. Mandy grunted and kicked out, dislodging Flossie and sending her across the floor towards Dick. The dog's collar snapped this time as Dick neatly sidestepped to allow the animal to slide through the door.

'*You'd* probably piss yourself if you had been defenestrated,' he observed.

Flossie was not finished. She picked herself off the floor — she had not got far to go — shook herself and then darted through to nip Mandy's other ankle. The little animal dodged her kick, skipped round Dick, shot through the front door and took off up the lane after Howard.

'What are you doing here, anyway?' asked Dick as they all

watched the dog through the window. 'Apart from breaking up my house and driving away my guests.' He turned to Sweetbriar. 'What was that about, by the way?'

'That was Howard. He was a friend of mine,' said Mandy. 'He made me extremely cross.'

'Yes, I can see that,' replied Dick drily. 'Your eyes flash and you flare your nostrils like a dragon.'

Mandy looked at him suspiciously. 'Are you calling me a dragon?'

Dick hastily raised his arms in protest. He had realized that it was unwise to provoke her. 'Certainly not. You don't look the least like a dragon. You're most attractive. Perhaps a bit of a fire breather.'

'Attractive?' repeated Mandy. She gazed at Dick with a musing look on her face. Lindy feared for him but Mandy had just had a lesson in emotional pain and was not yet ready to switch allegiance from the commander.

Dick misinterpreted the look. 'Yes, most attractive, I assure you,' he said heartily.

'I'll bear that in mind,' said Mandy even more musingly. Somewhere, in the snow-covered wastes of Siberia, a wandering wolf stopped in its tracks, cocked its ear and lifted its muzzle in a howl to the leaden sky.

Dick shuddered. 'Whoops! Somebody must have walked over my grave. Anyway what are you here for?'

'Your turtle,' said Lindy.

'Ah yes! My turtle. Follow me.' He led them into the hall, through another of the doors and along a lino-floored passage. He continued the conversation as he walked. 'I mentioned it to a friend of mine at the university and he's sending out a colleague of his, a palaeontologist, to take a look at it.'

'That's nice. We just want to have a look at it for the historical exhibition. It's going to be the centrepiece.'

'It's probably new to science, you know. If it is, it'll be named after the village and this place will become famous all over the world.'

'Really?' said Lindy. 'A bit like the Piltdown Man?'

'Yes, except that the Piltdown jawbone turned out to be a

41

forgery.' The passage ended in a room that had probably once been the farm dairy. It was now a store-room containing some battered tea chests and piles of newspapers that were rapidly reverting to their original pulp under the onslaught of damp. 'There!' said Dick proudly.

The two women inspected the turtle. It lay solidly in the middle of the floor, its back dark and sleek with the outlines of the segments of its shell clearly visible. 'Where's its head and its legs?' asked Mandy.

'The soft bits would have been eaten up by scavengers when it died.'

'It's certainly not the sort of thing Percy Bladderwort would pick up on a picnic,' commented Lindy. 'It looks very heavy.'

'It is. Well over a hundredweight. It's solid rock.'

'It's very impressive. I'm sure everyone will be most interested in it. Would it be possible for you to deliver it? I don't think I'd have the strength to move it.'

'It would be my pleasure. I'll make out a little label to go with it, saying what it is, where it was found and who has lent it.'

'That would be very kind,' said Lindy politely. 'But there's no need to go to all that trouble. I'm pretty sure everyone would know where it came from.'

'There may be tourists around and it wouldn't surprise me if the newspapers and television people did a story on it.'

'On that lump of stone?' asked Mandy dubiously.

'Oh yes. It's not every day that a new species of animal is discovered by science. Think of the excitement if the remains of an abominable snowman or the Loch Ness monster were found.'

'Hmm,' said Lindy. 'Surely the point about those is that they're still around?'

'So might this turtle be.'

Lindy sighed. 'Well, it surely won't be doing much swimming around in its present condition. Anyway, if you could bring the thing up to the church hall, I'd be very grateful.'

'It would be my pleasure. Would you like a cup of tea?'

They had a cup of tea during which Mandy generously relinquished her rights over Howard to Sweetbriar when they discovered a mutual passion for Black Forest gateau.

Dick decided to deliver the turtle the next day which was not quite what Lindy had intended as there was not yet a firm date for the exhibition and the church hall was locked. However, Dick had extra muscle in the form of Sweetbriar and Howard and they had not brought the thing all the way to the village perched on the back of a bicycle only to take it home again, so they persuaded Helga to house it underneath a bench by the wall of the public bar.

The pub became quite proud of its turtle. It lay below the deranged stag's head and gracefully accepted its role as a conversation piece. Kelvin prodded it. Flossie urinated on it. The commander barked his ankle on it as he slid hastily along the bench to avoid having to sit beside Mandy and everyone admired it except Jimmy who could not understand why there

was such a fuss about a 'girt big stone' even if it was supposed to be a 'possil'.

It stayed there until one lunchtime at the end of the week. Fridays were always busy since many of the farmers came in to boast about the deals they had made at market the previous day and they augmented the usual crowd of regulars in for their midday fix of booze and gossip. Strangers did occasionally come into the bar but they were expected, like children, to be seen and not heard, so Kelvin was understandably annoyed when one interrupted Helga while she was concentrating on pouring him a pint.

'Excuse me.'

'Wait your bloody turn, mate!' snarled Kelvin over his shoulder. He turned to look. 'Oh, sorry, miss.' The stranger was a short woman in her forties wearing thick stockings and sensible shoes with a pair of National Health glasses on her nose. Kelvin laboured embarrassedly on, much to the amusement of Jimmy who was listening in. 'I thought you were a man, you see. But I can see now that you're a lady. It's your voice. It could be either and I naturally assumed that it would be a man coming up to the bar to order drinks—'

'It just shows the danger of making assumptions,' said the woman with a tight little smile. 'I am certainly not a man and I am not here to order a drink. I'm a palaeontologist. Jessica Leach.'

Kelvin looked round the bar for a translator, but Malcolm could only come in at lunchtime once or twice a month when he played hookey from his job as an English lecturer. Kelvin played safe. 'Are you now? Very nice for you, I'm sure.'

'Does it hurt?' asked Jimmy, beginning the asthmatic wheeze which signalled a laugh. He was a devotee of bad television sitcoms.

The visitor ignored him. 'I'm here about Dick's fossil. He told me it was up here.'

'Why isn't he here himself?' asked Kelvin interestedly.

'He said he's been warned to stay at home today.'

'Warned? Did he say who by?'

'His biorhythms,' replied Jessica Leach drily.

44

'Good God!' muttered Kelvin.

'Anyway, I'd like to look at this fossil.'

'Is that what that other word meant?'

'A palaeontologist is one who studies fossils. Where is it?'

Kelvin became all action. He jumped down from his stool and cleared a way through the customers to the stag's head. 'Excuse me! Excuse me! This lady is the expert in fossils come to find out what kind of turtle ours is. Shift your backs!'

The crowds parted and many conversations were suspended so that people could hear her comments. Kelvin moved Mandy and the commander – they split in opposite directions – and slid the table out of the way so that the turtle could be clearly seen. She looked. 'Is that it?'

'Yes. Of course that's it,' replied Kelvin.

She raised her head and looked Kelvin coldly in the eye. 'You mean I have just driven thirty miles to see this?' She gestured contemptuously towards the turtle.

'Well, I'm sorry,' muttered Kelvin. He was a little indignant since he did not see that he had to apologize for anything. 'I'd've thought that it would be quite nice for a pally-thing like you to see a turtle. You don't get them round here much these days.'

Jessica Leach looked round at the patrons who were silent, sharing Kelvin's indignation. 'It's not a fossil. It's a bag of cement.' She paused for a second or two. 'If that is all, I would like you to kindly get out of my way so that I can leave this place.' Kelvin did not get out of the way, so she walked round him and through the door, slamming it hard behind her. A few flakes of plaster sloughed off the ceiling and clicked on to the tile floor.

'What did she mean, "a bag of cement"?' demanded Mandy. 'What on earth is she talking about?'

Lindy began to giggle, but put her hand over her mouth when she was sent a furious look by Kelvin. Her shoulders heaved instead. The odd snigger came from other patrons and they gradually spread round the room and turned into guffaws. Kelvin's face suddenly split in a huge grin and great cackles of laughter came out.

'What on earth is going on?' shouted Mandy into the uproar.

Kelvin pulled out a large red handkerchief and wiped his eyes. 'Dick's bloody biorhythms were right. If he was here, I'd kick his arse for him. It's not a fossil at all, Mandy. That old fool Percy Bladderwort must have left a bag of cement out in the rain and it went hard.' He broke off for another cackle. 'Those markings were made by the paper bag which has rotted away.'

It was one of the more memorable lunchtimes the pub had known.

Chapter Four

LINDY LABOURED long and hard over her exhibition. The fiasco of the turtle had a positive side in that the story travelled everywhere within a matter of days. Men and women, old and young, emerged blinking from the isolation of their farmsteads with photographs and artifacts that were relevant to the history of the village and pressed them into Lindy's hand. Mandy called on the commander in order to solicit contributions and, although he had hidden in a potting shed at the far end of his square patch of Brussels sprouts as soon as her 'Yoo hoo!' pierced his peaceful afternoon's weeding, she gave him a nasty turn by looming up at him in the doorway, blocking out the light, after Elfrieda had maliciously indicated where he was likely to be found. His hand had found a scallop-shaped axehead with which to ward her off and he had managed to send her away with it as an ancient relic dug out of his potato patch. He had actually looted it from a crumbling farmhouse in the Dordogne where he had stayed during a leave in 1958.

The centrepiece of the exhibition was a collection of photographs showing the local fire brigade back through the decades; the village during wartime; the genteel life of the squire's forebears, their horses and new motor cars; and village weddings with bewhiskered faces whose eyes still expressed the agony of the unaccustomed stiff collars. There were school rolls, church records, newspaper cuttings, property deeds, bits of *Domesday*, letters, bills and maps. There were artifacts – no turtle, it was true, but there was the commander's axehead, and some superb Victorian agricultural implements

47

which had been lent by a grumbling Kelvin. He had scavenged them so that he could dominate the neighbourhood after the Bomb when electricity and diesel became unobtainable. Bill produced his milk-bottle collection which covered the farms of the parish over one hundred years and even Mike Weaver, who could conjure a fifteen-pound salmon from a goldfish bowl, came up with some wicked poaching implements passed down from an ancestor who, to the eternal shame of his descendants, was caught with a stag and hanged at the next assizes. It was the catching, not the hanging, that was still shameful.

The exhibition, which was opened by Marcia, the squire's wife, was a huge success. Old people spent hours cackling over sepia photographs of church picnics, working out who was who and with whom had they done what in the years that had followed. Dusty old scandals whose protagonists had lain comfortably in the graveyard together for decades were gleefully resurrected as were ancient arguments about boundaries and deals that had gone wrong.

The village was really rather tickled to discover that it had a history. It had heard that it had, but it had never before seen it clearly laid out. The pub, which itself featured in the exhibition unchanged since the dawn of photography, talked long and proudly about it. The locals often felt, but never articulated, a feeling of inferiority when faced with the worldly wisdom of the incomers. People like the commander had sailed the seven seas and Malcolm and Stephanie Jarrett had been to university. But there were Morchards, Weavers, Loosemires, Carters, Mowbrays and Bagginses in the photographs. Their descendants were the insiders, the inheritors of this bit of the country and the incomers, for all their knowledge, experience and sophistication, could never become part of its fabric as were the natives.

The exhibition was supposed to last a week but it lingered on. It was the village's equivalent of the mouldering copies of *Burke's* and *Debrett's* that filled a shelf in the squire's library.

Leon Wolff was a significant strand in the past of the village, but he was not recognized as such when he first came into the pub. He was just another seasonal tourist in his sixties who had strayed off the beaten path, more interesting than most because his clothes and his camera clearly branded him as an American even before he came up to the bar to order a drink.

Kelvin decided to speak to him, doing him a rare honour since Kelvin thought of tourists as a lion would zebra: 'Afternoon.'

'Afternoon,' replied the American. 'Nice drop of rain, this morning.'

Kelvin looked at him curiously. It was not often that one could have an intelligent conversation with a tourist, let alone with an American. He decided to test him further. 'Aye. It was the warm rain that'll keep the grass growing for a bit yet.' He cocked an inquisitive eyebrow but the American did not miss a beat.

'Not too much, though. Good open autumn. That's what's needed.'

Kelvin smiled his appreciation, thrusting out his hand. 'My name's Kelvin Morchard.'

The tourist looked delighted, shaking Kelvin's gnarled paw

with enthusiasm. 'Leon Wolff. Did I do it right? Gee! I thought I would have forgotten. It's been so long!'

'Buy the man a drink, Commander,' ordered Kelvin. 'What do you mean, "do it right"?'

'Speaking the language. It took me months to get the hang of it.'

'He's already got a drink,' observed the commander.

'Well, buy him another.'

'You buy him another,' replied the commander churlishly.

Leon Wolff held up a placating hand, his eyes dancing with pleasure. 'No, I don't want a beer. I never could stand the stuff. You guys are just the same as ever.'

Kelvin had no idea what the visitor was talking about. 'What are you talking about?'

'I've been here before. I used to drink in this pub forty years ago. It's exactly the same.'

'The same? It's not the same.' Kelvin indicated a table by the wall – that which had concealed the turtle. 'That table was only put there six years ago and the walls were painted for the Queen's Jubilee. It was the Jubilee, wasn't it, Bill?'

'That's right. They were painted for the Coronation, too, weren't they, Jimmy?'

'They were painted, yes. But I think they were painted in the same colour that they were before. Forty years ago. You must have been one of the Americans?'

'That's right. I was at the hall for six months during the war.'

'You were in the chicken house?'

'Yes. I was a driver there.' The chicken house, which now housed the communards, had been half nursing home and half R&R centre for Americans who were suffering from battle fatigue. The men of the village had been less than sympathetic as its patients had all been fresh young soldiers fatigued not by shellfire but by their training. The GIs had spread their dollars around like fertilizer on a field. Where they spread their fertilizer, they also tended to sow their seed as well. This was less often talked about since an embarrassingly high percentage of the sons and daughters of the parish

50

now entering middle age bore no resemblance to their putative fathers.

'I don't remember you. When exactly was that?' asked Kelvin.

'The spring of '44.'

'Ah! No wonder you don't remember him, Kelvin,' said Jimmy, making a serious social gaffe. Some topics were taboo. During that spring the War Agricultural Committee had decided that Kelvin was not farming as effectively as the nation required. A farmer from a neighbouring parish had been told to do a better job while Kelvin worked in a sawmill thirty miles away. It was six months before he got his land back and the community tacitly agreed that such an embarrassing episode should never be mentioned again.

There was an awkward silence during which Kelvin turned crimson. It was broken by the commander who, of course, knew nothing of Kelvin's shame as it happened decades before his arrival in the village. 'Did you come here often, Mr Wolff?'

'A couple of times a week. When I wasn't dating one of the girls.'

'I don't think we'd better go into that,' said Bill grimly.

'You were one of the darts players, weren't you?' asked Jimmy.

'You remember!' said Leon.

'How could I forget!' Jimmy turned to the commander. 'There were half a dozen of them who thought they could play darts! We took pint after pint off them. It was wonderful!'

'Hitler's war. Golden days,' sighed Leon Wolff. 'We were all young then – most of us, anyway.' Jimmy had obviously not been young since the Great War.

'You survived the war?' asked Ivor politely.

'Yes. I made master sergeant.'

'Like Bilko,' contributed the commander. 'No doubt you got lots of medals?'

'Oh, sure. But that was a long time ago. I'm in stationery now. I was over here on business with a couple of days to kill and I thought I'd come down here.'

'Stationery? Writing paper and things?' asked Kelvin.

'That's right. I've got my own business in Chicago.'

'You're rich, I imagine?'

'Well, let's say I pay my taxes and don't complain.'

'And what are you going to do now you're here?'

'Just go round old haunts and recall old memories.'

'Where are you going to stay?'

'I'll work something out.'

'There ain't a hotel round here, you know,' said Kelvin.

'I'll stay at a breakfast establishment, then. It'll only be for one night.'

'You can stay with us,' said the commander. 'Elfrieda would love it. I visited New Orleans once on a destroyer. Met a chap called Lucius. Or was it Lucien? Doesn't really matter. Anyway you will stay?'

'Thank you very much.'

There was an amiable pause in the conversation. 'I wonder what happened to all the girls? There was one real doll. She must be an old lady by now.'

'That was Mary Yerbury,' said Kelvin reverently. 'She married one of your lot and moved to America. To a place called Bullock.'

'It was Buffalo,' corrected Bill.

'That's right – Mary. She was too rich for my blood. I had one special girl. But I'm darned if I can remember her name.'

'It's probably just as well,' said Bill.

'Oh, I don't know,' argued Kelvin. 'It would be quite nice for you to meet her again.'

'She was a cutie. She had a real ass on her.'

'So one would have imagined,' commented the commander drily.

'Where did she live?' asked Kelvin.

'On one of the farms. Down a long lane.'

'That cuts it down', replied Kelvin sarcastically. 'Virtually every girl had a Yank and lived on a farm.'

'And Mary Yerbury is the only one of them who moved out,' warned Bill. 'I think you'd well let it lie.'

'Oh, stop fussing!' replied Kelvin. 'It was forty years ago! Where's the harm in it?'

'There are some things from forty years ago that are best let alone. You ought to know that, Kelvin,' warned Jimmy.

'Look, forget it,' said Leon Wolff. 'If it's going to cause trouble, I'll leave it. She'd look like my old lady now, anyway – sixty-five, 200lbs and with a temper like a wolverine.'

Kelvin chuckled. 'She sounds like Lily Baggins and it's hard to think that she could have broken hearts in her youth.'

'Perhaps ... er ... Mr Wolff's girl friend was Lily Baggins?' suggested the commander. 'Had she an American?'

'They all bloody did,' growled Jimmy.

'Lily Baggins?' said Leon Wolff, wrinkling his brow behind the metal struts of the spectacles that crossed the bridge of his nose. 'I don't think that was her name.'

'Could well have been,' grunted Kelvin. 'I remember when that sanctimonious old fart used to sell nylon stockings in the market. And you lot didn't give those away for praying in church.'

Ivor, ever the diplomat, changed the subject. 'You must go and visit the exhibition in the church hall while you're here. There's quite a lot about the war. And I'm sure the communards wouldn't mind if you looked round the hall.'

'The communards? Like communists?'

'If they're anything at all.'

'I've never met a communist,' said Leon cautiously.

'Well, you'll be able to live a little, won't you?'

Leon Wolff stayed with the commander that night, saw round the commune next morning, the exhibition in the afternoon and presented the commander with a case of whisky as he departed to catch a London train in the evening. But he left a delicate situation behind him which arose from his tour of the exhibition. It had been highly successful as a £20 note had been stuffed by him into an empty vase which had been placed fortuitously on a table by the door – but he had done some recognizing. If Lily Baggins had not been minding the door at the exhibition, all would have been well.

Many old people had lent treasured artifacts and documents on condition that the exhibition would always be manned to prevent hordes of urban vandals descending on the church hall to rob and pillage. Mrs Baggins knew all about the American visitor and she knew all about Kelvin's description of her in the pub the previous night. She also knew something else.

Mrs Baggins pounced while the commander and Leon Wolff were absorbed in pictures of the Great Flood, an event which had occurred when the river had celebrated what the experts described as 'a hundred-year event' by rising gently and inexorably a full ten feet above its normal level. 'Have you seen the photographs over there?'

'I bet you're Lily Baggins,' said Wolff with a grin.

She peered at him suspiciously, the bright smile dying on her lips. 'I didn't know you, did I?'

'No.'

'Well, how did you know my name?'

'Mr Morchard – Kelvin – described you in the bar last night.'

'He did, did he? I heard about that.'

'No, no. I said at the time that you sounded just like my wife and it's true.'

'Oh. What's your wife like?'

'Just like you.'

Lily Baggins thought for a second. Honesty was one of her few qualities. Her eyes narrowed. Even Kelvin, normally as sensitive to the moods of another as a Chieftain tank, would have realized that her expression boded ill for him. 'There's a picture of me with the choir picnic before the war. Come and see if I looked like your wife then.' Any anticipatory excitement that the invitation may have triggered in the commander and Wolff was overwhelmed by the ferocity of the scowl on her face. They both hesitated. 'Well, come on, then!' Mrs Baggins beckoned at them. They exchanged glances before reluctantly following her to the section on church activities which was laid out on a table beneath the window. Mrs Baggins pointed to a photograph bearing a label beneath proclaiming that it was the 1939 choir outing.

Leon Wolff looked briefly at the line of girls in cotton

dresses, men in jackets and flat caps and the solemn children with shorts covering their kneecaps. 'Very nice,' he commented, straightening up.

'Well? Which one is me? Did I look like your wife then?'

'I didn't notice,' replied Wolff unhappily. 'Why don't you point yourself out to me?'

'Look properly!'

The commander gave Wolff a nod to spur him on. Local women were best humoured.

Leon Wolff shrugged his shoulders, bent over the photograph again and looked properly. He even ran his index finger along the row of faces. His finger stopped. 'Hey! That one was my girl!' He looked up excitedly at the commander. 'The one I was telling you about last night! What's her name? What happened to her?'

The commander moved to the table. 'I don't suppose it can do much harm. You'll be off in an hour or two.' He looked down at the face underlined by Wolff's finger. He sighed and took his spectacles from his pocket, placing them on his nose before raising his eyebrows to peer down again. 'I've no idea who that is,' he said, shaking his head. 'She's quite pretty, though.'

'She sure was. Would you know who she is, Mrs Baggins?'

Mrs Baggins sniffed. 'There wasn't any point in asking him,' she said, jerking her head towards the commander. 'He's not local. Let's have a little look.' Her finger went down alongside that of the American. 'That's me at the end, there. I was a soprano, you know. I bought that dress for 12s 6d. Your girl—' she moved her finger along '—that's Ruth Snow.'

'Ruth Snow! That was it. How could I forget? Snow, like her skin!'

'Who is she?' asked the commander.

'Was, I'm afraid. She died nearly twenty years ago,' replied Mrs Baggins. 'She was Bill's half-sister.'

'Oh, that's a real shame!' said Leon Wolff.

'It comes to us all. Some are just taken sooner than others. She had a peaceful end. Her heart gave out when she was chasing a heifer from her garden.'

The commander looked relieved. 'Well, that's that, then.'

'Yeah, I suppose so. She was a real doll, though.' The American gave a final sad look at the picture. 'It's probably just as well. If she'd been around, it would have either spoiled my memory of her or we'd still have something going. It was a real shame when we were shipped out. We only got twenty-four hours' notice.'

The commander cast a puzzled look at Mrs Baggins who had retired to her chair by the door with a satisfied expression on her face. There was something he had missed about the last minute or two, but he could not see what it was. He shrugged, dismissing the problem from his mind. 'If you've got to catch a train, Leon, you'll have to think about going soon.'

'OK. I'll just take a few pictures of the village. I've told them back home so much about this place that they'll want to see it.'

'I bet you didn't tell them everything.'

'Well, no,' admitted Wolff with a smile. 'Ruth I kept to myself.'

It was quiet in the pub during the early part of that evening. The click of the latch, the squeak of the hinges, the hiss of damp logs and the laboured, uneven tick of the wall clock were the dominating sounds as the few customers supped their drinks quietly, waiting to see what the evening might bring. There was always someone who would come in whose day had contained some incident or experience that would be worthy of discussion. The clientele was usually entirely male at that hour as the women were either preparing their menfolk's supper or washing up after it. It was the commander who started the ball rolling. He came in, rubbing his hands briskly together, his nervous energy stirring the peaceful apathy of those already there.

'What are you so cheerful about?' asked Malcolm.

'Leon Wolff,' replied the commander. 'I've just seen Mick and he's delivering a case of scotch in payment for my giving Wolff a bed for the night.'

'Huh!' grunted Bill sourly. 'They haven't changed. That's the way they'd win people over back in the old days.'

'Oh yes!' exclaimed the commander. 'He found out who his girlfriend was. It was your late sister, Ruth Snow.'

Bill's jaw dropped. 'Ruth! It couldn't have been. I mean, she was always as quiet as a mouse. If it had been one of her sisters, I might have believed it, but not Ruth. She never went out with a Yank. She couldn't have done.'

'Wolff identified her in a photograph in the church hall. He was very certain about it.'

'Nonsense! How would he have known it was her?'

'Lily Baggins. She was on the door and she was in the picture too.'

'Lily Baggins!' exclaimed Bill. 'Yes, she was always a friend of Ruth when they were young.' He paused for a moment. Then he grinned. 'Well, I'll be buggered. Ruth. Who would have believed it?'

Jimmy, sitting in his chair in the corner of the bar, began to wheeze with laughter.

'What's the joke?' asked the commander. 'Malcolm, what's so funny?'

'Don't ask me,' replied Malcolm.

The door clicked and squeaked to announce Kelvin who walked to his usual stool and watched while Helga poured out his pint. Bill and Jimmy were still grinning at each other. Kelvin glanced at them and then looked more carefully. 'What's the joke then?'

'Nothing, nothing,' responded Bill hastily.

Kelvin turned to the commander who spread out his hands apologetically. 'I don't know what's funny. I was just telling them about Leon Wolff's old girlfriend. Lily Baggins—'

'Lily Baggins!' Kelvin gave a great guffaw and slapped his hand down on the bar. 'I thought it might have been her. It must have scared the shit out of him! What happened?' He looked eagerly at the commander, his eyes dancing with delight.

'No, his girlfriend wasn't Lily Baggins. It was Bill's sister, Ruth Snow. He saw her in a photograph in the exhibition and Lily Baggins said who it was.' The commander, in spite of his reservations at gossip on this level, could not help smiling at Kelvin's glee.

Kelvin's eyes shuffled to a halt. 'Ruth Snow? What are you talking about?'

'It was Ruth Snow that was his girlfriend. She was in a picture of a pre-war church picnic. Lily was there as well.'

'It can't have been Ruth Snow,' said Kelvin decisively.

'It was,' insisted the commander. 'Leon Wolff remembered her name. Snowy, like her skin, was what he said.'

Bill and Jimmy caught each other's eye and creased up with laughter. The commander looked at them with some bewilderment. It was not that funny. 'I've had a feeling that I've been missing something about your sister's little romance.'

'I've a feeling I can guess what,' said Malcolm. 'Reader, she married him.'

'I beg your pardon?' said the commander.

'It's a quotation.'

The commander showed his irritation. 'For Christ's sake, will someone tell me what the big secret is?'

'The woman may have been born Ruth Snow, but she died Ruth Morchard,' said Kelvin. 'She was my bloody wife, God rest her soul.'

Enlightenment dawned. 'Oh, I see! That explains why Lily Baggins was so keen that Wolff looked at the photograph. She must have known about the romance at the time.' Astonishment crossed the commander's face as he thought about it. 'If you lot didn't know about it, Lily Baggins must have kept it a secret for nearly forty years! That's amazing!'

'Good old Ruth!' said Bill. 'She had a bit of a life after all. What was it that Yank said? Cute little bum, wasn't it?'

'Do you mind!' objected Kelvin. 'You're talking about my missus.' He creased his forehead. 'I never noticed that she had a cute bum.'

'You wouldn't have noticed if she'd had no bum at all!' said Jimmy.

'Well, you couldn't have ever described her as a woman that'd you'd really notice,' said Kelvin defensively. 'But she was a good worker.'

'Yes, she was a good worker. Her harvest loaf was always a real picture,' agreed Bill. 'And she brought up your Prudence the same way. Milking, is she?'

'Feeding the young stock, by now,' said Kelvin, taking a sip from his beer. 'You know, I don't really mind about Ruth. Not now she's been dead all these years. I might have had something to say if she'd still been around. But not now.'

'That's a very fair attitude,' said Jimmy, peeling the stub of a hand-rolled cigarette from his bottom lip.

'It is,' agreed the commander. 'But why has it been such a secret? I mean, you know how hard it is to keep a secret round here.'

'Beats me,' said Jimmy.

'It's funny when you think about it,' mused Kelvin. 'You live in a house with someone for twenty years and you can still learn something about them.'

'You're wife's been dead for twenty years too?' asked Malcolm thoughtfully.

'Yes. I suppose it's an anniversary or something.'

'That's forty years ago that you got married?'

Kelvin glanced at Malcolm sardonically. 'Christ! You're quick this evening.'

What was stirring in the recesses of Malcolm's brain began to do the same in the commander's. 'When was it that the Americans were here?'

'Forty years ago, of course. That Yank said so last night,' answered Jimmy. 'Oh!' he added quietly.

Kelvin twigged too and rounded on Jimmy. 'Here! What are you trying to say?' Jimmy did not answer immediately, so Kelvin did it for him. 'You're saying that my Ruth was walking out with that Yank just before she married me!'

'I didn't say anything of the sort,' replied Jimmy.

'Yes, you bloody did!'

Bill intervened. 'Look, don't get all in a lather. It should be fairly easy to work out what was going on. When did you get married, Kelvin?'

'That's easy enough. It was the January when that two-headed calf was born at West Barton.'

'That was 1944,' said Jimmy.

There was a short silence. 'I'm not sure that gets us very far,' contributed the commander awkwardly. 'The Americans would have all left round about D-Day which was June that year. But for heaven's sake! You'd have surely known about it if she'd been seeing him. I mean, it was the first six months of your marriage!'

'I had to go away for a while round about then,' replied Kelvin, looking into his glass.

'You! Go away! I never heard that you'd lived anywhere else than on your farm!' exclaimed Malcolm.

'It was the war,' replied Kelvin evasively.

'What? Are you saying you were in the army?'

'Not exactly. Some of us who did our bit are still not allowed to talk about it.'

Malcolm snorted derisively. 'Kelvin, come on! You're not

60

saying you were parachuted into France to show the Resistance how to lay a hedge or something?'

Bill stirred on his stool. Kelvin, for all his faults, was his brother-in-law while Malcolm was nobody. He had come from somewhere like Dorset or Dorking. 'You leave Kelvin alone. Your generation wouldn't be here if it wasn't for ours.' Malcolm wisely did not argue.

'Anyway,' said the commander briskly, 'it's all history, now. And Leon Wolff is probably halfway across the Atlantic on his way back to his wife. Even if your Ruth did have a bit of a fling all those years ago, she was obviously a good wife to you and gave you a fine daughter.'

'I suppose that's true,' admitted Kelvin.

'You were quite right, by the way,' continued the commander, deciding that it was time that the subject was changed. 'He guessed who Mrs Baggins was after your description – actually she wasn't too happy about that.'

'Serve the old bag right!' replied Kelvin. There was a short silence before Kelvin's evening proceeded to deteriorate further.

'How old is Prudence, now?' asked Jimmy.

'Prudence?' repeated Kelvin. 'I dunno. I suppose she must be getting on a bit. She can't be far short of forty. It's funny to think of her as middle-aged.'

Jimmy broke into a fit of coughing as a mouthful of beer went down the wrong way. The others looked fearfully at their drinks, the floor and the walls. Nobody dared catch another's eye. 'Forty,' repeated Kelvin slowly. 'Jesus!'

The commander glanced up from his study of a slug trail that glistened on the edge of the carpet by the window. Kelvin was being wracked by an emotional maelstrom, as powerful as on the occasion when he had dropped a bottle of whisky on the pavement outside the post office. The commander cleared his throat nervously. 'Look, Kelvin. Don't jump to conclusions.'

'Absolutely!' agreed Bill vigorously. 'Ruth would never have done that. It's ridiculous to think otherwise.'

Jimmy nodded his head in assent, showering cigarette ash over his immediate environment. 'Quite. Your Ruth was a good woman. And Prudence looks just like her. It's obvious that they're mother and daughter.'

'When's Prudence's birthday?' asked Malcolm. 'That might help clear things up.'

'It's in January,' replied Kelvin. 'It always saved money as her Christmas presents did for her birthday as well.' There was a ten-second silence as fingers counted off the months.

'Well, of course, that doesn't prove anything,' said Malcolm.

'It certainly proves something since I wasn't around in April.'

Bill sighed. 'I must say it looks pretty bad.'

'Bad? It's bloody outrageous! All these years I've treated Prudence as my own and that bastard was her father all along. She's been living in my house under false pretences!'

'You can't be sure of that,' protested the commander feebly.

'Wolff! That's what her name is. Prudence Wolff! She's not a Morchard at all. It's humiliating!'

'It's not your fault, Kelvin.'

Kelvin turned savagely towards the commander. 'It's not humiliating for me, you fool. It's humiliating for her! She's been thinking all these years that I was her father and it's been a bloody American all along. She's half-foreign! She may be just Prudence but I wouldn't wish something like that on a dog! Think how it's going to make her feel! An American! And she's been working on my farm all these years, pretending she's my heir and she's not at all! She's someone else's bastard!' There was spittle flecking Kelvin's lips.

Bill looked across the bar at Kelvin with stony eyes. His stare shifted to Malcolm. 'Kelvin went away during the war because the government gave his land to someone who could farm it properly,' he said flatly.

'Here!' shouted Kelvin, aghast. 'What do you think you're doing? Do you know what you're saying?'

Bill knew. 'You're a right bastard, Kelvin! She may be Prudence Wolff but half of her is a Snow and don't you ever forget it. If you don't treat her right, she'll walk out on you and then where would you be? She does all the work.'

'I'm not denying that she's got her good points. But she's

not got any claims on me. Not if she's not my daughter. She's got no rights to my farm. Not now.'

'She's legally your daughter, Kelvin. That's the law if you and your wife were married when she was born,' said Malcolm.

'Look! That Wolff is her father. She's not going to get Morchard land. That farm's been in the family too long for it to be given away to a Yank.'

'There's something else,' piped up Jimmy. 'That Yank was rich. He had a business and he gave the commander a case of whisky. If Prudence is his daughter, she'll probably inherit from him.'

That was something Kelvin had not considered and his eyes showed sudden torment.

Bill turned the knife. 'That's a very good point, Jimmy. Prudence'll probably be left a great deal of money. He virtually said he was a millionaire. Prudence could well become a millionaire herself.'

Kelvin's brow furrowed as he weighed this information. 'But he's gone back to America and he doesn't know anything about it.'

'There can't be many Leon Wolffs who own stationery businesses in Chicago,' Bill chuckled. 'I think this might be Prudence's lucky day after all. With her own money she'll be able to buy her own farm. She might even move to America.'

'Move to America? said Kelvin. 'She couldn't walk out on me – not after all I've done for her over the years.' Kelvin was not one of Nature's blood donors. Instead he was one of those rare people with incorruptible integrity. His every action was ruled by self-interest. If he had been clever enough to be able to conceal it, he could have succeeded in any sphere of human activity.

'For heaven's sake!' exclaimed the commander. 'I thought you were going to cast her out into the snow five minutes ago!'

'But that was before I found out that she was going to be rich. Do you really think he would give her money?'

The commander sighed. He had known Kelvin for only five years and could not believe that he understood him. 'If you are prepared to cut her off after forty years because she's not your daughter, by the same strange logic he will acknowledge her.'

'Bloody hell! If Prudence became a millionaire, think what I could do with the money! I could buy a new tractor! Or start having racehorses like you used to, Bill.'

'Don't forget, it would be Prudence who would become the millionaire, not you,' warned Jimmy.

'She's my own daughter! Well, she isn't of course, but you know what I mean. She'll see her old father right after all I've done for her. Anyway, I'm in charge of the money in my household and it's me who decides what's to be done with it!'

'She'll run her own life!' said the commander. 'She's a forty-year-old woman!'

The conversation had been so engrossing that the clock had ticked on and the fire had kept hissing without anyone taking any notice. More importantly, the latch also clicked and the hinges had creaked.

'Who's a forty-year-old woman?' queried Lindy, coming up to the bar.

'Prudence,' replied Jimmy before the men could close ranks on this delicate subject.

'Balls! She's thirty-eight. She was born in 1946.'

'What?' shouted Kelvin. 'She's forty. We worked it out. She was born in 1944, the year of the two-headed calf.'

'The one at West Barton? That was 1946 too. There's a newspaper cutting about it in the exhibition. Anyway, I know she's thirty-eight. I had her medical card out when I gave her a tetanus booster last week.'

Kelvin's expression slowly turned to one of great anguish. 'That's not fair. If she's only thirty-eight, she won't be a millionaire.'

'What are you talking about, Kelvin?' asked Lindy.

'We thought that she and that American . . .' his voice trailed into silence. 'Shit!' he said savagely.

'You are a stupid bugger, Kelvin,' said Bill into the heavy silence which followed. 'Lindy, may I buy you a drink?'

64

Chapter Five

IT WAS NOT just that Frank Mattock was rich that made him unusual in the parish – there were plenty of farmers whose land could have been realized for impressive sums of cash – but the fact that he had made his money himself. He made it obvious enough by clanking round the neighbourhood weighed down with gold bangles and chains which advertised his presence by winking and flashing in the sunlight as he drove his pedigree Holsteins between the fields of his ample farm. However, the village was surprised when he decided to enter the property business by buying up the old tithe barn that stood near the church.

It was not a tithe barn to thrill the shade of Pevsner: there were no massive stone walls or buttresses or hammer-beam roof. It was a more modest brick and timber structure befitting the few bushels of oats and barley that the surrounding parishes grudgingly yielded to the Almighty's servants at harvest time. It had recently been used to store five-gallon plastic drums, originally containing formic acid silage additive, which the parish council had decided would be ideal to use for distributing water during the frequent occasions when the village supply failed. They had been there for nearly six years, gathering layers of dust and mouse turds while the acrid stench from their interiors, in spite of frequent rinsing during the early months, still had the power to rouse a well-swooned Victorian maiden lady at a hundred paces.

At first it was assumed that Frank had bought the barn to expand his agricultural empire. There was some concern at this since he was not the most environmentally conscious of farmers. Butterflies faltered in their flight, stalled and spun to the ground when they crossed a hedge into the airspace above his land, because Frank believed in chemicals and saturated his acres with fungicides, pesticides and herbicides. The pub was not happy.

'What I'd like to know is what he's going to keep in there,' said the commander. He had wedged himself into a corner of the bar where Mandy could not get to him.

'Poisons of some kind, I expect,' muttered Malcolm.

'It'll be chickens. Lots and lots of smelly chickens,' replied Kelvin, who was quite happy at the prospect since he lived well out of the village. 'I've heard Frank say that he's often thought of going into intensive egg production.'

'Oh, that sounds quite nice, doesn't it, Commander?' said Mandy. 'It's nice to have a few chickens around. Mummy used to keep some during the war.' The other patrons looked at her speculatively. The idea of Mandy having a mummy and a childhood seemed rather incongruous. She ought to have sprung into existence, already lipsticked and eye-shadowed, out of a Christmas cracker and given a bollocking to all present at her incarnation for leaving the dirty pudding plates around.

'I think Frank was thinking in terms of thousands of chickens,' said Kelvin.

'The more the merrier,' responded Mandy gaily. 'The clucking is so soothing.'

'Stupid cow!' growled Jimmy, who could afford to be rude to anyone as he was protected by the armour of seventy-five years. 'Hens shit, and it makes catshit smell like lavender. Clucking indeed!' He took a gulp from his pint of bitter, dribbling a little on to his khaki shirt front.

'He'd need planning permission and it'd have to come before the parish council,' said the commander. 'He won't find it easy to fill the village with chickens.'

'How clever of you to think of that!' cried Mandy. 'We're so lucky to have you on the council to protect us!' The latch on the door of the pub clicked up and the door squeaked open. Mandy rolled her eyes like a ventriloquist's dummy. 'Talk of

66

the devil!' she whispered hoarsely as it opened to admit Frank.

He looked carefully round the pub, checking on who was present before moving to the bar and ordering a lager. Mandy looked covetously at the sovereign ring on his little finger. Frank had never really become part of the agricultural mafia of which Kelvin, Bill and Ivor were such stout members. It may have been that he was too young, still barely forty, or it may have been that he was too flashy, both in his dress and in his farming. The non-farming element in the village thought it was because he knew what he was doing. The others farmed by the seat of their pants, doing as they had always done and secure in the knowledge that a cow had been a cow and a grain of barley had been a grain of barley since before they were born and would remain so when they were naught but dust.

Frank did not have the same faith. He read books and magazines, discussed innovations with technical advisors and knew that the scrubby little shorthorns his father had chopped up in the back of the family butcher's shop which had gone out of business in the mid-fifties were very different creatures from his lanky, milk-gushing Holsteins.

'How much did you pay for the tithe barn, Frank?' asked Kelvin.

'£8,000,' Jimmy answered for him, scornful that Kelvin had to ask. 'What are you going to do with it?'

'You know that it is highly unlikely that the parish council will give permission for an intensive chicken unit so close to the centre of the village, don't you?' said the commander.

Frank took a long pull at his pint. 'So you reckon that I'd have difficulty with permission for chickens, Commander? Perhaps I should build a house next to the barn instead. Would I get permission for that?'

'A house? You want to build a house?' The commander burbled on for a bit as he and everyone else assessed the implications if Frank built a house. How much would it cost? What would he do with it? What could he sell it for? Think of the profit he could make! 'Oh dear! A house? Why should you want to build a house?'

'There could be a bob or two in it eventually. Or I could use it to house a farmworker.'

'You haven't got a farmworker,' objected Kelvin.

'I might need a cowman soon. What do you think, Commander?'

'There could be problems about it. Wouldn't you agree, Ivor?'

'There certainly would be,' put in Kelvin. 'Can't go building houses all over the place. Not with the sewers we've got in the village. When I was on the council, I used to complain about them regularly.'

'But you resigned, didn't you?' said the commander acidly. 'Another problem I can see is the preservation of the barn. We've got precious few old buildings left as it is. What with the sewers and worries about our heritage, I'd be very surprised if the council would give its permission.'

'Oh well. It wouldn't much matter. I was just wondering. It's chickens that I'll be doing,' said Frank.

'I've already said that chickens will be definitely out.'

'So you say, Commander. But I've had a word with a couple of district councillors and they said there'd be no problem. They said I wouldn't need any permission anyway because it's not a change of use. It's been an agricultural building for centuries and I intend that it should remain one – with 10,000 chickens inside.'

'You wouldn't dare!' exclaimed the commander. 'It would stink the village out!'

'It would, I know,' agreed Frank earnestly. 'That's why I just thought of putting up a house instead. It would be better for the community.'

'I think a house would be an excellent idea, under the circumstances,' said Malcolm.

Frank winked at him. 'Oh well,' he sighed, 'I suppose I may just have to settle for that.'

Kelvin and the commander had suspicions that they had been outmanoeuvred, but Jimmy and everyone else had been too concerned about being blighted by the miasma of hens to afford to indulge in the luxury of keeping Frank in his place.

'That's very good of you, Frank,' said Jimmy earnestly. 'There aren't enough people in this community who think of their fellow men.'

'Amen to that!' agreed Maud fervently. Her post office was near to both the church and the barn.

'Good,' said Frank. 'Mandy, is Keith very busy at the moment?'

'Over here, Frank,' said Keith, waving his hand. He was sitting beneath the stag's head. Most regulars avoided that bench as the stuffed head made them uneasy. Over the years its skin had withered back from the glass eyes to give it a manic glint as if it contemplated a spring from its hook to tear the throat out of any drinker who came too close. In the shadow of the twin threats of the decorporated stag and his wife, Keith was even more self-effacing than usual.

Frank walked over, pulling an envelope from the inside of his yellow anorak. 'I'd like you to take a look at this, Keith. It's a picture of the house I'd like to put up. I was wondering if you might have a look at it. I'll be wanting a builder and I think you've done a great job on your own house.' He handed over the paper. 'Let me know what you think of it.' He drained his glass, placed it on the bar, gave a tight smile to the commander and left, slamming the door behind him. The latch clicked down into the silence a few seconds later.

'Well, bugger me!' said Kelvin, expressing the general view. 'Who'd have thought it? He wanted to stick up a house all the time! But he must be off his rocker to ask Keith to build it!'

'What do you mean? Keith is a wonderful builder. Frank said he did a lovely job on our cottage and he's been very busy since then,' flared Mandy.

'But we couldn't have places like that all over the village, could we?'

'Why ever not? "Pixie's Bower" is a lovely cottage. It always looks a real picture, doesn't it, dear?' She nudged her husband who grunted acknowledgement from Frank's sheet of paper in which he was absorbed.

'It's a bit bigger than our cottage,' he said.

'Let's have a look,' said Kelvin.

69

'Bring it up to the bar where we can all see,' ordered the commander, clearing towels and ashtrays from the surface in front of his stool. Keith handed over the piece of paper and the commander spread it out on the warped and ancient oak of the bar. 'Heavens!' he murmured, after he had placed his reading glasses on his nose.

Kelvin peered and sucked in his breath with indignation.

'Cowman's cottage indeed! We can't have a place like this in the village. Who the hell does Frank think he is?'

'JR! That's who he thinks he is!' cried Mandy, making the commander start nervously as she placed her cheek close to his so that she could see. 'That's a picture of "South Fork". In *Dallas*.'

'A swimming pool right next to the churchyard is out for a start,' contributed Malcolm grimly. 'And he's not going to be allowed to knock down the barn.'

'The best thing to do is work out what we'll let him put up at the next council meeting,' suggested the commander. 'Something small that is in keeping with the traditions of the community. Something more appropriate for a cowman.'

'Something that he'll find difficult to sell to a weekender,' added Kelvin.

'Well, just so long as you don't make it too complicated,' warned Keith.

Contractors who build in cities can erect great sheets of plywood to hide their work and their mistakes from the prying eyes of the passers-by. The contract for Frank's house, although one of the largest feats of civil as opposed to agricultural engineering that had taken place in the village for a decade, did not stretch to such luxuries. Most inhabitants of the parish made sure they passed the site at least once each day.

It was something different. The scenery varied anyway with the passing of the seasons. Leaves appeared on the creeper which enveloped the church tower, only to drop off six months later. The single sunflower that Jimmy grew annually in his front garden was always something at which eyes attuned to

70

daisies and dandelions could marvel, while the gradual decomposition of his Ford Consul, which he had ceased driving five years earlier, could be closely followed from year to year.

However, there had never been anything like Frank's house. It was an intoxicating luxury and the villagers made the most of it. They did not merely eye it as they walked past. They walked round it, over it, through it with critical or appreciative eyes and passed advice, criticism and comment on its construction. The village took the house to its collective heart. Designed by the parish council, which had been Frank's intention all along, it was a square concrete box constructed from building blocks which represented the community's triumph over the threat of chickens. Some even saw it as a leap into the twentieth century. It was not every

village round about that could boast an example of modern architecture in its midst.

Under the eyes of the village, trucks came to deliver sand, cement, blocks and concrete. Drains went in, concrete was poured, and scaffolding rose. Everyone was entranced. Keith was a hero in the pub. This was no mere single-span concrete barn – all the rage at the obscure end of farm lanes – but a permanent addition to their everyday lives. Everyone had a critical stake in the business and bombarded Keith with advice. It was the commander who observed that there was no provision for a window in the bathroom and at 10pm helped Keith to pull down the blocks necessary to make a hole just as the mortar was setting. It was Dick who volunteered to monitor the wellbeing of the bats that lived in the tithe barn which almost kissed gables with the new house. It was Mrs Baggins who bustled through the front door of her cottage next to Jimmy's across the lane with two mugs of tea and two rich tea biscuits twice a day to give comfort to the workers.

There was one problem. The building inspector had been used to making a pleasantly moon-lit income by preparing plans for barns and house extensions on his patch for submission to the council. Frank had not needed his services and he was not happy about it.

The man dropped in shortly after the roof had gone up. Keith was away collecting some wood from the sawmill and had missed him and it had been up to his navvy, Jason Loosemire, to act as host and explain what had happened to Keith when he returned: 'He's not a cove I care for very much.'

'Yes,' said Keith impatiently. 'What did he say?'

'He shouted and waved his arms about for a bit when I dropped a block on his foot and then he went outside. I followed him after a minute or two when he had gone quiet and he was looking up at the roof, grinning like a Hallowe'en pumpkin. Then he went away.'

'The roof!' said Keith with alarm. 'He liked the roof! What's wrong with the roof?' He rushed out of the house, the metal on the soles of his boots denting the sap-filled wooden

72

floors and echoing round the shell of the interior. He splashed through the mud to the lane and looked back at the roof. 'What's wrong with the roof? It looks all right. Those tiles are straight. What did he say was wrong with it, Jason?'

'He didn't say nothing was wrong with it,' shouted Jason, leaning in the doorway. 'He was just looking at it and laughing.'

'Well, why didn't you ask him about it?'

'I told you. I didn't fancy him.'

Keith looked at him in exasperation. 'What's that got to do with it? Look, have you any idea why he was laughing at the roof?'

'Not a clue. Perhaps he was happy, thinking about his bird or something. He didn't say anything so there's nothing to worry about.'

But Keith worried, although neither his client nor his peers were particularly concerned. The civil engineering projects that they were used to relied upon baler twine as their principal ingredient, followed by recycled nails and any old scraps of wood that lay around. The roof seemed fine to Kelvin who had seen an entire home-built tractor shed collapse when a bullock scratched itself on the door frame, as it also seemed to the commander whose polythene growing tunnels carpeted the surrounding countryside like great undulating slugs after the first stiff breeze of autumn.

In spite of his concern, the house cruised ahead until Malcolm Jarrett went to have a look shortly before the scaffolding was removed. On Thursday Keith and his assistant kept going until eight o'clock to give those who worked during the day an opportunity to come to look at the house while the builders modestly enjoyed the admiration and the praise. Malcolm Jarrett's admiration was not actually worth a great deal. He was not a local, which was devaluation for a start, nor had he the countryman's eye for a structure. Everyone in the country can build if they are pushed; it is not an activity confined to contractors. Malcolm was also the nearest the community had to an intellectual so could not be expected to have any sense.

The men were cleaning up for the day when Malcolm arrived, wearing his gumboots. 'May I have a look around, Keith?'

'Be my guest,' replied Keith with a lordly wave of his trowel. By this time the walls and roof had been completed and work was underway on the interior, but the outside of the building was still clothed in scaffolding. Malcolm walked carefully through the doorway and disappeared from view.

'Are you going to the pub tonight?' Keith asked his assistant.

'Yeah, I suppose so. You coming along?' Jason would not normally associate with Keith. Being over thirty, Keith was geriatric and many years as a Reading butcher had left great gaps in his conversation. He could not discuss the way the salmon were running up the river, whether the squire's pheasants were worth taking yet or whether it was true that you had to go out twice with Lizzie Steer before she would let you into her knickers. However, Keith both paid him and felt that it was his duty as boss always to buy the first drink.

'Yes.'

'Well, I won't have time for more than a quick one.' Jason carefully made his mark to ensure he would not have to buy back. 'Going out.'

'Going out? Lizzie Steer?'

'How did you know?' demanded Jason.

'She told me,' replied Keith innocently.

Or was it innocently? Jason looked at Keith with suspicion. Keith was just a twit. Everyone knew that. But he had recently been rumoured to be a randy twit.

Malcolm had clambered around on the scaffolding to examine the upper storey and he now reappeared at the entrance to the house. Both Keith and Jason looked at him hopefully. Even Malcolm's opinion was worth something. 'Er . . . very nice, isn't it?'

'So they say,' replied Jason stolidly.

'You don't often see fireplaces on the first floor these days.'

'The fireplaces? No, I suppose not,' responded Keith.

'Aren't the chimneys meant to go all the way through?'

'What do you mean?' said Keith. 'Of course they go all the way through.'

'One of them doesn't. The chimney from the bottom is blocked by the fireplace on the floor above.'

'Don't be silly,' replied Keith, but his voice lacked conviction and he looked furtively up and down the lane to ensure that there was nobody of importance within earshot. 'Is it really blocked?'

'Yes.'

'Jason, that was your job. What the hell have you gone and done?'

'Just what I was told.'

'You weren't bloody well told to block up the fireplace.'

'I was just following the plans. If you can't draw up proper plans, it's your fault. Yours and Frank's. You should have got that council inspector bloke to do them.'

'If it was on the bloody plan that you should jump off the roof, you wouldn't do it, would you?'

'Of course not. I'm not daft,' replied Jason.

'Well, why block up the chimney, then?'

Jason seemed confused. 'What's that got to do with jumping off the roof? There was nothing about that on the plans but the fireplace upstairs was.'

Keith turned to Malcolm in resignation. 'Modern youth!' he sighed.

'Don't you take that attitude with me, Keith,' bristled Jason. 'I don't have to work here. I'd get bloody nearly as much from the Social Security as working here.'

'You're still collecting Social Security,' responded Keith.

Jason looked triumphant. 'Exactly!' he replied.

Both Malcolm and Keith appeared puzzled. Malcolm spoke after a short pause. 'There was something else that I didn't understand—'

'Bugger the chimney for tonight,' said Keith. 'Are you coming for a drink? I'll explain what you don't understand in the pub.'

Keith was now an important figure in the pub, receiving respectful nods of greeting from the others. With Frank's gold running through his economy, he quite often bought drinks for other patrons. He ordered a round and the three of them took the ritual first sip, smacking their lips with the faraway expression of men who were being men at the end of a hard day.

'What was it that you didn't understand, Malcolm?' asked Keith loudly. He was very happy with the role of advising Malcolm about the intricacies of his profession in an avuncular fashion.

'How are people going to get to the upper floor?'

'Of the house?' asked Keith, off balance at the inanity of the question.

'Yes. There aren't any stairs.'

'What?' shouted Kelvin. 'Of course there are stairs! I was up there this morning. You were with me, Commander. We were both up there.'

'Yes. That's right. We were discussing the bathroom.'

'Well, you must have climbed up the scaffolding, because there certainly aren't any stairs.'

Jason started to guffaw. 'He's right, you know. Keith forgot to put in a staircase. He's been running up and down the scaffolding and not even noticed.'

'So have you,' observed Malcolm mildly.

'Not my fault. I just work for him.'

'But you're supposed to be a builder too,' said the commander.

'Don't pick on me,' replied Jason with indignation. 'The whole bloody village has been traipsing up and down that ladder and this smart-arse is the only person to have noticed.'

Keith drained his pint and slammed it down on the counter. 'Damn!' He gave Malcolm a savage glance and stormed out of the pub.

Kelvin peered through the leaded lights of the window after him. 'He's going back to have a look at the house,' he announced.

Many of the customers in the pub walked the hundred yards to commiserate with him in this misfortune. Malcolm,

76

educated enough to know the likely fate of messengers who bore ill tidings, prudently stayed behind to chat up Helga behind the bar while Jason went off, rather nervously, to his tryst with Lizzie.

The building inspector dropped in the following week to spring his little surprise. He rubbed his hands together in pleasure as he emerged from his small, red motor car. He was a man in his mid-thirties with odd tufts of ginger hair sprouting from his cheekbones, his ears, his nostrils and above the collar of his shirt. Without clothes he would have looked like a short-armed orang-utan and he had a loud, booming voice which would have been very useful for communicating between the jungle treetops. Frank, Keith and Jason were present to respond to the 'Ho, ho, ho' which the sight of the cottage drew from him. He hummed happily as he toured the house. Keith, who had been looking forward to his visit with considerable foreboding, began to cheer up. The house was his life's masterpiece so far and he was very proud of it.

'Nice view,' commented the inspector, looking out through the living-room window at the tower of the church and the heather-purple moor that rose up beyond.

'We made up those windows ourselves,' replied Keith proudly. 'Seasoned ash. You can't buy that sort of quality off the shelf. Isn't that right?'

'Yes, they're very fine frames. Not quite what I would have specified—'

'There's nothing in regulations that says you can't use ash in windows,' interrupted Keith.

'I didn't say there was. Regulations are concerned with their size and the ceiling heights of the rooms.'

'I know all that,' replied Keith rather testily. 'And you won't be able to find anything wrong with them.'

'Oh good. Still, I always think it best to use someone who knows what he's doing when it comes to drawing up plans, don't you?'

'We knew what we were doing, didn't we Jason?'

'`S'right.'

The inspector rubbed his hands together again. 'Jolly good.

Mistakes can get very expensive.' He measured the doorframe with his eye.

'7 feet 6 inches. Not a fraction under,' said Keith emphatically.

The inspector smiled. 'They're supposed to be a minimum of 198 centimetres.'

Keith's jaw opened and shut in horror like that of a goldfish. Frank, who had been growing more and more twitchy at the bonhomie being shown, exclaimed, 'Bugger it. I knew there'd be something.'

'However,' continued the inspector smoothly, 'you don't need to worry about that since 198 centimetres is 6 feet 6 inches.'

Keith sagged against the wall. 'You did that deliberately, you bastard.'

The inspector chuckled, his beer belly vibrating. 'You ain't seen nothing yet. Shall we go upstairs?'

'What do you mean, "ain't seen nothing yet"?' asked Frank, but the inspector merely chortled. The natives exchanged uneasy glances. It was becoming evident that he had a Damoclean sword secreted somewhere about his person, but he kept it sheathed until they got outside. His suppressed excitement was such that Frank received an inkling of what it must have been like for an aristo on his last journey in a tumbril.

The inspector stepped outside and took several deep breaths, stretching out his arms to show a length of hairy ginger wrist at the end of each sleeve. He turned round to the house, merrily whistling *The Road to the Isles* through his teeth.

'It's the roof,' groaned Keith. 'It's got to be the roof.'

'The roof?' echoed the inspector with an innocent expression on his face as he lifted his eyes heavenwards. 'What about the roof? I'm sure it will show the same high standard of craftsmanship that you say everything else displays. Yes, I thought so. It looks fine.'

'You mean there's nothing wrong with it?' asked Keith incredulously.

'Wrong with it? I don't think so.' There was a gleam in his

eye that would have made even Lucifer pause before he unlocked his molten version of the Pearly Gates. The inspector looked back at the roof. He frowned like a pantomime villain. 'Oh dear, oh dear me. I'm not so sure about that. I shall have to check the plans in the car.'

'What?' demanded Keith. 'What do you mean?'

'The roof.' The inspector pursed his lips and shook his head. 'I could be wrong, but I'd better check.' He skipped merrily over to his car in the lane, flashing a beaming smile to Jimmy who was watching the proceedings under the guise of clipping his box hedge.

'Shit!' said Frank with venom. 'What's wrong with the bloody roof? If that sod is mucking us about, I'll have him.' Jason looked at Frank with admiration, coveting his ability to make a threat that sounded so certain of execution.

The inspector returned with the plans. 'I was afraid of that.'

'What?' demanded Frank aggressively.

'Look here.' He pointed at the plans with a hirsute digit.

Both Frank and Keith looked. It was the elevation showing the new house adjacent to the barn. 'What about it?' asked Frank.

'The height.'

'Oh,' said Frank as he, Keith and Jason looked at the roof which stood a few inches above that of the tithe barn. 'I see.'

'Well, I'm damned if I do,' said Keith. 'It looks fine to me.'

'It's supposed to be exactly matching the height of the barn,' said the inspector happily.

'Well it does, just about. It may be a tiny bit high, but I don't really see that it matters very much. Anyway how was I supposed to know that?'

'You may not have known it, but it was specifically mentioned in a letter to Mr Mattock. It was something that the parish council was extremely concerned about.' The inspector's eyes were twinkling with glee. ' "Ensuring that the new cottage blended in with our heritage" was how they put it when they were consulted by the planning department.'

'I completely forgot about it,' said Frank miserably.

'Oh well,' said Keith. 'No great harm done. We're sorry

about it. We'll get the council to change their decision if it'll make you any happier. They don't give a damn, really.'

The inspector pursed his lips in mock dismay. 'Oh dear me. It's not that simple. You can't just change a decision of the district council when you want to. That planning agreement has the force of law.'

'What do you suggest?' asked Frank humbly.

'Me?' If he had been Miss Piggy, he would have said 'Moi?' 'There's nothing I can do. Not now. It's much too late for that. It was a mistake not to have someone properly qualified keeping an eye on things in the first place.'

'All right, all right,' said Frank. 'I'm sorry. I should have hired you. Next time I'll make sure I will. But what happens next?'

'There's only one thing that can happen. It'll have to come down.'

'That'll be a shame,' said Jason. 'That barn's been around for a long time.'

Even the mightiest jungle giant of the rain forest would have vibrated to the hoots of delight that finally burst from the inspector's lips. 'It's not the barn that's got to come down,' he gasped, retreating backwards towards his car in face of the thunder in Frank's face. 'It's the house.'

'Oh, come off it,' said Jason. 'It'd cost a fortune.'

'Yes, it will,' smiled the inspector through his car window. 'I'll send you an official letter about it.'

'Are you serious?'

'Oh yes. I'm serious all right.'

'We could lower the roof and the ceilings in the bedrooms,' suggested Frank desperately.

'Wouldn't work,' gloated the inspector. 'It's the downstairs where you've got the extra height. Seven-foot-six-inch door-ways! That's where the problems start. Bye-bye!' Chortling, he started up his car and went off down the lane.

The pub was incensed. Frank was at fault, certainly, and there was some pleasure in seeing the community's most gilded citizen with egg on his face. It was also true that the parish council had insisted upon the symmetry of roof ridges in the first place. But that was only demanded so that its members could demonstrate that they had power. A far more important principle at stake was that of local independence. It was a village matter and up to the community to sort out: no jumped-up little bureaucrat could be allowed to interfere. But the official letter came and the appeal against its findings was refused. It was very simple: if Frank wanted his house, the apex of its roof ridge must match that of the barn in height.

Chapter Six

'BURN THE barn down,' suggested Kelvin, once the doors of the pub had been firmly locked behind the few strangers who had ventured in . After 11pm, business continued until the last man out washed up any remaining glasses and locked the back door behind him as he ventured out to face the dawn chorus. 'Then there wouldn't be any barn, let alone a roof for them to worry about.'

'That would be arson,' responded Percy, the local policeman.

'But I wouldn't claim on the insurance,' said Frank.

'Percy's right. It would be illegal, somehow. Trying to subvert the democratic processes of local government, perhaps,' contributed Malcolm. 'There's got to be another way. Can't you just make the roof a bit less steep, or something?'

'I wish we could. Quite apart from the cost of ripping it down and shortening all the timbers, there are all sorts of regulations about the slope of the roof and things. And that blasted inspector will not let us get away with a thing.'

'Slip him a couple of hundred quid,' recommended Percy. 'That's all he wants. If he's any trouble in the future, then I could have him for taking bribes.'

'I tried that on the telephone and got nowhere. He said it had gone above his head, and anyway he thought it was in his interests to do me.'

'*Pour encourager les autres* to get him to draw up plans in future, I suppose. Then you'll just have to take it down to the first floor and rebuild,' said the commander, 'and put the extra cost down to experience. I remember once when I was on a courtesy visit on a frigate in Asia – bloody hot it was but the girls were quite charming. Penang, Djakarta, Bangkok. It was one of those sort of places—'

'Oh shut up!' interrupted Mandy. 'Frank, there's a much easier way of doing it. It would cost you very little too. Look at it the other way round. Instead of reducing the house, why don't you raise the barn?'

'Raise the barn? What do you mean, dear?' asked her spouse. 'It would cost just as much to rebuild the barn as to rebuild the cottage.'

'Don't be stupid, dear. You wouldn't have to do any of that. Just put a hat on it. You could do it very easily. Just raise the ridge a bit.'

There was silence while the pub thought it over. 'It wouldn't work,' said Ivor. 'He's going to examine the place with a bloody microscope.'

'He'll be examining the house, not the barn. It won't occur to him to look at its roof.'

'He will when he finds that there are no obvious changes to the house.'

'Well, don't give him time. Hassle him when he comes. Keep him off balance.'

'You know, it might just work,' said Frank, hope dawning on his face.

'I could turn up in uniform and talk about receiving information about soliciting bribes or something,' contributed Percy.

'That would scare him shitless,' said the commander gleefully. 'Mandy, you're brilliant!'

'Oh, Commander!' breathed Mandy. 'I didn't mean it when I told you to shut up just now.'

The commander backtracked hurriedly. 'Well, perhaps brilliant is putting it too strongly, but it's certainly worth a try. We could ask the squire to go along too. He's a magistrate. With him and Percy breathing heavily in the background, the man'll be in and out of the village without even turning off his car engine.'

'What do you think, Keith?' asked Frank. 'Shall we give it a go?'

'Keith will give it a go,' replied Mandy.

Keith and Jason tackled the problem with confidence. One of the difficulties that they faced was the time element. It would have taken weeks to finish the rebuilding of the house whereas it was only a matter of a day to wire some corrugated-iron roof ridges to the top of the barn once they had marinated for a week in Frank's slurry pit to encourage weathering. Then work stopped to allow a credible amount of time to pass while the scaffolding round the house was shrouded in black silage plastic, just in case the inspector happened to do some spying.

He came. The commander was helplessly ensnared in the post office by a communard in a discussion about the nature of a carrot's consciousness, but through the window he saw the inspector's red car pull up in the lane in front of the new cottage.

Jimmy, however, was on the spot. He spent most of his waking hours, when he was not in the pub, tickling and teasing the soil in his vegetable patch to ensure that he won more classes than the commander in the annual horticultural show. He straightened up, after worrying at the root of an intrusive blackthorn from the hedge that separated his garden from a neighbouring field, to see the inspector park his car and stride purposefully towards the shrouding plastic. Although he did not see the commander gesticulating in silent horror through the glass between a poster about buying TV licence stamps and a warning about the dangers of colorado beetle, Jimmy knew where his duty lay. Thinking fast, he let out a mighty cry, clutched at his heart and leaned heavily on his garden gate. The inspector hesitated for a moment, torn between his curiosity and his duty. His curiosity won and he came over to Jimmy's aid.

'Are you all right?' he asked from a distance of about six feet.

'My heart! I think I'm going.' Jimmy slumped over the mossy stone of his wall. He rolled his eyes at the inspector.

'Help me to the house. Give me your arm.'

The average man would have already been jogging up the path with the moribund senior citizen borne tenderly in his arms. But Jimmy was a most unprepossessing senior citizen. Most of the trouble came from the fact that his elderly lurcher, Patsy, slept the night upon Jimmy's clothes which lay on the floor at the bottom of his brass bed; she had been incontinent for several years.

The inspector had the wind in his face and the afternoon sun behind him and could be forgiven for being reluctant to come closer than he had to. But he had to in response to a direct request for an arm. He extended it. Jimmy grabbed it with his skinny hand. 'Gotcha!'

The inspector lurched backwards in alarm. 'Geddoff!' he yelled, but Jimmy was holding on with the determination of the Ancient Mariner.

'Trespassing!' roared Jimmy. 'I saw you! Sneaking up to someone else's property. You're a burglar! Help! Help! Someone call the police!'

'Let me go, you fool! What on earth do you think you're

doing?' The inspector was reluctant to use much force to break free since Jimmy, even if he was not having a heart attack, was a poorly preserved septuagenarian. He had the sort of body that stands by the side of busy roads asking to be helped across. If it was offered violence, it looked as if it would pack up completely and that could lead to nothing but trouble.

The inspector shook his arm, but Jimmy held on, not quite sure what he ought to do next. He essayed another 'Help!', but it lacked the conviction of his earlier utterance. However, reinforcements were on hand.

The first to come to his aid was Patsy who had been dozing peacefully on the garden path a dozen feet away. The shouts of her master had woken her, but her senses were in such poor condition that she had not been able to identify their distance or direction. She hauled herself to her feet, carefully straddled her quivering legs and concentrated as hard as she could. Jimmy's second 'Help!' gave her the clue she needed. She swivelled her grizzled greyhound muzzle like a defective radar dish and homed in, all her old instincts creaking into action. She lumbered across the lawn and, with a remarkable example of the power of positive thinking, she managed to launch herself into the air across the garden wall. Patsy's granny had been an Irish wolfhound and the inspector now saw a large grey hearthrug sailing through the air towards him with obvious hostile intent, rather like a nasty alien from an episode of *Startrek*. The dog, who was filled with exhilaration at her best leap for at least eighteen months, struck the inspector full in the chest, knocking him from Jimmy's grasp and to the ground.

The inspector was winded; so was Patsy who lay on top of him for a few seconds until she had regained her puff. Then she recalled her duty and seized the nearest portion of her victim's anatomy – his wrist – between her jaws and gummed it, growling ferociously.

'Cool!' said Jimmy, peering interestedly over the wall. 'I didn't think the old girl had it in her!'

The inspector was not quite clear what had happened to

him, but he knew it was bad. He heaved his body, throwing Patsy from him, his wrist sliding from between her toothless gums. She landed in a dejected heap, knowing that she had enjoyed her last foray into canine ferocity. The inspector staggered to his feet. 'You did that deliberately!' he gasped. 'You were just trying to stop me looking at that house!'

'That's right,' agreed Jimmy who was enjoying the tranquillity born of the knowledge that, whatever the ultimate outcome, he had done his bit.

'Well, it won't bloody work. They're up to something and it's my duty to find out what it is.'

'Oh no, you won't,' announced the commander, who was in a bit of a lather, having sprinted the fifty yards from the post office with the communard at his heels.

'Oh yes I will,' replied the inspector, grimly refastening his shirt buttons and tucking his hair back under cover.

'Oh no you won't. By the authority vested in me as a member of the Emergency Volunteers, I have the power to forbid you access to designated areas and I hereby invoke such powers. Under the Emergency Powers Act of 1973 you need a magistrate's warrant to enter and, if you should ignore my instructions, you can be prevented by the use of deadly force.'

'Don't be ridiculous! I don't believe there is such an act, and even if there was it would only be a £10 fine.'

'I'll have you know I used to command a Polaris submarine,' replied the commander loftily. This was not actually true, but he had known someone who did.

While the inspector tried to work out the relevance of this statement and whether there was a threat implied, Jimmy clarified the situation. 'You get on home now, Mister, 'cos there is one of 'ee and three of we and one dawg.'

'Yes,' said the communard stoutly. He was one of the weediest of a weedy bunch. Elfrieda, the commander's wife, had once remarked on how slim the male communards were, particularly about the posterior. The commander put it down to permanent dysentery brought on by their revolting diet of beans and nettles.

The inspector looked at Patsy who was leaning on her elbows peering vaguely about her, at Jimmy, at the communard and at the commander. He raised his upper lip and puffed his moustache at them as a gesture of his contempt. It looked as if he had a large bloody butcher trout fly beneath his nose. 'Right! I shall make an official inspection of the premises tomorrow at 11am. And I'll make sure I have the police with me in case of any repetition of this ridiculous behaviour.' He dusted down his jacket as he retired to his car. 'And you, Sir!' He pointed a quivering forefinger at Jimmy. 'That dog of yours made an unprovoked attack. I shall lay a complaint and I intend to see that it is destroyed.'

'You'd better be jolly quick about it, otherwise Nature will beat you to it,' said the commander, looking down at Patsy who, still on her elbows, was mournfully contemplating the dozen long yards between her and the haven of the front doormat. The inspector started his car and accelerated away with Jimmy waving two gnarled fingers after him.

By eleven o'clock the following morning, everything was ready. It had been rushed, but a team of volunteers had been working on the house and the barn since shortly after dawn. They had glued moss on parts of the new roof ridge of the barn and the commander, with a stroke of genius, had plaited an extra dozen feet of ivy into the plant which already covered the gable end so that it embraced the ridge, making it look as if it had been there for decades.

The squire had put on his Guards tie, a sure sign that he was going to take his duties seriously. Percy was stamping his boots in the lane, chatting with Jason, while Keith and Frank finished the dismantling of the scaffolding, giving last critical looks at the barn. The squire went over to Jimmy who was in his front garden so that he would not miss any of the fun.

'Where is this damn fellow, eh, Jimmy?' he asked.

'I reckon we frightened him off yesterday. You should have seen my Patsy, Squire. She knocked him flying!' Jimmy looked fondly over to the doormat where Patsy was stretched out as usual.

'I hear that there may be a bit of trouble about that.'

'I hope so. The vet was on his way past to a calving at Ivor's a couple of days ago and I waved him down to take a look at her. He said she'd only got another few months before it would be right to put her down. £5, it'd cost me. £5 to kill my own dog!' Jimmy shook his head sadly, the smoke from his cigarette weaving a figure of eight in the still morning air as he did so.

'£5! Good Lord!' said the squire sympathetically.

'I've always shot my dogs before. It don't seem right to have to pay someone else to kill your own dog.'

'I know what you mean. My wife had a fall in 1971 on the first meet of the season. The animal broke its leg and she insisted on shooting it herself.'

'I remember that. That was a fine stag, killed just above the old weir, that day. I got its liver.'

'That's right.' The squire did not hunt but he respected the important place that the staghounds occupied in the local culture. His own pleasure lay in the slaughter of about 2,000 pheasants a year.

'I was hoping, Squire, you being a magistrate and all, that when Patsy goes to court, you might order her to be destroyed. That means she'll die a hero like, and I won't have to pay for it.'

The squire patted Jimmy reassuringly on the shoulder. 'A bit like a soldier dying for his country, eh? I'll see what I can do. If you get sent a summons, make sure you tell me the date and, even if I'm not on the bench, I'll leave word about it.'

There was the sound of a car engine coming down the lane. The squire turned to look. 'Ah!' he said rather nervously. 'This looks like the fellow now.'

The fellow was in his red car which drew up alongside Percy. The squire strode over to join them with his hands clasped behind his back, looking rather like Prince Philip.

'Good morning,' said the inspector, looking round at the welcoming party. 'I'm glad the law is present.'

'I'm not actually the law,' said the squire, 'although I am a magistrate.'

'Well, *you're* certainly the law, Constable. My name is Partridge. I'm the building inspector and I'd like to report that I was threatened by a man in his fifties with a bushy grey moustache yesterday. Right here.'

'I don't know anything about that,' replied Percy.

'That old man was a witness,' said the inspector, pointing to Jimmy. 'In fact he threatened me as well and his dog attacked me. I've already laid a complaint about it.'

'In that case it will be investigated in its due time,' replied Percy placidly. He was on familiar ground here as a goodly proportion of his official duties consisted of smoothing over feathers ruffled during clashes between opposing cultures — hunters *v.* saboteurs, farmers *v.* ramblers, villagers *v.* tourists. 'But I'm not here to talk about that, I'm here to ask a couple of questions about certain allegations concerning the corruption of public officials.'

Partridge cocked an inquiring eyebrow. 'Has that remark got anything to do with me?'

'I didn't say that, but if the hat fits . . .'

'Quite,' agreed the squire, nodding his head sagely.

The inspector examined the two of them carefully, assessing the nature of this attack. He had had some of his actions questioned in the past, but only by incomers who were trying to extend their newly bought cottages and did not understand the local customs. Country people knew all about the little perks of his job. Everyone either defrauded the Inland Revenue or the Social Security and it was in nobody's interest to demand too searching a scrutiny of the standard of integrity in their public officials.

'What exactly do you mean?'

'Well . . . er . . . you know.'

'No, I don't know.'

Percy sighed heavily. 'If you want me to spell it out, it was about that conversation you had with Frank over there.' He nodded his head towards Frank who was doing his best to keep out of the way during this stage of the business, just in case something went wrong.

The squire and Percy had a tiger by the tail. The inspector

smiled, a sight that made them both uneasy. 'You're Percy Chilcott, aren't you?'

'Constable Chilcott to you, Sir.'

'You've got a sister who lives out near Muddiford. I was passing there the other day and I saw that they've just put up a garage. Without planning permission.' He clicked his tongue. 'Awful pity if the authorities got to know of it. Don't you agree, Constable?'

Percy sighed a great sigh as he saw another rock being added to the cairn of compromise that is the human condition.

'Well, I haven't got a sister,' stated the squire. 'At least, not down here. I've got one up in Scotland. Married a Catholic. Lives in one of those icy castles with a positive farrow of children. Does it to keep warm, I suppose. The Eskimos do it in igloos a lot.'

'It's all right,' said the inspector kindly. 'As long as the constable has a sister, you don't need any relations at all.'

'Really? Is everything sorted out then?'

'Yes, Squire,' replied Percy. 'We know just where we stand now. You were a great help.'

'Oh good. Well, I might as well wander off now.' The squire wandered off, pleased that he had fulfilled familial obligations to his people once again. 'Everything's sorted out,' he told Jimmy happily as he walked past. 'Spot of fishing now, I think. The salmon are running, you know.'

'Good luck to you, Squire,' replied Jimmy, who had a twelve-pound fish, complete with pitchfork holes, simmering in a kettle on his pre-war Aga.

'Now we've got rid of him, let's take a look at this house,' said the inspector briskly. 'Judging by our little talk, it may be quite interesting.'

'I wouldn't know about that,' answered Percy. 'But I think I'd better be getting on with my duties now.'

'Oh no you don't. I demanded police protection, remember?'

Percy looked at him, his eyes those of the picture of Dorian Gray after an early trawl through Limehouse by its subject. 'I don't reckon you need any protecting, Sir. That silly red moustache of yours should give people plenty of warning to leave you well alone. If you'll excuse me, Sir, I'll just go and have a word with Mr Mattock.' Percy touched the brim of his helmet and walked heavily over to Frank to impart the news that the inspector had not only not been nobbled, but was also fully alerted to the probability of skulduggery. Jimmy hobbled out from behind his wall to fill the hiatus left by the departure of the squire and Percy.

'Morning.'

'Oh, it's you. Morning,' replied the inspector, who had reached into the back window ledge of his car to collect his yellow safety helmet. 'No heart attacks today?'

'Where's Percy going?'

'I don't know, but he's got his tail between his legs. Where's that matelot friend of yours?'

'The commander? He's gone into town to sell some tomatoes.'

'That's a shame. I hoped he might be around to see this. I'm sure you'll make sure he hears about it, though.'

'Hears about what?'

'How I made your friend rip his damn house down. This bit is always exciting, listening to them squirm when they make excuses.'

Jimmy examined him as white corpuscle would a bacterium. 'You're a nasty sort of a fellow, aren't you?'

'Piss off, Grandad,' replied the inspector.

'Piss off yourself. Anyway, they've done what you told them to.'

'What?' The inspector turned for the first time to look at the roof ridges. His jaw dropped. 'Jesus! I don't believe it! How on earth did they manage that?'

'Aha!' crowed Jimmy. 'That surprised you, didn't it? It doesn't matter how they did it, just so long as it's done. Now you have to give it your approval.'

'I don't understand. There's got to be something going on otherwise what was all that business about yesterday? And why was that daft policeman coming the heavy with me?'

Frank, seeing the inspector looking at the roof, decided that it was time he went over to hear the worst. 'Good morning,

Mr Partridge,' he said glumly.

Partridge turned a bewildered face towards Frank. 'The roof. How did you do it?'

Frank interpreted bewilderment as the expected accusation and decided to come clean. 'Corrugated iron', he replied briefly. 'I'm sorry that—' The rest of what he was about to reveal was drowned out by Jimmy who deemed that the moment was right to do his duty once more. 'Aah!' he yelled, clutching at his heart.

'Oh not again!' complained Partridge, stepping swiftly backwards a few paces. 'What do you mean, "corrugated iron"? How can you reduce the height of a building with corrugated iron?'

Frank heard but failed to understand the import of the inspector's remark as he was transfixed by Jimmy's performance. Unlike the inspector, he had not seen it before. Jimmy stopped clutching his chest but his face was suddenly contorted in an enormous, agonized grimace. It was only when the spasm was repeated, even more violently than before, that Frank realized that Jimmy was winking and then managed to work out why. He felt a tiny spark glow amid the damp kindling of his hopes.

'Corrugated iron! Ah! Yes! Nice morning, isn't it? Very good of you to come. See? We managed to lower the building all right.'

'You won't get away with it. You must have reduced the ceiling height upstairs and that'll make them lower than you're allowed.'

'We didn't lower the ceilings.'

'Well, what did you do then?'

'Don't you go telling him,' interrupted Jimmy. 'He's just here to make sure you abide by his silly rules. You don't have to tell him your trade secrets.'

'Don't worry,' Frank reassured him. 'If you can't find out for yourself, Mr Partridge, I'm certainly not going to tell you.'

'So you're still not prepared to co-operate? Right, we'll just have to have a look. I've been doing this job for twenty years. You won't be able to keep any secrets from me!' The optimism in the inspector's voice had taken on a note of defiance which was not lost on his audience. Feeling more cheerful by the second, Frank led the inspector to the house to join Keith and Jason and they all went in.

'Ha!' cried Partridge, unable to conceal his disappointment. 'You haven't lowered these ceilings.'

'That's right,' agreed Keith. 'We haven't had to make any changes here.'

'Let's go upstairs, then.' Partridge almost trotted through the hall to the stairs, taking them two at a time.

'If you were doing your job right, you'd be taking a proper look around down here,' shouted Jason reprovingly at his ascending backside.

'There's no point,' it replied, 'if the whole place is coming down.' Keith and Jason climbed after him. He had his steel rule out and was running it up the bedroom wall. He checked it and checked again. 'The roof!' he cried, feverishly. 'You must have reduced the height of this roof. We specified the pitch. You aren't allowed to alter it.'

'The trapdoor is in the bathroom,' said Keith equably.

'But I'll need a stepladder. It's no good not providing me with a ladder. You have to give me every assistance on my inspection. I'd just be back with a court order and a sensible policeman.'

Keith was enjoying himself. He, like Frank, doubted if they would get away with this stratagem but there were compensations whatever the outcome. 'We've got a stepladder in the bathroom all ready for you.'

'Oh! You have, have you?' The inspector squared his shoulders. 'We'll soon see about that.'

'Exactly,' said Jason.

Partridge suspiciously examined the ladder to ensure that it was not booby-trapped. He grasped it firmly in both hands, shook it as if it were a thicket of jungle bamboo and climbed resolutely upwards. He paused at the top to raise an enquiring eyebrow at Keith, who pointedly retreated outside the bathroom door to flick a switch which flooded the loft space with 500 watts of illumination. There was foreboding in

Partridge's face as he finally disappeared through the bathroom ceiling.

'E.T. going home,' croaked Jason, sitting on the avocado-green lavatory. Keith gave a comfortable chuckle and they waited placidly for a minute or two until a shadow over the trapdoor announced the re-appearance of Partridge. 'All right,' he hissed, his spittle being atomized through the fine sieve of his moustache to drift down the beam of light into the bath. 'I give up. How did you manage it?'

'We lowered it,' replied Keith, speaking softly since he was witnessing one whose cup of triumph had been cruelly dashed from his lips.

'Lowered it! I can see you bloody lowered it. But how? This roof slope is exactly as specified.'

'Of course it is. We're craftsmen, not cowboys.'

'But you must have had it too steep before!'

'Perhaps we did and perhaps we didn't.'

'It would have cost a fortune to take it down and replace it!'

'If it did, it's not your problem, is it?'

'I'm coming down.' He descended, turning to peer into Keith's face when he reached the bottom. 'That's it, isn't it? It cost a fortune, didn't it? You had to work day and night, didn't you? And all that business with the scaffolding and that old man and the policeman was just to wind me up, wasn't it?'

'If that's the way it was, it's none of your business, is it?' remarked Keith.

'Exactly,' agreed Jason, receiving an approving nod from Keith for using the word in its correct context for once.

'I won, then, didn't I?'

'I didn't know we were in a competition,' replied Keith. 'Is the inspection over, then?'

'Not till I see Frank Mattock.' Partridge pushed past and clumped down the stairs, darting suspicious glances to his right and left. There was small comfort for him. Keith may have been a little shaky when it came to the big picture, but detailed finishing was his speciality. He could hang a hundred horse brasses along a wall at precisely six-inch intervals by eye alone.

Outside Frank was pacing up and down nervously, worried that either Keith or Jason might lose their nerve and babble out their guilt. Jimmy had tried to pace as well, but had given up and was now resting his backside on the bonnet of the red car.

When the inspector appeared in the doorway, Frank tried to muster a confident smile, but managed only to look shifty. The inspector came over to him. 'I'm sorry it had to be this way, Mr Mattock.'

'What way?' asked Frank guardedly.

'That you had to spend so much extra money on lowering your roof, of course.' The inspector sensed that he had missed something, but he could not identify what it was. 'What else did you think I meant?'

'Ah, yes! That way! Yes, it has really taught me a lesson. Next time I do some work, I'll know who to get to draw up plans. You can rest assured on that. I've certainly learned my lesson. Oh yes. I've learned my lesson all right.' Frank put an unconvincing arm round Partridge's shoulder and steered him towards the car.

Partridge stopped. 'You're not angry! None of you are angry with me! That's what's wrong! Why aren't you angry?'

'You're only doing your job' – Frank suddenly saw quicksands – 'you bastard!'

'You're up to something. You should be yelling at me, not being so damn reasonable. I've just cost you thousands of pounds. There's something funny going on here. That copper was trying to put the squeeze on me and he sure as hell wasn't very practised at it. He must have had a good reason.'

'No, no, none at all,' protested Frank.

It was unfortunate that the inspector had been a few minutes late for his appointment. If he had been on time, he would have been gone by the time the church clock suddenly hammered the tenor bell in the tower to signal the half-hour. Its vibrations gave this year's rooks the excuse for which they were waiting to leap from their perches on the top of the clump of beeches at the end of the churchyard and wheel, cawing, into the sky under the indulgent eye of their parents.

'You're pulling a fast one, somehow. I don't know what it is, but it's something,' continued the inspector.

Frank began to burble. 'It's nothing,' he said. 'Really, truly, it's nothing. I couldn't pull something on you, now, could I? You're Mr Partridge, isn't he, Jimmy? You're a right hard-nosed bastard. You've cost me a fortune. I hate you, I really do, don't I, Jimmy? Jimmy?'

Jimmy was not paying attention. It was just as well that Partridge was, because there was an expression of horrified dismay on the old man's face. Frank turned his head to follow the line of his gaze. It ended on a trio of the young rooks. They had had enough of wheeling and had come to roost on the roof ridge of the barn and, to their raucous surprise, the commander's plaited ivy had unplaited. A green curtain swished away from the roof to leave, gapingly visible, the naked gap between the original line of the roof and its addition.

'Urrggh!' remarked Jimmy.

Frank could not help but agree: 'Urrggh!'

'What?' asked Partridge, who still had his back to the incident.

'Urrggh!' Jimmy repeated and rather wearily clutched at his chest.

'Oh no, please, not again,' begged Partridge. 'This is getting boring.'

Jimmy was afraid of that, but he had an extra prop to add to the efficacy of his distraction display. 'Urrggh!' he cried again, rolled his eyeballs, and began to drum his heels on the paintwork of the car against which he was resting.

'Watch it, you old fool! Mind my car!' Partridge sprang forward and jerked Jimmy off his perch. Jimmy staggered forward but he knew, if he showed sufficient purpose, that he could win the day with his heroism and put Frank many pints in his debt. He grimly came back in, his army surplus boots poised to thud into the door of the car. 'What the hell do you think you're doing? That car's council property! Stop it!'

'Get your vehicle out of here!' shouted Frank, sizing up the situation. 'When he gets like this, he can't help what he's doing.' Frank put his arms round Jimmy, pinioning him loosely, and supported him towards the back of the car – away from the barn. Partridge hesitated, so Jimmy squinted through a half-closed eyelid and made contact with a rear light. The crack of splitting plastic was the clincher. The inspector scuttled round to the driving seat of his car and jumped in.

'Don't forget to send me a certificate,' shouted Frank happily. 'You might as well send me a bill for your light as well. You're too smart for us. We tried to pretend that it was easy to lower the roof, but we couldn't fool you.'

Partridge afforded himself one final poisoned look at Frank before he put his car in gear and disappeared down the lane, drawing seed parachutes from the willowherb that swayed in the hedgerow at his passage.

Jason walked over to Jimmy. 'You wicked old devil!' he said admiringly. 'I wouldn't have believed it if I hadn't seen it!' As Jimmy blushed beneath his dirt and wrinkles, Jason leaned forward and gave him a smacking kiss on his cheek.

'You disgusting young bastard!' Jimmy clapped one hand to his cheek as though it had been branded and swiped with the stick in the other at Jason, who skipped away with the fluid ease of youth. Jimmy turned to Frank: 'That's got to be worth at least six months of tick in the pub, Frank.'

'How much do you drink?' asked Frank.

'I never have more than one pint of beer an evening, do I, Jason?'

'Never more than one pint,' grinned Jason.

'All right. I'll tell Helga that the next six months of your drinks are on me – as long as you promise that you'll have no more than one pint of beer a night.'

'Thanks.'

'Well done, you two,' Frank continued. 'It's been a great day for the village.'

'And your pocket,' said Jason.

'Well, I'm not complaining. I'd better get back to the farm. I've got a hundred heifers to dose.' Frank walked contentedly over to his car, parked near the lychgate.

'Would you two like a cup of tea after all that excitement?' asked Jimmy.

'Thanks', said Keith.

'No more than one pint, you old bugger! I've seen you knock back a bottle of whisky when you've had money in your pocket.'

'He said he'd pay as long as I didn't drink more than one pint of beer a night. He didn't say anything about scotch.'

'He didn't say anything about you not buying me beer, either.'

'Nor'e did. He'll pay for his bloody roof yet, or I'm not the Jimmy I think I am!'

And he did.

Chapter Seven

'THE RUSTLE of money.'

'The baying of a pack of hounds in the distance.'

'The whistle of a bosun's pipe when you go on board your first command.'

'The rush of beer from a hand pump.'

'The squeal of a rabbit when a ferret grabs hold of her.'

The topic for discussion at the WI meeting that evening had been 'The Most Beautiful Sound in the World'. The crackle of a log fire had been the winner among the ladies, but the men in the pub showed a wider choice.

'Yuk! I don't like yours, Gerald,' said the commander. 'That's horrid!'

'You can't have heard it,' replied Gerald, his pint tankard almost hidden in his huge hands. Gerald was a farmer in his forties who wrested a living from the edge of the moor by brute force, of which he had a large amount. The consuming passion of both himself and his wife, Mary, was field sports. 'It makes the hair on the back of your neck prickle. I like my shooting and I like my hunting, but ferreting's what I like best of all. It's so sort of intimate.'

'I can't imagine what the fun of it is,' replied the commander with a shudder.

'Haven't you ever been ferreting?' asked Gerald.

'No.'

Kelvin tut-tutted. 'Surely you must have done when you were a nipper? Everybody goes ferreting when they're kids.'

'Not in Eastbourne, we didn't.'

'Well, you missed something. In the old days, ferrets were

proper ferrets. People really bothered about them and made them really tame. They're wild as hawks these days.'

'I've got a ferret at the moment that's the best animal I've ever seen. Bloody amazing animal it is. Shove it down a hole and the rabbits pop out like rats from a burning rick,' announced Gerald smugly.

'Fat chance,' said Kelvin with scorn. 'I haven't handled the beasts for twenty years but the old skills have died out. I had a ferret that would sip milk from my tongue.'

'Good grief!' exclaimed the commander. 'What a bizarre picture! Why on earth would you want it to do that?'

'It shows how tame it is.'

Gerald shifted his large buttocks on the stool. He hid his muscle under a layer of protective blubber which spilled over the belt of his trousers and bulged, hairily, through the buttonless gaps in his cotton shirt. 'You and the commander ought to come out and see her in action some time.'

'How about tomorrow morning?' asked Kelvin. Prudence had strained her back shifting ten tonnes of fertilizer. With her *hors de combat*, there was nobody to do Kelvin's work for him so he could take time off. 'You can come, can't you, Commander?'

'I don't think I can. I've got to do some weeding.'

'Don't be silly. The weeds'll still be there tomorrow but the chance of a bit of ferreting won't be. We'll both come, Gerald.'

'I don't know that I can manage tomorrow. I've got 300 sheep to sort out.'

'I've got a warren in one of my hedges that's like the ones you used to get before the myxomatosis. I was going to get Jimmy to help me gas it, but if you could come out tomorrow . . . ' Kelvin was one of nature's Machiavellians, but this was child's play as he knew he was on to a racing certainty.

'Really?' queried Gerald eagerly. 'I couldn't miss a chance like that. What sort of time?'

'About half ten. OK, Commander?'

'I don't see why not. It's all experience, isn't it?'

The commander liaised with Kelvin at the top of his farm lane in the lay-by which allowed the milk lorry to pull in to empty

Kelvin's tank without blocking the road. They both had their shotguns. Gerald's Land Rover was soon audible and visible above the hedgerows since it was without a silencer and trailed a blizzard of straw, twine and empty paper sacks that had once contained half-hundredweights of cattle nuts. They watched in silence as it rattled round the corner, sheepdogs peering over and round the cab from the back, and pulled in behind the commander's Subaru. Gerald got out, clutching a green felt bag, and snarled at the dogs who hung their panting heads over the tailgate of the vehicle.

'You've got a real treat coming, Kelvin,' he announced.

'Let's have a squint at the bugger, then.'

'Hang on,' said Gerald, swinging the bag gently away from Kelvin's grasping hand. 'You'll frighten her. She doesn't know you. I'll open it for you.' He delicately loosed the drawstring and peered slowly inside, making a kissing sound with his lips. He held the bag out to Kelvin who peered inside.

'Huh! It doesn't look much. Damn thing looks a bit dopey to me. Are you sure it's not been overfed?'

Gerald snatched the bag away. 'Overfed?' he snapped. 'It's in fighting condition, you ignorant old bugger. Just let me point her to a rabbit hole.'

Kelvin hefted his gun to his shoulder. 'Well, what are we hanging about for? We'll soon see.' He led the way to the opposite side of the road and through a muddy gateway into a field that looked as if it had been made over to the cultivation of rushes and thistles. They squelched a couple of hundred yards across to a hedgerow that separated the field from a tangled beech wood.

Gerald examined it in silence. 'There are a few holes here, I suppose.'

'What do you mean, "a few holes"?' said Kelvin indignantly. 'It's not a hedge any more. It's one of them Tom and Jerry cheeses.'

Gerald delved into a poacher's pocket inside his green jacket and pulled out a handful of nets. 'Let's get on with it, then. You block up holes this side and I'll go the other.'

The commander hunched his shoulders against a biting

wind that scudded the clouds above the trees. He watched Gerald carefully negotiate the gap between a couple of healthy young oaks that were sprouting in the unkempt hedgerow while Kelvin crabbed across the base of the bank in front of him, carefully tying nets over fifteen yards of holes. 'What did we bring the guns along for, Kelvin?'

'To shoot rabbits with, you fool!'

'But aren't they supposed to get stuck in the nets?'

'It's a smart rabbit that'll get through a net that I've laid out, but it's possible. A big old buck can be travelling when it hits the net and some will go round the ends.' He straightened his back with a groan. 'No wonder I gave up this game years ago. Still, it's nice to watch a good animal work and it's exciting waiting for the rabbits to come out.'

There was a yell from the other side of the hedge. 'Are you ready, Kelvin?'

'Yes!' called back Kelvin. 'Commander, you stand one side of the nets and I'll stand at the other, and for Christ's sake, wait till the rabbit is out in the field before you shoot it. They can come out damn fast and I don't want you waving your gun at me.'

The commander, as well as being cold, was now rather nettled. 'Kelvin, I may not take my gun to bed with me, but I know what I'm doing.'

'Good.' Kelvin raised his voice: 'Get on with it, then, Gerald!'

'She's just going in now!' yelled Gerald. 'Go on, my beauty. Get down there. Go on!'

Kelvin thumbed back the hammers on his gun with a double click that had chilled the hearts of generations of small furry and feathery creatures on the farm ever since his grandfather had bought the weapon, second-hand, to mark the coronation of Edward VII. 'This is the bit I like,' he said with a grin. 'It's so bloody exciting, isn't it?'

'Yes, I suppose it is,' agreed the commander with an answering smile. He was disarmed to hear Kelvin actually admit to a spontaneous emotion. 'You never know what or when.'

A rabbit erupted from its burrow behind Kelvin. His gun leapt to his shoulder and discharged, to the detriment of a clump of rushes about eight feet in front of him. He swore, pulled the trigger again and there was a click. 'Bloody cardboard cartridges!' he roared. 'They get damp in them if you keep them for a year or two. Why can't they make them out of plastic like everything else?'

The commander laughed. 'When did you last buy any? They've been plastic for years.'

Kelvin paused in the act of reloading his gun to deliver a crushing retort, but none came into his mind. A rabbit nipped out of the hedgerow and scampered past him. The commander chuckled. Kelvin glared at him. 'It would be more use if you shot the blasted animals rather than just sniggering at them.'

'They're not coming out my side.'

'Behind you!' shouted Kelvin.

The commander swung round, the barrel of his shotgun hunting for a target. A rabbit had emerged from a burrow. It gave one horrified glance and dived back underground before the trigger was pulled. The commander smoothly adjusted his aim and blew another to a better world. 'I got one, Kelvin!'

'Big deal!' came the scornful reply. 'It's like shooting ducks in a barrel.'

'How many ducks have you shot?' asked the commander.

'And I thought I told you to wait until the brutes were out into the field before you fired. That last one was not even out of its burrow. If you can't be a safe shot, you've no right to be out.'

'That was perfectly safe shooting and, anyway, you yelled "Behind you", ' responded the commander in annoyance. Another rabbit emerged from under Kelvin's feet. His thumb slipped on the hammers of his gun as he pulled them back to cock and the left barrel exploded, punching a tight pattern of shot through the hedge. '—Which is more than can be said for that!'

'That was an accident,' replied Kelvin defensively, raising his voice above a roar of rage from Gerald.

'You amaze me! I thought you were trying to shoot him deliberately,' said the commander.

There was silence for a couple of minutes with both hunters remaining tense, waiting for more prey to present itself. Kelvin shifted his feet, the mud squelching beneath his wellingtons. 'There are a damn sight more rabbits down there than we've seen so far. That ferret isn't doing its job.'

'If there are that many of them, perhaps they've ganged up against the beast and beaten it up or something.'

'Don't be stupid.'

There was another damp silence. The trees of the wood overhung the field and the wind shook chill teardrops from the leaves down the back of the commander's neck. 'How long do we have to wait?'

'I dunno,' responded Kelvin. 'If there aren't any more rabbits there, Gerald should try the ferret somewhere else. I'll give him a shout.' Kelvin walked over to the hedge. 'Gerald! There's bugger all going on over here. Bring up your ferret and let's try further along.'

Gerald's face reared into view through the lattice-work of brambles. 'There's bugger all going on over here as well. The ferret's down there somewhere, but I don't reckon there are many coneys around.'

'Pull her out and let's try a bit further along.'

'OK. Did you get many?'

'One or two,' replied Kelvin, airily.

'Huh!' grunted Gerald. 'Apart from the one aimed at me, there were at least another three shots.'

'True, but the rabbits were bolting fifty yards up the hedge. There are none in the nets which there should have been if your ferret was doing her job.'

'I've been offered £250 for that animal.'

'It just proves there are plenty of idiots around.'

The commander shivered and stamped his feet. 'Can we get on with it? I'm cold.'

Kelvin turned from the hedge and broke his gun, laying it on the wet grass. 'We'll get these nets in, Gerald.' He and the commander unpegged the nets from the front of the burrows and piled them by Kelvin's gun. 'Where's your rabbit?'

'Er . . . actually it fell back down its burrow. I fired a bit too soon.'

'Well go and get it, then,' ordered Kelvin scornfully.

'I had a look when I got the nets and I'm afraid I couldn't tell which burrow was which.'

'It's just as well you've got someone to wipe your arse for you,' said Kelvin. 'I marked the hole when I saw it put its head out. If I pick it up, can I have it?'

'Feel free. But let's get on with it. Standing around in a cold wet field is not my idea of a fun afternoon.'

Kelvin walked up the hedgerow, a sneer on his face as he considered the barrenness of spirit of someone who could casually give away a rabbit he had just shot. He walked to the burrow, pushed his arm inside it and pulled out the corpse. He held it above his head, brandishing it at the commander. 'Ha!' he yelled. 'There's a damn good dinner there!' Although the commander was twenty-five yards away Kelvin could sense that there was something amiss. It may have been the

106

fact that he nearly dropped his gun or the high-pitched whimper that escaped between his lips. 'What's wrong?'

The commander shot a furtive glance at the hedge and back at Kelvin. 'The rabbit!' he called hoarsely, walking swiftly across.

'What?' Kelvin looked for the first time at the animal which dangled, slackly, by his side. 'Jesus!' he whispered. 'It's not a rabbit.'

'I didn't think it was,' said the commander miserably.

'It's a fucking ferret. It's Gerald's fucking ferret.' It was Kelvin's turn to look fearfully at the hedge. 'What the hell did you go and shoot it for?'

'I didn't do it deliberately, for Christ's sake! I thought it was a rabbit. You did too. You yelled at me to shoot it. What are we going to do?'

Kelvin dropped the ferret and backed away from it. 'It's nothing to do with me, mate. You shot the bloody thing.'

'You told me to,' hissed the commander. 'We're in this together.'

'We're bloody not. Gerald'll tear your head off. He's not

having mine off too. Take my advice. Own up and get it over with.'

'I'll go one better than take your advice. I'll do what you would do under the circumstances.'

Kelvin fingered his gun nervously. 'What's that?'

'I'll tell him it was you that shot it.'

Kelvin grimaced in horror. 'You wouldn't! I'd tell him the truth!'

'Which one of us do you think he'd believe?'

'You bastard!'

'Here!' came a voice from down the hedge. 'Have you seen my Betty?'

Kelvin turned to the commander. 'Hide the damn thing! Quick!' The commander nipped smartly across to the hedge and deposited the departed wonderbeast back down its rabbit hole.

'Have you seen my Betty?' repeated Gerald.

The commander emitted a squeak of alarm as there was now only the thickness of the hedge between them. 'Betty? Betty? Who's Betty?' he asked wildly.

'The ferret, of course. If there were no rabbits left down there, she should have been out by now. What's wrong? You sound a bit funny.'

'Nothing's wrong. No, I haven't seen your Betty.'

Gerald appeared on top of the hedgebank. 'It's not like her, you know. She's never stayed down like this before. I can't understand it.'

'You should have put a bell round her neck,' said Kelvin. 'She'll be down there eating a rabbit and she won't be coming out until she's finished.'

'But I fed her just before we came out!'

'Have you brought a spade to dig her out?'

'No. I tell you, she never stays down.'

'She'll be out and into the wood then. She'll be long gone. You'll never find her. We might as well go home.'

'She's still down there. There aren't that many holes the other side and those that I didn't net I stopped up.' Gerald looked broodingly down at the commander. 'Give me a rabbit and I'll paunch it and try to lure her out.'

'A rabbit! Yes, a rabbit. That's a good idea. Kelvin, he wants a rabbit.'

'Well he can't bloody well have one. We didn't get any.'

'No! That's it! We didn't get any!'

Gerald looked puzzled. 'I thought you said you'd got a few, Kelvin. What were you shooting at apart from me?'

'It was the commander and he kept missing.'

Gerald sighed. 'What a bloody shambles! Stick your head down a hole and see if you can hear her.'

Kelvin did as he was requested. The brambles prevented Gerald from climbing down from the hedgebank to join him but he watched as Kelvin prostrated himself before Betty's burial chamber with his gun by his side, for all the world like an elderly Druze militiaman when the muezzin presses 'Play' and the speakers blare from the Beirut minarets. 'I can't hear anything,' said Kelvin after a few seconds.

'I'll go and listen my side.' Gerald disappeared.

Kelvin peered over his shoulder. 'Has he gone?' The commander nodded. Kelvin rose to his feet. 'Even if there had been any underground noises, I wouldn't have heard them through that ferret. I think you'd better get it out of there. He'll be down this burrow himself before he gives up on it.'

The commander put his arm down the hole and retrieved the muddy, bedraggled fleshy envelope of Betty. He trotted 150 yards down the hedge and stuffed it down another hole. He was flushed and panting by the time he returned to see Kelvin climbing one way through the hedge and Gerald coming the other. 'Right, Commander. I'm going off to get a spade. Kelvin's going to watch the other side of the hedge and you watch this.'

'How long will you be?'

'Not more than twenty minutes.'

The commander lifted his arm in a half-hearted farewell as Gerald hurried off up the field. 'Kelvin, this has all the hallmarks of becoming ridiculous.'

'Has he gone?'

'Yes.'

Kelvin heaved himself back over the hedge. 'It is bloody ridiculous. But it won't be if he digs it up.'

'Can't we produce the remains when he gets back and say that it tripped when it came out of a hole and broke its neck, or something?'

'Not when it's half its head missing. It couldn't have landed with a thump like that off those little legs.'

'Let's say someone else came along and shot it.'

'Why? Who was it? And what were we doing at the time?'

'Well, you suggest something, then.'

'I would suggest that we keep bullshitting if we want to keep healthy. He loved that bloody animal.'

The sound of the Land Rover's return gave Kelvin plenty of warning of scramble back over the hedge and take up watch and they both continued to evince concern as the spade made several abortive forays into the underworld during the following hour. After that they just stood around and waited for a while. It was 1.30 before they found themselves back in the pub, putting chattering whiskies to their mouths.

'What have you three been up to?' inquired Jason Loosemire.

'Ferreting,' replied Kelvin shortly.

'Any luck?'

'No. It got lost.'

'It's my best ferret,' said Gerald. 'It's terrible.'

'Not Betty?' asked Jason in shocked tones.

'Yes.'

'What a shame! I lost my Horace last week. Where did you lose Betty?'

'That hedge by Gliddon's Wood.'

'That's where I lost mine!'

'What!' shouted Kelvin. 'How dare you go down there without permission!'

'The wood belongs to the squire,' protested Jason. 'It's got more rabbits than anywhere else.'

'But this side of the hedge is mine.'

'I no more went your side of the hedge than you went the squire's side this morning.'

'The bare-faced cheek of it! Do you hear? He's admitting he's been poaching. I'll set Percy on you, Jason!' threatened Kelvin.

'Psst!' said the commander.

'What is it?' asked Gerald.

'No, not you. I was wanting a quiet word with Kelvin.'

'Me? What is it?'

The commander raised his eyebrows in exasperation. 'I said a *quiet* word.'

'Can't it wait?'

'No, it bloody can't! For heaven's sake!' The commander dragged Kelvin away from the bar and towards the fire. 'That ferret of Jason's. It could have been that one that I shot and not Betty at all. I thought it a bit funny that the thing came out so quickly. If it was Jason's, it could have been lonely and come out when it heard our voices.'

'So what?'

'Don't you see? Betty could still be there.'

'So what?'

'We could go back there and she could easily be there waiting for us.'

'Do you want to go back there? Back to the wet and cold? All for some vicious little rodent?'

'Is a ferret a rodent?'

''Tain't a cow or a fox, so it must be a rodent.'

'No.'

'Yes, it is.'

'I meant I don't want to go back to the cold and the wet.'

'Then keep your mouth shut.'

'Have you sorted everything out, then?' asked Gerald as they returned to the bar.

'Yes, replied Kelvin. He drained his glass.

'In that case let's get back there and see if Betty has come out yet.' Both the commander and Kelvin groaned. Gerald's eyes narrowed. 'You both care about Betty, don't you?'

'Oh yes, we cared,' said the commander, having watched the way the sod had flown from Gerald's spade and the

111

muscles on his back had rippled his heavy oiled-cotton jacket. 'We cared . . . er . . . care very much.'

'I should hope so. No sportsman would leave matters as they are.'

'Quite,' said the commander almost immediately.

'Let's go, then.'

'My leg,' said Kelvin, clutching his leg. 'It's my knee. Jason, you can take my place.'

'All right. I might find my Horace.'

'Let's go, then,' said Gerald.

The commander could have saved his poisonous look, for Kelvin did not even turn to say goodbye as he was busy getting in another drink before closing time.

The rain had passed over by the time they returned to the hedgerow, although the wind still howled mournfully through the honeycomb of tunnels and craters left by rabbit and shovel. There was no sign of life for the first half an hour. Then there was. 'There she is!' shouted Gerald. 'Up the hedge about 150 yards.' The hair on the back of the commander's neck prickled as he followed the outstretched arm to see a ferret emerge from the burial burrow. 'Quick! Before she goes down again.' The commander held back, fearful of what manifestation of the supernatural should be found and how much of it would be obviously missing due to shotgun wounds. 'Aah!' Gerald's hoarse cry as they approached skidded the commander to a halt. He watched cautiously. 'She's dead! My Betty's dead! That bastard must have killed her!' The commander began to edge quietly backwards. Gerald turned, his face working with emotion. 'Commander, come here!'

'No, look. I'm sorry, Gerald. It was an accident,' babbled the commander.

'An accident! Nonsense! It's bloody murder!' Gerald loomed before the commander, grabbed him by the collar of his jacket and dragged him over. The commander felt as if he'd been hooked by the jib of a crane. He struggled, but unavailingly. 'Look!'

He looked. A cry burst from his lips. There was Betty, or

most of Betty. Standing over her was another ferret chewing at a sinewy bit of her thigh. It looked up and peered at the witnesses with an expression of benign goodwill on its face.

'That's my Horace!' cried Jason.

'Kill the bastard!' shouted Gerald viciously.

'It's not Horace's fault,' said Jason, picking his animal up and thrusting it inside his jacket, leaving smears of blood on his shirt front.

'Kill it! Ferrets will fight and can kill each other, but look at Betty!' A great shuddering sigh of sadness shook his huge frame. He swallowed, shaking his head. "It's not right that she was torn to pieces. That's not natural. A ferret that can do that to its own kind is a bloody menace. You want to get rid of it before it attacks again. It could be a baby next time.'

'I suppose you're right,' said Jason sadly, feeling inside his shirt.

'Hang on a minute,' said the commander. 'I think we may be in danger of over-reacting here. It's not likely to come across many babies down a rabbit hole, after all. And we don't know for sure that it killed Betty.'

Gerald picked up the corpse and held it in his hand. 'You stick to what you know, Commander. That brute killed Betty all right. You can see the bite wound on the back of her neck.'

'But Betty may have been dead already and Jason's ferret may have just stumbled across her body.'

'Commander, you'll never make a decent countryman. You're too soft. Ferrets don't just die. Something or somebody has to kill them and that Horace was caught in the act. It's a shame, but there it is.' Gerald swung his arm and Betty sailed far above the hedge, above the trees, and came to her final rest deep in the wood.

Jason took out Horace and held it in front of his face. 'You never were much of a ferret, were you?'

'No!' said the commander. 'Don't do it!'

Gerald sighed again. 'We've no choice. A ferret that kills like that can't be used again.'

'Well don't use it again. Keep it as a pet or something, but

113

don't kill it. You can't kill it just like that. There's a reasonable doubt about its guilt.'

'There isn't unless you know something that we don't know. I'll tell you what. If you want it to live so badly, Jason can give it to you. As long as you keep it by itself in a cage, it can't do any more damage. That'd be all right by you, Jason?'

'Sure,' replied Jason with a shrug. 'The commander can have it if he wants it.'

And the commander got it. It escaped from its orange box that night and disappeared, but not before killing ten of Elfrieda's chickens. Kelvin was the only person who found it funny.

Chapter Eight

AUTUMN IS the end of the agricultural year. Nature has done with her growing and creatures from squirrels to farmers check their stores of nuts, hay or silage to ensure that they have enough for the hungry months ahead. Full barns did not mean prosperity for just the farmers and squirrels, however. With a bit of luck they could lead to a bit of extra income for some of the young male villagers as well – up to £5 an hour, double the going rate for working in the garage, the cafe, on the farms or vaguely piling bricks on top of each other as they added desultory extensions to the houses of the village.

The source of this prosperity was one of the foundations of the community's civic pride. It had its own fire station, the only one for miles. Other villages may have been larger. Some may have been sufficiently pretentious to change the name of their elected rulers from parish councillors to town councillors. There was even one nearby hamlet which not only had fifteen street lights to the village's two, but had gone so far as to paint yellow lines along the edge of some of its streets to pretend to visitors that it could afford to pay traffic wardens; but this hamlet had no fire station

It was a source of great status to be or to have been a fireman. It was great fun too. There was enormous pleasure to be had from thundering round the countryside, lights flashing and klaxon blaring, a delightful surge of adrenalin coursing through the veins, wondering what excitements were to come. And there was also the money. The firemen had a network of informants, often girlfriends, who reported the faintest trace of smoke. The firemen had bleepers nowadays, but everyone looked back with nostalgia on the days of the old siren whose wail had echoed round the valley, wheeling the rooks like Junkers 88s above the cottages and fields, to summon the crew and alert the whole community to the drama.

The fire engine waited until the first half-dozen of the men sprinting through the village or roaring down the lanes in tatty vans, with doors flapping and seatbelts flying, had jumped, properly uniformed, on board; then it was off, tyres screeching, siren braying, scattering ducks and tourists while the crew stared straight ahead with steely jaws and grim purpose on their faces which broke only to jeer at their tardier colleagues whom they passed on their way through the village.

Mick, who ran the village cafe with his wife, was the fire chief and he ensured that his lads were kept well in training and had plenty of work to do. He made it clear to the community that he expected the brigade to be called out at the

116

least threat of a chimney fire or the smoulder of an electrical socket and everyone co-operated as best they could, although his penchant for blasting unattended bonfires with high-powered hoses caused some ill feeling, particularly since blackened, half-burnt debris could be sent hurtling into neighbouring gardens or smeared over pink-painted cottage walls. However, everyone knew it was important that the crew should be able to produce figures to prove that infernos were as frequent in the area as summer showers: this source of excitement and revenue for the community had to be justified.

It all remained rather unreal because nobody ever got hurt. In the 150-year period during which there had been known to be a specialized fire-fighting force of some description in the village, no fire had ever damaged any human being. The odd animal was roasted before its time and once the fire engine had crashed on its return journey resulting in a couple of broken limbs, but that was a natural hazard of return journeys. After a fire of any reasonable quality, it was only right that the nearest pub should be visited for a post mortem and a chance to water dry throats, so progress back to base was always rather erratic.

Spring and summer provided most of the bread-and-butter work for the brigade, but it was autumn that produced the jam. Autumn was the barn fire season. In the old days of a couple of decades ago, the countryside was pimpled by ricks, delightful constructions that burst into flames with enthusiasm when they were damp or when they received visits from the old-fashioned village idiots for whom arson was the normal mode of self-expression. It was one of the tragedies of progress that, just at the time when the brigade finally gained the mobility of a modern appliance, both the village idiot and the rick went out of fashion. The idiots became the handicapped and people looked after them, while hay and straw was baled up and stored under cover.

Progress could not alter the Laws of Nature, however. If hay was stored before it had dried out properly, it still heated up and could still catch fire. One needed to be a pretty lousy farmer to allow this to happen, but there was no shortage of lousy farmers in the neighbourhood which led to plenty of work for the firemen. In the autumn, headquarters would be shuffling round their fire crews like Fighter Command during the Battle of Britain, moving fire engines halfway across the county to meet emergencies as they occurred. There was just such a crisis in progress the afternoon a barn went up only a few hundred yards from the pub.

The village machine was already out attending a flashy insubstantial affair that was roman-candling inside a patch of gorse, the sort of fire for which it is hardly worth unrolling the hoses, except that this one had been reported by the householder nearest to the blaze who was known to be the widowed mother of the assistant under-secretary of state at the Home Office with responsibility for the fire service.

Back in the unprotected village, the pub telephone rang towards the end of the midday session – although it did not so much ring as chirrup in the approved modern manner. Helga behind the bar picked it up, listened to it for a second and held the receiver out to Kelvin. He peered suspiciously at it before taking hold. It not only chirruped but also looked as if it would snap if grasped carelessly in a horny agricultural hand.

'Yes? . . . Prudence! What the hell are you doing telephoning me here. You're supposed to be spreading muck this afternoon. . . . What? . . . A fire? Jesus! A fire! Where? . . . Oh, that's not so bad. Have you telephoned the fire brigade? . . . Don't be so damn silly. Of course it's an emergency. Get on with it. I'll be home in a minute myself.' He slammed down the receiver. 'Stupid woman!' he muttered.

'What was that about, Kelvin?' asked the commander.

'Prudence,' he reported. 'She says the hay in the Dutch barn is on fire and she doesn't want to dial 999 in case it makes trouble. Women!' He returned to his drink.

The commander looked at him curiously. 'Aren't you concerned? If my property was on fire, I think I'd want to do a bit more than sit at a bar drinking beer.'

'There's bugger all I can do about it, Commander. If the

118

barn is burning, all I can do is piss on it. The fire brigade are the right people to deal with it. That's what they're there for and that's what we pay them for.'

'But it might spread. Prudence might do something silly and get hurt. Anything could happen.'

'No. The barn is well away from any other building.'

The only other proper agriculturalist present was Bill and he had known the ways of Kelvin for decades. 'What was your hay like this year, Kelvin?' he asked innocently.

Kelvin had his glass halfway up to his mouth but he paused to look suspiciously across at Bill. 'What's it to you?' he said.

'Nothing at all. Weren't you making hay that week in June when those two cows of Frank Mattock's were killed by lightning?'

'I might have been,' replied Kelvin cautiously.

'And you took weeks to repair the roof of your barn. It must have got very wet, your hay. Can't be much good.'

'Well, that's where you're wrong,' answered Kelvin. 'Best hay I've made for years. And the biggest crop.'

'It would be, wouldn't it?' said Bill. The civilians in the pub were not quite clear as to the purpose of this exchange, but Bill's next question threw a bit of light on the matter. 'You're well insured against fire, of course?' It was not so much the question, but the cynical chuckle that accompanied it. That, together with Kelvin's reaction.

He turned red. 'None of your bloody business!' he blared.

Bill was not fazed. 'If you want a bit of advice, Kelvin, you'd better be careful. We all know what you told Frank to do with his barn next to the new cottage.'

Kelvin looked briefly and contemptuously at Bill, but his reply was silenced by another volley of chirrups from the telephone. Helga picked it up, listened for a second and mutely stretched it out towards Kelvin a second time. Muttering under his breath in protest, he slid off his stool and came over to take it from her. 'What is it now?' he demanded. He listened for a few seconds. 'Yes, I know the barn is on fire, you've already told me that. Has Mick arrived yet? . . . . He hasn't? Good!'

'What's good about that?' whispered the commander in some surprise.

'It's hay that's on fire,' replied Bill. 'When Mick shows up he's going to douse the lot in water which'll make it useless and leave Prudence to clear it all up. The more that's burned to ashes, the less there'll be to clear up.'

'I'm surprised Kelvin minds about giving Prudence extra work,' murmured the commander.

'He wants her to fell that wood on his southern boundary before it gets too wet to get a tractor down there, and it could take a week to clear up the hay if the fire brigade gets there too soon.'

'I see.'

'No!' shouted Kelvin suddenly. Conversation stopped as everyone turned to look at him. 'You'll do no such thing. It . . . er . . . would be too dangerous. Look, I'm coming straight home. Don't do anything until I get there.' He put down the telephone and hurried over to his pint and drained it with one draught. He slammed his empty glass down on the bar, belched and wiped the sleeve of his jacket across his lips. 'I'm off then,' he announced. 'Prudence is beginning to panic.'

'You mean she wants to put the fire out,' suggested Bill, getting to his feet. 'I'm coming along too.'

As it happened, the entire pub had been itching to rush up the road to Kelvin's farm so that they could see the fire, but it had seemed a little impolite to do so while the victim of this dramatic catastrophe continued to sit imperturbably at the bar. There was a general dash for the door.

A fire is one of life's most exciting spectacles. Kelvin's barn was a good fire, almost a great fire. There was a large pall of smoke towering up above the trees while the lane down to his farm was choked with the cars and Land Rovers of his neighbours who had come along to enjoy the thrills and the entertainment. The vehicles which brought the customers from the pub had to pull on to the verge near the top of the lane –

120

all except that belonging to Dennis whose passenger was Kelvin. He pulled out into the centre of the lane and parked across it. The vehicles emptied.

Dennis was not happy. 'What did you want me to park there for?' he demanded. 'Nobody else is going to be able to get in or out.'

'There looks to be quite enough people getting ghoulish pleasure from my disaster,' replied Kelvin as the group set off down the lane towards the smoke.

'He's no fool, our Kelvin,' contributed Bill. 'With your vehicle there, how is the fire engine going to get down?' Kelvin chose to ignore the remark. 'Incidentally, Kelvin, if you're hoping to persuade your insurers that you made decent dry hay, it's a pity that the smoke is so black.'

'What do you mean?' asked Kelvin.

'That's a very good point,' agreed the commander, pausing to pick up a nail lying on the grass hump in the middle of the lane and chuck it into the hedge. 'It's a bit like when they elect a pope. They use dry straw which makes white smoke when they've agreed on one and wet straw to make black smoke when they haven't.'

Kelvin looked at the great bank of smoke that was rolling down the narrow valley cutting through the farm. 'It's not all that black.'

'Any engineer officer would be proud if he could create a smoke screen of that density and that darkness,' scoffed the commander. 'You could hide the Grand Fleet behind it.'

The barn, with its open sides and rounded, corrugated-iron roof, stood about forty yards away from the house and the rest of the farm buildings. Watching it burn were about twenty human spectators, being fussed over by Percy, and about the same number of cattle. The latter were lining a field downwind of the crackling conflagration and their enthusiastic coughing when the smoke billowed over them would have been the envy of any concert audience.

Some of the barn's spectators had seen their fill of smoke and crackle and turned their backs on the fire to watch Prudence who had hitched a tractor to a venerable cast-iron wagon, used to carry water into the fields in the days before water was piped to troughs. She had filled the wagon and was now snailing her way towards the barn. The interest lay in estimating the quantity of water that would be left by the time she reached her destination. At every bump and rut – and there were plenty of those about – the wagon lurched, sending a bucketful or a full-blown tsunami over the edge. There was also some discussion about her intentions, once she had reached her destination, between Frank Mattock and Gerald Mowbray, both farmers whose land ran with that of Kelvin.

'I reckon she's going to get the water out with a bucket,' said Gerald.

'Don't be daft. There's got to be 100 tons of hay there. Using a bucket would be like trying to shovel shit out of a cubicle shed with a teaspoon. Anyway, she wouldn't be able to get close enough. She'd fry in the heat.'

Gerald shook his head. 'She wouldn't fry, she'd more likely roast.' The wagon casually despatched a cubic foot of water at the back of Prudence's neck. 'Or boil. Perhaps she reckons she'll be protected from the heat by the amount of water on her.'

'No, she won't use a bucket. She must be going to tip it as close to the fire as she can get and try to swamp the flames.'

'That'd do no damn good, it'd just damp the outside of the bottom bales and, anyway, look at the state of the wagon,' argued Gerald. 'It won't have been tipped for nigh on fifty years. That tipping mechanism will have rusted solid. No woman is ever going to have the strength to shift it. Not even a woman like Prudence.' There was not a lot of Prudence, but what there was had earned the respect of the local agricultural community. 'Wiry' was a word that was often used to describe her, 'barbed wiry' by those who had come up against her in a deal for she had inherited her father's devotion to the cause of squeezing every penny out of every opportunity.

'You could shift it, Gerald,' said Frank. Gerald was a man of mighty thews. His speciality was flooring recalcitrant bullocks with a blow of his fist to the centre of the forehead.

'Shift what?' interrupted Kelvin. He had briefly inspected

the blazing barn and then surveyed the surrounding scene before coming to join his two fellow farmers.

'Oh, hullo, Kelvin, shame about your barn, but it was obviously a pretty awful bit of hay,' greeted Frank.

'Nice fire, though,' acknowledged Gerald.

'It was the best hay I've ever made,' said Kelvin indignantly.

'Best hay you've ever made!' jeered Frank. 'What the hell made it burst into flames if it was so damn good?'

'It was good,' insisted Kelvin.

'You're on a difficult one there, Kelvin,' said Gerald. 'Hay burns either because it's too wet when it's made or else because someone put a match to it. It's your choice, I suppose.'

'That's right. It's my choice. Hullo, Percy.'

Percy had seen Kelvin approach and had come hurrying over, looking important. Apart from Prudence, he was the only person present who seemed to think there was some kind of crisis going on. He shook his head worriedly. 'It's a bad business, this. It'll be another ten or fifteen minutes before the fire brigade gets here, I'm afraid.'

'Ten minutes!' said Kelvin with satisfaction. 'It'll be really blazing away by then.'

'That's right. They were called away to another fire, you see. It's just one of those things. Hay a bit damp, was it, Kelvin?'

'It damn soon will be unless I do something about Prudence. Excuse me a minute.' Prudence was creating something of a stir amongst the audience. She was in the process of negotiating a way through their ranks and the profligate behaviour of her water bowser was more than they had bargained for. Kelvin squelched through the mud towards her and tried to communicate over the crackle of the flames and the clatter of the tractor engine. She shook her head, leaned and cupped her ear. Kelvin raised his voice, looking irritated. She shook her head again. Kelvin took a deep breath and began to bellow.

Several small things happened simultaneously. Prudence decided to stop the tractor engine so that she could hear her

father. She did this economically, if in an unorthodox manner, by suddenly letting her foot off the clutch, thus inducing a stall. For a brief moment Kelvin was thoroughly audible. '— The insurance money, you stupid cow!' could be clearly heard for a fifty-yard radius. Percy pricked up his ears and sharply drew in his breath. Then the laws of physics relevant to the tractor's sudden halt came into inexorable effect. Kelvin watched helplessly as most of the remaining contents of the trailer rose four or five feet into the air and glittered in a brief moment of glorious existence against the low afternoon sun that managed to pierce the bank of black smoke before hurling itself accurately upon him.

The fire introduced a selection of alarming creaks to its repertoire of sounds as the heat began to take effect on the corrugated iron on the roof of the barn, but it had temporarily lost its position at the centre of the stage as its audience wiped tears of joy from their eyes at the sight of the spluttering Kelvin standing with the cargo of the cart cascading off him like meltwater from an iceberg. Even Prudence was moved to crack a rare smile as her father snorted water from his nostrils like a spouting dolphin, too surprised to show his customary fury. The only dissenter from the general delight was Percy. He had a gleam in his eye as he pushed through the revellers towards Kelvin, the words 'insurance money' still echoing in his ears. He pulled out a clean white handkerchief, neatly folded eight times as may well have been laid down in Police Regulations, and handed it to Kelvin. The latter, beginning to regain his composure, took it and dabbed his face briefly before dashing it to the ground and stamping it into the mud. Rage was clearly beginning to build.

Percy looked down at his handkerchief. 'You shouldn't have done that,' he said reproachfully. 'That handkerchief was police property.'

'What? A bloody police hankie? I'm sodden and you give me a hankie? What the hell's the good of that? If you're a bloody policeman, why don't you do your job? This lot here,' Kelvin spread his arms round at the crowd, 'they're all trespassers. Get rid of them. Everyone's laughing at me.'

'Trespass is a civil offence. You'd need a court order before I could do anything about it. Anyway, not everyone is laughing at you.'

'Yes, they are.'

'I'm not. I don't laugh at people when I'm on duty, especially when I'm investigating a possible offence.'

'Well, get on with it, then. I'm going to the house to get changed.' He turned to Prudence and shook his finger at her. 'And you let that fire well alone. It's not doing you any harm. So leave all the hero stuff to Mick and his lot, if they ever get here.'

'What were you saying to Prudence about insurance money just now?' asked Percy.

Kelvin turned from Prudence to Percy. 'What the hell is that to do with you?' he demanded. Kelvin never defended when he could attack.

The spectators had not only turned away from the fire but had also moved towards Kelvin and Percy and now surrounded them in a loose arc with the fire controlling the open side. 'He thinks that you started the fire for the insurance money, Kelvin,' Jimmy piped up. Jimmy was extremely old and it was quite understandable that he may have begun to lose his marbles. Even so, he had made a remarkably crass remark. The spectators wanted to hear if Percy would have the bottle to come out with the question himself and nobody wanted Jimmy to feed him his lines. There was some scornful tut-tutting and a bit of muttering and Jimmy looked a little abashed.

Percy turned to frown at him. 'I'd be grateful if you'd keep your mouth shut, Sir.'

The commander whispered in Gerald's ear, 'Sir? I've never heard him call Jimmy "Sir" before. He's being extremely official.'

Percy used his 'Sirs' in the old-fashioned country way. Those whom he considered gentry received them automatically and all other locals were known by their christian names. There was a speculative, almost wolfish gleam in most of the spectators' eyes, like the look in the eyes of a cat when it hears the first rustle in the wainscot and senses that the game's afoot. Kelvin picked up on it too. 'If you want to talk to me, Percy, you can come into the house because I'm not going to stand here and catch my death.' He stumped off in the direction of a set of dry clothes and, after a brief dither while he thought about his duty to protect the public from the dangers of immolation, Percy hurried off in pursuit of his first possible arsonist for at least a decade.

A fire, *per se*, is not enough. There needs to be human interest to add spice and hold the spectators' attention. If there is not the ultimate thrill of danger to person or persons, then it needs a distraught owner to stand around wringing his hands and being plangent or, at the very least, the possibility that it might spread. Kelvin had gone indoors; Prudence was trailing disconsolately back towards the tractor shed with her empty water cart; while the fire itself was settling down to chew its way steadily through the contents of the barn. Apart from a few rats which were scuttling out of the blaze as the heat

126

reached more intimate areas of the pile of bales, there was precious little to get excited about. It was also after 3pm and there were chores to be done and no sign of anyone to bring out cups of tea.

Just as the audience was becoming restive with one or two of its members peeling away to trudge reluctantly back up the lane towards the road, the sound of a siren became intermittently audible above the fire. It brought Kelvin bounding back out of the house, hastily tying a piece of baler twine round his middle to keep his jacket closed. The fact that the jacket still had a full set of buttons on it was irrelevant as Kelvin was a traditionalist. Percy was in hot pursuit and neither of them seemed particularly happy.

'Get away from me!' snarled Kelvin over his shoulder. 'I'm buggered if I'm going to let someone else into my bedroom when I'm changing my trousers.'

'If you don't talk to me now, you'll have to talk to me down at the station,' replied Percy, puffing after him. 'Where do you think you're going?'

'Mind your own blasted business. Anyway you had no right to come into the house without a warrant.'

'Slow down,' commanded Percy. 'Where do you think you're off to?'

They made an odd couple. Kelvin was scuttling away from the fire across the yard, still trying to do up the buttons on his trousers. It looked as if he were heading for a small track that led towards Gerald Mowbray's farm.

'Gerald!' called Dennis from his shooting stick, on which he had parked himself. 'Have you any idea where Kelvin thinks he's going?'

'No idea,' replied Gerald, mystified. 'He may've gone round the twist.'

'How will we be able to tell the difference if he has?' asked Frank rather gloomily.

'Come on,' said Bill scornfully. 'You lot know Kelvin better than that. It's obvious, isn't it? He's making sure that Percy isn't around to clear the cars out of the lane so that the fire engine can get down.'

127

The stratagem was unsuccessful as Prudence was coming the other way, having put away the tractor. 'The fire engine's here, Father!' she yelled. Even Kelvin realized that it would look suspicious if he continued to run. He stopped and Percy stopped behind him, breathing rather heavily.

'What was that she said?' demanded Percy. Kelvin had no need to answer. The siren had stopped at the top of the lane but Mick must have switched it on again as he saw the obstructions. It blared out, its orchestrated cadences cutting through the disorganized crackle of the flames. Percy dithered again. He had Kelvin within his grasp and yet he was being summoned by the urgent demands of the siren.

'What was it that you wanted to ask me, Percy?

'Sorry?' said Percy distractedly, his eye looking up the lane from where he was expecting the fire brigade to appear.

'I asked you what it was that you wanted to talk to me about. You've been chasing me for the last ten minutes.'

Percy turned back to him. 'Oh yes. I wanted to ask you about the insurance on the barn.' The siren sounded again. 'What's Mick up to?' asked Percy. 'Why doesn't he come down?'

'I don't know,' replied Kelvin. 'What about the insurance?'

Percy made his decision. 'It'll have to wait. I'd better go and see what's going on up the lane.'

'I may not want to talk to you later on,' said Kelvin sniffily.

Percy turned on the majesty of the Law. 'If I want to interview you later, I'll most certainly interview you later. And I'd be grateful if you did not leave the district until I've talked to you.' Kelvin gaped at him as he moved away. Percy paused and turned. 'Have you got a passport?'

'What the hell are you talking about, you silly bugger?' said Kelvin.

'Don't you call me a silly bugger, Kelvin Morchard. I just want to make sure you don't try to escape justice. We can't have you skipping off to South America or somewhere.'

'Well, you are a silly bugger. A piddling little fire in a hay barn and you're treating me as if I was a Great Train Robber. No wonder you failed your sergeant's exam so many times that they wouldn't let you take it again! You haven't got enough brains in your head to police a church social!'

'Don't you dare talk to me like that!' cried Percy, raising his voice. 'You're not talking to *me*, you know. I'm on duty and you're talking to a policeman.'

'The policeman is talking like a bloody fool and he's on my property without my invitation or permission. I'm quite willing to talk to my friend Percy, but I'm damned if I'll give the time of day to an idiot like you.'

'You damn well watch yourself, Kelvin!' warned Percy through clenched teeth. 'You're playing with fire!'

Not surprisingly under the circumstances, this remark elicited a roar of laughter which did nothing to improve Percy's temper.

'I could have you here and now for insulting behaviour or . . . or conduct likely to cause a breach of the peace.'

The siren had been switched off but, above the noise of the fire, there was clearly heard a grinding sound which could only have been caused by the fire engine taking drastic steps to clear a path for itself.

'Bloody hell!' Dennis had risen from his shooting stick and stared up the lane before turning to Percy. 'For heaven's sake, stop messing around and go and do your job. That fire engine has just smashed up my Land Rover!'

Percy aimed one last shaft at Kelvin before returning to his duty. 'If you think you're going to get back in the skittle team, Kelvin, you've got another think coming!'

Kelvin jeered. 'If you think you're going to remain captain of the team, it's you who's going to get a surprise!'

'We'll finish this later,' stated Percy. He raised his voice to the assembled multitude. 'If anyone has a vehicle that is blocking the lane, now is the time to move it before it's moved for them.' Half a dozen spectators hurried across the yard, past the burning barn, with Percy following after them at a heavy trot. He was taking more exercise this afternoon than he was used to.

Kelvin turned back to look critically at the conflagration. 'What do you think, Frank?'

Frank looked as well. The fire was still doggedly going about its pre-ordained business, eating up the bales and smoking furiously. Within the last few minutes the flames had spread all over the surface of the hay, although much of it was obscured by smoke. Frank inspected it with an experienced eye. 'I should think you'll be OK. There doesn't seem much point in trying to put it out.'

'I hope you're right. But you know what Mick's like. Shall I get Prudence to make us a cup of tea?'

'You'd better have a word with Mick first. He'll be here in a minute.'

'Aye, I suppose I'd better.' They waited in companionable silence, watching the fire. Its quality of devotion to the task of ensuring its own death as quickly as possible by destroying its own means of existence excited some pity in Kelvin's stony heart. 'It would be a right shame if Mick spoilt it by pouring water all over it.'

'It makes such a filthy mess,' agreed Frank. 'And what's the use of a barn full of wet and smoky hay? Although I suppose it was already pretty damp before the fire started.' Kelvin failed to demur, so Frank continued, 'I must say, I don't quite know what Percy's going on about. It's obvious that the fire started because the hay was damp.' There was a speculative look in his eye as he stared at the flames. 'What's more to the point would be if you knew the hay was heating up and, if you did, whether the law says you should have done something about it.'

'Difficult one to prove, even if it was illegal. Percy's got no chance,' replied Kelvin.

At last the fire engine came roaring into the yard and its crew jumped off. Mick had a white helmet and those of his underlings were yellow, although the black tunic and yellow trousers he wore were similar to the others'. He stood with his hands on his hips and surveyed the scene. Kelvin and Frank came over.

Mick greeted them laconically. 'That piss-head Dennis is threatening to sue us for bashing up his Land Rover.'

'Us?' said Kelvin.

'Yes. You for telling him to park it in the middle of the lane and me for pushing it out of the way.'

'I see. And what has Percy got to say on the matter?'

'Not to worry. He wasn't there and my lads will say that the handbrake on the Land Rover was bust and it slid into the fire engine.' Mick would have made an excellent administrator for Big Brother. He believed that truth was entirely subjective and was what you wished to believe it to be. 'What do we do about this fire of yours, then? Have you got any chemicals or fertilizer in there?'

'Just hay. I think the best thing would be to let it burn out,' said Kelvin hurriedly.

'Insurance job?' queried Mick. 'Trying to get some decent hay in with the money?' He watched his minions unreeling their hoses, to Kelvin's increasing agitation. The stream that ran through the centre of his farm was about 100 yards from the burning barn and, with some degree of difficulty due to having been winkled out of a pub towards the end of their gorse fire, the firemen were linking hoses to reach over the fields towards it. 'Tricky one, that. Our job is to put out fires. Unless it's not worth it because of the risk to my lads. Very hot, hay fires. That roof'll be buckling soon. Could even begin to melt.'

'It looks very risky to me,' agreed Kelvin. 'Anyway, the fire's not doing anyone any harm and it would make a filthy mess if you tried to put it out. I'd be very grateful if you let it alone.'

Mick turned away from the fire towards Kelvin. 'Would you, now? Grateful. How grateful?'

Kelvin began to prevaricate. 'Well, you know, I'm not a rich man and with a disaster like this and—'

'—me listening in as well,' added Percy, who had joined them.

'This is nothing to do with you, Percy,' said Mick. 'Why don't you sod off and let the fire brigade deal with its own affairs?'

'I think that everything Kelvin's up to today is probably my affair. There's something very suspicious about the origins of this fire.'

'Suspicious?' mused Mick, turning back to the barn. 'Now there's a thing. Both you and Kelvin realize, of course, that it's my job to discover whether there is anything suspicious about it or not. It's a pity you're not rich, Kelvin.'

'It would be wrong to say I was poor, of course,' said Kelvin hurriedly. 'It all depends how you define rich.'

'That's easy,' replied Mick. 'Rich is the fellow who's got a bit more money than yourself. You, for instance, have a couple of hundred acres and a potential insurance settlement of several thousand pounds. I have only a cafe and a rather fierce wife.'

'She is pretty fierce,' agreed Kelvin. More and more local women were becoming tired of their roles as hewers of wood and drawers of water, which had been their lot since the Norman Conquest, to the baffled alarm of their menfolk whose culture and evolution had not equipped them to deal with a female sex that no longer recognized its secondary role. 'I miss the wife, God rest her soul, but I'm quite glad that I'm a widower. Prudence does for me fine.'

'You wouldn't catch me with a wife,' agreed Percy. 'My mother does for me.'

'—And her scones are quite something. You don't need a wife if you've got a mother who can make scones as good as hers. My Prudence makes a very nice fruit cake, but she's no good at scones.'

Percy had an idea. 'If I got my mother to make scones for you, would you exchange them for clotted cream?' Kelvin looked dubious. 'Go on,' continued Percy coaxingly. 'It would be fair exchange. You've got cows and lots of cream and I've got the scones.'

'We sell scones and clotted cream in the cafe,' contributed Mick hopefully. 'You could always come round to us. They're only 95p for two.'

'People?' asked Percy.

'No, scones.'

Percy weighed up the possibilities. He sighed. 'It's not the same, though, is it? The whole point of scones and clotted cream is that you have lots of cream left over and can dip your

132

finger into the bowl and lick it. Your Beryl does individual portions of jam and cream and the tourists don't know any better. I'd rather do a trade with Kelvin.'

'You sound as though you're talking about a lot of cream,' said Kelvin dubiously, conscious of time passing and flames flaming. 'How do you reckon we might work it? How many scones to how much cream? After all, although your mother's scones are better than most, they don't cost very much. It's the cream that pushes up the price. Isn't that right, Mick?'

'That's right,' confirmed Mick. 'I buy my cream from Ivor and he charges a shocking price.'

'That's one of the reasons I don't come to the cafe,' explained Percy. 'He's got Friesian cows and you really want good thick Jersey cream. Nice and yellow with the consistency of cold treacle.'

'My cows aren't Jerseys,' said Kelvin.

'Your cows aren't anything in particular, but I had a look in the tank at the top of your lane and the milk looked nice and yellow.'

'What the hell were you doing poking your nose into my milk tank?' demanded Kelvin. 'And when was it?'

'Last week some time. It's my job to know what goes on in the parish. It could have been anything in your tank.'

'Anything? What the hell do you expect to find in a milk tank except milk?'

'I heard of one farmer who stuffed the body of his dead wife into his milk tank,' said Percy darkly.

Kelvin and Mick looked at him incredulously. 'That's as bloody silly a story as I've ever heard!' snorted Kelvin. 'Nobody would do a thing like that. If you stuck a body in a tank, you'd have all your milk rejected by the dairy as sure as fate. And another thing, if I have any trouble with the dairy in the next day or two about my milk, I'll tell them it was you opening up the lid and dropping your bogeys into it. If they complain about poor hygiene, I'll tell them to take it up with you.'

During this dissertation on the art of scones and clotted cream, the fire crew had succeeded in linking their hoses to the stream and were waiting for Mick to give them the word. He recalled his duty. 'Well, I suppose we might as well get on with putting out this fire of yours, Kelvin.'

'I'd much rather you didn't,' implored the latter. 'It's doing nobody any harm and it'll burn itself out in a couple of hours.'

'You get on and do your duty, Mick,' contributed Percy pompously. 'You've got my backing if there is any come-back.'

Mick sighed, looking apologetically at Kelvin. 'I'm sorry, Kelvin. Look at it from my point of view.' He gestured towards the firemen and the rest of the spectators. 'This lot all want me to put it out. My lads like nothing better than a nice, straightforward barn fire. All those people watching are expecting it of me and that great nit' – he indicated Percy – 'has every intention of being awkward if we do nothing.'

'Bloody right I do!' said Percy with relish. 'There's something definitely suspicious about this here fire and Kelvin's attitude.'

'How about if I got on the phone to the insurance company and they said it was all right to let it burn out?' asked Kelvin desperately.

'Don't be daft,' replied Mick. 'No insurance company's going to say that.'

'At least let me try,' responded Kelvin. 'Look, just give me a couple of minutes on the phone and then you can spray water as much as you like.'

Mick thought for a few seconds. 'OK, Kelvin, you've got two minutes and then my lads'll get on with it.'

'Here!' cried Percy. 'You can't do that. You start squirting your bloody hoses right now.'

'Look, Percy, I've told you already: I don't tell you how to do your job and you don't tell me how to do mine,' said Mick patiently. 'Two minutes is neither here nor there.'

Percy knew he could not shift Mick so he turned to Kelvin. 'No nonsense, mind. If your insurance man says yes, I'll want to talk to him.' Percy had had to raise his voice as Kelvin had already dived into the house. 'Silly old bugger,' muttered Percy after his retreating back. Mick went over to the lads to explain the situation to them and to discuss their tactics once they went ahead with their extinguishing. A stir of expectation ran through the crowd, which had begun to become slightly restive due to the inaction of the fire brigade. Even the spectating cattle kicked up their heels in excitement and careered briefly round their field before coming back to a snorting halt along the fence.

Percy placed himself in the porch of the farmhouse studying his watch, ready to burst through the door as soon as the time was up, but Kelvin appeared in the doorway with fifteen seconds still to go, brushed his way past without giving him a glance and walked slowly out into the yard towards the fire engine. Every eye was on him.

Percy came pattering after him. 'Well?' he demanded. 'What did he say?'

Kelvin stopped. 'I am not telling you anything. I'm going to tell Mick. It's nothing to do with you.'

'He said no, didn't he?' jeered Percy.

'It's none of your business,' replied Kelvin firmly.

'He said no. Don't deny it. That'll teach you!' It was not often that one could see a policeman in uniform actually dancing with glee, but Percy was capering in front of Kelvin rather like a large puppy. Kelvin looked at this exhibition with phlegmatic distaste, showing no inclination to go over to let Mick into the insurance company's decision. So Mick came across to find out the news for himself.

'Well?' he demanded.

'Well what?' asked Kelvin innocently.

'He said no. Go on, admit it. He said no,' crowed Percy.

'He said nothing of the sort,' replied Kelvin.

Percy paused in mid-caper, one leg poised rather ludicrously. His face showed first dismay, then incredulity, then anger. 'Balls! I don't bloody believe you. He said yes?' Kelvin opened his mouth to reply, but Percy did not give him a chance to speak. 'Anyway, you can go and phone him right back. If you remember, I said I would want to hear for myself, and by the time I've had my say he'll be saying no or I'll resign from the bloody force.' Kelvin made to say something again. 'Go on.

135

Admit it. You're lying. I don't believe he said any such thing.'

'Percy, why the hell don't you shut up and let Kelvin speak?' said Mick mildly. Percy shut up and the two of them looked expectantly at Kelvin. The latter glanced from one to the other.

'Well?' demanded Percy.

If Kelvin was about to say anything, which looked fairly unlikely, it would have been drowned by a double blast from the siren on the fire engine. It made everyone from Percy to the smallest of the watching cattle jump. 'Jesus!' exclaimed Mick, turning on his heel to glare at the fireman in the cab. 'What the hell does he think he's up to?' The figure in the cab was gesticulating wildly. Mick trotted the few yards across to the fire engine.

Percy, breathing heavily, glared from Kelvin to Mick to Kelvin again. Everyone else was now looking at Mick who listened briefly to his man in the cab and then signalled to the rest of the crew who hurriedly began to reel in their hoses. He strode back to Percy and Kelvin. 'It looks as though you're off the hook, Kelvin. There's been a 999 call about a grass fire up on the moor.'

Percy was aghast. 'You can't go away and leave this because of some bloody grass fire. It's been pouring with rain the last day or two anyway.'

'The bloke who phoned up said that he and his family were on a picnic and the fire had them surrounded.'

'Nobody has a picnic at this time of year and, anyway, if the fire had them surrounded, how did he get to a telephone?'

'He said he just happened to have one of those new-fangled radio telephones in his car.'

'What a load of nonsense!' said Percy angrily.

'I know,' agreed Mick. 'The chances are it is a hoax call, but we can't afford to risk it. We never can. Think what would happen if we left a family of tourists to burn! It would be lousy for business. If you'll excuse me.' Mick was off. The hoses were reeled in; the lads stood on the running board like Keystone cops, steeled their jaws, and looked into the middle distance as the fire engine engaged gear. Blue light flashing and siren blaring, it roared off up the lane, spraying a plume of mud and cowdung from under its wheels.

Percy turned, slitty-eyed with frustration, to Kelvin. 'You jammy bastard! That insurance man told you to put the fire out didn't he?'

'I couldn't find his number, so I didn't get through to him.'

'Who did you phone then?'

'I didn't phone anyone.'

Jimmy still had not learned to keep his mouth shut. 'Yes you did, Kelvin. I heard the bell out in the yard tinkle. You must have used the phone.' Most of the farms had outside bells so that the farmer could hear the telephone ring when he was out ministering to his beasts. Percy looked puzzled; the rest of the spectators merely frowned at Jimmy.

'Who were you on the phone to, Kelvin? Percy asked.

'I must have jogged the receiver with my sleeve when I was trying to find the insurance man's number,' replied Kelvin innocently.

Percy knew Kelvin well enough to realize that the given explanation was almost certainly not the correct one, but he was not a lateral thinker. Everyone, including Kelvin, looked curiously at him, wondering when he might manage to add two and two together. Percy darted glances at his onlookers, trying to work out why he was the object of so many pairs of eyes. He rubbed his chin thoughtfully, his mind ruminating gently over all the inputs that had recently come its way. The fire might as well have given up and gone out for all the attention that it was getting.

'Very nice for you, Kelvin, that Mick was called away,' said Percy. The audience held its breath. 'I bet it was a hoax call. These bloody kids are a real pain.' Jimmy began to moan softly. He had understood at last and the tension created by the ponderous workings of Percy's brain cells was getting to him. He shut up when Gerald Mowbray kicked him on the ankle. Suddenly it happened. All the cogs fell into place with such force that Percy's head jerked to one side under their impact. 'Christ Almighty! That telephone call to the fire brigade. It was you who made it, wasn't it, Kelvin?' His denial was inaudible beneath the muted cheer from the gallery. 'What?' demanded Percy.

'I said no. I didn't telephone anybody.'

'You're a lying bastard! Of course it must have been you. It's just too convenient. What kind of an idiot do you take me for?'

Rhetorical questions of that nature are most unwise. Kelvin looked slowly round at the audience who were daring him to come out with the truth. When it suited his own interests, however, Kelvin knew exactly how to play things. 'I made no telephone call, Percy. Even if I had done, which I did not, there is absolutely no way that you could prove it was me. I bet it isn't a false alarm, anyway. There probably is a fire up at Higher Down.'

Gerald Mowbray opened his mouth. 'Higher Down? Who said anything about Higher Down?' Kelvin heard Gerald Mowbray and turned a delicate shade of grey. Everyone else heard Gerald Mowbray and held their breath – everyone, that is, save Percy. He was busy on another track.

'I'll prove it if it's the last thing I ever do!' he roared. 'I'll trace the telephone call. I'll make voice prints. Nobody can make a fool of me like that. Just you wait, Kelvin Morchard. I'll get you.'

'Oh, go to hell, Percy. If you can catch me, then do what the hell you like, but until then go away and stop wasting my time.'

'Right!' said Percy, breathing heavily. 'Right! I'll be off now. But I'll be back. Mark my words, I will return.'

'You and Fu Manchu,' replied Kelvin, ensuring that he had the last word. Percy, his lips tight with frustration, turned on his heel and stalked off up the lane towards his bicycle and his mother's scones.

The fire was left to its own devices for the rest of the afternoon and early evening while people went home to catch up on their chores. They reassembled after dark when Kelvin broke out several bottles of his home-made wine for a fire party and the spectators, who included half of the crew of the fire tender, caroused on into the evening, seated on barrels,

138

warming their toes on the gently decaying barn. They watched the sparks floating into the air while the bats flitted in and out of the firelight, harvesting moths and other insects attracted by the abnormal brightness and warmth in the autumnal evening. The cattle lay down along the fence to cud, their eyes reflecting the glow of the embers.

'It was a damn good fire even if Mick didn't put it out,' said Dennis, belching contentedly.

'Bit of luck about that hoax call,' added the commander.

'That reminds me!' exclaimed Mick. 'The emergency operator asked the caller for his number.'

'They always do,' agreed the commander.

'That's right, they always do. Anyway, the number the caller gave was yours, Kelvin.'

There was silence, broken only by a soft thump as the ghost of a hay bale rolled over, jetting sparks into the sky.

The commander sighed. 'Ah well, nobody can remember everything.'

'I put Percy off when he asked about it,' said Mick.

'Some say otherwise, Mick, but I've always maintained

you're a decent sort of a bloke,' said Kelvin, looking deep into the fire.

'That's nice of you to say so, Kelvin.'

'And I'm sure I can find a bit of cream for you now and again. Really cheap.'

'That'd be right neighbourly of you,' replied Mick.

Chapter Nine

'IS IT HARDY, dear?' asked Elfrieda eagerly as her husband
fine-sprayed coffee across the inside back page of *The Times*.
The commander was wont to chortle or sigh occasionally over
breakfast as he perused the deaths column, but a snort of such
proportions could only mean a demise of outstanding quality,
possibly even that of the retired admiral whose adverse report
had caused the untimely end of his career. The commander
had been racked by jealousy when he had discovered that
even the densest of his contemporaries now sported an MVO
for elbowing an impertinent *paparazzo* off a jetty during one of
the honeymoons spent on the royal yacht.

'No,' replied her husband. 'It's us!'

'What? Us in the obituaries! What are you talking
about?'

'No, we're not dead. It's this advertisement under "Holidays
and Villas". It mentions the village! It's got our phone
number. I mean, it's a local number.'

'Whose is it?'

'137.'

'137? That's Mrs Baggins!'

'No, she's 127. Who on earth could it be?'

'Well, read the blasted advert and find out, then!' Her
increasing shortness with him the commander put down to
feminism rather than to his own growing preference for nursing
beer in the pub over that for nursing his seedlings. He threw
her a dirty look above the top of the paper.

'I was just about to, dear.' He cleared his throat. ' "Find
yourself in beautiful surroundings." '

'Well? Don't stop.'

'That's all there is. That and the phone number. What do you think it could mean?'

'It's a mistake. They must have left out a line.'

'No, they can't have done. Surroundings is on two lines, although I suppose the word could be surrender. "Find yourself in beautiful surrender in our fascinating surroundings." Perhaps it's someone trying to advertise bed and breakfast. Imaginative use of our native tongue is not a notable local characteristic.' His face lit up. 'No! Of course! It must be the communards. Find yourself in the sense of finding your soul, like Kelvin said he did when he looked down the barrel of that poacher's gun when he was a special constable.'

'But the communards haven't got a phone.'

'Oh. Well, who on earth could it be?'

'Ring up and find out.'

The commander shook his newspaper nervously. 'I couldn't just ring up. It would be frightfully rude.'

'They wouldn't have published their phone number in the personal column if they didn't want to be phoned up,' responded Elfrieda reasonably.

'Yes, but not by neighbours. They could have stuck up a notice in the post office window if they wanted us to phone. I'll ask in the pub at lunchtime. Someone there is bound to have rung up to find out by then.'

'The only problem is that most of that lot have enough trouble when it comes to reading the *Sun*. They certainly won't have read *The Times*.'

'Don't worry. The advert could be etched on a microchip placed on the dark side of the moon and the village would know ten minutes after sunset.'

It was Saturday and so there was a good turnout of locals enjoying the sight of Helga trying to explain to a family of foreigners that their six-year-old could not be served with a drink, when the commander bustled importantly into the pub. He waited until the bewildered guttural noises that the visitors were making faded as Helga shut the door behind them before he made his announcement. He thought he would start quietly.

'By the way, whose phone number is 137?'

'You been looking at that advert? It's bloody silly if you ask me,' replied Kelvin.

'Oh.' The commander felt decidedly deflated. 'Whose is it, then?'

'It's the Jarretts. Malcolm's organizing a weekend on the moor. He said they're camping out so that they can tune into their essence, but it's bound to rain. I told him that there was no point putting an advert up in the post office because nobody from round here is going to do anything like that. He's charging £12.50 too!'

'I actually saw it in *The Times* this morning.'

'I mean, who's going to pay £12.50 to walk on the moor when they can do it for nothing?'

'I can't imagine,' replied the commander gloomily.

'And who would want to go there even if they could do it for free? It's just steep ground, bogs and scrub. You'd have to drain and lime it before you could plough and it just wouldn't be worth the expense.'

' "Heather and a rolling landscape with wooded combes" is what they call it in the tourist brochures,' murmured the commander.

'You go looking for missing sheep up there and you'd soon find the place is one of God's mistakes. It's only good for breaking the necks of tourists.'

'It would do you good to take a weekend in the open air, Kelvin.'

'Couldn't do it, even if I wanted to. It's the beginning of Operation Bulldog that weekend.'

'Operation Bulldog?' inquired the commander.

'That's right,' replied Kelvin importantly. 'All the nation's defences are on full alert and we're practising for when the Russians invade. As head of the Emergency Volunteers, I'm commandeering Gerald Mowbray's bacon wireless.'

'Don't tell me. Let me guess,' said Lindy.

Kelvin looked mystified. 'What's with you?'

143

'I know, Commander!' exclaimed Lindy delightedly. 'Ham radio! Oh, that's a real goody, Kelvin.'

Kelvin shrugged. 'Yeah, that's it. His farm is going to be my command post.'

Malcolm marketed his weekend with subtlety. He knew that, faced with a phalanx of cynical faces in the pub, he would have no luck at all. On the telephone he could isolate prospects and flatter. 'Commander, I was hoping you might come along next weekend on this stroll I'm organizing.'

'Actually, I was hoping to watch *Dynasty* on Friday—'

'—We need a man of your skills and experience along with us. There'll be some young ladies who will be very grateful to you if you come.'

'Young ladies? Grateful to me?'

'For your money you get a free breakfast every morning and we've got a carefully planned itinerary.'

'Young ladies? Have you ... er ... met any of them? They're not like Mandy, are they?'

'Lord, no. They're really nice people. Lovely figures, too.'

'Well, in that case, I might be able to manage it. I can always get *Dynasty* videoed by Ivor.'

'He's coming too.'

'Is he, by God! It was just the young ladies, I bet. Ha ha. Do I have to bring a sleeping bag? I'm a bit past that sort of thing, you know.'

'Ho ho,' concurred Malcolm. 'Come along on Friday at about 10pm. Just bring yourself and some sensible clothes. Everything else has been taken care of.'

'Sounds quite fun. Bags I a bed in with the young ladies, eh?'

'It's a men-only weekend. But the wives will be very pleased that a man of your calibre will be going along. See you Friday. Bye.'

'Shit!' said the commander as he slammed down the telephone.

'What's wrong with you?' asked Elfrieda who was passing

144

through the hall bearing some tobacco leaves, part of their latest crop, towards the airing cupboard.

'I've been conned into going on this weekend that Malcolm's running.'

'That'll be nice. I'll be able to have a couple of days to myself. I might throw a party.'

'Well, don't count on many men being around. Half the male population of the village will be off on the moor before Malcolm is finished.'

In the event only the commander, Ivor and Keith turned up at the Jarretts' cottage on a wet Friday night. The commander and Ivor were dressed almost identically in Barbour jackets, corduroy trousers and green gumboots. The only variation was the commander's choice of a deerstalker as opposed to Ivor's flat cap. Keith wore a blue nylon padded anorak and black gumboots. Malcolm greeted them at the door. They noticed uneasily that he was sporting knee breeches and the heavy woollen socks that are worn by the active variety of tourist who is usually enveloped above his calves in an orange kagoule that rustles and crackles like the sails on a storm-driven windjammer as he tramps his way through the village, his eyes fixed on the cloud-covered moor a mile or two beyond.

'Come in, come in,' greeted Malcolm cordially, ushering them in. Both he and his wife went jogging and swallowed lots of authentically dull food purveyed in large brown paper bags by a shop that still called itself 'Health' rather than 'Whole'. This made them both look fit but Kelvin had observed that it seemed to cause them to belch and fart a good deal, although the former appeared to be a necessary part of their culture as the eructations were emitted with pride.

The visitors filed through into the sitting room which had been laid out with the sofa and chairs lined up facing one way and lines of cushions on the floor. 'Sit down, please.' Malcolm indicated the sofa and they sat themselves nervously down on the oatmeal hessian covers. Malcolm took the chair opposite, from where he could control the meeting, and stared pleasantly at them.

145

After half a minute's silence, the commander cleared his throat: 'Harrumph!' Malcolm continued to look benign while Ivor and Keith turned to the commander, expecting him to say something to break this rather odd quiet. The commander picked up their vibrations. 'Have you got anything to drink?'

'It wouldn't be wise.'

'Oh.' There was another hiatus. 'How many people are you expecting?'

'Twenty-three.'

'And what exactly are we going to do?'

'Let's wait until everyone's here and then I'll tell you – there again, perhaps I won't.' Malcolm smiled enigmatically. Ivor yawned theatrically, picked up a magazine from the top of a pile on the polished wooden floor, which was scattered tastefully with numdah rugs, and put it back down again when he saw that it was a copy of *Alliance News*.

'Are we allowed to talk?' asked Keith.

'Of course,' smiled Malcolm. 'You can do what you like until everyone else comes.'

'Good. What exactly is the point of this weekend? You were rather vague about it on the phone.'

'Yes,' agreed Ivor. 'I'm not sure—'

'I'd rather we waited until the others are here before we talk about what we're going to do,' interrupted Malcolm. 'It will save saying everything twice.'

There was another short silence. 'Where's Stephanie?' asked the commander.

'I sent her away for the night.'

'Gosh!' exclaimed the commander admiringly. He would no more dare send his wife out for the night than wear a tie with a Windsor knot.

Malcolm reddened. 'Actually, she wanted to go out. She's gone to the theatre with some friends from work.'

The silence stretched to twenty minutes before the doorbell rang. Ivor put away the hoof knife that he used in idle moments to scrape the accumulations of mud, dung and tractor oil from beneath his finger nails and looked up expectantly as Malcolm went off to answer its summons.

146

There was a tramping in the hall and a trio of bespectacled men of around thirty entered the room. They had the same woolly socks as Malcolm and all carried rucksacks which they placed on the floor. The bell rang again and the room gradually filled. The locals, recipients of curious looks from the others, huddled together on the sofa, as a murmur of conversation in half a dozen accents from Newcastle southwards discussed mountains they had conquered, mighty expeditions they had endured across barren plateaux and argued the merits of various types of dubbin for their supple boots.

Malcolm called the meeting to attention. 'Right!' he said briskly. 'I didn't get anyone from our advert, although there were a few phone calls, but this weekend we're going to tune into our emotional strengths. We're going to strip away all the dross of civilization and tap into the essence of our collective manhood.'

There were excited 'rhubarb' noises from the bulk of the congregation while the commander's murmur of 'Heavens!' earned him a few dirty looks from those close enough to hear.

'In a few minutes, we shall be splitting you up into groups of five and then you will be making a night march to a pre-arranged rendezvous point.'

'But it's pouring with rain!' exclaimed Ivor.

'It'll make it all the more interesting,' said Malcolm.

'Where will we sleep?' asked the commander.

'You won't tonight,' said Malcolm cheerfully, 'unless you get to the rendezvous point early, which is in a nice warm barn.'

'Good God!'

'There are also a couple of wobblies that we'll be throwing at you. You will not be told where you're being dropped and myself, Peter here' – a man with smoothly swept-back blond hair and an out-of-season tan smiled coldly – 'and Tom' – Tom had the sleek, doctored-cat look of someone who prospered undemandingly in the City – 'will be touring round the area all night and, if we catch you, you will be dumped five miles further away from the rendezvous point.'

Before the three locals had been able to do more than exchange looks, let alone confer in private when they would have been able to give each other the courage to walk out and return to their nice warm beds, Malcolm read out the names of the groups, bracketing Ivor with the commander but allowing Keith to fall among strangers. The party adjusted their kagoules and tightened the laces on their books. Leaving the cottage they obediently boarded vehicles and were driven away into the leaden, moonless night.

There is a unique desolation of the soul which comes in the depths of the English countryside when a motorist *perdu* reaches a crossroads and finds that he has has heard of none of the four villages to which the signpost points. Being ejected from a vehicle into stormswept darkness with one feeble torch for illumination conjured up much the same in sensation in Ivor's group, particularly when a ten-minute grope revealed that they were at a crossroads without any signpost at all.

Ivor and the commander made straight for shelter and stood disconsolately beneath the drips of a scrubby hedgerow while the experienced weekenders discussed the matter in whispers from the other, exposed, side of the lane.

'Turn on the torch so that I can read the map,' ordered one of their companions, Roy from Huddersfield in a yellow anorak.

'If we turn on the torch, the patrols might see us and we'll be caught,' replied another. Judging by the area of dark from which his voice emanated, the commander decided that it must have been Hugh who was about 5 feet high with a face like a piglet. Hugh came from London. 'And anyway, if we get the map out, it'll probably disintegrate in the rain and then we really will be in the shit.'

'We'll just have to risk it. We won't get very far if we have to stand here all night and we've been dumped with these two. Have you seen their feet? They've got gumboots on.' That was the third who was tall and thin with boots so supple with use that one could see his toes wriggle beneath the leather in a manner that seemed faintly obscene. The map was unfolded; the torch gave light and a conference ensued.

'Have you got any whisky on you?' muttered the commander to Ivor as the cough of a sheep in the field behind their hedge distracted the experts into twittering excitement.

'What was that?'

'It's Malcolm!'

'It's not fair! We can't be caught already. Quick! Put out the torch! Everyone into the ditch!' Three dark shapes rushed past the commander and Ivor. It had been heavy rain and it was a main ditch, so the water was a foot deep over a muddy bottom. They made quite a splash.

'I've only got one bottle. What are these people doing in the ditch? And why are you whispering?' asked Ivor.

'I've only got one as well. I'm whispering because I bet these people have got none at all and I don't want to dissipate it and I've no idea what they're up to in the ditch.'

'Sshh!' hissed the ditch.

The commander sneezed. The sheep coughed again. There was consternation. 'That's torn it!' said Hugh, the piggy one, savagely. 'I knew we'd drawn the short straw with these two in our group!'

'Excuse me!' said the commander to the ditch politely. 'What are you doing?'

'We're hiding.'

'Why? I thought we were supposed to be going to that barn.'

Another sheep bleated. Sheep do not all say 'meeah' – if they did, they would all sound the same, which would remove the only point of making the noise at all. Some sheep howl, some yelp, some squawk, some sound like the most derelict of winos trying to hawk phlegm from the wreckage of his lungs, and some sound like Mrs Thatcher. This particular animal had a mellow growl.

There was a muttered conversation from the ditch. Then the sound of them hauling themselves out. Eyes were becoming used to differentiating between sky-dark and the padded-cell blackness below the horizon and the three silhouettes were visible above the line of the hedge.

'All right, Malcolm! We give in!' shouted Hugh, as the sheep growled once more.

'Oh, I see!' exclaimed Ivor. 'There's no need to worry. That's just a sheep.'

'A sheep?'

'A sheep.'

'That's not a sheep, that's a human voice,' stated Hugh patronizingly.

'Meeah!' said another voice in the accents of an ovine Richard Burton.

'Oh. Well, all I can say is that you've got some bloody funny-sounding sheep down here.'

'We probably have,' responded Ivor equably. He would quite happily defend his purse, his daughter's innocence and possibly even his nation from verbal abuse, but sheep noises could look after themselves. 'How long do you want to stand around here, by the way?'

'Until we know where we are. We don't want to set off in the wrong direction, do we?'

'Why don't we find out where we are then?'

'We can't. We don't know where we are on the map.'

'Give me the torch,' ordered Ivor. It was passed over and he flashed his way a few yards down the lane to a gateway and shone it through. He gave a grunt of satisfaction. 'That's not too bad. It shouldn't take us more than a couple of hours to walk to the barn. The moor's a couple of hundred yards up this lane and we can pick up a footpath there. Shall we get going?' Ivor strode briskly off into the darkness.

The commander joined him, but the others showed reluctance. 'How do you know all that from looking through a gate?' shouted Hugh suspiciously.

Ivor turned and called back, 'I recognized the grass. If you live in the country, you grow to know different grass like you people in towns recognize buildings.'

'Oh.' There was a note of surprised respect in Hugh's voice and they followed in silence along the tarmac road surface.

The commander mulled things over for a few hundred dark yards. 'You didn't really recognize the grass, did you?' he whispered.

'It was the sheep,' replied Ivor.

'You asked the sheep?'

'In a manner of speaking. They're Dick Hunniford's which means that the field must be his fifteen-acre meadow.'

'You can tell who owns a sheep just by looking at it? That's just about as good as recognizing grass.'

'It's not difficult when there's a large 'DH' in blue dye on their backs,' replied Ivor mildly.

It was a gentle if soggy stroll across the edge of the moor to the rendezvous point which was reached by 3am. They enjoyed a peaceful few hours amid the hay bales.

Peter decided to make a move at 6.30. He walked over to the barn, his hair gleaming in the watery morning sunshine, to stand looking up into the dim heap of bales. 'Right, everyone out!'

'Is breakfast ready?' demanded the commander after Peter had shouted for some time. He peered down, showing little inclination to move.

'No.'

'I'm not getting up until it's breakfast time. Here!' he said accusingly, 'you've had a shave! If you were scouring the lanes for us all night, when did you have time to shave? I bet you've had a bath too.'

151

'I haven't.

'You twister! I can smell your Essence of Athlete aftershave from here.'

There were murmurings of support from the other three but it was *sotto voce* as they had no desire to face court martial for insubordination. Peter was not prepared to surrender authority to the contents of the barn.

'You have thirty seconds to come down or there will be no breakfast for you,' he ordered.

In spite of the threat, it was a good twenty-five seconds before the incipient mutiny crumbled and the three slid down the hay bales with the commander and Ivor following more circumspectly behind. Another of the groups, whose members had arrived later on, clambered down from the eaves at the other end of the barn. They drew up in a ragged line opposite Peter who regarded them coldly. He had his hands behind his back and bounced gently on his toes. 'I think you lot need a bit of exercise before breakfast.' There was a chorus of groans. 'Everyone into the orchard behind the barn. Hugh, come and help me carry stuff from the camper.'

Ten disconsolate people, most of them tired, gritty, wet and potentially foul-tempered, trailed through the nettles and long grass into the orchard to a roughly scythed circle where they stood to watch Hugh, playing teacher's pet, and Peter carry in a large rug-covered bundle which they dropped on the ground with a clatter.

Peter put an arm inside and drew out a long sword. Ivor and the commander exchanged a wary glance as Peter flexed his arm with the authority of the Black Prince before Crécy. 'Steve!' he called. 'Let's have a bit of a warm-up.'

Steve was tall, fair and bearded. He pushed his way through and selected a sword, waving it above his head. His resemblance to a Viking berserker was marred only by his pebble-lens spectacles. His sword, like the others, was a piece of roughly shaped wood about a yard long with a crosspiece at the hilt. Before the wondering gaze of the commander and Ivor they came on guard, saluted and circled each other before emitting screams of rage and falling on one another, parrying and thrusting at each other's vitals.

'Jesus wept!' exclaimed the commander. 'What on earth do they think they're up to?'

'It's duelling with English broadswords,' explained Hugh. 'Peter thought it up on a weekend in the Yorkshire Dales. It's purpose is to put you in touch with your male aggression.'

'Is that so?' remarked the commander, wincing as Peter rattled Steve's ribs with a slashing swipe that the latter failed to avert. He continued to watch, open-mouthed, as the contestants, who were now breathing heavily, clattered their wooden blades while they slashed away with no apparent concern for each other's wellbeing.

The commander started violently when Ivor nudged him in the ribs just as Steve did the same to Peter. Ivor nodded towards the roadside where Father Loosemire, just beginning his letter round, was peering over the hedge from the roof of his van to discover the source of these hoarse cries and the peculiar clattering sound. 'Hell!' said the commander as he and Ivor moved smartly behind the trunk of a gnarled apple. 'We'll be a laughing stock in the village if he recognizes us.'

After a couple of minutes it became clear that Peter's sword-play would prove decisive. He had a determined grin on his face, baring his teeth like Errol Flynn, as he drove Steve back with successive blows until the latter slipped to fall flat on his back, the sword spinning from his hand. Peter prodded him in the belly, driving the breath from his vanquished opponent and held the tip of the sword against his heaving chest. For a dreadful moment, both the commander and Ivor thought that Peter had regressed to Hammer Horror and was about to skewer Steve as one would a vampire. They would have leaped forward to protect him had not a hee-hawing laugh from Father Loosemire over the hedge reminded them of the wisdom of preserving their anonymity. The laugh also broke into the battle haze clouding the brain beneath Peter's hair which was still sleek with an emulsion of sweat and brilliantine. He turned towards the hedge with a snarl, lifting the sword above his head. The commander feverishly wondered what was appropriate: not a Tarzan yell, not 'All for One and

153

One for All', nor even 'God for Harry! England and St George!' Peter must have been wondering as well since he opened and shut his mouth a few times before merely managing a hoarse roar. It was enough for Father Loosemire. Uttering a cry of alarm, he scurried into his van before this lunatic could attack and roared off down the lane, his mind busily honing and polishing the experience into an anecdote that would absorb the discerning audience of the pub.

'Right!' said Peter. 'That's how you do it.' His eyes swept the watchers. Ivor had stepped out from behind the tree with the disappearance of the post office van but the commander, an older campaigner, elected to stay where he was. This defence was sufficient to protect him from a casual inspection, but Peter's eye carefully winkled him out. 'You!' he barked, extending the point of his sword straight at the commander. 'Come out here and have a go!'

The commander needed no more than a split-second to consider his response. 'No.'

'Come on,' repeated Peter impatiently. 'I won't hurt you. You'll be all right, won't he, Steve?'

'He'll be fine,' groaned Steve, using a fallen branch to haul himself to his feet while one hand protectively hugged his battered ribcage.

The commander laughed incredulously. 'There is absolutely no chance of me hitting someone else with those ridiculous weapons. Or being hit myself.'

'They're not ridiculous!' said Malcolm who had come down to observe. 'We've been using them for years and they really tell you about yourself. Come out and try it.'

'Certainly not! I had better things to do even when I was a schoolboy.'

'You dirty little bugger!' responded Malcolm with a laugh that came from the subculture of the pub rather than from his persona as organizer of a self-seeking weekend. 'Ivor, you come out and have a go. Peter won't hit you. He just wants to demonstrate the scoring strokes to those who've never done it before.'

'Scoring strokes!' sneered the commander. 'You must think

we're bloody mad. Ivor! Where are you going?' Ivor walked awkwardly towards the centre of the circle, peeling off his jacket. He did not look as if he would give Peter much trouble. As Kelvin had once said, Ivor needed to stick matches in his ears before he had a bath to stop himself slipping down the plug hole. 'I fenced for Cirencester.'

'Oh, did you?' said Peter. 'Well, this isn't fencing. Stand there and I'll show you the scoring strokes.' He showed the scoring strokes: an upward stab to the base of the throat and the heart with a downward lunge into the bowels and the groin. Lesser strokes were incapacitating slashes at the joints.

'Pick up a sword and let's try,' said Peter. Ivor carefully selected the smallest sword, being closest to the *épée*, and flexed his wrist experimentally. Although he looked an inferior species of animal to Conan the Barbarian, many years of tugging the foremilk out of cows a couple of times a day had

155

preserved the strength and suppleness of his wrist and so he appeared quite professional as he took his guard and parried the first mighty swipe from Peter. It was the last mighty swipe. Ivor looked like a Disney cartoon character tottering away from an upswinging garden rake. The vibration from the parry and the sting in his fingers caused his sword to drop from a numbed hand and he stood there hugging his palm in his armpit as Peter, chanting 'One and Two', smacked him smartly on the knee and poked him in the belly, before standing back to admire his prone figure.

'See?' said Peter, turning his back on Ivor. 'It's very easy. Everyone pick up a sword and let's see you all work up an appetite.' The orchard rang like a bodger's battlefield as grown men circled, slashing at each other with their wooden swords, uttering squeals of apprehension and aggression.

The commander threaded his way through the mob to Ivor who was sitting on the grass, nursing his knee. 'You are a silly bugger! At your age, you ought to know better. Oh, hullo, Keith.'

Keith had only just arrived. He looked dreadful: gaunt, covered in bramble scratches, burrs and goosegrass, with a six-inch barbed-wire slash across the knee of his trousers. 'What's going on?' he asked, looking round at the battle.

'They're stripping away the dross of civilization,' replied the commander.

'They're all bloody mad. They must be as knackered as I am! What's up with you, Ivor?'

'That prat Peter thumped him,' replied the commander. 'Why don't you go and sort him out?'

'I think I might just do that. I've had about as much as I can take from this lot.'

Keith picked up Ivor's sword and plunged through the mob towards Peter. The latter was toying with a small, bald man who had his back to a tree and a terrified expression on his face as he defended himself desperately from the attacking blade as it crashed into the trunk, inches from his genitals. Keith had obviously summed up the chivalrous spirit in which the battle was being fought as he crossed the grass. With a great 'Huzza' he jabbed the point of his sword into Peter's backside just as tears of humiliation were springing up in the eyes of his victim.

It may have been the effect of launching his attack on the run, or his judgement may have been affected by his lack of sleep, for even Ivor forgot his wounded knee to draw in breath with a hiss of horror as Keith slammed in his weapon. The effect on Peter was immediate: he screamed in agony, dropped his sword, clutched at his buttocks and rolled on the ground.

Combat gradually ceased as cavaliers, pirates, musketeers and Scarlet Pimpernels – even the odd samurai, specializing in a two-handed style – had their fantasies interrupted by the shrieks. They formed a grimly curious circle round him, resting on the hilts of their swords like Crusaders, satiated after a bit of good rape and pillage.

Keith was more into violence as a countryman than he had been in his days as a pork butcher in Reading; even so, he was appalled at the effect of his blow. 'Christ! I'm sorry,' he stammered. 'Are you OK?'

'Of course he's not OK,' said the commander. 'You jabbed him on the coccyx. It really wasn't the most honourable way to attack.'

'Bloody effective, though,' admired a spectator.

'You stupid bloody shit!' gasped Peter.

'I've said I'm sorry,' said Keith helplessly. 'There's not a great deal more that I can do.'

'Cows don't make half as much fuss when you break their tails,' said Ivor, who had wasted no time in hobbling over to appreciate the drama. 'Oh, it's all too easy to do,' he continued, responding to a couple of raised urban eyebrows. 'If you want them to go forward, you push their tails up above their backs and you have to be very careful or the bone snaps.'

'I am not a fucking cow,' moaned Peter. 'Although I think something may have broken.'

The commander inspected Peter as he writhed on the ground. 'Hmm. You do look a bit pale, but I should think you're probably just bruised. However, we could always ram a splint up if you really think something's broken.' Ivor and the commander exchanged a contented smile. 'They do say that sticks and stones may hurt your bones,' he continued remorselessly. 'I knew it would be dangerous to play with those swords. Let this be a lesson to you.'

'Go away,' groaned Peter. 'Please, all of you. I want to be alone.'

'That's Garbo,' said Keith.

'What is?' asked Ivor.

' "I want to be alone." '

'But she didn't get a wooden sword up her arse, did she?'

'Malcolm, take them all away!' pleaded Peter.

'You mean we've finished playing with the swords?' asked the commander.

'Yes,' said Malcolm briskly. 'What about some breakfast? After that, and when Peter's licked his wounds, we can go on to something else.'

'Breakfast! Now that sounds like a good idea, but I'm not sure I'd recommend that Peter licks his wounds,' said the commander. 'Or whether we should abandon an injured member of the party.' His protestation of concern would have carried more weight if he, Ivor and Keith had not immediately turned their backs on Peter and headed rapidly through the orchard towards the barn. The rest of the party, shepherded by Malcolm, followed, leaving Peter to find out what kind of man he might be when it came to coping with pain.

Chapter Ten

BREAKFAST DID little to convince the commander that he had made a wise decision in coming on the weekend. Keith seemed to be quite enjoying himself, while Ivor's way of avoiding involvement was through constant complaints. 'Call this food? I wouldn't feed it to my pigs!'

'You can't expect miracles when you feed twenty people off one camping stove and small campfire. I think we're lucky to get beans as well as half-raw bacon,' replied Keith.

Malcolm had at least chosen a reasonable place to make camp. The lichen-covered grey stone barn had been part of a farm whose house had long been demolished, although the outbuildings were still in use. Behind it lay the orchard and to its front was a stretch of grass-covered hard ground which had been the old yard, from where a lane led back alongside a stream to the public road. Beyond the orchard and on the other side of the river, the fields rolled up to the moor with tiny thistledown sheep dotted across the grass and heather. They were sitting on a fallen sycamore, a decent distance upwind of the fire which was fuelled by a sackful of artificial logs smelling as if they had been marinated in sump oil. Ivor had his leg carefully stretched in front of him to favour his injured knee. 'Do you know what we're supposed to be doing after this?'

'More cowboys and Indians, I should imagine. They've got shields and bows and arrows in the back of one of the Land Rovers.' The commander stared morosely at the majority group by the fire, hungrily watching some frozen sausages that remained obstinately willy-pink in the frying pan above the fake logs. He wrinkled his lip as he tasted the tea that had been sploshed into a tin mug for him. 'It amazes me. You can eat food on a destroyer that has been cooked during a force twelve gale and wouldn't shame an adulterer's bistro in Soho, while this is one of the worst meals I have ever experienced. How do you mess up baked beans, for instance?'

'It's not difficult when you try to poach them,' responded Ivor. 'Oh look! Here comes Peter. He must be feeling better.'

Peter was walking delicately back from the orchard towards the campfire. He moved like Robert Mitchum, as if there had been a slight interruption in communication between the upper and lower halves of his body, but he still managed a charming smile as he came over to the tree stump in response to the commander's beckoning arm.

'Feeling a bit better?' asked Ivor solicitously.

'Yes, thank you.'

'Good. I'd be a bit careful over breakfast if I were you.'

The commander looked puzzled. So did Peter. 'What do you mean?'

'The beans.'

'The beans?'

'Yes. In your condition you don't want any sudden shocks or explosions.'

'Is that why you wanted to talk to me?' asked Peter bitterly.

'No. I want to know what we're doing today – and don't give me any of that mystical secrecy bullshit.'

'Just walking.'

'Just walking?'

'Well, just about. It's a race between each group to capture a hill fort at the head of the river. Malcolm and I will defend it and there'll be a debriefing session there this afternoon at four.'

The commander raised an interrogative eyebrow. 'Is that all? No nasty little googlies that you'll tell us about after-wards?'

'No.'

'No?'

'No. Each group will be armed, of course.'

'Ah! Armed! Bags I the machine guns. Ivor and I can shout "Rat-tat-tat" and the other groups can fall down.'

'Your group has been allocated quarterstaffs. Each group can attack any other group it comes across en route.'

The commander rose to his feet and felt the seat of his trousers. He sighed. 'Well, dear boy. You can do what you like, but I am rather tired, rather dirty, rather fed up and I have now got a wet arse. I am going home. Are you coming, Ivor?'

'Yes.'

'How about you, Keith?'

Keith gnawed his moustache. 'I'd like to, Commander. But I said to Mandy that I'd be out until tomorrow evening and, you know, I wouldn't like to put her out.'

'My dear chap,' replied the commander, 'I quite understand. Elfrieda has gone off to a conference of Women in Socialism. So you'd be very welcome to spend the night with me.'

'You can't all go home!' said Peter. 'You'll change the spiritual balance of the weekend.'

'Tough!' remarked the commander.

'Well, you can bloody well walk home. I can't spare a Land Rover.'

'So be it. It's only a few miles and I suspect we'd walk us a damn sight further if we stayed.'

'You're afraid of getting hurt,' sneered Peter.

'Damn right I am,' answered the commander with some spirit. 'I could end up like you, walking around as if I'd been rogered by half the Home Fleet.'

'You're chicken!'

'Cluck cluck!' agreed the commander. 'Being wounded for one's country is one thing but it's quite another to be damaged in some Noddy weekend like this.' He picked up the haversack which contained his whisky. 'Ivor, Keith, we might as well get going. If we're quick, we'll be back for opening time.'

As the conversation had become more heated, so their voices had carried to the group by the fire who had come up to add their support to Peter's point of view. 'Huh!' snorted

161

Hugh. 'It didn't take you very long to discover what sort of a bloke you are.'

'I knew already,' replied the commander. 'Excuse me.' The crowd parted to allow the trio of deserters to pass through its midst.

Malcolm's was the only face that did not wear an expression of contempt. He caught up with them fifteen yards from the rest of the party. 'I'm sorry about this,' he said rather awkwardly. 'I shouldn't have pressured you into the weekend.'

'It doesn't really matter,' answered Ivor. 'It was our own fault for coming along.'

'Malcolm!' called Peter accusingly.

Malcolm looked back irresolutely. Ivor patted him on the shoulder. 'Get back to your playmates. I think it's in everyone's interest that we don't say too much about this back in the village.'

Malcolm looked relieved. 'I think you're right. Anyway, have a nice walk back and I'll see you next week some time.' He returned to the group as the commander and the other two ambled off along the side of the river.

They did not make it by opening time. The commander's brief look at the map had shown only half a dozen miles between home and their breakfast site, but they were not crows and the moors went up and down a bit. Some of the ups were very up and some of the downs, had they been alpine ski-slopes, would have been marked by black warning flags.

The crest of the third significant up they had tackled within a couple of hours was marked by an Ordnance Survey cairn and Ivor sat gratefully down in its lee to wait for the other two who were toiling below him, their hands grasping at the roots of the heather and bracken as they sweated their way up the hill. The commander was first to join him, followed closely by Keith. They lay beside each other, breathing heavily.

'You should have looked more closely at the map,' gasped Keith.

'I know,' admitted the commander. 'But it's too late to choose another route now. I should think we've still got two or three hours to go.'

'I think it's time we lightened our load,' suggested Ivor. 'Let's have a wee sensation.'

'A what?' asked Keith.

'Whisky.'

'Did someone mention whisky?' said the cairn against which they were leaning.

Keith and the commander were too exhausted to react but Ivor jumped for all three of them. 'Christ! Who said that?'

'It was the cairn, I think,' replied the commander. 'Judging by its accent, it's an American cairn. However, there is a possibility that it wasn't the cairn at all, but merely somebody round the other side of it. Ah!'

The 'Ah!' was the exclamation of a man whose theory had stood the rigours of experiment as the speaker entered his field of vision. The latter was an American, which was obvious from his uniform and the fact that the stripes on his sleeve were upside down. 'Have you guys got whisky?'

'Yes,' said the commander.

'Would you be interested in a trade for a bottle of Myers?'

'Myers?' queried Ivor.

'Rum, begod!' exclaimed the commander. 'That's what I would consider an interesting trade. Have you got much rum?'

'A dozen quarts.'

'How quaint,' murmured Ivor, who now thought in litres like a good dairy farmer.

'A dozen quarts!' exulted the commander. He raised himself up on his elbow and looked at the new arrival. 'If you don't mind me asking, what is an American serviceman doing hiding behind a cairn in this God-forsaken spot?'

'It's not that bad,' argued Ivor.

'It depends on your point of view,' replied the commander. His point of view had been forged by a twenty-minute hike up the side of a steep hill. However, when he cast a jaundiced eye, he had to admit that it was picturesque. They were on the edge of a marshy plateau that stretched across the barren heart of the moor. The heather rolled down to the sea a dozen miles away in one direction and to the misty summits of the next range of hills across miles of fertile farmland in the other.

'We're here because of Operation Bulldog. It's an exercise to test NATO defences.'

'Ah yes!' said Ivor. 'That's the thing that Kelvin was so excited about. But what has that got to do with sitting on top of a hill with a dozen quarts?'

'We're a radio unit.'

When nothing else was forthcoming, Ivor looked at the commander who tapped the side of his nose. 'Oh, I see. We could be Russians.'

'You can never be too careful in a foreign country,' said American. 'My name's Willard. Come and meet the boys.'

They levered themselves to their feet and walked round the low tumulus in front of which the survey mark had been placed. There was a neatly camouflage-painted hut sitting incongruously behind it. 'How on earth did that thing get here?' asked Ivor. 'There isn't a road for three miles.'

The American caught their dumbfounded expressions. 'Chuck brought it in under a chopper yesterday.' He opened the door to reveal a couple of colleagues sitting in front of a bottle-gas heater. They were holding glasses and staring gloomily at a couple of pornographic magazines on the table in front of them. They turned as the door opened. 'We've got some visitors, boys,' said Willard. 'They got some whisky.'

'They got any women?' asked one.

'No women.'

'Shit! What are they doing here? Are they Red Force?'

'Are you?' Willard asked the commander.

'No. We're just going home.'

'Lucky bastards! Find something to sit on and have a drink.'

They had a drink and then another. They were all fast friends a couple of hours and a couple of quarts later. 'But what are you actually doing here, Billy Joe?' asked Keith, putting his arm round Billy Joe's shoulders.

'It's about as crazy as what you're doing here, Keithie baby.'

'Shit, Billy Joe,' interrupted Willard. 'We're supposed to be top secret. Tippity-top secret.'

'Who are these guys going to tell?' replied Billy Joe, flinging his arms wide in an expansive gesture, almost knocking Keith off the camp chair that had been provided for him. 'The fucking sheep?'

Keith put his hand on his heart. 'I promise we won't tell the fucking sheep.'

'See?' said Billy Joe to Willard. 'I told you these guys were OK. Anyone can end up playing cowboys and Indians with a bunch of jerks. It's not their fault.' He leaned confidentially across the table. 'We're here to guide in the attack this afternoon.'

'What sort of attack?' asked Keith somewhat nervously.

'Wheee!' said Billy Joe, skimming a rather shaky hand over the table top. 'We've got the whole US airforce coming along to bomb some goddam hilltop. We're here to tell them where to go. Wheee!' His speeding hand knocked the commander's glass and spilled a few drops. 'Sorry.'

'It's quite all right,' replied the commander. 'But surely they know where to go before they take off?'

'Half of the guys who fly those things don't know their right from their left.'

'Yeah,' agreed Willard. 'If it wasn't for us, they'd probably bomb London by mistake.'

'They don't use real bombs, do they?' asked Keith.

'Hell, no!'

'In that case, would it be all right if we stay to watch when they come over? It might be quite fun.'

'Hadn't we better be thinking about getting on our way?' protested Ivor.

'No, we're OK,' replied the commander, glancing at his watch. 'I think we could get to Frank Mattock's farm in an hour and he could run us into the village.' He emptied one of the rum bottles into his glass. 'Tell me, Willard, how low do the planes go when they make their bombing runs? What exactly goes on?'

'Depends. We've got one bunch in F11s and they take a

165

pride in taking the tops off molehills. We've got them and some Tornadoes this afternoon and they'll come in one by one in separate waves to zap the target. Wheee! It's quite a sight when they come in.'

'Hmm,' said the commander thoughtfully. 'And where is it exactly that they are supposed to be going today? And what time are they due?'

'The target is some hill or other over there.' Willard waved his hand vaguely westwards. 'They ought to be here at teatime.' He nudged Ivor who was sitting beside him. 'Hear that? Teatime! I can talk Limey real good!'

'Hmm,' said the commander once more.

'Hmm,' agreed Ivor. 'If you're thinking what I'm thinking, it's a jolly interesting idea.'

'What are you thinking?' asked Keith.

The commander poured Willard another whisky from their diminishing supply and leaned forward confidentially. 'How exactly do you guide them in?'

'On the radio. They're supposed to have a map reference. We watch them go by as well and if they're going the wrong way, we give them directions. What's all this about?'

'It occurred to me that it might be possible to change the reference.'

'Gee! I don't know about that. Hey! Billy Joe!'

Billy Joe had gone out of the hut to urinate and was declaiming from the top of the cairn that the wigwam of Nokomis stood by the shore of Gitchee Gumee. He broke off. 'Yeah? Whaddya want?'

'You got the reference for this afternoon?'

'No.' He returned to *Hiawatha*.

'Hell, I must have it then.' Willard shuffled his fingers though his pockets, pulling out a crumpled envelope. 'Here it is!'

'I'm glad about that. Can you change it?'

Willard looked dubious. 'I can do if there's an emergency. But I ain't needed to yet. It's supposed to be in sight so's I can report that they really wasted the enemy.'

'If you need an excuse, you could say the hunt were in the

166

area of the original target and you didn't want to frighten the horses.'

'The hunt? You mean lots of guys in fancy red coats? That would be neat! They'd love to send that to the Pentagon as a reason for a change of target zone. But what's the point of changing the target?'

'Yes, what's all this about?' asked Keith plaintively.

The commander smiled. 'Peter is holding his hill fort against warriors with swords and bows and arrows. It would be rather nice to call in an air strike against him.'

Keith gave a long sigh and sagged back in his canvas chair. 'Ohhh! That's beautiful!' He turned to the American, his moustache wiffling with yearning. 'Please, Willard.'

Willard rubbed his chin thoughtfully. 'I don't see why not. It would sure spoil your guy's day. What's the target like?'

'Let's have a look at the map.' The commander pulled a dog-eared tourist map of the moor from his pocket and traced back the stream to its source. 'There! That must be it. There's only one hill fort in the area.'

'Let's see that,' demanded Willard. 'Hey! Look at the contour lines! It must stand up like a pimple on a hooker's ass at the top of that valley. Yeah, that looks fine. The only snag is that we won't actually be able to see the strike from here.'

The commander studied the map, spread on the table in front of him. 'That's true. But if we go over there, we ought to have a good view. We can tell you how well they . . . er . . . did their zapping.' He indicated the edge of the plateau on the paper. About a mile west of the hut, the ground dropped steeply into the valley.

Willard traced his finger over the map. 'It should be perfect. The aircraft'll make their run up the river and hit that castle place at the top. Is it a real castle like they have in Disneyland?'

'No, it's just a mound with a few rocks on top. It's prehistoric.'

'Shame! It'd be great for the flyboys to bomb a real castle.'

'It's just practice, remember,' said Keith.

The Americans had to stay in the hut with their radio, but

the other three left later in the afternoon, allowing twenty minutes for a gentle stroll across to their vantage point. There was a convenient scattering of boulders on which they placed cushions lent for the occasion by their American friends. The commander brought out a flask: 'I didn't want to waste this before. It's a single malt which is really rather fine.' He had a neat little stack of silver cups in a leather case and he carefully filled them and handed them round. He placed his own cup carefully on his boulder, took his binoculars – also borrowed from their hosts – and put them to his eyes. He scanned the valley up to the hill fort which was half a mile away. He gave a grunt of satisfaction. 'Ah! I can see them. There are a few figures actually on the top and there's others milling round below it. They look as if they're playing tag.'

'They're probably having their war,' said Ivor contentedly.

'It's really very pretty up here,' observed Keith looking round at the view. 'It's a shame that Mandy and I don't come up to the moor more often.'

'It's not really Mandy's sort of thing, is it?' suggested the commander. 'At least, not with you. Me, perhaps, but not you.'

'I suppose you're right,' agreed Keith wistfully.

The commander looked at his watch. 'They should be coming over any second.' He held up his hand. 'Hark!' They hearkened. There was a sound of distant thunder. 'Timing's not bad. Although I suppose it's only a few minutes in one of those things from East Anglia or wherever it is they live.'

'There!' pointed Keith. Its wings swept back, a slim jet skimmed up the valley below them. Beneath the greeny-brown camouflaged wings, the points of four missiles were visible. The thunder of its engines cracked the air as it raised its nose to skim the ramparts of the mound before climbing towards the sinking sun. 'By God! That's a sight and a half! That must be one of the F111s they were talking about!' The end of his feverish comment was drowned by the next aircraft, the vibration of whose passing seemed to resonate in their bowels as it streaked over the top of the hillock.

The commander put the binoculars back to his eyes.

'They're all flat on their faces!' he shouted. 'Even the ones at the bottom of the hill!'

Keith jumped up and down with excitement as jet after jet screamed up the valley. As the last echo of the last plane rumbled into silence, he turned to the others, his eyes shining. 'To think we did that! I've never known anything like it! I'd love to be able to do it again!' He gave a sudden shriek of delight as the whisper of approaching engines suddenly became a roar. 'The Tornadoes! I forgot the Tornadoes!' The Tornadoes were smaller and stubbier than their predecessors, but more than adequate for their task. Through the binoculars, the commander could see tiny figures running away from the fort as the first aircraft of this second attack crashed through the air just above their heads, then another and another, their huge noise almost having a life of its own divorced from the tiny planes.

The valley returned to silence once more save for the shocked crowing of a cock pheasant in a wood a couple of hundred feet below them. Keith sat back on his rock, groped for his silver cup and downed its contents in one gulp. 'That's the finest thing I've ever seen!' His lips were quivering with emotion.

The commander shot him a quizzical look round the binoculars. 'Steady on, old chap! I hope neither Reagan nor Gorbachev thinks the same as you.' He scrutinized the scene below. 'However, I think it can be safely said that we won today's battle. Gentlemen, shall we return our binoculars and go home?'

'Shall we tell Malcolm that we were responsible?' asked Keith.

"Oh no,' said Ivor.' I think it would be much nicer if we didn't. Let's keep it a secret.'

Kelvin laughed so much when he told Malcolm on Monday evening that his false teeth fell on the floor of the pub and broke.

Chapter Eleven

'I THINK IT'S a disgrace,' said Stephanie Jarrett firmly, sinking her teeth into one of Mrs Baggins's rock buns. Like her husband, Stephanie was an intellectual, so the other women paused in their conversations to listen. Women's Institute meetings had changed in character quite recently. They used to be highly traditional, serving the needs of the older women in the parish – lots of competitions for the best jams, the prettiest teatowels, and lectures from members about visiting the Tower of London while their husbands were getting drunk at the Smithfield Show.

Then it changed, thanks to the local newspaper. It had always carried reports of the area's WI meetings under the heading 'Ladies' Groups'. A fresh editor had cast a critical eye at the grey columns of funerals, auction reports and the lists of those done for possession of cannabis or non-possession of television licences and decided to liven it up a bit. In the first editorial in living memory he had announced his improvements. In the classified advertising section motors were moved from after property to before, and the column which included WI reports was no longer headed 'Ladies' Groups' but 'Women's Groups'.

The shifting of 'Cars for Sale' had no discernible impact upon the community, but the other change did. A Women's Group was a very different animal from a Ladies' Group and light-years away from the Ladies' Circle to which the yuppier spouses of the Round Table members belonged so that they would have a chance to wear expensive evening dresses at their annual dinner-dances where they gyrated the night away to the accompaniment of pina coladas and a trio of middle-aged men in gold lamé who sang *Yesterday*, *My Way* and *Viva L'España* to remind them of their summer holidays.

The term Women's Group had serious overtones. It conjured up topics like abortion, feminism and muesli-flavoured, hand-woven, recycled lavatory paper, and this attracted fresh members to the WI, including Stephanie Jarrett who had a sociology degree and Elfrieda who was not only against nuclear weapons but had actually been to Greenham Common. It was rumoured that the commander now had to iron his own shirts.

'What's a disgrace?' asked Mrs Baggins nervously. She was afraid that it might be her rock cake to which Stephanie was referring.

'That we seem so inward-looking in this community.'

The subject under discussion was 'Charity begins at home', not quite as potentially explosive as 'Lesbianism as a political issue' which was promised for the following meeting. This was already the subject of caucuses amongst the older members about what it meant and what they could possibly contribute to it.

'For example,' continued Stephanie, 'I heard Dennis say that he had refused to put anything in the plate when the collection in church was going to African refugees because he thought that we ought to take care of our own first.'

'Well, he may be right,' replied Mandy, one of the stalwarts of the old WI who was rather enjoying the new look. Mrs Baggins still hankered nostalgically for the days when she won a contest for putting the greatest number of objects inside a matchbox.

'I doubt it,' argued Stephanie. 'But that's not what I object to. It's the fact that so many people round about say things like that and then do nothing for any charity closer to home.'

'Marcia gives a buffet lunch at the manor for the World Wildlife Fund every year,' said Mandy.

'That's not quite the same as giving to the starving in the Third World and, anyway, most people only go to the manor for social rather than charitable reasons.'

'I think you're being unfair,' contributed Lindy.

172

'Well, just ask around. Find out how much people know and how much they give and to what.'

The pub was interested in what went on at WI meetings. Just as it had been awed by the number of things that Mrs Baggins had managed to stuff into her matchbox, even though it was a Swan Vesta box, so it mulled over Stephanie's accusation. In essence, it was true that people did look inward, but not because of heartlessness. They did not feel themselves part of the international community. Even those in a village half a dozen miles away were considered to be foreigners, while anything that appeared on television or in the national press might as well have taken place on Mars. The state of the greenfly on the roses in front of the pub was of much greater interest than what went on at arms control talks in Geneva.

However true it was, nobody liked to admit it. 'I think we're very generous in this village,' said Bill. 'Remember in the spring when the school wanted some gym equipment? The kids did a sponsored spelling test and they raised nearly £100.'

'Yes, that's quite right,' agreed Ivor. 'And the village hall fund grows year by year.'

'Look at the jar on the bar,' said Keith. They looked at the large glass sweet jar crammed full of pennies which were given to the Guide Dogs for the Blind every Christmas. It made them all feel a little better.

'I think that proves Stephanie's point,' said Helga from behind the bar. 'She is just saying that people here only give when it's close to home. Giving for gym equipment and to the village hall is just giving to ourselves.'

'But you can't say the same about that jar,' responded Keith.

Helga looked at it. 'You can hardly suggest that the odd penny from your change for a pint of beer is a great charitable sacrifice.'

'It's not just the odd penny!' exclaimed Kelvin who was peering in through the side of the jar. 'See that silvery bit?' They all followed his pointing finger. 'That's got to be the edge of a 20p piece.'

Keith picked up the jar, with some difficulty, to give it a shake and make sure that there really was a piece of cupro-nickel in there. The glint of silver disappeared in a sea of pennies. 'I can't see it,' he complained.

'Well, it was there all right. That's what I call really generous. I wonder who put it in there? It wasn't me, was it, Helga?' Kelvin asked anxiously.

'Don't be silly,' scoffed Ivor. 'You'd never put in 20p.'

'If I hadn't got my glasses on and if it was fairly late in the evening I might. Anyway, it must have been one of the customers and it proves my point that we're a generous lot here.'

'It was put there by a rep from one of the brewers,' said Helga tartly. 'I once saw Frank Mattock give 2p, otherwise nobody has given more than a penny. You've never put in anything, Kelvin.'

'Thank Christ for that!' exclaimed Kelvin with relief.

'You ought to be ashamed of yourself, Kelvin,' said the commander who, up until then, had been holding his peace.

'Why?' demanded the latter indignantly.

'Your attitude. I knew a seaman who raised £500 for Oxfam when he was only eighteen by getting sponsored for walking to John O'Groats. It may have been Land's End, but it was certainly somewhere like that.'

'Silly bugger!' muttered Kelvin under his breath.

'£500! I could really admire a man who could do that,' said Helga. She was a spectacularly beautiful woman, somewhere in her forties with a glamorous 'Mittel European' background who had somehow come to take over the pub. Business had boomed when it was realized that she was not interested in converting the place to a tourist's gin palace and was prepared to allow gumboots into the public bar. She had every male in the village licking her hand and wishing they had the opportunity to lick more interesting portions of her anatomy. She exploited this devotion shamelessly, making one man strive against another to achieve her favours and, since she was a thoroughly nice woman, her influence in the community was wholly beneficial – as, initially, in this instance.

'Admire a man who could raise £500?' asked Kelvin.

'Oh yes! It would show that he had a beautiful soul if he'd do that for other people.'

There was a short pause. 'I could raise that easy, if I wanted to,' said Kelvin.

'It wouldn't be that hard, I'd've thought,' agreed Ivor and the other men present murmured that they were of the same mind.

'You're all wonderful!' breathed Helga, who had learned that she had to lay it on with a trowel during the year or two she had been in the pub. She winked at Stephanie who picked up the baton.

'That's easy for you lot to say, because you're all talk and no action,' she said. 'When it comes to doing anything practical, you're all hopeless.'

'I'm not all talk!' said Kelvin.

'Right then,' said Stephanie briskly. 'You'll raise £500 in sponsorship for Oxfam.'

'I didn't say I'd do that,' replied Kelvin evasively.

'Kelvin!' cried Helga. 'You wouldn't let me down.'

'Well, no,' he agreed miserably.

'Excellent!' cried Stephanie. 'And the rest of you will do something as well?' Grudging although it may have been, there was definite assent.

'But what will we do?' asked Ivor. 'We can't do a sponsored spelling. Some of us would never get any money.' The locals were experts at deciding the worth of a bullock or the tonnage of grass on a field, but 'readin'n'ritin' were not their strong points. 'Rithmetic' was different as it was needed to count up money.

'That's true,' agreed Kelvin. Literacy was a clerkish talent and slightly effeminate.

'I'll organize one of the things that the teenagers at school do when they're sponsored.' Stephanie taught at the comprehensive school in the nearby town.

'All right, you do that. But make sure it doesn't need too much learning,' said Kelvin.

'Or too much exercise,' added Bill.

'Right,' said Stephanine. 'I'll have something worked out by lunchtime on Sunday.'

After church on Sunday was an important social occasion in the pub. Very few would have actually gone to church but more would dress up in their Sunday best to visit their local hostelry.

The publican had always put out free peanuts and crisps and Helga enriched the event by adding sausages on sticks and canapés.

Stephanie and Malcolm Jarrett turned up with Napoleon, the pimply teenage son of Mandy and Keith. He began to stuff sausages into his mouth with grim concentration, annoying other customers who would have liked to do the same if it were not for the fact that age had made them self-conscious.

Conversation flowed easily. The men had almost forgotten about their money-raising pledges and the suggestion that a new drain should be put in the gutter outside the post office was by far the most relevant topic of the moment. It had been tossed around in the parish council for several months from where it had recently emerged to be debated in public. Stephanie waited her moment. She decided that it had come when Kelvin snapped at Napoleon after he had finished off the sausages and was moving into the solitary bowl of cashew nuts.

'By the way,' she said casually. 'I brought along Napoleon because he was sponsored for £50 last year.'

Napoleon managed to smile proudly and chew at the same time. The commander had bought him a pint of orange juice to force him to fill his mouth with something other than cashews, but he was using it to wash them down, thus increasing his speed of intake.

'For eating large amounts, I suppose,' commented Ivor with some distaste.

'No, nothing like that. I thought he was jolly brave.'

'So did I,' agreed Helga. She presented Napoleon with a warm smile. It was wasted on him as he was picking his teeth, but noted enviously by everyone else.

176

'I'll do the same and I bet I get double the money,' said Kelvin stoutly.

'If you're man enough,' smiled Helga.

'Man enough to do what he can do?' questioned Kelvin incredulously, nodding towards Napoleon. The latter was at the gangly stage and his fashionable drainpipe jeans accentuated his general air of weediness.

'Anything he can do, I can do better,' hummed Helga.

'You'd better be careful what you get yourself into, Dad,' warned Prudence. The stolid fruit of Kelvin's loins was rarely seen and even more rarely heard. She came to the pub on Sunday with her father but had rarely been observed to do more than belch discreetly after a couple of glasses of mild ale.

Kelvin had obviously not expected advice from that quarter either. Startled, he looked at her. 'What's with you, then, Missy? Do you not think your old father knows what he's doing? There's nothing he can teach me. 'Course I'll do what he's done.' He turned to the other male regulars. 'We all will, won't we?'

With a combination of Kelvin's crude stick and Helga's seductive carrot, all agreed.

'You are all wonderful!' said Helga. 'And the money you raise will go to help the world's hungry?'

'If you think that's the best place for it, then that's where it will go. I'll show you what generosity is. Commander, if you sponsor me, I'll make sure that Prudence sponsors you.'

'That sounds a fair enough offer,' agreed the commander. 'But what exactly did you do, Napoleon?'

Napoleon chewed, swilled, swallowed and answered. 'I went round and got everyone to fill in my form and they paid up afterwards.'

'Yes, I know that, but what did they sponsor you to do?'

'A parachute jump.'

There was complete silence in the room, broken only by Jimmy pawing at the commander's arm. 'What did he say?' he asked plaintively.

'Jesus Christ!' replied the commander shortly.

Jimmy considered for a few seconds, before turning to

177

Helga across the bar. 'I don't understand. What does he mean by that?'

'It's all right, Jimmy,' replied Helga. 'He said parachute jumping.'

Jimmy looked annoyed. 'Well, why did he say "Jesus Christ", then?'

'Think about it,' answered Helga. Jimmy thought about it and began to shake. A wheezy laugh, not unlike the death rattle of a donkey, escaped from him, driving the smoke from the hand-rolled cigarette, which was permanently attached to his bottom lip, towards the commander in a series of rancid puffs.

Jimmy was seeing the bright side of having a gammy leg, emphysema and being into his seventies.

Those who would be unable to claim medical exemption were still absorbing the implications and were startled by Prudence opening her mouth. 'A parachute jump! Oh, I've always wanted to try a parachute jump. Can I be sponsored as well, Stephanie?'

'Of course. All these men have volunteered but, as you're the first woman, I'll put £1 down myself.'

Kelvin was aghast. 'Prudence! What's wrong with you? A parachute jump! You're off your bloody head!'

'You're going to do one too,' replied Prudence.

'I'm bloody not. If you think I'm jumping out of a sodding aeroplane, you're insane.'

Helga knew that she had to employ every aspect of her genius. 'Kelvin, you promised!' she said reproachfully, a little sigh, as delicately sensual as the zephyr from a hummingbird's wing as it sipped nectar from the blossom of a hibiscus, escaping between the warm gules of her lips. Of the imperatives that drove Kelvin, lust came after cowardice, gluttony, vanity, avarice, envy, malice, sloth and a host of others. She realized that she was being too subtle and so leaned over the bar to display her cleavage and placed a soft hand on his grey-stubbled cheek, tracing a finger down to the point of his jaw. 'Kelvin, I'd be so disappointed.' He wavered slightly and she pressed her advantage home. 'How would you

178

like a drink on the house?' She was assaulting on several fronts. Lust, avarice, gluttony and vanity were all under attack. The other men looked on in concern. With Kelvin crumbling, what possible chance would they have?

'Mum's going to have a go. It's easy, if you've got the bottle,' sprayed Napoleon through a shrapnel-shower of roast ox-flavoured crisps.

'Mandy? Is Mandy doing a parachute jump?' asked the commander incredulously.

'That's right,' smiled Stephanie. 'She's bought a yellow jumpsuit for the event.'

All the men, save Kelvin, looked worriedly at each other. He was looking down the front of Helga's blouse as she pulled him a pint.

'I'm not sure that this is a particularly good idea,' remarked Ivor. 'It's a young person's game, you know. We chaps are not as physically resilient as we used to be.'

'There's no need to worry. We had a grandmother in her seventies doing a jump for the school last year.'

'It takes a bit of bottle,' swaggered Napoleon. 'Fatty Hutchings who's in our class said that she felt really scared when she stepped out of the door of the aircraft. She's just a kid, though. She was really scared of *Driller Killer*.'

The bottomless pit that was before the patrons of the pub yawned wider and wider with every word spoken. Stephanie carefully gave them the little push. 'I've sent an announcement to the local paper about it and they will be sending along a photographer on the day.'

The commander sighed, knowing that he was trapped. 'When's it going to happen?'

'I thought in a couple of weeks. I'm told it's a quiet time for the farmers which means everyone will be able to make it.'

'Will you sponsor me, Helga?' asked Kelvin hoarsely.

'Of course, darling. I think you're wonderfully brave. I shall come along too. Napoleon and I can sponsor each other.'

That was it. There was no more that anyone could do about it. Ivor had the last word on the subject. He sank his pint and smacked it down on the bar. 'Oh shit!' he remarked crisply.

It was extremely naive to expect Kelvin to jump from an aeroplane. There was a bit of speculation when he failed to appear in the pub the following Thursday lunchtime, but it was put to rest that evening when he limped proudly through the door. His foot was in plaster. Bill looked at him and sighed.

'What's happened to your foot, Kelvin?' he asked resignedly.

'It was Ramrod. Bloody animal. It's really most annoying.'

Ramrod was his elderly, foul-tempered bull, mostly Friesian, which spent the best part of his time in a small shed that could have doubled as the Black Hole of Calcutta with the addition of a yard's depth of dung. The animal had the run of an adjacent pen where he performed his duties, but he preferred to stand inside his shed where he thought evil thoughts and rolled his eyes in fury at the sparrows which scavenged round his feet. With advancing years, Ramrod had grown casual about copulation and sometimes lay along the back of his spouse and daydreamed. In that instance, Kelvin would take a sprig from a convenient clump of nettles which grew beside the pen and tickle the animal's testicles. It had a galvanic effect but did nothing to add to the *tendresse* between master and beast.

'I suppose that means you can't jump,' continued Bill.

'I really don't know how I can,' Kelvin said, trying to look disappointed.

'What happened?' asked the commander, taking on the role of inquisitor.

'The bull stood on my foot.'

'I see. And why is it in plaster?'

Kelvin looked at the commander. 'It's broken, you bloody fool. Why else do you think it would be in plaster?'

'Let's just get this quite clear. The bull stood on your foot and broke it. What exactly were you doing at the time?'

'Standing behind the bull, of course. I was whipping its arse with some nettles and it stepped back.'

The commander did not know the fine print of Kelvin's relationship with Ramrod but he had trodden inadvertently on too many spectacularly bizarre examples of local mores and behaviour to wish to know more. After a brief pause, he moved hurriedly on with his line of enquiry. 'And where was Prudence when this happened?'

'Prudence? I dunno. I think she was helping out with dipping sheep next door.'

'I see,' said the commander. 'What happened then?'

'I went to hospital and had it plastered up, of course.'

'Ah!' said the commander triumphantly. 'And how did you get to hospital?'

'In my van—'

'—But how did you drive with a broken foot?'

'Very, very carefully,' replied Kelvin without hesitation. He had had a lifetime of bluff and counterbluff in the hard school of agricultural dealing and there was no possibility that an innocent like the commander could catch him out. 'I really am very disappointed. I was looking forward to the experience and, of course, raising lots of money for Stephanie's darkies.'

'How long will it be before the plaster comes off?' asked Helga.

'Why?' asked Kelvin suspiciously.

'Just wondering.'

'Hmm.' Kelvin thought for a few seconds before replying. There was no obvious benefit to him in not giving the right answer to Helga's question and this worried him. If people told the truth in response to a question, you would never know what to believe. Vagueness was safe. 'It depends how it gets on. I shouldn't think it'll be on for more than a few weeks.'

'I was just thinking that there's no reason why you shouldn't enjoy a jump of your own when you're better.'

The inhabitants of the bar looked at Helga as if she was mad. Even Kelvin. It was just possible that Kelvin had really broken his foot and, if he had, it was just possible that it had happened fortuitously. Much more likely was that the foot was intact under its white covering or that Kelvin had been attempting a bruise that had got out of hand. Whatever had happened, he was certainly not going to waste such an excuse.

Kelvin laboured unsmilingly on. 'Even when the plaster comes off, there'll be no telling how long it will take for the

EXCUSED PARACHUTING

foot to get back to normal. In fact, at my age, it may never be quite right and it could well break down again when I'm least expecting it.' That was almost enough, but you never knew with Helga. 'I'm quite sure that my medical advisor would never allow me to parachute again.'

'Again?' queried Ivor with a disdainful curl to his lip.

Kelvin turned his attention to Ivor with relish. 'But you can be quite sure that I won't miss the jump. I'll be along to give all the help that I can. I can imagine what that moment when you step out into thin air might be like. The howling of the wind and the hard ground rushing up to meet your body. It can't be all that much fun. After all, even Fatty Hutchings was quite concerned about it.'

'You bastard!' said Ivor, turning rather pale.

'It's a cruel, cruel world,' said Kelvin cheerfully.

Chapter Twelve

THOSE WHO had agreed to jump had lived long enough to understand that the future, however dreaded, was bound to become the present at its appointed time, and so there was phlegmatic acceptance in the air when the day finally dawned. Even Kelvin, who gave the commander and Ivor a lift in his van to the airfield, could not generate much fear in them on the journey, although he did his best.

'It's a good thing I'm bringing the van along,' he had ventured into a strained silence. The silence was actually due to a deep concern about the quality of Kelvin's driving which was being felt by his two passengers. 'I said, it's a good thing I'm taking the van,' he repeated rather more loudly.

'What?' asked the commander. He had his hands on the dashboard and both feet braced against the floor. They were not braced as hard as he would have liked as, due to the condition of the vehicle, they were quite likely to pass through into thin air.

Kelvin, under the impression that he was bemused with terror at the prospect before him, turned to the commander to savour the emotion. The van was not travelling fast but, with Kelvin's vague supervision totally withdrawn, it lurched drunkenly across the narrow lane to ricochet off the opposite hedgebank. 'Damn!' muttered the driver, spinning the wheel to bring it back on course.

The commander cleared his throat. 'Kelvin, if you kill us before we get there, you'll spoil your chance of seeing us killed when we make our jump.'

Kelvin looked shocked. 'I don't want to see anybody get

killed. I just want to see you all thinking you might be killed. A bit of suffering, that's all. Mind you,' he continued musingly, 'I do owe Ivor £65 and I wouldn't have to pay if he didn't make it. Saving £65 would go a long way towards helping me to cope with my distress.'

'I'd have thought 10p would be a big help. For £65 I'd expect you to've done the job yourself,' said Ivor caustically.

'That would be against the law!' stated Kelvin disapprovingly. There was a pause while they all calculated the distance between the van and a rabbit which darted out of the hedgerow across their path. Kelvin fought to regain control of the van after he had swerved towards it. 'I'm glad I brought the van along,' he repeated doggedly.

'I'm not,' moaned Ivor from the back.

'I'm glad I brought the van along because it can double as an ambulance on the way back.' There was silence. 'Or as a hearse,' Kelvin added hopefully. He kept trying, but his passengers refused to rise. The van turned out on to the main road, cutting across a stream of traffic and rattling up to 50mph for the last few miles towards the airfield. He was feeling rather depressed when they arrived.

Even the commander, who had crunched down on to the decks of aircraft carriers in his time, looked askance at the limp windsock dangling over the molehill-scattered length of grass and the rickety barn which was, apparently, the hangar. 'I hope their planes all have MoT certificates,' Ivor remarked nervously. 'I mean, it's not exactly Heathrow.'

'We won't be up there for long and there's no need to worry about the landing,' comforted the commander, eliciting a snort of laughter from Kelvin who rather wished he had thought of that line first. The van bounced across the grass to pull up alongside the other cars already parked by the barn and its passengers emerged to follow the sound of concerned voices which were coming from the building's interior.

The hangar seemed to have been converted from a small warehouse which, in its turn, had incorporated the original barn at one end. There was only one aircraft at which they were all staring with alarm. It was clear what the problem

was. It was a small and extremely tatty biplane about twenty-five feet long, painted a faded green. It was a two-seater with one seat set behind the other and both open to the sky.

'Good grief!' said Ivor. 'That thing looks lethal. I'm not going up in something like that.' He turned to Napoleon, who had come along to give people the benefit of his expertise. 'I thought one was supposed to have static lines and things like that. Are we expected to climb out on to the wing like some bloody circus act and dive off? I think it is quite outrageous that we should be called upon to go up in that. I vote we go home.'

That was the best idea that anyone had had for weeks and his suggestion was hastily endorsed. It took Kelvin, standing in the doorway of the barn and flapping his arms as if to divert a stampeding herd of cattle, to prevent them rushing back into their cars, twittering with relief at their narrow escape from a thoroughly nasty experience, and driving off home. 'Stop!' he thundered just before the retreat became a rout. 'Friends!

What is wrong? Where is your pride? Think of those more unfortunate than yourselves who stand to benefit this morning from your activities. Can you let those . . . er . . . kiddies down?'

'Kelvin, for heaven's sake! Would you fly in that thing?' demanded Ivor as he tried to sidle round the outstretched arms.

'Of course! If only I could. Nothing would give me greater pleasure. If I had not hurt my foot, I'd be up there like a shot.' He emphasized his determination that this should have been so by stamping his plaster-covered foot noisily on the ground. 'But I can't.'

'In that case, mind your own business,' said Mandy tartly. 'And get out of the damn way!'

'There's got to be a mistake, Kelvin,' contributed Napoleon. 'There's no way that this lot can be expected to climb out of that thing and jump.'

'Mr Morchard to you, sonny!' snapped Kelvin. 'And children should be seen and not heard.'

'Ah! But out of the mouths of very babes and sucklings hast thou ordained strength,' Napoleon surprisingly replied.

Kelvin was spared the need to cap Napoleon by the arrival of another car, its body a delicate filigree of rust. The driver of the wreck emerged and retraced the path of his vehicle, tidily picking up pieces of it that had become detached when it had taken to the grass. He was a bald, painfully thin man in his forties with a concave chest, a great beak of a nose jutting from his face on which was perched a pair of thick-lensed spectacles, and he wore a jumpsuit rather like Mandy's, although his was blue and faded rather than yellow and new.

'What the hell's that?' asked Kelvin.

'That's Budgie. He's a nuclear scientist,' said Napoleon.

'He doesn't look as if he's been eating his Trill!'

Budgie had collected a sidelight amongst other things, and put them into the boot of his car. He slammed down the lid and came over to the barn. The boot slyly re-opened behind him. 'Hullo,' he said, surveying the scene. 'You're a pretty funny-looking lot,' he remarked.

'You're a bit of a joke yourself, mate,' responded Kelvin reasonably.

Budgie looked at Kelvin and then at his plastered foot. For a man who seemed as if he must have had sand kicked in his face for much of his life, he showed few signs of being downtrodden. 'I don't know what the hell you've come here for. You're not going up with a foot like that.'

'Are you something to do with this business?' asked the commander.

'If by "business" you mean the jump, the answer is yes. I'm the jump master.'

'Are you now?' remarked the commander grimly. 'In that case I should inform you that we have decided that none of us are going up.' He looked defiantly at Budgie.

Budgie shrugged. 'Suit yourself.'

'Don't you care?'

'Why the hell should I? You're the people who wanted to jump.' He turned back towards his car. 'I'm off home, then.'

'Don't you want to know why we won't go up?' asked the commander, rather miffed that so little interest was being shown in such a momentous decision.

Budgie, already beginning to walk back to his car, stopped and turned back. 'Not particularly. Quite a lot of people turn chicken when it comes to it. It's no skin off my nose.'

'That's a relief,' muttered Dennis to Helga, thinking about the amount of skin that might come off a nose the size of Budgie's.

The commander ploughed doggedly on. 'It's nothing to do with being chicken, as you put it. Only a lunatic would risk their lives in a set-up like this.'

Budgie smiled. 'Look, I don't need to hear any excuses. I quite understand. It's nothing to be ashamed of, although I'd rather you'd decided to back out earlier so that I could've done something more profitable with my day. I only came because Stephanie said that quite a lot of money would be raised.'

The commander turned rather red. 'I don't think you've quite got the point. It's nothing to do with us being scared.

187

It's just that everything here looks *contrapted*.' Everyone nodded agreement. Budgie's car suddenly let the air out of one of its tyres, sagging even closer towards the tarmac with the gusty sigh of relief of a fat man subsiding on to a toilet seat.

'Oh bugger!' said Budgie. 'The spare went last night.'

'That's just the sort of thing we're afraid of,' said the commander, grateful to the car for choosing such a well-timed moment to provide him with evidence to buttress his case.

'What the hell are you talking about?' asked Budgie, dragging his eyes back from the car to the commander with irritation.

'If your bloody car behaves like that, what the hell is that wreck of an aeroplane in there going to do?' He indicated the machine squatting in the background with a jerk of the thumb.

Budgie looked at him with scorn. 'Don't pretend you thought we'd use the Gypsy Moth there. It's being restored – it hasn't even got an engine in it.'

'Oh,' said the commander, uncertainly.

'There's a nice spanking new plane flying in here this afternoon,' continued Budgie. He smiled, 'Look, I really don't mind. Nobody's forcing you to go up.'

Ivor spoke up. 'You mean we'd be parachuting from a decent aeroplane?'

'Of course. And the parachutes are virtually new and they're all checked twice.'

The change in attitudes was magic. Kelvin's desperation and depression lifted from his head like a cloud and sailed across the intervening few yards to settle on the commander, Ivor and Dennis. Even Mandy, who had been coming to an unpleasant understanding that her new jumpsuit carried with it certain responsibilities, was finding the silver lining rather hard to spot.

'That's all very well,' the commander blustered, 'but you can't expect us to hang about here all morning, waiting for some chum of yours who might fly by later on this afternoon.'

'You tell him,' agreed Mandy.

'You won't be hanging about,' smiled Budgie grimly. 'You've all got to be taught how to fall – like this.' Budgie suddenly crumpled at the knees and did a complicated little shimmy which resulted in a somersault, his feet slapping down in a patch of mud which splashed Mandy's jumpsuit. He got up, brushed himself down and smiled once more at the commander. 'You'll enjoy that, won't you?'

'Jolly impressive,' agreed the commander, gnawing nervously at the tip of his moustache.

'Has anyone got a tissue?' asked Mandy. Prudence rootled around the pockets of her nylon milking overall and passed over an udder cloth which Mandy pointedly used to rub the mud carefully into her suit. It was an extremely colourful garment, light yellow at the crotch with the hue gradually darkening as it spread out to her extremities. It was rather like one of those paintings by de la Tour, lit by a single candle. 'I don't see why we have to do that sort of thing,' she continued. 'It looks awfully undignified.'

'I can assure you that it's a lot more undignified if you break your leg on landing,' said Budgie.

'Or your neck,' added Kelvin, beginning to get back into the swing of things.

'Is it decided, then, that we're going to do this jump?' asked Dennis gloomily.

'I'm afraid so,' confirmed Ivor.

'I feel like the bloke in the electric chair who has just been told of his reprieve when the prison governor comes rushing in shouting "April Fool!" '

'Right! Quiet please!' ordered Budgie. 'We've got a lot to get through before you make your jump.' His audience looked at him in trepidation. 'You!' he pointed at Kelvin who jumped, unused to being addressed by a man accustomed to command, particularly one who looked as unimposing as Budgie.

'Me?' he asked.

'Yes. Go to my car and you'll find some parachute harnesses on the back seat. Rig them up on that frame.' He indicated a horizontal iron bar about ten feet long, supported on a couple of wooden posts six feet high in one corner of the shed.

'Why do I have to do it?' complained Kelvin.

'Because I'm not having you hanging around all day like a priest in a whorehouse. If you're going to be here, you might as well make yourself useful. When you've done that, you can start brewing up some tea. You'll find a stove and everything else in the back.' He turned. 'Everyone else, please sit down on those benches over there and we'll get started.' Budgie strode over to a blackboard propped up against the wall and began to draw diagrams.

'He's got a bloody cheek!' spluttered Kelvin. 'I've a damn good mind to tell him who I am. Just because he is daft enough to jump out of aeroplanes, he thinks he can order folk around.' Grumbling, but softly so that Budgie would not hear him, he limped pointedly out of the shed and towards the car.

Budgie may not have been everyone's idea of an intrepid sky diver, but he was good enough for Prudence, particularly as she had never seen her father do as he was bidden with quite so little fuss. There were stars in her muddy brown eyes and her spectacular bosom rose and fell rapidly within the confines of her milking overall. 'I like him,' she announced as everyone seated themselves on the benches. 'But why should he think that Father was like a priest?'

'In a whorehouse, dear, no use to anyone,' replied Mandy.

'Oh, I see.' Prudence thought for a moment and emitted a great guffaw of laughter. 'He's very witty, too.'

'Very witty,' agreed the commander. 'I bet he's a barrel of laughs when he chucks people out of the aeroplane.'

'You!' said Budgie, turning from the board to point at the commander. 'Pay attention unless you want to end up as a smear on the runway.'

'Barrel of laughs,' agreed Dennis, under the cover of another guffaw from Prudence, earning her a thin smile from Budgie which made her blush.

Stephanie arrived in the middle of the day, bearing a large hamper. The problem of lunch had been interfering with the concentration of Budgie's bench-bound audience who abandoned him in mid-sentence and descended on the hamper. It contained pasties, sausage rolls, home-made cakes and bottles of parsnip wine, for which Stephanie had a growing reputation in the community.

Budgie gracefully accepted the pasty and glass of wine brought to him by Prudence and, at her request, launched into a dissertation on quarks and neutrinos as she sat at his feet, her mind flicking between the charming way that he tugged at his hair when he became excited and the difficulties he would face in adapting to life as a farmer's spouse after they were married, particularly with a father-in-law such as his would be.

Budgie broke off as Dennis and the commander glumly came over to join them. Dennis was clutching a whisky and the commander was braving the parsnip wine, but neither of them was hungry. 'Looking forward to this afternoon?' asked Budgie.

'At least we'll soon have it over with,' replied the commander.

Budgie bit deep into his pasty and chewed carefully as Prudence picked up his scattered crumbs from the concrete floor with a dampened finger tip and popped them into her mouth. Budgie opened his mouth. 'Jerfth fthhusth,' he said, spraying bits of pastry from between his lips. Prudence looked at them and decided to leave them where they lay.

'I beg your pardon?' asked Dennis, fishing a small piece of chewed potato from his whisky.

Budgie swallowed. 'There's a German lad coming in this afternoon to join us for the landing training. He's been badgering me to teach him to jump for weeks so I asked him to join us. He's flying in with Charles on the Cessna.'

'German?' queried the commander, wrinkling his nose.

'Charles?' asked Prudence.

'Cessna?' added Dennis, just so that he would not be left out.

They waited patiently for answers as Budgie chewed his way through another bite of pasty. For such a skinny human being, he had evolved a remarkable capacity for packing large amounts of food into his mouth at one time.

'Yes,' he said eventually, before taking another large bite.

'What do you mean "yes"?' asked the commander, irritated.

'Prffly phthls,' replied Budgie.

Dennis appraised him thoughtfully. 'If we asked him questions, he could tap the floor with his foot. One tap for yes and two taps for no.'

'Splutthus,' said Budgie. He made an attempt to swallow and turned red in the face.

'I'd say he's bitten off more than he can chew,' contributed the commander.

At this point Prudence retreated, moving along the floor on her bottom so that she was out of range of all but the largest lumps that were propelled from Budgie's lips.

Dennis looked inquiringly at Budige. 'Who's Cessna?' he asked. Budgie stopped struggling to close his mouth and succeeded in conveying disgust through his eyes and a wrinkle of his nose.

'You are a fool, Dennis,' admonished the commander. 'A Cessna is an aeroplane, isn't it, Budgie?'

Budgie nodded vigorously, swallowed convulsively and, before anyone could prevent him, stuffed the remaining third of the pasty into his mouth.

The commander sighed. 'Charles – is he the pilot?' Budgie nodded. 'And this German. Is he all right?' Budgie shrugged. 'Is he like Helga?' Budgie gave the commander a strange look.

Dennis helpfully interpreted. 'He would look extremely odd if he was like Helga.' Budgie nodded appreciatively.

'I didn't mean physically like Helga. I wanted to know whether he had been in this country for a long time or whether he was still quite . . . er . . . German.'

'You're not prejudiced against Germans, are you?' asked Dennis loudly.

The commander cast a worried look across at Helga to ensure she was not within earshot. 'No, of course not. But

192

some of them can take life a little too seriously.'

'We're not throwing a party, so I wouldn't have thought it'd matter if he was a bit po-faced.'

Just then the sound of an aircraft was heard and they all went to the door of the hangar to watch the Cessna come buzzing over the tops of the trees, to land on the grass strip of the runway. It lurched across the bumps and potholes towards the small patch of concrete that had been laid in front of the hangar.

'I wonder what the pilot will be like?' mused Prudence, beginning to have second thoughts about Budgie as a life partner as she picked a few crumbs from her hair.

'It's a very small aeroplane and the runway looks very bumpy,' said Mandy, with the experience of a couple of flights between Palma and Luton to draw on.

'I'm sure everything will be all right,' reassured the commander. 'Budgie knows what he is doing.' He glanced back at the jump master who was still munching away in the hangar. From somewhere he had dug out a doughnut and had artificial cream smeared all over his face. The commander cleared his throat nervously and returned his attention to the aeroplane which, with a final flourish of the engines, rocked to a halt in front of the hangar where its two occupants emerged. The pilot was slim, cavalry-twilled, thirty-five, cravated and wrapped in sunglasses. His passenger was in his late twenties, well over six feet tall, with blond hair, broad shoulders and wearing a dazzling white pair of overalls. The sun emerged from behind a cloud as he climbed out and stretched. He gleamed.

'He looks like an angel!' exclaimed Prudence.

'More like a recruiting poster for the *Luftwaffe*,' the commander replied sourly.

'Good afternoon,' said Dennis as the pilot walked delicately up to the group.

'God, I feel awful. I'll never do that again,' he replied.

'Do what?' asked Mandy.

'Fly with a hangover like I've got at the moment. Booze and coke really aren't the best thing the night before flying. I didn't think I'd be able to make it. Has anyone got some aspirin?'

'I've got some in my handbag,' said Mandy.

'I implore you to bring me a handful!' Although he was in shadow and wearing sunglasses, he still shaded his eyes with his hand to look at her. 'Better still,' he continued. 'I'll come inside with you and have a little lie-down until you want to start leaping about the sky.' He tottered into the darkness of the hangar. Then he stopped and turned, nodding towards his passenger who was now bouncing across towards them, his golden curls forming a nimbus round his head: 'Make sure you keep that prick away from me!'

Dennis watched him give Budgie a wide berth and lie down on an old sofa behind the biplane. 'Oh dear, oh dear, oh dear,' he sighed. 'The more I get into today, the less I like it. It was bad enough when we just had to face a parachute jump, but it never occurred to me that we'd be putting ourselves in the hands of Laurel and Hardy.'

'What's so bad about mixing booze and coke?' asked Mandy. 'I love it with rum.'

'It's all right if you're drinking it. I suspect that Charles was probably sniffing it,' replied Helga.

'Really? What an odd thing to do! He's lucky he didn't drown himself.' Mandy gave the beautiful German a dazzling smile as he reached the hangar.

He smiled back. 'The top of the day to you. I am Helmut Krause. I am going to be a parachutist because I am strong and brave. Are you old persons here to be looking at me?'

'Jesus wept!' exclaimed the commander with horror. 'He's one of them!'

Helmut Krause looked stiffly at the commander. 'I would be knowing you that I like womens. I am well appreciated for my loving of ladies' bottoms. You are most uncourteous to say that I am men's man. I strike at dishonourers!' Helmut raised his fist in a symbolic striking.

'Mad, too!' gasped the commander, missing the symbolic nature of the gesture and skipping behind Prudence for safety.

194

'Nutty as a pumpernickel. God preserve us! Helga, can't you reason with him in his own language?'

'I don't speak German. I am from Rumania.'

'Really?' said Dennis with interest. 'I had always thought you were German or Austrian.'

Prudence was now face to face with Helmut. He may have fulfilled the commander's criteria for insanity, but she had lived with Kelvin all her life and hers were less rigid. Prudence knew cattle, not people, and Helmut, unlike Budgie, would have made a prince among bulls – excellent conformation, the probability of a good conversion rate and, by his own admission, an interest in the craft of procreation without which a bull is merely beef. She was not quite certain about how to indicate that her milking-overall-clad posterior was a bottom for the loving, but she thrust it out anyway, jarring the startled commander back a pace.

The movement drew Helmut's attention to Prudence and her relevant portion. 'You are not old like the others. Are you to be watching me?' he asked.

Prudence looked puzzled so Mandy, miffed at being considered old like the others, helped her out. 'I think he wants to know if you're here to watch him jump, not just to look at his beauty.' She sniffed. 'I don't know who the hell he thinks he is. He obviously keeps his brains in his biceps and his balls, unlike the commander.'

'Helmut Krause, pretty woman.'

'Well, Helmut Krause. We are all here to make a parachute jump. All except Kelvin over there.'

'You josh with me,' replied Helmut incredulously. 'It is young men who are strong and brave like me who do this thing. Old bones will break like dry sticks when they hit the ground. I know bones. I am a chiropractor.'

'Dry sticks!' quavered the commander, his imagination shuddering. 'Budgie!' he wailed. 'Could you come here a minute?'

Budgie had by now done his eating and was on to his teeth-picking. He ambled over, his middle finger working away on a wisdom tooth. He gurgled interrogatively.

'Budgie, do we have to do our jump with Helmut? I'm sure he's very nice and everything, but he's going to have a dreadful effect on morale. Tell him to go away, please. I think I speak for all of us?' The commander looked at everyone else. 'Except Prudence.'

'I told you the man was a prick.' Charles's voice came from the shadows of the biplane. 'I wouldn't mind a drinking coke, by the way, if anyone has got one.'

Kelvin, who had been avoiding being given any further work by skulking in his van with a copy of *Farmers' Weekly*, sensed some drama and appeared in the hangar doorway.

Budgie took his finger from his mouth. It glistened. 'What's wrong with Helmut? He looks a clean young man.'

'He's saying that we'll all end up with broken legs, for a start.'

'Not all of you,' Budgie demurred, eliciting a gleeful snort from Kelvin who could not have put it better himself.

'For heaven's sake—' the commander started, but he was interrupted by the voice of Charles.

'Don't worry, old son. You'll be all right. Budgie's only joking.'

'Are you?' asked the commander.

Budgie answered with an enigmatic smile. 'It's time you were taught the practical side of the business. Will you all please go outside on to the grass.'

Helmut did all that had been expected of him during the two hours' training. When he fell, his rolls were impeccable, bouncing immediately back to his feet without touching the ground with his hands, to sneer at his fellow fallers who would still be thrashing about on the grass. He counted the seconds between the simulated leaving of the aircraft and the simulated pulling of the ripcord on the emergency parachute so loudly that Charles, still recuperating inside the hangar, yelled at him to shut up as his booming voice was setting up sympathetic resonance in the corrugated iron of the building's walls. When he actually simulated the pulling of the simulated ripcord of the emergency chute, he cried in a mighty voice and smote Dennis, who was practising more diffidently beside him, smartly in the pit of the stomach.

By three o'clock, Budgie decided that his pupils were as ready as they were ever going to be. He divided them into groups of four for their first leap. The first batch consisted of the commander, Mandy, Helmut and Prudence, who were chivvied into the belly of the aircraft where they squatted on the floor, the bulk of their parachutes precluding them from taking their places on the seats. With an expression of grave disquiet on his face the commander looked through the gap in the side of the fuselage, from which Budgie and Kelvin had taken the door, at those who were due on the next drop. Mandy was more concerned that her harness was too tight. Prudence, who had been waggling her bottom at Helmut like an unco-ordinated wagtail for much of the day, was still looking appreciatively at him as he raised his arm to the onlookers with the craggy confidence of Kirk Douglas saluting to the crowd before starting combat in the Colosseum.

The noise of the engine was loud inside the aircraft, but not loud enough to drown out Helmut who, with shining eyes, was declaiming like an Old Testament prophet in praise of himself rather than the Lord. 'Ha! You will see. I will fly like a bird. I shall roll correctly when the ground strikes my feet, but I shall land so gently that I still can stand. See me, people: no virgin in a parachute shall do it like me!'

'The mind boggles,' said the commander drily. Having someone like Helmut around certainly took his mind off speculating why Budgie suddenly uncrossed his fingers and regained colour in his cheeks as the aeroplane hopped, skipped and finally jumped uncertainly into the sky, the ground disappearing from view at alarming speed.

'Yes!' cried Helmut. 'I shall boggle too as I fall like – how do you say? – like a star which flies through the sky seen by Halley. Like a comic! Yes, I shall fly like a comic!'

'Oh, for Christ's sake, shut up, you fool!' snapped Mandy. 'Wait until you are out of the aeroplane and then you can babble away as much as you like.'

'You are frightened, yes?' asked Helmut with Kelvin-like sympathy. 'Have no fear. I shall show you the way.'

Ten minutes after take-off, Budgie stood up. Holding carefully on to the roof of the aircraft, he walked the couple of steps through to the cockpit and had a quick word with the pilot before coming back.

'Right!' he shouted. 'Who's first?'

Helmut sprang to his feet. 'I!'

'—Said the fly,' added the commander.

'*Nein*, the comic,' said Helmut.

Budgie clipped the static line on the back of Helmut's parachute to the ring bolt on the roof and clapped him on the shoulder as he climbed gingerly through the doorway. The style of exit had been carefully explained and even more carefully listened to. Left hand on the edge of the doorway, left foot on the step that was attached to the aircraft just below the doorway, then a lurch outwards so that the right hand could clutch the strut below the wing while the remaining limb was left to dangle in space. This left the body spreadeagled alongside ready for a yell from Budgie at which one let go and followed one's line of sight to the ground beneath.

Helmut carefully climbed out of the plane, his crash helmet the same snowy white as his overalls. The commander shut his eyes as his stomach began squat-thrusts in protest at the risks it would shortly undergo through no fault of its own.

'Go!' yelled Budgie, leaning out to smack Helmut on the arm.

There was a hoarse cry above the roar of wind and Budgie stepped back, turning towards Prudence. 'Are you next?' he shouted.

'Yes,' said Prudence, struggling to her feet.

The commander tapped Budgie on the knee and indicated the hole in the fuselage. Helmut, his face contorted in a rictus of fear, was clinging with both hand to the base of the doorway, trying to haul himself back into the cabin.

'I said "Go!" ' yelled Budgie.

"I am not an insane. It is too far long down.'

The commander was surprised to find that he had instinctively clutched Mandy who was sitting beside him. She

had clutched back and he glanced sideways to find his own expression of appalled terror reflected in her face. Helmut heaved himself up in the doorway.

'I said "Go", you yellow bastard!' Budgie put his boot on the centre of Helmut's chest and pushed. The commander and Mandy watched helplessly as Helmut was whisked out of sight by the slipstream. Budgie leaned out for a few seconds to follow his progress before he pulled himself back. 'Right. Next!' Prudence moved across to the doorway, her expression revealing neither apprehension nor disappointment at the craven behaviour of her intended. The commander briefly reflected that courage may have been a quality to be bred for in the bulls of Andalucia, but Prudence would be seeking one who was tractable and docile. Budgie clipped her line to the bolt and she stepped out of the aircraft as if she were stepping out of a bus. 'Go!' yelled Budgie, and she went.

Budgie turned, his eyes raking the rest of his prey. 'You!' He indicated Mandy. 'Come on!'

'Fuck off!' replied Mandy, holding tightly on to the commander's hand. 'If you think I'm moving from this floor, you must be mad.'

'All right,' said Budgie mildly. 'Nobody's forcing you.'

'You mean you're not going to throw me out?' asked Mandy.

'Of course not. I am not a barbarian. The other chap was out of the aircraft and he had to go. But you can do what you like.'

'Oh,' replied Mandy, rather deflated.

Budgie turned to the commander, raising an interrogative eyebrow. The commander considered. Short of being locked in a small room with Kelvin for eternity, there was nothing that he could think of that could fill him with greater apprehension than the concept of jumping out of the aircraft. On the other hand, there was his reputation and honour to consider, not to mention those who would benefit from his sponsors' money. If Prudence could do it, so could he, and the idea of showing himself a better person than Helmut was almost irresistible. It was Budgie who tipped the scales by removing the word 'almost'.

'One thing's certain,' he shouted in the commander's ear. 'It'll be a damn sight safer to jump out rather than risk landing with Charles in the state he is.'

The commander rose to his feet feeling like Sidney Carton on his way to doing a far, far better thing, and Budgie clipped on his line. He stepped to the hole in the fuselage and leaned out to grasp the strut. His hand missed and he overbalanced to somersault out of the aircraft. 'Hell!' he said to himself phlegmatically, as he tumbled through the air, thinking vaguely that he ought to be counting, pulling ripcords and doing all the other things that Budgie had been drumming into him. However, he was much more interested in wondering why he was not seeing his whole life flash in front of his eyes before he hit the ground. He was doing his best to help by trying to recall his earliest memory when he felt a jerk and looked up in surprise to see a parachute canopy sailing serenely in the air above his head. He looked round at the scenery below as the sound of the aircraft's engine faded into silence and decided to start enjoying himself.

Back on the ground, the spectators watched the parachutes drift down. Prudence landed on the edge of the runway and stood up immediately to begin rolling up her parachute as she had been taught. Helmut touched fairly near the hangar and, true to his prediction, he landed on his feet with hardly a flex of the knee. He was shouting before he hit the ground: 'It was magnificent! I fly like a comic or a hawk!' He gathered his parachute to his bosom and walked over to his audience. 'Did you not think I was like a comic?'

'Oh yes,' agreed Dennis. 'You were like a leaping young lion or a hart panting for the pool.'

'Like a hart. That is good. You are fortunate that you will soon be in the sky.'

Prudence had come over and was standing by. Dennis turned to her: 'What was it like?'

''S'alright, I suppose. The commander might be in a bit of a

pickle, though.' The commander had drifted over the edge of the airfield and had landed amid a herd of heifers. One might have thought that the animals would be used to curious aerial happenings in the field next door but they had seized the opportunity to charge round and round the field with their tails in the air while the commander lay prone beside his collapsed parachute.

'He's killed himself!' exclaimed Kelvin, rushing towards his van and starting it up. Dennis dived into the passenger seat and, with Helmut hanging on to the running board, they bounced across the field towards the fence.

'What's that noise?' asked Kelvin as they cleared the edge of the runway.

Dennis looked out of the van window. 'It's the plane. I can't think what the pilot's playing at. He was just above us. Oh dear, I think you may have driven across the runway when he was trying to land.'

'The silly bugger must have seen us and we had right of way. We were on the runway first.'

'I'm not sure that it works that way,' replied Dennis. They stopped by the fence. Helmut cleared the low barbed wire with an elegant bound. Kelvin, in spite of his gammy foot, was only just behind him, while Dennis was more circumspect and crawled through. The commander sat up as they approached and Kelvin's face crumpled with disappointment. Dennis felt that, if Kelvin had reached the commander in time, he might well have struck him with a stone to keep him down.

'What the hell's wrong with you?' demanded Kelvin. 'Lying around like that! We thought you had done yourself a nasty injury or something.'

'I winded myself. I quite thought I was dead for a bit and, when I found that I wasn't, I rather wished that I had been.' The commander sighed and rose shakily to his feet. 'Thank God that's over, anyway.'

'What happened to Mandy?' demanded Kelvin. 'Did her parachute fail to open or was she cut in half by the propeller?'

'I'm afraid it was nothing exciting like that. She just decided that she didn't want to jump.'

'That's shocking!' exclaimed Kelvin, who had come to the same decision a lot earlier.

Dennis and Helmut rolled up the commander's parachute for him while he watched the Cessna come in for its second, uncluttered, approach to the airstrip. 'It wasn't really her fault. After Helmut's performance, I can't say I felt much like jumping myself.'

'Helmut's performance?' asked Kelvin, eagerly. He was scrabbling a bit. He really wanted the dirt on one of the locals which he could embroider at great and scandalous length during the sunlit years of his retirement. With nothing else really juicy being fed to him, Helmut might have to do.

Helmut swiftly moved in with a pre-emptive shut-out. 'I fly like a bird, yes?' he said to the commander. 'I show clearly the great spirit of manhood?'

It was that questioning note in his voice that made Kelvin lick his lips. He looked eagerly at the commander. The latter sighed. He couldn't bring himself to do it. 'The great spirit of German manhood, certainly.'

Helmut stiffened, a war between national and personal pride ricocheting between the hemispheres of his brain. Personal won. 'Like a bird,' he said weakly. 'You too are a brave and gracious person.'

'How kind of you to say so,' gracioused the commander. 'Now, if you would carry my parachute to the van and hold the fence for me so that I can get through . . .'

Kelvin sniffed. There was something he had missed but he could not quite work out what.

Napoleon, Helga, Dennis and Ivor were Kelvin's last chance so he followed every move of the second trip, burrowing for uncertainties and weaknesses amongst the participants. He watched them select their parachutes with beady eyes, passed comments on the inadequacy of their crash helmets and pointed out Charles, sneaking a surreptitious few pulls on a bottle of vodka to steady his nerves after the last landing. But all agreed that a pissed pilot with his nerves intact was better than a shattered one with a hangover.

The light wind had died between the first and second flights and so those on the ground were able to watch four parachutes snap into existence above them as Budgie jettisoned his cargo. Kelvin sighed: at least last time only three had opened, leaving room for some delightful speculation.

Three thumped into the grass by the runway and regained their feet with varying degrees of grogginess. An errant breeze sighed gently up to the fourth, Dennis. Just when he was trying to recall whether he should roll left or right on landing, it stealthied beneath the parachute and puffed, imparting both lift and momentum.

Whereas Helmut had spun like a teetotum as he tugged his toggles in a frenzy of activity to prove that he had control, Dennis hung on the parachute straps like a sack of potatoes. Looking as unmoved by his fate as the corn before a combine, he drifted over the heads of the spectators and landed with a crash on the iron roof of the hangar. Kelvin was the first to react. It may not have been as exciting as a golden fireball at the end of the runway, but beggars could not be choosers. Ever an optimist, he rushed towards the hangar door, hoping to find Dennis neatly filleted, lying beneath a jagged and bloody hole. There was no sign of him, so Kelvin ran outside hoping to see him splattered across the roof.

The anarchic zephyr was not quite finished with the parachute. The silk bellied briefly once more, lifting off the roof across which it had been tastefully draped. It carried Dennis with it, rumbling him across the corrugated iron to the gutter and tumbled him the dozen feet to the ground.

The commander congratulated Kelvin on his forethought in bringing his van to act as an ambulance. Kelvin should have been delighted but he wasn't, since the patient stretched out in the back, as the commander rattled carefully through every pothole, was himself. Dennis had landed safely when he was blown off the roof, but only because Kelvin had been underneath his point of impact. Kelvin had a broken collarbone.

Within a week he was overheard telling a tourist in the pub

that he had sustained it while parachuting. It was only another couple of weeks before he was talking about what it felt like during his jump to the commander and Dennis. The pub pondered on the Nature of Truth. One Truth was that he did not jump; another was that he had persuaded himself that he had; and the third, the one that ultimately counted, was that he had carried his conviction round his cronies in the livestock market and made them stump up £300 in sponsorship. The last was the only Truth with a price tag, so, of course, it was accepted.

Chapter Thirteen

'BUT WHAT CAN I do about it?' demanded the commander. 'I thought I was getting somewhere up to that parachute jump, but now she's coming at me again like an express train.' The commander had endured an undeniably difficult few months since Mandy had decided that he was the one for her. 'It's not as if she's after me the whole time – in many ways I wish she was, because I'd at least know where I stood. But she can go for a day or two and be quite rude to me – just like normal – and then she'll come at me again like a randy tarantula. I tell you it's bloody terrifying. And with Christmas not all that far away, there'll be lots of parties and it'll be a misery.'

'It's a shame for you,' consoled Kelvin, who felt that he ought to react since the other two in the bar, Jimmy and Bill, were sitting slackly on their stools, enjoying that peaceful vacancy of mind in which the locals had the ability to pass hours at a time. A couple of months ago they would have listened with interest to the commander's complaints, but they had seen it happen for themselves, and a sight of the commander's terrified face when her 'Yoo hoo!' pierced through the hubbub of a social gathering told them more than his words.

'But what can I do?' the commander reiterated with despair. 'It's colouring my whole life. I almost dread coming in here because she might come in too. And I haven't been near the post office for a week. The last time I tried to go, she was standing in her doorway waving at me as soon she saw me!' He shuddered.

Kelvin looked blank. 'What's so awful about that?'

'She was wearing a pink nightdress that barely came to her knees!'

Kelvin was impressed. 'Heaven's above!'

'And that's not all. On her feet were a pair of those slippers – mules, I think they're called – and they were made out of white fur with a red pom-pom on the instep.'

'Heaven's above!' repeated Kelvin. 'And what did you do?'

'What else could I do? I turned and ran.'

Kelvin thought for a few seconds and sighed. 'I don't suppose there's much else you could do.'

'That's my point. Can't you think of anything?' the commander pleaded.

Kelvin considered. Initially he and the rest of the community had enjoyed the commander's understandable apprehension at being the object of Mandy's desires but it was now clearly beginning to wear the man down. That did not matter in itself, but it had turned him into a bit of a bore. 'You've become a bit of a bore,' said Kelvin.

'With that damned woman coming at me with the determination of a Mountie, do you bloody wonder?' cried the commander.

Bill turned his eyes towards the victim. 'Tell her to piss off.'

'Piss off? Tell Mandy to piss off? Even if I could tell a lady to piss off, just how do I go about it with Mandy?'

Bill looked nonplussed. 'Just open your mouth and tell her, of course.'

'Mandy?'

'I don't see why not. She's just another woman.'

Kelvin's sense of equity felt constrained to intercede. 'Be fair, Bill. You could hardly call Mandy "just another woman".'

'Quite!' acknowledged the commander curtly. 'In fact, there are precious few of the fair sex round here who could be so described.'

'Except Prudence.'

'With the possible exception of Prudence,' admitted the commander. He spun round as the door opened, but it was

207

only Malcolm who came to the bar, rubbing his hands briskly together. 'Cold, this evening.'

'Winter drawers on,' said Kelvin as he had said a couple of times each autumn for the last forty years.

'What's fresh?' asked Malcolm, pouring himself a pint and putting the money in the till.

'The commander's moaning about Mandy again,' said Kelvin.

'Still? Why don't you tell her to piss off?'

'Jesus!' exclaimed the commander.

Malcolm had the grace to look contrite. 'Well, no, perhaps you couldn't do that. But you do seem to have been going on about it for some time. I'm amazed you don't do anything about it.'

The commander literally shook, like a man suffering from an ague. 'What? You stupid sod! Tell me what! It's all very well for you lot to tell me that I ought to be doing something, but none of you come up with any ideas!'

'You never asked me,' replied Malcolm huffily.

The commander turned wild eyes towards him. Life was quite clearly getting him down. 'You think you may be able to help?'

'Well, yes, I suppose so. It's merely a question of breaking down the problem into its constituent parts.'

'Like what?' demanded the commander eagerly.

'Well . . . um . . . let's think.' Malcolm paused. 'Mandy fancies you and you don't fancy Mandy. That seems to be the basis of it.'

'Yes. We know that. But how does that help?' asked the commander.

'It lets us know what we have to work on. Here we have two separate areas which might be changed. We can either try to make Mandy stop fancying you or else make you fancy Mandy.'

'It would be very convenient if we could make the commander fancy her,' said Kelvin. 'Remember, we wanted someone to take her on in the first place.'

'No! Certainly not! I don't want to fancy Mandy.'

208

Malcolm put a consoling hand on the commander's shoulder. 'There's nothing to worry about. If we make you fancy her, you'd want to.'

'But—'

'How could you make him fancy her if her doesn't?' asked Kelvin. 'Old Granny Chilcott had a line in love charms which she sold to the local maids so that they could snare their man. But I never heard that they did much good.'

'Commander,' said Malcolm patiently, 'just imagine for a second that Mandy really was the object of your desires.' The commander did his best, but his imagination was not up to it. Few imaginations would have been. Malcolm understood his difficulty. 'All right. Forget about Mandy. Who do you really fancy?'

Bill and Jimmy came out of their dark-brown studies to look curiously at the commander as he leafed through his mental catalogue. 'Well . . . er . . . your Stephanie comes to mind. She's a very fine-looking woman.'

Malcolm's eyebrows arched in surprise. 'She is? . . . . I mean, I know she is. Well . . . I suppose you'd better imagine that Mandy is Stephanie. No.' He broke off. 'Look, couldn't you think of someone else you fancy? It feels uncomfortable using my wife as an example.'

'Yes, I'm sorry. It just slipped out. I'll think of someone else.' His brow furrowed.

'Well?' demanded Malcolm after a few seconds.

'I'm sorry, I can't think of anyone else,' replied the commander sheepishly.

'There are probably 2,000 million women in the world. You can surely think of one to lust over apart from my wife.'

'It's that running shirt she goes around in,' apologized the commander. 'It really is rather impressive.'

'I know Keith admires her when she's out joggling. And so do I,' contributed Kelvin with relish.

'It's jogging,' said Malcolm worriedly. 'Keith? You've heard Keith talking about it?'

'By "joggling" I mean "joggling". I don't think Keith has tried it on, but he'd certainly like to.'

Malcolm took a deep breath. 'Commander, imagine that Mandy is not Mandy but Brigitte Bardot.'

'Right!' agreed the commander. He leant his arms on the bar to concentrate.

'We don't have a possessive relationship, but Stephanie wouldn't look at Keith. Surely not. No . . . the only time in the last few weeks when she went off by herself was that weekend and Keith was with us.'

'How long do I have to go on imagining Brigitte Bardot?' asked the commander, cocking an eye towards Malcolm.

'Oh, sorry . . . er . . . what was it I was trying to say?'

'I haven't the faintest idea.'

'Don't ask me,' said Bill in response to an inquiring look. 'I didn't understand a word of it.'

'Oh, bugger it. Let's try something else. If we can't make you fancy Mandy, we'll just have to make her stop fancying you.'

'That sounds much more the sort of thing I'm after. What do I do?'

'Be rude to her.'

'Look, I can't. Quite apart from getting my head bitten off, the poor woman's in love. One can't just rudely reject that. I imagine she's got human feelings like anyone else. I want her to reject me. That's the decent way to play it.'

Malcolm sighed. 'I admire your sensibilities, but you're asking for a great deal. Think what she feels when you jump through windows whenever she comes into a room. A quick clean break would be much kinder in the long run.'

'For heaven's sake! I've made it clear enough for any creature this side of a rhino! And she and I will probably be living in the same community for some time to come. I don't want to make a huge enemy of her.'

Malcolm held up his hand. 'OK. If that's the way you want it, you'll just have to make yourself sexually unattractive to her in some way, but retain her friendship.'

'That's it! That's exactly what I want! How?' The commander leaned forward eagerly.

'The best way is to turn gay.'

It was as if someone had sunk his fist into the commander's belly. He sagged back on his stool. 'Damn you! he said savagely. 'I thought you were going to come up with a sensible suggestion.'

'It is a sensible suggestion!' replied Malcolm indignantly. 'It may be a bit devious, but if you pretend to be gay, it's bound to change her attitude towards you. You go out to Julian's tomorrow and get some tips on how to act gay.'

'It's ridiculous!' scoffed the commander. 'Quite apart from anything else, I'm married and it's obvious that I'm . . . er . . . normal.'

'Oh, I don't know,' contributed Kelvin. 'Your Elfrieda is one of those Peace Women these days and you just have to see them on telly to realize that they're all a bit funny. It would be quite likely that you might be a homo because I've heard that two homos often get married. I'd find it quite believable if someone told me you were a homo.'

'How dare you!'

'Of course, you being in the navy helps too. Everyone knows what sailors are like.'

The commander, purple with indignation, cast around savagely for a crushing retort. 'You . . . you sheep shagger!'

Kelvin sucked in his breath in mock horror. 'That's a terrible thing to say!' He winked at Jimmy and Bill who were also enjoying the commander's discomfiture.

The commander noticed the wink and slid down from his stool. 'There are some things that are just not amusing,' he said curtly. 'I'm not staying around here to be insulted. I'm going home.' He nodded icily to Malcolm, ignored the others and walked over to the blackened oak settle by the fire to pick up his coat. The others watched him with interest since he had left a good half-pint of beer in his glass on the counter. He turned as he reached the door to cast another disdainful glance at the bar just as Kelvin was stretching out towards the glass in order to beat Jimmy to it. 'Here!' he shouted. 'That's my beer! Leave it alone!' He moved swiftly back to the bar, just as the pub door opened behind him.

'Yoo hoo, Commander!' His hand froze just as the glass

reached his lips. The heads of everyone else swivelled towards
the door. Mandy loomed in the doorway in a high-neck
angora sweater whose colour matched her red tweed skirt. She
was also wearing red plastic boots with a pair of deeply
dimpled knees bulging over the top.

'Ah! Mandy!' said the commander nervously. 'I'm just off.
See? I've got my coat on.'

'Well, you can just take it off again, can't you?' replied
Mandy gaily. 'Now I've got you, I'm not letting you go that
easily! It's been days since we've had any time together. I've
been beginning to wonder if you've been avoiding me!' She
wagged her finger.

'Oh, no . . . er . . . well,' stuttered her victim.

'Grrr!' growled Mandy with a little pout. 'I could eat you
up!'

Kelvin thumped the bar in his delight. 'That's it, Mandy!
The bugger's really been lusting after you! You should hear
what he's been saying.'

'For heaven's sake, Kelvin! Stop talking such tommy rot!' The commander's voice rose to a squeak as Mandy's hand sneaked beneath his coat and sharply nipped his bottom. 'Mandy! Control yourself! Stop it at once!' But Mandy merely laughed.

'Malcolm!' cried the commander despairingly, as her fingers encircled his wrist and she dragged him off to the far side of the settle by the fire. 'I'll do it! I'll do it!'

The hotel, which lay a couple of miles downstream of the village, gave the community a touch of class. It was an authentic Victorian fishing hotel, bulging with stuffed trout, brown Windsor soup and slumbering generals. The only note of incongruity was its proprietor, Julian, an outrageously camp London interior decorator, who had inherited the establishment from a bewhiskered aunt who had run it for thirty years. He had been there for four years and the hotel was thriving since the generals had all discovered that their wives became putty in the face of his flattery and preferred to hang around the hotel, hoping to be stroked by Julian, rather than follow them out to the river or demand to be taken round the National Trust properties within driving distance.

Julian was ambivalent about local custom. He liked the amount of money that the villagers could spend across his bar, but his elderly gentlefolk rubbed shoulders uneasily with Kelvin, Jimmy and their like. It was not a class conflict but little mannerisms that could give rise to complaints, such as the way Jimmy would cough up the tarry deposits from his lungs and shoot them accurately on to the toe of his boot, or Kelvin's habit of sipping from other people's drinks if their backs were turned. Nevertheless, he greeted the commander, Kelvin and Malcolm from behind the reception desk with a warm smile as they pushed through the heavy, mahogany front door and settled down to wipe their feet as he had taught them on the enormous coir doormat that guarded the entrance hall.

'Good evening, you lot. This is a rare honour. Is it Helga's night off?'

'Nice sweater, Julian,' commented Malcolm. Julian vied with Mandy in the pyrotechnics of his dress. His jersey was sky-blue with an arching salmon knitted in from shoulder to waist.

Julian was delighted to tell them about it, coming out from behind the desk to show it better. He pirouetted on white calf shoes. 'It is pretty, isn't it? I saw it in a shop window just off the Via Veneto in May and what could I do ? It was crying out to me! Who else in the wide, wide world could it have been meant for?'

'Pretty rough-looking salmon. It looks like a kelt to me,' remarked Kelvin, examining it critically.

'You want sea-lice on a sweater?' asked Julian scornfully. 'If you go to the bar, I'll come through and serve you in a couple of minutes. I'm just making out a bill.' He went back behind the desk and Malcolm led the way through to the bar. It was empty save for one ancient guest in plus-fours who was snoring in a chair by the window with a copy of *The Field* open on his lap. The rest of the hotel's occupants would be slumbering in their beds, recovering from their day's exertions on the river and preparing for the steak and kidney pudding on the evening's menu.

'It really is a pretty dire place to come for a drink,' commented the commander, glancing at the prints by Lionel Edwards and Cecil Aldin on the wall.

Malcolm looked out over the lawn in front of the hotel which stretched down to the river. 'Well, it doesn't really matter since you're not here for a drink. We might be, but you're here for information and instruction.'

'I must say, I'm finding this extremely embarrassing.'

'It's your own fault. You must be the only sailor on the seven seas who needs to be told how to act the gay.'

'Bloody homos,' muttered Kelvin. 'You know what I did today? I castrated twenty lambs with my teeth – and they're not my own teeth either. I'd like to see one of those bloody homos do something like that.'

Malcolm's face creased with pain. 'Oh dear, Kelvin, you can be positively rococo, sometimes.'

Julian came striding gaily into the room. 'Rococo? What do you mean, Malcolm?'

'Kelvin's talking about biting the balls off sheep.'

Julian stopped in his tracks and groaned. 'You know, I sometimes feel I should sell up and buy a garret in San Francisco. You peasants can be so earthy that you're positively subterranean.'

'It's just Kelvin,' reassured Malcolm.

'It isn't, you know,' replied Julian with a sad shake of his head. 'Anyway,' he continued, lifting the flap to get behind the bar, 'now you're here, what would you like to drink?' Julian's resident clientele liked its liquor hard and usually brown. His only draught beer was drawn straight from the barrel and tasted like ferret widdle. It won frequent awards at Real Ale festivals. Malcolm was the only member of the community who could stomach it.

'Whisky.'

'Whisky.'

'I think I'll have a pint of your best.'

Julian selected a glass and trickled a sullen pint from a dusty barrel, plonking it guiltily on the counter in front of Malcolm. The contents looked like one of those table lamps of the sixties with globules of unidentifiable matter swirling around in amniotic fluid. He and the other two watched, their lips curling with disgust, as Malcolm picked up his beer, took several swallows and banged it back on the bar. 'Your ale is a credit to you, Julian.'

'So it has been said.'

'By whom?' challenged Kelvin.

'Well . . . er . . . by Malcolm here for one. And . . . and . . .' Julian smacked the side of his head, 'the last customer who had some. I've forgotten who it was.'

'It was probably Malcolm the last time he was in here,' sneered Kelvin.

'Of course!' exclaimed Julian. 'You're absolutely right! It was Malcolm. I don't suppose we can really count him twice.'

Malcolm looked dubiously down at his beer. 'I haven't been in here for several weeks.'

'Well, there's not very much call for it, you see. But it's awfully nice to know you like it so much.'

The commander cleared his throat. 'Actually, we're here for a purpose – I'm here for a purpose, anyway.' He paused. 'It's difficult to know quite how to put it.'

'For heaven's sake, do try, dear boy. I can't stand the suspense. That's £2.30 for the drinks.'

'Well, you may have heard that I've got problems with Mandy.'

Julian gave a little shiver. He could have been a character in a sitcom produced by a provincial commercial television station had it not been for the shrewd, sardonic eyes through which he viewed the world and his more comely apprentice chefs. 'Yes, it must be quite thrilling for you! She seems so outrageously butch.'

'Perhaps,' agreed the commander cautiously. 'I've been trying to put her off without success for weeks and Malcolm came up with this idea that if I made out I was gay, then she'd leave me alone and we . . . er . . . thought that you might . . . you know . . .' The commander's voice trailed into embarrassed silence in the face of Julian's incredulous expression.

'What a ridiculous palaver! Why on earth don't you just tell her to piss off?'

The commander's hand shook so violently that he spilled a few drops of whisky. Since he had already wet his lips with it and it had only been a standard pub measure in the first place, he was understandably concerned. 'Bugger!' he exclaimed, carefully licking his hand. 'Look, if anybody else tells me to tell her to piss off, I shall carry out violence on sensitive portions of his anatomy.'

'Oh dear!' said Julian. 'We are touchy, aren't we? Sorry I spoke.'

'It's all right. It's just that nobody seems to be taking the situation seriously.'

'Perhaps because it's not too serious a situation,' suggested Julian.

'It's bloody serious. It's interfering with my life.' The commander had a tendency to become maudlin. He might

216

well have dropped the odd tear into his whisky if he had not been afraid of over-diluting the tiny quantity that was left.

Julian raised his hand to scratch the back of his head. He sighed. 'All right, I accept that. But honestly, Commander, don't you think it's going a little far to proposition me? I'm awfully sorry, but I can't really say that I fancy you.' There was a snort from the chair by the window. The ancient guest was demonstrating that his hearing was still in good working order. His eyes remained closed, making it the mildest of protests.

The commander was working himself into a bit of a lather. 'No, no, no. Good God, no! What a revolting idea! I never suggested anything of the sort!'

'Commander!' exclaimed Julian, his eyes those of a down-trodden inmate of Battersea Dogs' Home, although the effect was spoiled with a wink at Kelvin. 'What a thing to say!'

'I don't mean it personally,' babbled the commander. 'If I was like that, I'm sure I'd love to.'

'Then if you want to be like that, we have no problem, have we?' Julian gave the commander a winning smile. 'Oh! This is going to be so exciting!' Julian pouted and wriggled his shoulders in a way that made the commander blench. His hand automatically lifted his glass, only to find that its contents had evaporated. Julian was right there, pouring another drink straight from the bottle: 'Have this on me.' Kelvin stirred on his stool and shifted his glass along the polished wood of the counter towards Julian. It was ignored as the commander gulped down his drink and then took a deep breath to calm himself.

'Let's start again. I'm sorry if I haven't made myself clear.'

'Oh, but you have.'

'No, Julian, I haven't. I really truly haven't. The important bit was "pretend". I want to pretend to be a poofter so that I can put Mandy off. I only want some tips on how I should do it.'

'You don't like me!' exclaimed Julian.

'No, no, no. I do like you. I really do. But,' he added

217

hastily, as Julian met his worried gaze with eyes that shone like fairy lights, 'not in that sort of way.'

'How about giving me a drink?' interrupted Kelvin.

Julian turned. 'Look, Kelvin. The day after you give me something for nothing, I shall give you a free drink.'

'That's not fair! You've poured the commander a whisky which is at least a triple!'

'A triple? Was it a triple?'

'Yes, it damn well was! In fact, it was nearer a quadruple!'

Julian went to the cash register. 'Four whiskies. That's £3.20. It is your round, isn't it, Kelvin?'

Kelvin hesitated. 'Yes! No! That's not the point. The commander didn't order it. It was free!'

'It most certainly was not! And whether he ordered it or not, he's drunk most of it. That's £3.20.'

'In that case, it's Malcolm's round.'

'I'll chalk it up on your account, Malcolm,' said Julian.

'What are you talking about? He hasn't got an account. You won't let anyone have an account here.'

'I've just opened one for Malcolm,' replied Julian blandly. 'But there's no need for him to rush to pay.' He turned his head from Kelvin, who was spluttering indignantly at being out-manoeuvred, back towards the commander. 'Look, Commander, I was just pulling your leg. I would no more fancy you than you would Mrs Baggins. I think your idea is ridiculous, but if you must do it, just flap your wrists and behave like any of the TV queers.'

The commander showed relief. 'Oh! You mean you didn't really think I wanted to . . . er . . .' He laughed heartily, but a shadow flew across his face. 'You're not saying that I'm no more attractive than Mrs Baggins, are you? I mean, you might say that about Kelvin here, but not me.'

'Oh dear!' sighed Julian, turning to Malcolm.. 'These two are like Tweedledum and Tweedledee. Can't you take them away with you?'

'I'm sorry,' Malcolm apologized. 'I know what it can be like if you don't see them every day. But the commander would really appreciate any help that you might be able to give. He's really most insecure about the whole business.'

'That's right,' confirmed the commander. He hung his head, more to check whether Kelvin was trying to sneak some of his whisky than to demonstrate insecurity. 'I know it's a bit of a cheek, but you're the horse's mouth, as it were.'

Julian sniffed, looking at the commander with calculation before coming to a brisk decision. 'Right, my jolly matelot friend. I believe there's going to be Marcia's charity lunch up at the manor next week.'

'Yes,' said the commander warily. 'It's in aid of the World Wildlife Fund.'

'Just you make sure you turn up. And you can buy me a packet of David Shepherd Christmas cards so that Marcia will let me out the door afterwards.'

'Why? What are you going to do?'

'What you asked. I'm going to persuade Mandy that you're as gay as Tinkerbell.'

'Can't you just give me tips?' pleaded the commander.

'When I do a job, I do it properly.'

'But you won't create some sort of dreadful scene, will you? It's an embarrassingly public place.'

'Ah! You don't want to come out of the closet. Is that it?'

'Yes,' blurted the commander, nodding vigorously. 'That's just how I want it.'

'But the closet door to be just a teensy-weensy bit ajar so that Mandy can peek through?'

'Yes, I suppose we must allow that, but we don't want her to see anything too upsetting when she peeks, eh?'

'We'll see what we can do.' The quality of Julian's smile did little to reassure the commander.

Chapter Fourteen

MARCIA'S LUNCH happened every year and she invited everyone who did not give her the impression of being liable to pinch the silver. This had included Kelvin, but the previous year he had turned up late in a state of intoxication and, although he did not pinch a spoon, he had pinched her bottom with the ruthlessness of a lobster, so he was still *persona non grata* at the manor.

The lunch was a decorous affair. Gentry from up to thirty miles distance donned their Viyella shirts, hairy ties and pearl necklaces to mingle easily with the locals for some of whom it was the equivalent of a royal garden party. The horsehair sofas, and the worm-ridden tables which flanked them, were pushed against the walls of the drawing room while trestle tables, borrowed from the church hall, were covered in sheets and food of that peculiar variety that is never met except upon such occasions – pieces of cheddar married to pineapple chunks atop crispy biscuits, celery choking beneath cottage cheese with the texture of wet Polyfilla, miniature sausage rolls with a few grains of meat swaddled in layers of soggy pastry. The goodies – teatowels, playing cards and the like – lay in ambush on either side of the front door, womanned by Mrs Baggins and by Barbara, the widow of a colonial judge who had been forcibly retired after sentencing an African to be flogged and hanged for poaching.

The turn-out at the party was the best for years. Discussion of the impending denouement of the relationship between the commander and Mandy had been so widespread that even the budgerigar which sat suspended in its cage in the window of the cafe was in on it, causing the commander to blush by screeching 'Who's a pretty boy?' whenever he walked past. Nobody wished to miss the fun.

By 1pm there was an air of expectancy in the manor. Nobody was buying and nobody was eating, although there had been a run on the wine. The furthermost flung of the visiting country gents of both sexes milled in an uneasy group near the window, sensitive to the febrile atmosphere but unaware of its cause. Mandy had the commander by a glass case containing a stuffed tapir, oblivious to the twelve-foot *cordon sanitaire* which the party had tacitly thrown round them. She was ogling him over the rim of her glass while the commander had his eyes nervously riveted on the door.

Julian arrived at 1.15. His entrance had the impact of that of Pizarro at the court of Atahualpa. Conversation amongst the locals faded into silence, isolating the voice of the middle-aged daughter of an earl who was regaling her peers by the window: '—the fucking animal refused a perfectly ordinary little hedge. It was so humiliating as Bunty knew it had cost me an arm and a leg. Damned creature was used to the pistes up in Leicestershire. I say! Why has everyone gone quiet? And who's that ghastly little poof? Is he frightfully famous or something?'

Julian stood framed in the doorway. He had dressed for the occasion with some skill, wearing a brown three-piece tweed suit, although the effect was marred by the yellow waistcoat and a large badge which stated 'I am AIDS free.' The other guests parted like the Red Sea, leaving him two clear paths radiating from the doorway – one towards Mandy and the commander and the other towards the window in case he felt like an altercation with milady whose last two sentences had fallen into the silence like an anvil into a millpond. Julian looked down the left-hand tunnel towards the commander and Mandy. She had turned and seemed puzzled. As the only person within paper-streamer range of the commander who did not know what fate had in store for them, she had every right to wonder why her companion was looking at Julian as a rabbit would a stoat and why the others round about had the air of a Roman crowd when the lion spotted a succulent Christian across a packed arena. Julian smiled a wintry smile and plunged into the crowd towards the table where the squire was dispensing drinks.

'He must be going to wait for a little while,' said Ivor.

'But why?' asked Gerald Mowbray, glancing at his watch. 'I don't want to stand around here all afternoon. I've got an artic loaded with straw coming this afternoon.'

'You don't have to stay,' said Lindy tartly.

'Nor do you, missy. You're supposed to be coming out to look at old George's leg at two. If Julian don't get on with it, you'll be late.'

'My appointments are my business.' Lindy refused to gossip, otherwise she was quite normal.

'They're mine too when I have to give the old bugger an hour off to wait for you.'

Similar scratchy conversations were taking place all over the room. The audience had expected swift action. 'What's going on, Julian?' asked the squire, as he proffered a glass of red wine. 'I haven't missed it, have I?'

Julian sipped the wine and grimaced as it slunk over his palate. 'I thought I might like a drink first, but I was wrong.'

The squire raised his voice. 'It's all right! He's going to do it in a minute!' he called.

'Do what?' came a plaintive cry from the window. 'This is a most peculiar sort of party. I can't think what Marcia's playing at.'

'Julian!' ordered the squire. 'Go and tell Lady Daphne what's going on. It's a bit unfair to leave her in suspense.'

'I'll go,' said Keith, who was standing within earshot. He wriggled swiftly through the crowd with the adroitness of the one in 300 million that succeeds in fertilizing the ovum.

Dennis took the opportunity to pass Julian a glass of whisky as the squire looked after Keith thoughtfully. 'That might be quite a good idea,' he said. 'Daphne has always prized enthusiasm above all other virtues in her lovers and one hears that Keith may be just the ticket for her.' He shook his head gloomily.

'Nice enough fellow, Keith. But a chap had to have something before the women would let him into their knickers in the old days.'

'It's the modern decline in morality,' agreed Julian drily.

The squire cocked an eye at his badge. 'You're right, but I don't mind buggers. Had plenty of them in the regiment and most of them were quite charming.'

'Thank you,' said Julian even more drily.

'Don't mention it. Would you like some more wine?'

'No, thank you.'

The squire grunted in disappointment. 'You'd be doing me a favour. Marcia will have me drinking the stuff for weeks.'

'Speaking of which, our hostess approaches.'

'Julian! Have I caught you in time?' Marcia was looking flushed.

'What do you mean?'

'Don't be silly! Have you done the dirty deed for the commander yet?'

'No.'

'Oh good.' She turned to her husband. 'Nobody's buying a damn thing. They're all waiting for Julian and then they'll be out the front door like lemmings.'

The squire looked round the room. 'You may well be right, dear. But I don't know what I can do about it.'

'Give them a little speech. Thank them all for coming and that sort of thing and then tell them that Julian won't be doing his thing until they've all bought something.'

The squire was aghast. 'How can I say that? They'd probably lynch me, anyway.' The mood of the party was beginning to change. Julian had played it shrewdly, but he was in danger of allowing anticipation to turn into frustration.

'I'll say something, Marcia. After all, it is me that they have come to see.'

'Yes. I've something to say about that. It's all very well to pack the house, but they're supposed to be here because they want to preserve wildlife.'

'Think like a Jesuit, Marcia. The ends justify the means.'

'But the means are the ends. If we don't get the means, the

Chinese mountainsides will be carpeted with dead pandas.'

'Oh dear!' remarked Julian mildly. 'There seem to be many responsibilities descending on my shoulders all of a sudden. I have a sudden urge to discharge them. Excuse me.' He put a hand on the table and climbed up on a chair. He clapped his hands for silence as Marcia looked worriedly at the chair. The furniture of the manor had been an important breeding habitat for woodworm for centuries. The conversation died to a buzz and then into silence.

'Ladies and Gentlemen, I'm sure we all know why we're here by now.' There was a murmur of excitement. He was going to make a speech.

'He's going to announce that the commander is a poof!' exclaimed Ivor. 'That's subtle!'

There was a sudden cry from the opposite corner. 'Julian! *No!*'

'It's all right, Commander.' Julian raised a propitiatory hand. 'I would like to thank everyone for coming and our particular thanks go to the squire for lending his lovely home once again and to Marcia for providing this delicious lunch. However, I can assure you that it was not my hotel that did the catering.' There was a polite laugh: a little barbed but adequately witty seemed to be the consensus. 'Marcia informs me that unless you all go and spend your money in the hall, our planet will be smothered in decomposing pandas. I shall wait patiently here as you do so. I won't do anything until you're all back.' There was a delay of several seconds while the audience assessed Julian as he stood with folded arms on the chair, a slight smile playing about his lips. Then it broke in a great surge towards the doors. Julian watched them stream through into the hall. 'I'd get back to your post, Marcia.'

'Yes, I will. Thank you very much. I'll wink at you or something when the time is right.' She turned to plunge into the sea of people.

'What a peculiar speech!' said Mandy. 'And why was Julian making it?'

'I can't imagine,' the commander replied.

'Are you all right? You look a little flushed.'

'It's just the heat,' said the commander, fishing a handkerchief from his pocket and wiping beads of nervous sweat from his forehead.

It was fifteen minutes before the roar of the market place died down and people trickled back into the sitting room clutching their knick-knacks. Julian had stayed by the drinks table to demonstrate that he was keeping his side of the bargain until Marcia waved her arm at him above the crowd. Once again the sea parted, revealing a stained brown carpet, now decorated with discarded gherkins and the odd dollop of cottage cheese, stretching towards the small pool of conversation to which Mandy and the commander were contributing. The commander watched him approach, an expression of resolution on his face. This moment was the culmination of months of hope and a week of nail-biting anticipation. He knew that what was to follow would be a grim, unpleasant business but, as a trained warrior, he realized that one sometimes had to endure the agony and humiliation of battle in order to achieve a lasting peace. He had done his best to ensure that everyone knew he was not really gay, whatever happened.

Julian processed along the ranks with his hands behind his back, nodding and smiling at friends and pausing every few yards to drop a sentence or two of greeting to a privileged guest. The squire, appropriately, walked a few deferential paces behind in attendance.

Julian emerged into the clearing surrounding the commander's group. The commander took a deep breath and cleared his throat. 'Harrumph! Er . . . hello, dear.'

Mandy swivelled to see who the commander was addressing and hit a smear of lumpfish roe. Julian stepped nimbly backwards as she flailed her arms before crashing forward on her hands and knees. Keith knew there was trouble brewing. Left to herself – and those surrounding were showing little interest in helping her to regain her poise and her feet – she would incandesce her surroundings in a holocaust of invective which would render the execution of their carefully constructed plan impossible. Mandy's outbursts of vituperation could only be enjoyed out of doors, otherwise the spectator risked immolation. He shimmied through the crowd, doing his spermatozoa impression, to her side and wrapped her in solicitude.

'Mandy!' he cried, as he hauled her to her feet. 'Are you all right? Oh dear! You must have fallen right on a cream cheese and anchovy canapé!' He dabbed at the stain with his finger. 'No! It's the garlic dip! We'll have to get a new dress.' Mandy stood, looking about her like a bull facing the banderillero. The Lady Daphne, who had followed Keith through the crowd dragging a young man of good but vacant looks in her wake, was unwise enough to laugh. It gave Mandy her target. 'Shut up, slag!' she snarled.

'Well really!' The Lady Daphne did not know the danger that she was courting, but others did. The squire retreated hurriedly from the area of peril, using as an excuse the need to gather up the contents of Mandy's handbag which had burst open upon impact with the floor, scattering lipsticks, half-litre bottles of scent and deodorants, powder and paint over a good part of the room. 'How dare you speak to me like that, you ridiculous person!'

'Ridiculous! You call me ridiculous!'

'Darling!' interrupted Keith feebly.

'Keep out of this, you useless turd!' snapped Mandy.

The commander was standing behind the infuriated Mandy, hoping that out of sight meant out of mind. His proximity to the emotional napalm that was roaring out of her had driven the Grand Plan from his mind and he was concentrating on nothing more than his own survival.

Julian, however, was cast in the mould of Cromwell, Churchill or Paisley. He knew a crisis when he saw one and dealing with them was part of his trade. He assessed the situation with a calculating eye, seeking both the best way to distract Mandy before she tore the throats out of those in her vicinity and still achieve the purpose of the afternoon. 'Commander! Are you all right?'

The commander let out a small squeak of fear at having attention drawn to him. 'Eh? What? Yes, of course I'm all right. Why shouldn't I be?'

Julian laid a hand on the commander's arm. 'Oh! Thank God! I couldn't have coped if you had been hurt.' He moved forward and, in full view of the company and less than six feet away from Mandy, he kissed the commander lightly on the cheek. It happened too quickly for the commander to take evasive action; his hand flew to his face and his guilty eyes first to Julian and then to Mandy. Julian was looking quietly pleased with himself. Mandy was not, but at least her mind had been taken off her immediate troubles.

'You're queer,' she stated flatly. 'You're nothing but a nasty little queer. I might have bloody well known it.'

'Not a nasty little queer,' protested Julian. 'He's nice and really rather attractive.'

'You keep quiet,' said Mandy without taking her eyes off the commander. Nor did at least another fifty speculating pairs round about. 'Why didn't you tell me you were queer?'

'You shit, Julian!' whispered the commander. 'I said let Mandy peek. Not rip the cupboard door off its hinges in front of half the world.'

Julian looked at the commander and shrugged. 'Under the circumstances I had to do something rather drastic. I've done

227

what you wanted. It's up to you now.'

'Commander!' roared Mandy. 'Answer my question. Why didn't you tell me?'

The commander looked at her, looked at the crowd round about which was looking back at him with hungry interest. He turned to Julian with mute appeal in his eyes.

'You were embarrassed to bring it up,' prompted the latter encouragingly.

'I was embarrassed to bring it up,' parroted the commander. He grimaced as he finished his sentence and fired a dirty look at Julian who shrugged. It did sound a bit feeble. Mandy certainly thought so.

'You bloody little wimp! You fooled us all! Even my blasted husband said you fancied me!' The mob sighed its pleasure.

'Well, I did – I mean I do, of course. I'm not that queer.'

'He'd have to be bloody queer to fancy her,' remarked the Lady Daphne to general murmurs of agreement, once it was clear that Mandy had not heard her.

'You bastard! I've been wasting my time over you for months and you're not even attractive! I'll kill Keith. Where is he?' She looked round, but her husband had melted into the crowd.

The commander frowned once more. 'You mean you don't fancy me?'

'Christ, no,' answered Mandy, witheringly. 'Your moustache is even worse than Keith's. But if you're my age and married to someone like him, you don't look a gift horse in the mouth.'

'I always check a gift horse myself, in case it might be pregnant with ill-disposed Greeks,' contributed Julian.

'You shut up!'

'Sorry.'

Mandy glared at the commander. 'At least most queers are honest these days. I hate the sneaky ones like you. I'm cancelling my sprouts order, you fairy.'

'Mandy! I'm not gay!'

But she tossed her chin contemptuously and walked through the crowd to the door.

228

'Well, it worked,' said Julian as conversation started up behind her.

'But it was all unnecessary,' moaned the commander. 'She thinks I'm gay. And she says I'm unattractive. It's awful.'

'It doesn't really matter. There are worse things that can be thought about you.'

'I need a drink,' said the commander. 'This is a nightmare! Half these people don't know I'm not gay. What can they be thinking?' He turned and bumped into Lady Daphne's escort. 'What do you want?' he demanded.

'I was just coming to say that you handled a difficult situation extremely well.'

The commander looked for irony but found none. 'Thank you.'

'I thought you might like a decent drink.' He pulled a glass flask covered in crocodile skin from the inner pocket of his tweed suit. 'It's from a little distillery on my uncle's estate. It's just the ticket when one's shooting.'

'Aha!' cried the commander. 'Life looks up a bit. You're a man after my own heart!'

'Oh! I do hope so. I find you rather beautiful in a rugged sort of way.'

The commander turned to Julian, stifling a sob. 'What have you done to me?' he whispered.

'Don't be depressed. He finds you attractive!'

'Yes! That's true. I'm not like Mrs Baggins, am I?' He turned back to Lady Daphne's escort. 'Thank you, but go to hell and take your whisky with you.'

'But I thought—'

'You thought wrong. Talk to Julian about it. I'm going to the pub. Come on, Ivor.'

The pub was still open when the commander and Ivor arrived. Bill was by the bar along with Jimmy and both were staring ahead of them at the wall in silence. By the fire was Mandy, batting her eyelids at Kelvin who was clutching his whisky like a talisman. She had seen the commander enter but ignored him. The commander looked at her with a happy sigh. 'Perhaps it was worth it. I'll buy you a beer, Ivor. It's like coming home.'

Bill turned. 'Hullo, Commander.' He jerked his thumb towards the fire. 'It must have worked all right. She bought him a free drink as soon as she came in. Have you heard about the Mattocks?'

'No.'

'Shocking it is. Hilda Mattock poured sugar into the petrol tank of that Mary's little red car.'

'Mary?' queried the commander delicately.

'Frank's relief milker. Her with the big bosoms and a backside like a Large White sow.'

'You know what's so nice about living here?' said the commander.

Bill frowned. 'What?'

'It's the right things that are important.'

Bill shifted in his seat uncomfortably. 'I don't know about that sort of thing.'

Mandy's tinkling laugh broke the silence. The commander stiffened, but relaxed again. He sighed happily a second time. 'It'll soon be Christmas. Can I buy everyone a drink?'

230

Any Fool Can Be A Yokel

Chapter One

THE CLOCK in the church tower had stopped. It was a church clock with all the necessary trimmings. It had its moping owl; it overlooked the graveyard where the rude forefathers of the hamlet heaved the turf in mouldering heaps. Its tower had even been ivy-mantled until a decade earlier when it had been decided that Virginia creeper would be less damaging to the stonework. It was more appropriate anyway, since the building was dedicated to the beautiful St Wilgefort who had grown a beard to discourage suitors and retain her virginity. But the clock had worked for a good couple of centuries, tolling out the days and seasons for the good folk of the village who lay or got laid in its shadow.

They had grown to depend on it. Its mellow chime was less obvious than it had been in the past as it was often drowned by the noise of traffic or the slurping of ice-cream-eating tourists who wandered the streets of the village, gawping at the thatched cottages and leaning over the medieval bridge to look at the trout which disported themselves in the river below. But its chime was still important. During the still watches of the night, it rang down the wooded valley and bounced off the steep hillsides. Then the clock's habit of losing eight minutes a day came into its own, persuading shy virgins, admittedly as rare as unicorns in the parish, that it was not time to return to their cottages and farmsteads quite yet, and allowing the pub to stay open for a few more precious minutes which, by the day before it was wound, would have stretched to a useful three-quarters of an hour.

The clock had stopped a couple of times before. The most

serious occasion had been during the war when the sexton had suffered a severe attack of delirium tremens brought on by a surfeit of scrumpy. He had been convinced that the Germans were about to invade and had barricaded himself in the church tower armed with tins of stewed plums and an air-gun with which he proposed to shoot birds which he would then tie to the lightning conductors to be flash-fried during thunder-

storms for his meals. He had chosen the glorious Spitfire summer of 1940. While the Few carved their legend in the skies over Kent, the cloudless heaven above the village was tainted by the subtle odour emanating from a hundred rotting sparrows. This was eventually overlaid by the awesome bouquet of the excrement resulting from an exclusive diet of stewed plums which rained down on the ground from the top of the tower.

On that occasion the clock had just not been wound. This time it was broken. The commander, who ran a market garden at the bottom of the village, had wanted to try his hand at bell ringing. He had become bored by grandsires and treble bobs after a couple of hours and most of a bottle of gin, and had attempted to play the sailor's hornpipe, but he had swung from the clock weight instead of a bell rope by mistake. When the verger had next climbed the spiral staircase to the top of the tower to spend his usual sweaty fifteen minutes amid the cobwebs and bat droppings in turning the handle that brought the weights up from the floor, they refused to come. Something was bent.

The verger reported the matter to the pub. This was the hub of village life where most of the influential figures of the neighbourhood gathered once – if not twice – a day in the public bar to consult with each other on matters of local concern. The pub despatched Frank Mattock to repair the clock. Frank was a farmer, now in his forties, who had risen from being an assistant slaughterman to owner-occupying dairy farmer through an astonishing run of good fortune which began with the premium bonds, progressed through the pools and had had its most recent manifestation in a disgustingly large sum of money won from the *Reader's Digest* in one of those free contests that every sensible person throws in the rubbish bin as soon as they come through the letterbox. Frank had a tendency to put on weight, a fact that was always evident as he also liked to go around in white shirts unbuttoned to the navel which showed off his hairy, tubular torso and the chunky jewellery that usually bounced away on top of it. Frank, like all farmers, could mend anything. Give a

235

farmer a hammer and a piece of baler twine and he would confidently approach the faulty guidance equipment on a space shuttle.

Frank hit the clock mechanism once or twice and slid his crowbar into the works, levering it a few times so that some bits dropped off and shattered on the church floor 50 feet below. He then reported his failure back at the pub. An expert quoted £500, which was a large sum of money, to repair the damage. The commander was not going to pay: he had only bent something; and Frank said that *he* could not be held responsible for metal fatigue – one bit had shattered after only a single hammer blow. The vicar, a dangerous radical who had once proposed sending the proceeds of the Sunday collection to the families of striking miners, was approached but he thought that the clock might as well stay broken since everybody who wanted to know the time had a watch already. The village was faced with the need to find £500.

One would not have thought that the raising of such a sum would have presented many difficulties. The average English village conceals an astonishing amount of money. Take the land alone. The parish had a couple of thousand acres of farmland, most of which was owned by a dozen or so individuals who could be seen nightly in the pub, nursing half-pints in their gnarled hands and wearing gumboots and trousers held up with baler twine: there was £4 million or so there. Then there was the village itself. To the irritation of most of those who had been born there, it was beautiful. The river which ran through it chuckled and sparkled. Many of the streets were cobbled, winding, narrow and given an added dimension by the millstreams which popped up here and there for a few yards before plunging back beneath the ground through neatly arched stone tunnels. Most of the cottages were thatched and lime-washed pink, green or white and looked as if any one of them could easily have housed Red Riding Hood's grandmamma or a gargantuan Squirrel Nutkin. The entire picture-postcard conglomeration was set at the top of a steep-sided valley whose thickly wooded slopes made an eminently satisfactory backcloth for all the amateur photographers who snapped the same things from the same angles every year.

If only, bemoaned the locals, the village was ugly. Dot a few slag heaps around; knock down the string of seventeenth-century cottages that lined the banks of the river and ask a fashionable architect to fill the space with modern living modules – anything that would drive the tourists away and give all the residents a bit of privacy. However, the picturesqueness of the community brought in money. The tourists may have clogged the pavements with their peeling bodies and their cars may have filled the roads like flocks of mechanized sheep, but they were sheep that could be fleeced. Those who did not work on the land worked on the tourists and took money off them through cafes, souvenir shops, garages and bed-and-breakfast establishments. And the prettiness of the place brought in the wealthy retired, drunks every one, who enabled the village grocer to sell expensive guavas, pawpaws and smoked salmon as well as Chateaux Latour, Lafite, d'Yquem and twenty different varieties of malt whisky. The village was rich but did its best to conceal the fact. One could never quite be sure that one of those innocent-seeming tourists might not be a tax inspector.

The pub was discussing some serious business. Nothing mundane like money or politics, but a good titillating local scandal – the staff of life. Bill slowly supped a mouthful of beer from the thin-walled glass that had been standing on the oak bar against which he had been leaning. He replaced the glass and smacked his lips to remove the line of froth that had stuck to them. He turned back to his attentive audience of fellow drinkers, enjoying his recapitulation of the events so far: 'Well, David Carter is having a dalliance with Maureen Reed.'

Everyone knew this already and had done for a week or more, but there was a sucking-in of breath from the others. David Carter, his wife and their three small children lived only a few doors up from the pub. 'He must be near thirty-five and she is only twenty-one,' continued Bill. There was a shaking of heads. 'Mary Mowbray's younger sister is Sharon

237

Carter – David's wife – and she and Angela Reed, Maureen's mother, have been best friends ever since they left school. But not now they ain't!' Bill paused on that triumphant note. There was complete silence from the others – elderly farmers, gamekeepers, farm workers and a smattering of ex-tourists who had bought property and settled. The only sound was the measured ticking of the clock, the hiss of damp wood from the sullen fire that smoked reluctantly in the inglenook and the faint sounds from the juke box that thumped away all day and night in the tourist ghetto of the lounge bar through the thick cob wall.

'Granny Reed and Granny Carter have fallen out too. And they're sisters and have always said they'd never had a cross word between them since they were two!'

Kelvin pursed his lips sanctimoniously. He, like Bill, was an elderly farmer. Bill had retired, in theory, which meant that he lived off deals and land rents. In fact he did very well at it and was rumoured to keep great wads of notes inside the dirty trilby hat that never left his head. Kelvin still actively farmed which meant, in his case, that he told his daughter what to do each morning before going off to market or out on some other errand. 'It's a right bad business,' he said.

Bill had not finished yet. 'And yesterday morning, right in the street, Stephanie Jarrett saw George Carter strike his son and call him a stupid bastard.' A mass clicking of tongues ensued.

'I hear that Maureen is having to move out of the village to let things cool down a bit,' said Keith. He was a butcher in his fifties who had caused a great stir when he had moved to the village a couple of years earlier and, with his wife, had prettified a perfectly innocuous cottage so that it looked like the sort of place that Hansel and Gretel might inhabit in a Disney cartoon.

It was a wonderful scandal and it had to be spelled out in every salacious detail at each social gathering, after which all its ramifications and possible scenarios would be examined. Once the essential facts had been set out, the imaginations of everyone could roam free and flesh them out where they felt like.

The village enjoyed a *brouhaha* of these dimensions every decade or so and had done for several centuries. They were colossal while they lasted, a source of deep pleasure and satisfaction to everyone in the village who was not directly involved. But the place was small; people had to continue to live together and scandals always blew over with, perhaps, a shuffle of the pack of human cards before they settled down again. The very smallness of the village always prevented too much calumny being cast at the sinners. If one became too self-righteous, there was the risk that some dark secret from one's own past or that of one's father or grandfather might be recalled as a reproof to one's hypocrisy. It was amazing how many 'sisters' existed who were in reality daughters, the result of harvest indiscretions during giddy girlhood. There was even an entire generation, born during the war, whose paternity owed considerably more to the convalescent home for battle-fatigued American soldiers than to the regular swains of the village who could not compete either financially or charismatically with those exotic foreigners who spoke like they did in the films that were sometimes shown on Saturday night in the church hall.

This latest scandal was lumbering along its predictable path. Maureen would have to leave the area for a year or two before returning to marry and settle down to produce children and prepare packed lunches for whichever farm worker would end up as her husband. The pub customers puffed at their pipes in companionable silence as they remembered their youth when they too had possessed the capacity to become the central figure in such a scandal.

'Sex,' said Bill suddenly. The others cocked a pensive eye at him. 'If this village has got to get some money to pay for this here clock, something to do with sex is the best way to raise it. Everybody is interested in sex. The young want to know all about it. Most people want to know how to do more of it and those like us want to remember how it was.'

'That's true,' agreed Kelvin. 'There's money in sex. Look at Nellie.' Everybody thought about Nellie. Thirty years ago, when anyone complained that the village was staid or dull,

Nellie would be pointed out. She lived in a cottage equidistant from three villages and cycled round the countryside serving her exclusive clientele. Nellie and her bicycle were available for hire; she was the district's sole representative of the demimonde. Even in those days, Nellie had struggled to make a good enough living for herself and the four children which were the byproducts of her chosen profession; there were too many enthusiastic amateurs around. But her customers had grown old with her and had remained loyal. She had given up riding her bike and could often be seen striding along the road to the village in her woolly balaclava with wispy grey hair poking out from underneath, a ridiculously unglamorous figure with her bright little face highlighted by large round spectacles through which she peered shortsightedly at the world around her. Nowadays her clients visited her in their battered motor cars and on their tractors, but the local convention was that nobody knew about it. Nellie was treated as a colourful figure from the past and was cherished as the only practising hooker in six parishes.

'You could hardly say that Nellie has grown rich on sex,' objected Jimmy. He was the oldest man in the village and, as such, occupied the Windsor chair that sat by the fireplace. He was a tiny, bandy-legged old man who would have been far more comfortable on the stool he had been used to all his drinking life, but he had enough of a sense of history and duty to do what was expected of him.

'She's done all right,' replied Bill, idly rolling himself a cigarette with one hand, a widespread skill learned on tractors. 'We only want £500 for the clock and she must bring in a damn sight more than that each year. So there's willingness to spend money on sex round about.'

'True enough,' admitted Jimmy. 'But her money comes from people like Kelvin and there aren't many like him.'

Kelvin began to splutter with outrage. The fact that he was one of Nellie's friends could hardly be a secret since the battered, doorless ex-post office van that he drove around was there to be seen parked outside her door on alternate Wednesday nights and it could even be heard as it blared through the village with its defective exhaust on the way there. There was not much he could say in denial and Bill saved him the trouble of trying.

'We've got to tap into the female market. The women folk don't spend nearly enough money on sex.'

'Ah, but if they did, it would be our money,' replied Jimmy, which was a bit of a cheek on his part since he and most of those present were either bachelors|or widowers.

At this point the door of the pub opened and Lindy walked in. One of the curious aspects of village mores was that women were always treated as gross inferiors and drudges only so long as they allowed themselves so to be. The ordinary housewife was scarcely of more import than a milch-cow until she decided to nag or assert herself, whereupon her husband would crumble and the other men of the village would regard her as a terrible force of nature. If a|woman took a job or became prominent outside the home, she was treated as an equal or superior by the most chauvinistic or arrogant of the locals. It was as if she lost her gender. Women, in the eyes of the average local male, was the word given to those females who stayed at home to smooth the lives of the superior sex. Once they broke out of that mould, they became something different. The usual courtesies due to their sex were dropped and they were expected to exchange opinions and blue jokes with anyone.

Lindy was the epitome of this latter stage of womanhood. She was married and had two small children but she brought in the bulk of her family's income through her job as district nurse. At the end of her day, she liked to come into the pub for a quick lager while her husband cooked the dinner. She was a short woman in her thirties, highly efficient at her job and had the dedication to walk through the winter snowdrifts in order to change a dressing or to comfort one of her elderly patients. She was built rather on the lines of Dolly Parton, but the locals would no more dream of lusting after her than they would after the parson.

'What are you lot talking about?' was her greeting.

'Sex,' replied Bill succinctly.

'Ah! You mean the David Carter business.'

'No, we weren't talking about that,' replied Bill.

Lindy gave him a sceptical glance. 'You must have been the only people in the village who weren't. Gossip keeps this place going.'

'It's not gossip,' replied the commander loftily. 'It's the study of human nature which is the foundation of all art and culture.'

Lindy let that one go. 'In that case, what about sex?'

'We were thinking about ways to raise the money for the clock bill and sex seemed to be one of the few interests shared by everybody that we could think of that might be exploitable.'

'I don't see how you can make much money out of sex round here,' objected Lindy. 'Nellie has got the market sewn up. Ask Kelvin.'

Kelvin began to splutter again. 'I strongly object to remarks and insinuations like that being made about me.'

'I don't see that you've got much to complain about since they're true,' replied Bill brutally. 'No, what we reckon,

242

Lindy, is that we ought to get the women involved. People like Kelvin pay money and Maud at the post office sells lots of dirty magazines each month, but they're all for the men. The women don't spend on anything like that.'

'We're too sensible as a sex. Don't you agree, Helga?'

Helga had just come through from the lounge. She was the current landlord who had taken over the pub just under a year ago and was very different from the usual run of country women. She was an Austrian in her mid-forties and still startlingly beautiful. She was blonde with high cheek bones and wide-set blue eyes and exuded sexuality with the prolific ease of a fountain gushing forth water. She was not a dumb blonde but carried herself with an air of sophisticated central European decadence. She evoked Bond-filled casinos, luxury express trains and black satin sheets. She had earned her living as an actress and, from the few hints that she dropped, she seemed also to have been one of the very last great *poules de luxe*, which was probably how she came to afford to buy the pub.

Initially, the locals had found Helga extremely hard to cope with. If one were male, a conversation with her at a party was an overwhelming experience as she was extremely tactile. For the first two minutes as she greeted you, her hands would be everywhere, stroking and patting and seemed to rummage into every orifice of your body. You felt as if you were being assaulted by a swarm of butterflies. Even as simple an act as offering her a smoke would take on immense sexual significance as she caressed the proffered cigarette first between her fingers and then rolled it sensually between her lips before taking the hand which offered a light between her own and sliding her fingers round the shape of your knuckles and up to the wrist. It left the local men with steam coming out of their ears and the women with daggers from their eyes.

Then it was realized that Helga was no threat. This was her natural way of behaving and she was scrupulous at never doing more than flirt with anyone who was married. If one of the wives of the village saw her husband in a spider-like clinch with Helga in a corner at a party, she did not mind. It was of less significance to Helga than shaking hands and she left the husband in the sort of condition that promised an interesting evening once the wife had got him back home. Helga considered Lindy's point. 'I agree. It is men who make such a fuss about sex. Women do it while men just talk about it.'

When Helga came out with a remark like that, one did not argue, any more than one would with Einstein on the subject of relativity. People were also mesmerized by her voice which was exaggerated Garbo. Like everything else about Helga, it first appeared that she put on this seductive tone and accent by design, but it was entirely natural. It was even a handicap as it had considerably reduced the range of acting parts that she had been considered for in this country. By the time she retired a couple of years before she came to the village, she had become restricted to 'beautiful foreign spies' and Bulldog Drummond-type villainesses.

'What is it that you want to know about sex, anyway, Willie?' Nobody but Helga called Bill by that name. It came out as 'Weelee'.

Bill blushed. Most men blushed when Helga addressed them. It was an embarrassed reflex caused by the carnal thoughts that she invariably aroused. 'I was thinking that a good way to raise money to pay for the clock would be to get some money from the ladies. The Rotary Club made a fortune when they got hold of a stripper in town. Perhaps we could get in a male stripper.'

'A stripper? That would be wonderful, particularly if it was you, my dear.' Bill blushed even deeper. Much of Helga's charm came from the fact that she did not take the way she looked seriously and made fun of the effect that it had on other people. If a remark like that had been made by anyone else, Bill would have been mercilessly mocked, but his cronies held their peace for fear of attracting a machismo-destroying remark from Helga.

'I wouldn't pay money to see a stripper,' said Lindy.

'No. Most men are so disappointing when you see them without their clothes on. It is so much better to leave them with their pride and their cod-pieces intact.'

'I don't wear a cod-piece,' said Kelvin, always slow to learn.

'That is very clear to see, darling.' It came out as 'dorlink'. 'However, I see no reason why we ladies should not have a knicker party.'

The men looked uneasily at each other. 'What *is* a knicker party?' queried the commander.

'You know what a Tupperware party is?' asked Helga. The commander nodded. 'It is the same as that. Except they do not sell plastic containers but all sorts of wonderful things.'

'Like what?' questioned Kelvin.

'You know, beautiful underclothes, vibrators. Things which will make us and our menfolk better lovers. All that sort of stuff. Some of it can be very enjoyable, you know.'

Bill didn't know. It was doubtful if any of those born in the parish would. The commander might know a little about that sort of thing since he had been in the navy and presumably had had a wife in every port. Sex, locally, was a function carried out in the dark in pyjamas on alternate Saturday nights. There was a lot of it about but, after the first careless passions of youth when some experimentation might have been in order, no missionary would be shocked by what he might see. He might, however, be unsettled if he knew the identity of the coupling couples.

There was a pause in the conversation after Helga had revealed a hint of the delights that might be on offer at a knicker party. The locals were rather shaken but they were not going to reveal that to Helga or to each other. Kelvin was the first to put into words some of the *angst* that the others were feeling.

'It won't give our womenfolk any funny ideas, will it?' he asked anxiously. If Nellie had never demonstrated any funny ideas to him, despite her long and varied career, then such things must be few and far between within the locality.

'Oh, Kelvin, don't be so fuddy-duddy. Making love should be fun. Don't you agree?' said Helga. Kelvin had never made love; he had only copulated, so was hardly the right person to ask. 'What about a knicker party, then?' demanded Helga. 'If you want to raise some money, I am sure that I could organize something for the ladies of the village that they would enjoy.'

The establishment of the village began to shuffle their feet and blow through their lips. Bill put their doubts into words.

'I'm not sure that the gentle sex round here are quite ready for that sort of thing. They're not like they are in the city, you know. We menfolk want to protect them from the decline in moral standards.'

'Don't pay any attention to him, Helga. You go right ahead with it,' said Lindy. 'I know the women round here a damn sight better than Bill and this lot, and they would love it.'

'Now look here, Lindy,' protested Bill. 'Don't you go putting any daft ideas into Helga's pretty little head.'

'Oh, Willie. You are so sweet. You are jealous. You would

246

like to come along to the party yourself. Don't worry, I'll make sure I give you a private showing all of your own and I won't let on to anyone what you buy.'

The solidarity of the opposition began to crumble. 'Here,' said Kelvin, 'if you're going to give Bill a look, I'd like to come along too. And I'm sure most of us would like to as well.'

'In that case, let us have a knicker party for everybody,' said Helga, flinging her arms up in the air. 'I think it would probably be better if we split the sexes though.'

'I don't see why,' objected Kelvin. 'The ladies might like it if their menfolk were beside them to protect them from being embarrassed.'

'It's not the ladies being embarrassed that I'm worried about. It's the men,' replied Helga.

'Don't be daft,' said Kelvin scornfully.

'Helga's right, you know,' said Lindy. 'I think many men would be a bit uneasy to hear women talking openly about sexual matters.'

'Nonsense!' insisted Kelvin stoutly. 'Anyway, the ladies round here just wouldn't talk about things like that.'

'I know at least half a dozen women not very far from this bar who think that their men leave a lot to be desired as lovers.'

The bar was fairly full with several separate groups talking quietly amongst themselves, but all conversation throughout the room ceased immediately. The men pricked up their ears to hear what Lindy would say next and none dared catch the eye of another.

After a short pause, Kelvin cleared his throat nervously: 'Well, I'm all right. I ain't got a woman. Anyway, when would you talk about things like that?'

'You may not have a woman to yourself, Kelvin. But Nellie's a good friend of mine,' said Lindy. The commander gave a guffaw. 'As is your Elfrieda, Commander.' The commander looked thoughtfully into his beer. 'And, you know, we don't just talk about flower arranging at WI meetings. It's astonishing what comes up.'

'Or doesn't come up when it should do,' added Helga.

Bill pulled his handkerchief out of his pocket and trumpeted loudly into the silence. 'Grenville's got a good crop of kale along the top road this year,' he said.

Kelvin eagerly swivelled on his bar stool to look at him.

'I've seen that. I reckon he's hoping to hold a few of the squire's pheasants in there this season.'

Helga and Lindy exchanged a smile which everyone pretended they had not seen as conversations hesitantly restarted.

And so it came to pass that a date was set for the party. It had been hoped to hold it in the church hall, which was the normal venue for events of such importance, but the vicar had expressed grave uncertainty about the bishop's views on such a use for an adjunct of God's house, even though Helga explained to him that frilly knickers were nowhere condemned in the scriptures, not even by St Paul.

The party was then snapped up by Ivor. There was a large chunk of Ivor that had never grown up. While he was a farmer, a sometime county councillor and a member of the board of visitors at the county prison, he still found time to be the prime customer for the rack of dirty video films that had recently been introduced as a sideline in a little room behind the counter of the post office. He had bought most of the magazines which were also on sale there and the range of goods had been extended with the express purpose of retaining his custom. Ivor also took an exhaustingly gleeful delight in dirty jokes. It is traditionally supposed that these find their way, almost by osmosis, into the collective consciousness of all the dirty-joke-telling segments of the world's population at the same time. But Ivor proved it otherwise. Not only did he tell dirty jokes; he invented them as well. Kelvin once said that he had heard one of Ivor's jokes, a subtle play on the bishop-and-actress theme which also involved a fork-lift truck and a monocle, from someone at the market, but most of them were so filthy as to be incomprehensible to everyone else except the squire, though he was so imbued with the concept of *noblesse oblige* that he laughed at everyone's jokes whether he understood them or not.

Ivor had intended to hold the party in his sitting room, but word had gone round very quickly about the sort of entertainment that was going to be on offer, and it was decided to move the venue from his farmhouse to the manor where there would be more room. The squire considered that this might threaten his dignity but Ivor said he would resign his chairmanship of the local Conservative Association if the squire refused, which would mean the latter taking over and, faced with such a threat, he had caved in immediately.

The drawing room of the manor provided an august setting for the party. The grand furniture had been sold off several generations earlier and the collection of paintings had declined to a couple of likenesses of sour-mouthed ancestors that those in the process of founding dynasties had refused to buy and claim as their own. However, provided one ignored the damp stains on the plaster, the odd broken floorboard and the fact that the chimney smoked abominably, it was still an impressive room, despite a few cracked window panes and holes in the panelling caused by the ravages of deathwatch beetle. It was large enough to house the majority of the local adult population who had come along to see what was on offer.

In spite of the ominous nature of Lindy's comments in the pub, which had spread rapidly and secretly to all the males in the community, most of the men had turned out for their party which was to be held first. In exchange for a £1 note each arriving guest was handed a glass of ill-flavoured red wine by Ivor as he came in through the door. The church clock was an excellent cause. The wine had to be decanted as it had been bought by Mick, who ran the local cafe, at a fire-damage sale when a nearby cash-and-carry had burned down after the wiring had been chewed by rats. As the labels had been severely burned – all that was legible was the word 'English' on a few of them – and most of the corks had become loose when the wine had boiled, it had seemed less trouble all round to remove it completely from the bottles. The quality of the wine was not critical as the guests were normally confronted with beverages distilled from the detritus of the hedgerows, quite often pre-sprayed with herbicide which meant that in excess quantities they made effective lawn weedkillers.

The knicker demonstrator at the men's party was a friend of Helga. She was apparently a professional, a full-time knicker-party demonstrator, who had very kindly agreed to pass over her commission to the clock fund, the only condition being that Helga should collect her from the train and have her to stay for the weekend. She was due at 8 pm, which just allowed time for Ivor to go round with his decanter and replenish the glasses. The first evidence that most people had of her arrival was a great booming bellow which silenced all conversation. 'Men! I am having nothing to do with any men!'

Beneath the air of ribald jollity, there was a vein of deep uncertainty among those present and the contempt that came sizzling from the doorway did nothing to alleviate this. People turned to look. Helga, her friend and Lindy, who was carrying a large suitcase, were standing on the threshold. The demonstrator was not what most people had been expecting or even hoping for. Instead of a *Viva Maria* fantasy in frilly clothes, they were confronted with a gorgon. She was much the same age as Helga, but was as different as a carthorse from an Arab. She was certainly blonde and busty, but she was big: not fat, just tall, her hair drawn back in a tight bun above shoulders that would have not been out of place on an American footballer. She wore a pink dress that could have covered tepees for a whole tribe of Indians.

The squire had put a trestle table at one end of the room and this was the platform from which the party was to be run. Helga and the gorgon pushed their way through the guests and the room became silent as they climbed on to the table, using a couple of chairs as ladders, and turned to face the audience. Helga introduced her friend as Lesley Parker-Brown and the woman-mountain rose to her feet to a hearty round of applause. The trestle table creaked ominously as she shifted her weight, surveying the gathering.

'Pay attention, please,' she started, to a rapt audience. 'This party is going to be fun for you all,' she said grimly. 'I am told that Helga has said we intend to show you knickers. This is true but, in addition, there are many other sexual aids and devices that I shall be demonstrating. Normally, as Helga has said, these demonstrations are just for women and we girls thoroughly enjoy ourselves, but you are men which may create certain difficulties. Accordingly, anyone who misbehaves will have to answer to me and I shall eject them from the room. Forcibly, if necessary.' Her eyes swept across the audience. One could have heard a fly fart in the silence. 'Is that clear?' Nobody responded. 'Is that clear?' she repeated, in a voice that would have quelled King Kong. There was hasty agreement from the assembled guests.

'Excellent. Now, these goods are not for the prudish or faint-hearted, so I would suggest that anyone who feels that such things as dildoes, ticklers and extremely revealing undergarments might be embarrassing or offensive to them should leave now.' One could have now heard that same fly's stomach rumble as people strenuously avoided each other's eyes. A couple of young men in the audience nudged each other and one did a poor job in stifling a snort of laughter. Many looked at them enviously as they had the sexual security of youth and probable virginity at their disposal, but Lesley was not to know this. Her cold grey eyes quartered the audience and picked them out with the efficiency of a pin extracting a snail from its fragrantly garlicked shell. The snort became a curious strangled grunt as it froze on the perpetrator's lips. Lesley cleared her throat: 'Sex can be fun, but it is nothing to snigger about.' The two boys blushed deeply and, in the silence which followed, the fly's belly emitted a deafening rumble. The commander, standing by the door, drowned it out in an aside to Ivor. 'I think I'm going. I see no reason why I should stand here and be treated like a primary school child who has just messed his pants. Do you think I could have my money back?'

'For heaven's sake! Don't be so mean. Go, if that's what you want, but at least leave your £1 in the kitty. Remember it was you that bust the clock in the first place.'

'That's right, Ivor,' muttered Kelvin, sidling up just in case he missed anything. 'You tell him. Remember he's drunk the

251

wine and that's what the money was paying for.'

'Don't be absurd,' retorted the commander. 'I saw that wine before it was decanted. If Mick was not paid to take it away, he was robbed!'

'I thought it was quite nice, meself,' mused Kelvin. He was being more discreet than the other two in speaking with his hand in front of his mouth in case the gorgon should spot him. 'It had a round fruity taste, I thought.'

Ivor and the commander turned to look at Kelvin with astonishment. 'What have you been reading?' asked Ivor.

'One of Prudence's magazines,' replied Kelvin. 'By the way, how can a taste be round?'

'It's when you take a good mouthful and it rolls round beneath your tongue – hence "round",' replied the commander. 'Now, about my £1 . . .'

The three of them had been so engrossed in their conversation that they had failed to observe that the gorgon had stopped speaking and was staring at them in fury. The fly and everybody else had, and had been watching the pink tepee cover begin to quiver as the pressure of its owner rose towards the point of explosion. It came. She opened her mouth and let out a mighty roar and, at the same time, she stamped her foot. The table had been suffering considerable discomfort ever since she had clambered aboard it and it had bravely borne its load for as long as it was able, but now it could hold out no more: it gave a loud groan of distress and collapsed.

It is a well-known fact that if one drops a mouse down a mineshaft, it will walk away from the bottom, whereas if one drops a horse down the same shaft, it will messily explode. The same forces of physics applied when the table gave way. Helga let out a squeak of dismay and subsided gracefully into the arms of the squire who had been standing close by, hoping for a peek up her skirt. It had been a vain endeavour since Helga was wearing trousers. Lesley, on the other hand, came down like a factory chimney with half a ton of dynamite to help it on its way. Jimmy had been standing near for much the same reason as the squire and the descending Lesley brushed him aside like a piece of chaff before hitting the floor with a thud that rattled the teeth of every woodworm in the building and brought a squint-eyed squire from an earlier generation crashing down from his vantage point above the fireplace.

There was a moment or two's silence, as in the aftermath of any great natural disaster, before Lesley's bellow of rage and distress was drowned by the clatter of agricultural hobnail boots on the wooden floor as people rushed forward to assist. The squire managed to fight off those who wished to help with Helga while Lindy gave Lesley a cursory examination, diagnosing a severely sprained ankle, and directed a dozen or so bystanders to grasp her by her appendages and carry her from the room. Ivor helpfully held open the door as they staggered past and Lesley ceased her groaning long enough to shoot him a glance that would have melted his spectacles, had he been wearing them.

While Lesley was being treated somewhere in the bowels of the decaying mansion, there was a hiatus at the centre of events. Into this gap sailed Helga. The squire had her seated in an armchair and was enthusiastically patting her hand since it was the only piece of naked flesh that he could reasonably lay his hands upon, but she fought her way free of his sticky grasp. She took firm hold of the suitcase that held Lesley's stock and slammed the lid shut on the fingers of Kelvin who had just realized the fact of its abandonment. She then stood on the armchair and clapped her hands sharply together. 'Pay attention!' she called, turning heads that had moved hopefully towards the large earthenware jug which held the decanted wine. 'It looks as though Lesley is out of action for the rest of the evening, so we can either cancel the party or else I can have a go at demonstration. What do you all want?'

'Will you model for us?' asked Kelvin optimistically.

'You dirty old bugger!' replied Helga cheerfully, to the distress of a local Methodist lay preacher who must have come to the party in error. Helga was a much jollier – if more ignorant – hostess than the expert. She decided to use the armchair as her pulpit and roped in the squire as her

253

assistant. His function was to hold up the suitcase of goodies while Helga delved inside. As he swayed dangerously backwards under the awkward weight of the case, Helga pulled up the first object to cheers from the guests who were feeling like reprieved prisoners since the departure of Lesley. It was made of pink satin and appeared to be about 3 or 4 inches square. Helga looked at it doubtfully and indicated to the squire to hold up the suitcase once more while she made sure that she had not left most of it behind. She held it up for the audience's inspection. They looked at it with expectation while she consulted a label which provided a significant percentage of the object's substance.

'This is . . . er . . . a . . . Fifi.' She looked hopefully at the spectators who did not seem to be much the wiser. She correctly deduced that 'Fifi' was not a term the local males normally applied to anything in particular and re-consulted the label.

'Well, what does it say?' yelled Kelvin.

' "Fifi. Machine washable," ' replied Helga unhelpfully. 'I think it must be a *cache-sexe*.'

'What's a *cache-sexe*?' asked Bill.

Helga looked round the room for help. It can surely have not been because she felt embarrassed but because her command of the less-used nooks and crannies of the English language was not extensive. Everyone looked at Malcolm, a man with a degree, as the obvious person to supply the needed information.

'It's a sort of lady's jockstrap,' supplied Malcolm, reddening slightly under the warm gaze of so many pairs of eyes. The eyes shifted back to the *cache-sexe*.

'How do you wear it?' asked Bill. Helga gave him a quizzical look, but it was obviously a genuine request for knowledge. She turned it over carefully in her hand and a couple of strands of satin fell away from it. 'Ah! I have it now. You tie it on like this.' She tied it on like that, unfortunately over the top of her trousers, but the spectators got the general idea clearly enough as she swivelled her hips from side to side so that everyone could see. She clicked her fingers to break the squire out of his trance and he lifted up the suitcase from which she extracted the catalogue. 'A Fifi costs £2.35. Does anyone want to buy one?' She looked at the catalogue again. 'They only come in one size.'

'Well, they would, wouldn't they?' said the commander reasonably.

Nobody wanted a Fifi, so Helga took it off and rummaged around for something else. Her hand came up with a rat. She screamed and dropped it back into the suitcase. If it was a rat, it seemed to be dead and so Helga gingerly prodded it to ensure that it remained comatose and picked it up again between finger and thumb. Her face cleared. 'Ah! It is another *cache-sexe*.' She looked at the label. 'This one is called "Pussy".'

The commander's nose wrinkled in distaste. 'That's not very subtle.'

'I doubt if one can expect all that much subtlety in this sort of situation,' said Ivor.

'I suppose not.' Nobody wanted to buy a Pussy, nor a Cancan nor the rather bizarrely named Margery which was somewhat shocking since it had a hole where one would have thought its wearer would least have wanted one. Kelvin had had enough.

'Let's have something more exciting than all these hankies,' he said loudly. Everyone seemed to be in agreement, especially Helga, so she burrowed further down into the suitcase and came up with something more substantial. This was a nightie – even Kelvin recognized it as such – but it was not the sort of nightie that was donned by the average farmer's wife after she had slipped off her Wellington boots beside the bed and groped beneath the pillow. This one was a bright scarlet, foaming with lace of the same colour, with filmy net over the parts where the interesting bits were most likely to be. This was more like it and there was a gasp of appreciation from the voyeurs.

'Coo!' said Kelvin almost involuntarily. 'I wouldn't mind one of those.'

Helga looked at him critically and then back at the

garment. 'It would not really suit you, Kelvin dear. It would clash with your complexion.'

'I didn't mean I would want it for myself,' said Kelvin. 'I mean, it's for a lady, isn't it? Not for the likes of me.'

'I wouldn't be in too much of a hurry to give a thing like that to a lady, Kelvin,' said the commander. 'But if you didn't want it for yourself, who was it for? Nellie?'

Kelvin blushed deeply.

'Poor Kelvin,' said Helga sympathetically. 'Leave the poor man alone. It is not fair to mock him for being romantic.'

Kelvin blushed even deeper. 'I'm not romantic,' he protested.

Nobody but Helga was willing to argue with him. He was about as romantic as a haddock but she persuaded him to lash out nearly £10 on the nightie which gave all present considerable food for thought. Extracting money from Kelvin was more difficult than passing a camel through the eye of a needle, so his need of such a garment must have been very great.

Helga continued to burrow deep into the suitcase. Underneath the topsoil of filmy negligees and g-strings, she discovered a mysterious stratum of mock-leather boxes. With the triumphant air of one who has uncovered a nugget of gold in the gravel of a Yukon river bed, she freed one from the clinging embrace of rayon, satin and nylon that crackled and flashed as it reluctantly gave it up. It had two words emblazoned in gold on its lid. 'Triple orgasm,' Helga read out. There was a suck of indrawn breath from the audience. This was a bit more like it. It must contain one hell of a pair of knickers. Helga opened the box and held it up to the audience to show its contents nestling in a cocoon of red plastic. It contained four mysterious pink objects and an ordinary torch battery. There was a buzz of speculation as to what their purpose could be. The commander did his best to look knowing as he had his reputation as an international sexual sophisticate to maintain, but everyone else, including Helga who might have been expected to have experience of most aspects of love making, looked stumped. Helga picked up the leaflet which was enclosed and read it out to the respectful silence.

' "A titillating trio of vibrating egg for her, ring for him and porator for both." ' Her voice ended on a puzzled note and she looked doubtfully back at the contents of the box. 'I do not understand,' she said. 'What, for instance, is this word "porator"?' She looked round the room to a succession of blank gazes. 'Does anyone know?'

The squire, beneath his suitcase, spoke up. 'There's a dictionary behind Ivor in the bookshelf.' It was a big dictionary too. One that had provided food for bookworms as well as thought down the century since it had been published, but the word was not in it.

Kelvin was worried about something else. 'Why should her want a vibrating egg?'

The commander was at least up to that question. A group of youths edged closer to share in the enlightenment. 'It's for a woman to put inside herself and then it vibrates.'

Kelvin looked puzzled. 'What's the point of that? And why should it be shaped like an egg?'

'The vibration is stimulating,' explained the commander carefully, 'although I've no idea why they should make it egg-shaped.'

'It might do something for a hen, I suppose,' said Kelvin.

Helga was removing the items from their box for closer examination. The ring was obviously the ring. There was a rocket-shaped object which was presumably the porator, but what earthly use it might be to both parties was not clear, and the egg was fixed with a piece of string to an object that looked vaguely like a baby's dummy. She looked baffled. 'Does anyone want to buy these? They are only £12.50?' There was a stony silence. Helga sighed. 'Perhaps we ought to go and ask Lesley what these things are for.'

The box was replaced and Helga rummaged around for something else. This time she came upon a small bottle which she held up for all to see.

'And the next object is a bottle. A bottle,' murmured the commander.

Helga squinted at the label. ' "Booby drops?" ' she said, looking round with a wild surmise.

'Keep reading,' said the commander.

She kept reading in tones of increasing incredulity. ' "Booby drops – a drop rubbed into the nipples makes each one a sucker's paradise. Banana, chocolate or strawberry flavours." ' She paused. 'I think that is the most disgusting thing I have ever heard.'

Her audience was not enjoying it very much either. They had come round for a bit of a laugh, but were finding that there was precious little fun to be found. They practised on the craggy uplands of sexual experience and they were finding the steamier swamps of the lowlands rather unsettling and faintly obscene. Helga next came out with a bewildering array of vibrators. Her audience had heard of those and were rather shocked at their graphic modelling. When she came out with Maximum Big Man Cream – an eight-week course for a large, firm, full organ – there were some who felt that a gross of jars might be no bad thing, judging by the size of some of the vibrators, but Helga sampled it by tongue and said that it was nothing more than cold cream.

Then came an array of rubber goodies – each looking more like a medieval torture implement than the last. Somehow the humour of the situation was being lost. Helga succeeded in extracting some money from people when some of the joke items came up, but her disgust tended to show through. Sales were not helped when the commander pointed out that the surprise element of most of the jokes would be lost, since most potential recipients were already present in the room. The party closed with a short speech of thanks from Ivor who did not seem to be much happier than anyone else and the men of the village, rather chastened, trooped out of the room.

In the hall, the women were gathered for their party. There was a vain attempt by some of their spouses to pull them away from the forthcoming experience but they had little success as the wives had been stoking up in the pub beforehand and were in the right sort of mood to enjoy themselves. Most of the men went back to the pub to have a consoling drink.

'None of the stuff was really shocking,' Bill said, once he had fitted his haunches into the depression that he had made on his stool down the years and had a pint nestling cosily inside his hand. 'But a lot of it was rather silly.'

'I've a feeling that much of it might have been shocking if we could have only worked out what it was all supposed to be,' contributed Ivor. 'I did quite like Kelvin's nightie, all the same.'

'Did you buy anything?' asked Kelvin.

'Yes,' replied Ivor rather hesitantly.

'Well, let's have a look, then,' said Kelvin.

Sheepishly Ivor pulled out from his pocket a flimsy-looking rubber ball which was subjected to a silent scrutiny.

'It doesn't seem to be very much,' said Kelvin. 'What's it for?'

'It's not actually for anything,' replied Ivor.

'You must have spent good money on it, so what does it do?'

'You squeeze it,' said Ivor.

'Ah!' said the commander, 'you squeeze it. How fascinating! I didn't see Helga hold up that.'

'No, she didn't, actually.' Ivor made to put the object back in his pocket but his wrist was held by the commander.

'OK,' the commander said, 'so you squeeze it. Then what happens?'

'Nothing very much.'

'I know!' cried Kelvin. 'He's got one of those inflatable women there. I've heard about them, but I didn't see any up at the manor. I was rather looking forward to seeing some . . . so long as they were nice and big.'

'It's got to be a very small inflatable woman that Ivor's got there,' said the commander, looking down at the object in Ivor's hand. 'Squeeze it.' Ivor reluctantly did as he was bade and, before the wondering gaze of the barflies, the thing obligingly produced a 6-inch erection: pink, with a red tip. 'Good God!' said the commander. 'You went and spent your money on a thing like that?'

'I thought it was rather fun,' replied Ivor defensively. 'It only cost £2.50.'

The commander turned sadly back to the bar. 'Think of the drinks you could have bought me for £2.50.'

'But it was in aid of the church clock,' said Ivor.

The pub sat in morose silence for some time, reflecting on the events of the evening. 'I don't reckon that it was a good idea letting our women see some of that sort of stuff,' announced Kelvin.

'You could be right,' said Bill, 'but it's too late to worry about it now.' He glanced at his watch. 'It'll probably soon be over anyway.'

Kelvin was not to be mollified. 'I don't know what my Prudence will make of it at all,' he said with a shake of his head.'

'I think she'll be all right,' reassured Bill. In the silence of the bar, we sat and thought of Prudence. She was Kelvin's only child and was agreed to be a good worker. This was the highest accolade that could be bestowed by the older generation. The trouble was that times had changed and such a virtue was no longer appreciated as it had been in the old days. Modern youth liked pretty faces and sweet natures in their girlfriends and Prudence had neither, so much so that even her agricultural potential as sole heir to Kelvin's stretch of England had been insufficient to tempt any suitors when she had been in her prime a decade earlier. The fact that her husband would have had to put up with Kelvin as a father-in-law may well have had some bearing on her remaining in spinsterhood.

Suddenly the latch clicked and the pub door was flung open with a crash to admit Lindy with a couple of other women and a blast of cold air which tore into the rather pleasant fug that had built up. They were in high spirits. '£350!' exulted Lindy.

'What!' exclaimed Bill.

'Yes. You useless men could only raise £50 amongst you. It's just as well you had us to rely on.'

'How come you made so much?' asked Ivor.

'We brought in Lesley. She is rather nice, you know, and she explained what everything was while Helga modelled it.'

260

'Oh no,' groaned the commander. 'Why couldn't she have done that for us?'

'It was thanks to the squire's wife,' explained Lindy. 'She took one sip of the wine and brought out some of her own instead. We all got rather merry.' She confirmed this with a belch and a shriek of laughter.

'Who bought what?' asked Ivor with interest.

'Ah! That would be telling. I'm sure you'll find out in good time.' That did nothing to relieve the faint air of apprehension among the assembled males.

'Is my Prudence all right?' asked Kelvin.

'Prudence? She had a whale of a time. She bought two vibrators and a pot of bust-enlarging cream.'

'Prudence!' gasped Kelvin. 'She can't have done!'

'She damn well did. Prudence has a secret life, you can be sure of that, Kelvin.'

Prudence's was the only purchase that ever became public knowledge. There were certainly some very tired and some very thoughtful men around the village for the next week or two, but they were too secretive ever to compare notes.

The church clock had been ticking away for some weeks, just like it always had done, before the subject of the party came up in the pub again. It was triggered by Helga saying that she had had a letter from Lesley. Kelvin had smiled a slow smile. 'Do you remember those things that Prudence bought at he party?' Everybody did. 'The bust cream was useless. She wanted it to put on the udders of the cows and nothing happened at all.'

After a pause, Ivor delicately prompted him: 'And the vibrators?'

'Ah, now they were different. Very useful, they were.'

'In what way?' asked Ivor, surprised.

Kelvin looked at him craftily. 'I don't think I ought to tell you. It wasn't what you think. She's a sharp maid, my Prudence.'

'Oh, go on,' cajoled Bill, his curiosity now aroused. 'We'll keep it a secret.'

'You've got to promise, mind. And buy me a drink if you want to copy the idea.'

'We promise!' chorused those present.

'All right, then. Prudence wanted those vibrators for the two great water troughs in my yard, the ones that always freeze over. She's wired them to the mains through transformers and every time it looks like being frosty she puts them on and they jiggle the surface of the water and stop it freezing. They work a real treat.' Kelvin looked smugly round the awe-struck faces.

'She's no fool, your Prudence,' said Bill eventually.

'Cheap-rate electrics too,' said Kelvin. 'Giving you lot the idea is surely worth a pint, isn't it?'

'What'll you have, Kelvin?' asked Ivor.

Chapter Two

THERE IS fishing and fishing. The sport enjoyed in the north of Scotland, where you stand in your waders watching the salmon queue up to take your flies while some wise gillie drivels on in the background about water conditions and passes round flasks of whisky, is not common. The great majority of anglers in this country go in for coarse fishing where they chuck bits of bread and maggots into scummy water in the hope of catching fish with names like tench, carp, gudgeon, rudd, roach, chub or perch, all of which sound like the noises made by a rugby team regurgitating their beer and curry after an evening spent celebrating a win.

Fishing round the village, while not coarse, could scarcely be described as fine. The river and its many tributaries were certainly full of trout and even the odd salmon, but the snag was that there were so many trout that any fly foolish enough to land on the surface of the water would be torn fin from fin by a pack of starving fish. Anglers had to pull out a dozen or so before they could be sure that they would fill up an empty pilchard tin. It was game fishing, but a far cry from the sport to be found on the Dee, Don or Spey.

It was made even more suspect by the process of battery-rearing trout. After dairying and sheep rearing, one of the biggest industries in the area was fish farming. Great stewponds full of fat rainbows dotted the landscape, marked by the crowds of wheeling herons and cormorants above them like the vultures of Africa above a dead elephant, waiting for the farmer and his shotgun to go away so that they could drop down and feast themselves on this remarkable avian delicatessen.

Curiously, the greatest predator of the fish farms, apart from the epidemics which swept through them like bubonic plague through the ghettoes of medieval Europe, was the wren. It was so small that virtually no chicken wire could keep it out and it foraged round the hatchery trays, rearing four or five broods a year on the fry.

The fish could be harvested in a variety of ways. Almost everyone who cultivated fish let out rod space to the tourists. They were very useful since their presence kept the other predators at bay. If a pond were lined with villainously camouflaged fishermen from Brum and Leeds, all the other fish thieves made themselves scarce. They were not only useful as scarecrows, these fishermen, but they were profitable in themselves. They could be hit for a tenner a day for the privilege of standing by one of the ponds and charged per liveweight pound for everything they caught at a price comfortably above that which a fishmonger dared to ask.

The illusion of man-the-hunter was sometimes rather difficult to achieve on the stewponds. Game fishing, after all, is supposed to be a testing battle of wits between man and fish, and the denizens of these ponds were used to coming to the bank to beg for their food a couple of times a day all of their lives. It could be rather embarrassing when a newly arrived angler, creeping along behind bushes so that he would not frighten the fish on his way to a good position, was followed down the bank by hordes of voracious trout, most of which were poking their heads out of the water or blowing bubbles at the unfortunate man so that they could get his attention long enough to ensure that he would chuck his bait at them and not their neighbours. Fortunately, the type of fisherman who frequented the stewponds knew no better. He might be equipped with £1000's worth of rods, nets and tackle and throw flies constructed from entire macaws at the fish, but the fine art of river fishing was way beyond his ken. Something fat and simple that jumped on to his hook and made him feel like a cross between Captain Ahab and the last of the Mohicans was what he was about.

As well as the rivers and ponds, there were a couple of lakes

264

in the neighbourhood. Historically, water had never been in short supply for the local population. Enough came down from the sky and occasionally bulged out of the rivers, drowning large tracts of the landscape, to provide ample for the needs of the people and the farms round about. But the summer millions who came down were something new. Their thirsts had to be satisfied somehow and two reservoirs had been built. One lay about a dozen miles outside the village where a valley had been blocked by a mighty curtain of concrete, backing up the rather insignificant river that had flowed through it until it became a dozen square miles of water that reacted violently to the constant and unpredictable moorland winds by throwing up waves which broke strongly on the cow pastures of the shore. It was still a curious half-world between water and land. Lanes and barbed-wire fences marched solemnly into the water to disappear beneath the waves and emerge on the opposite bank half a mile away.

The water was still an alien presence, grafted on to an ancient landscape. There was no beach, just a lifeless fringe of mud where the waves had pounded at the turf and drowned the grass. Forests still poked above the water, providing perches for cormorants rather than wood pigeons and, in the height of the tourist summer, drowned farms complete with their modern concrete single-span buildings still rose, dripping, from the lake. Just as the land seemed uneasy with its new neighbour, the water itself looked unused to its surroundings. No islands emerged to give it substance. No reeds fringed it to give it definition. No houses clustered on its banks or poked their piers and jetties out into it. It looked no more natural than water in a bath.

This bleak prospect had some use. The fish farmers found a splendid new market as the water authority bought from them scores of thousands of trout a year for release into the lake: they had created one of the largest stewponds in the country and, with 15 miles of shoreline, the tourists and their tackle could sometimes appear to be shoulder to shoulder round its circumference. The farmers whose land had been swallowed up found these trout something of a comfort. It was very easy to leave nets or baited traps moored to one of their old hedgerows and keep their freezers well stocked. There was a warden whose job it was to prevent this sort of thing, but he was a refugee from a car factory in the Midlands who had no hope of curtailing the activities of these sly countrymen with a lifetime of experience to assist them, who had passed the halycon days of their youth poaching under the noses of gamekeepers.

After a year or two of its existence, the reservoir began to be developed. A yacht club and a windsurfing centre were built and the pancake of water became populated by capsized dinghies and windsurfers, shivering in their wetsuits as they scudded before the gales. The water authority built a jetty a tied a dozen rowing boats to it which were let out to the fishermen. They organized fishing festivals and competitions that attracted people from hundreds of miles away. Although the reservoir was some distance from the village, this was right out on an unpopulated part of the moor and so it was the nearest local conurbation, if a village of two or three hundred people could be described as such.

In spite of this new addition to the amenities of the area, nobody from the village used to visit it until the commander decided that this was something that ought to be rectified. His birthday was coming up, he went around telling people, and he thought it would be a good idea to organize a party for all his friends. There was some reservation about this. Although the commander had been in the village for five years and had managed to establish himself firmly as an amiable eccentric in the most respectable rural tradition, there still lingered memories of his arrival. For a month he had been insufferable. He had gone round in a pair of immaculate cavalry twills, trying to bully and cajole the villagers into running their lives and affairs in ways that he considered efficient. He had been broken, of course, by the enormous weight of tradition and apathy, but not before he had made himself thoroughly unpopular and it had taken a couple of years of suspicious observation to make sure that he really had become a harmless drunk before the villagers were prepared to take him

266

to their collective bosom. Now here he was trying to organize everyone again.

'I would like to take all my friends up to the reservoir on Saturday so that we can do some fishing and have a barbecue,' he announced in the pub.

Lindy looked over with interest. 'That sounds fun. Can I bring the family?'

'Certainly,' said the commander. 'How about you, Kelvin? Will you come and bring Prudence as well?'

'Why?' asked Kelvin. Since he never did anything without a selfish motive, he naturally assumed that everyone else was the same.

'Why? I thought she might enjoy it. Heaven knows, she doesn't appear to get much chance to enjoy herself.'

On the rare occasions when Prudence came to the village to collect her father's pension from the post office, she would hurry through with her eyes averted so as to avoid the agonies of trying to overcome her shyness to make conversation.

'No, I wasn't thinking about Prudence—'

'Surprise, surprise,' murmured Lindy.

'— I was wanting to know why *I* should come.'

The commander raised his eyebrows in surprise at the question. 'Because I'm inviting you, of course.'

'Will it cost me anything?' The rest of the pub was listening with close attention. Kelvin, with his rhino-like skin, was putting all the questions that the rest were too polite to state out loud and could only wonder about.

'Of course it won't cost you anything,' snapped the commander indignantly. 'It's going to be my birthday party.'

'Will I have to do any work?'

'Look,' said the commander in exasperation. 'All I'm doing is asking you to come to a party. I'm not asking you to interview me.'

'Hmm,' ruminated Kelvin, 'it doesn't sound much like a party to me. Up at the reservoir. Parties are things that you have at home in the evening. Not miles away and during the day.'

'Well, I'm sorry,' said the commander. 'I thought it might

be a bit different and could be fun. You don't have to come.'

'I didn't say that I wouldn't come,' said Kelvin hurriedly. 'I just wanted to know what it would be like.'

'Well,' said the commander, 'I thought that a couple of dozen or so of us could go up there and take out a few boats and do some fishing and then, if it's a nice day, we might go over to that little corner on the south side that was so difficult to get to before and have a barbecue.'

'What about drink, though? Would you be expecting guests to provide their own drink?'

'Certainly not,' said the commander hurriedly. While a few connoisseurs like Dennis would inevitably turn up with their whisky – in Dennis's case, safely screwed into a flash in his pocket – the main bulk of them would bring brews made from potato peelings, rhubarb, and the less poisonous of the native wild flowers. This would lead to a ghastly unbalanced affair, during the first half-hour of which guests consumed as much as possible of the drinkable foreign wines and all the spirits in the hope that they would be inebriated enough not to mind when the approaching drought forced them to move on to the drink that they had brought themselves. On one memorable occasion, the vicar, who had just come back from a duty-free excursion to Boulogne, had provided so much free good wine that the party he gave had to finish abruptly after an hour as most of the guests were too helplessly drunk to participate any further.

'No?' said Kelvin, his eyes gleaming. 'You mean you will provide all the drink yourself?'

'Yes,' said the commander.

There was a sharp intake of breath from Jimmy and the ever-present cigarette that dangled from his withered lips was almost sucked back into his mouth. He broke into a fit of coughing before noisily spitting on to his shoe. Helga had stopped him from spitting on the pub floor but was unable to stop him spitting. 'You'll pay for proper drink for everybody?' he asked incredulously. 'That'll cost a terrible amount of money.'

'I've just had a win on a horse,' said the commander.

268

'Balls!' said Bill. 'You don't know one end of a horse from another, and anyway you never bet.'

The commander looked pained. 'If you must know, my old nanny, who's now in her eighties, send me £200 for my birthday.'

'And you took it?' said Dennis disapprovingly. He was a farmer of sorts, but enough of a gentleman farmer to have been reared by a nanny as well. 'You'd deprive someone like that of £200? The poor old thing is probably senile and didn't know what she was doing.'

'You think I ought to send it back?' asked the commander. 'I must say that when I first opened the letter and saw the cheque, I did wonder if she might have made a mistake. But it didn't bounce.'

'Course you shouldn't send it back,' said Bill, worried at the prospect of losing an afternoon's free boozing. 'That would make the poor old thing very unhappy.'

'Well, she was an employee of my parents. And now she has only a tiny pension to keep her going.'

'All the more reason why you should not give the money back,' said Bill reassuringly. 'She'd be too proud to take it, quite apart from thinking that the reason you didn't want it was that it came from her and that her money wasn't good enough for you.'

'That's a very good point,' said the commander thoughtfully. 'That's the reason I didn't return the cheque straight away.'

Dennis snorted in derision.

'You don't have to come to the party if your conscience is bothering you,' said Bill, rounding on him.

Dennis held up his hands placatingly. 'I didn't say anything.'

'I didn't say you did say anything,' replied Bill. 'But I didn't say you didn't.'

'Shut up, you two,' said Lindy. 'Commander, I think your idea for a party is quite splendid.'

'I'll feel just like a bloody tourist,' muttered Kelvin.

On the appointed day, there were a full two dozen villagers mustered in the car park by the reservoir. In a curious reversal of the usual roles, the tourists looked like countrymen and vice versa. All the Midlands fishermen had their heads bowed down under the weight of the fishing flies in their hats, while the browns of their thick tweeds and shiny anoraks made them look like mobile cowpats as they trudged past, festooned with rods, tackle pouches and landing nets, towards their patch of reservoir bank. They gazed with contempt upon the squire's long khaki shorts and the primitive fishing implements that were carried by the locals.

The commander had reserved three boats for the day. The idea was that we should row across the water to the picnic spot and then allow those who wished to fish to fish and those who wished to lie around in the sunshine and get drunk to do just that. There was a knot of disgruntled anglers on the jetty, the end of which was a prime fishing position, and they saw no reason why they should have to stop their frantic casting to permit access to the craft. Kelvin, playing the special constable, cleared the fishermen away, however, and we loaded the boats with plastic containers of cider and the little

mummified bodies of pheasants provided from the commander's larder, still exuding their freezer chill through their plastic cocoons. It was one of those lovely summer days without a breath of wind to stir the hot air with the water mercury-still except where rings from the rising trout spread out across the surface.

The commander took charge of the flotilla, giving land lubbers a quick course in oarsmanship, passing out instructions forbidding passengers to stand up and checking who might be the swimmers in case anyone fell overboard. With the line of fishermen on either side of the jetty looking contemptuously on, the party set off. The commander was admiral of the fleet with the booze safely stacked in the bilges of his vessel. Lindy was in charge of the food and number two boat which was populated with the most sensible and cautious members of the party – almost all women – who had chosen to sail with the captain in whom they might have the greatest degree of confidence.

The heavy mob was under the charge of Dennis. Dennis had been appointed to the job when he had told the commander that he had once seriously thought of taking up rowing when he had been at school, but his boat was only a few yards off the jetty when it became apparent that he had not thought about it too deeply. The boats could carry eight people apiece and Ivor and Keith had been appointed to take first stint at the oars.

'Where's the rudder?' demanded Dennis, looking around the stern where he had seated himself.

'I don't think there is one,' replied Ivor, who had a sheen of sweat on his face after half a dozen strokes.

'Of course there must be a rudder. All boats have rudders, otherwise you can't steer,' retorted Dennis scornfully.

'They don't seem to have one on the other boats', said Keith.

Dennis's boat was supposed to be following in their wake, but it was already 20 yards behind and beginning to slew to port, enabling Keith to have an unimpeded view.

'I feel sick,' said Jimmy.

'Don't be so bloody silly. You can't possibly feel sick. You'd be as likely to feel sick in your bath,' said Kelvin. 'Mind you, perhaps you do feel sick in the bath, which is why you never have one.'

Jimmy was undoubtedly turning green. 'I think I'm going to be sick,' he insisted.

'Don't worry. You won't be,' reassured Ivor, whose rowing position just in front of Jimmy made him extremely vulnerable.

'How do you know?' asked Jimmy.

'Well, we're on a lake and you don't get lake-sick. There's no such thing. You can only get sea-sick, so you're bound to be all right because we're not at sea.'

Jimmy brightened immediately. 'I didn't think of that. So I can't be feeling sick at all, can I?'

'That's right,' said Ivor.

'The man's a bloody moron,' muttered Kelvin. The boat had now travelled in an almost complete circle and was heading back towards the jetty. 'I think you'd better do something, Dennis,' continued Kelvin, 'otherwise we're going to have a crash.'

Dennis had been peering down into the water over the back of the boat, trying to find the rudder, and he raised his head to look at the jetty and the interested bunch of fishermen who had been following our progress. 'Quite right. Ship oars!'

Keith gnawed his moustache worriedly as he caught a crab. 'What does that mean?'

'It means stop rowing,' said Ivor.

Keith dug his oar into the water and the boat lurched away from the jetty round the axis of his oar.

'That's it!' exclaimed Dennis. 'I remember now. You steer by pulling harder on one oar or the other.'

'You could always take another oar and use that as the rudder.'

'That's an excellent idea! Is there a spare oar lying around?'

We all looked round the boat and under the seats but there was no spare oar.

'Ask one of the fishermen to chuck one over from another of the boats.' They were close enough to the jetty to allow the fishermen to hear and one of them picked up an oar and hurled it, torpedo-like, towards the boat. It caught it amidships with a thud and Dennis gracefully retrieved it. We got underway again. Dennis stood up in the stern, dug his oar in and began to sing *O Sole Mio*. Kelvin and Malcolm joined the other two on the oars and the boat began to scud across the surface while Jimmy, his sickness now forgotten, dug out a fishing line and trailed it over the side with a large piece of cottonwool on the end concealing a hook. It was really very pleasant in the sunshine.

Then, halfway across, Kelvin staged a successful mutiny. As Dennis was taking a long swig from his hip flask, the boat veered violently off course, nearly tipping him overboard. It coincided with Jimmy hooking a whale. There was chaos. Keith and his fellow rower caught a crab which tumbled them off their seats while Jimmy, screeching with excitement, hauled powerfully on his line. As Dennis flailed his arms for balance, he lost his oar over the side and everyone began to shout at each other. Fortunately, Jimmy's whale turned out to be Dennis's oar, but by the time that we had sorted ourselves out, Kelvin had firmly pushed the protesting Dennis down to the other end of the boat. The crew looked at Kelvin with some apprehension.

'Right, you lot. Who remembers seeing the film *Ben Hur*?' There were murmurs of denial from everyone. 'You know. It was that one with the guy with a big chest and a chariot race.' This time there were a few nods of recognition. 'Right. Well, in *Ben Hur* they had a dirty great rowing boat with lots of people on the oars and there was a black man with a drum at the back who was banging away and they all had to row in time. So I'm going to get Jimmy to bang on the bottom of the boat and you lot on the oars have to keep in time with him.'

Jimmy struck up a nervous hand: 'What'll I bang with, Kelvin?'

'Anything you like, so long as it makes a noise. Now the rest of you sit completely still so that you don't rock the boat and we might get somewhere.'

'How about a newspaper?' asked Jimmy.

Kelvin looked at him in irritation. 'You can't make a decent bang with a newspaper. Use your initiative, man. They had a drum in the film. Find something like a drumstick.'

'Has anybody got a drumstick?' asked Jimmy, plaintively.

'Use your knuckles,' said Kelvin. 'Now, everybody ready? Right Jimmy, bang!'

The oars dipped as Jimmy banged. They waited for the next bang but it did not come. They looked round to see Jimmy rocking on his seat, moaning as blood trickled down his fist.

'For Christ's sake!' yelled Kelvin, Fletcher Christianing away. 'Bang, you daft old goat!'

'I've hurt my hand, Kelvin,' moaned Jimmy.

'Well, use the other one, then.'

'But if I hurt that, I won't be able to open any bottles.'

'Why don't you just say "bang"?' suggested Ivor.

'That's a good idea,' agreed Kelvin.

So, with Jimmy saying 'bang', we slowly tacked our way across to the other side of the reservoir.

By the time our boat finally grounded on the muddy shore, the commander and the others were already making camp. The favoured spot was the unflooded half of a small clearing that had been in the middle of a rather scrubby coniferous plantation, the water side of which had been felled before it had been flooded. The brambles now grew thick throughout and, although the commander had had sufficient sense to requisition a couple of scythes, there was a rather rebellious group standing on the shore while they waited for space to be created in which they could set up the fire and lay out the chairs. It looked wise to avoid the area for a half-hour or so.

'We'll go and get some fish,' said Kelvin, after surveying the scene. 'We'll see you back in an hour.'

'Would you like a few pigeons?' Dave asked the harassed commander.

'Yes, anything would be useful. Before you go fishing, Kelvin, it would be a help if you could get the fire lit.'

Dave was a country boyo through and through. Many of the young round about were interested only in sex, motor bikes and space-invader machines and hankered for the low city life, but Dave had fully imbibed the old-fashioned lore of his ancestors and found his pleasures in watching deer and poaching pheasants and fish. He had once come out of a local fish farm with 60lb of prime trout in response to a dare. This particular farm had been established by a foreigner from up country somewhere. He was utterly paranoid about poaching, but there had not been enough of a challenge to interest the locals until he had thrown down the gauntlet by surrounding his ponds with chain-link fencing and releasing a couple of homicidal Alsatians to roam around inside looking for intruders whom they could tear to pieces. Dave had picked up the gauntlet. He borrowed a bitch that was on heat, cut a hole in the fence to push her through and, while the guard dogs had the time of their frustrated lives, he leisurely filled a couple of fertilizer sacks with fish. Percy, our local policeman, had then advised the farmer to remove all his poaching deterrent and Dave, and others like him, had not bothered to go back.

Watching Dave catching pigeons for the barbecue without a gun was likely to be educational, so I tagged along as he went off into the larches behind the clearing.

'How many pigeons do you think the commander would like?' he asked.

'I should think half a dozen would be ample,' I said. 'After all, he's got all those pheasants and Kelvin and his chums might catch a few fish.'

'I suppose so. Let's make it eight just to be on the safe side.'

'You seem to find pigeon catching very easy,' I remarked as we came to a stop beneath a tree.

'Yeah. I did this wood a few weeks ago. I think I've got twenty-odd pigeons here. There are a couple in this tree.'

'How do you know?'

'I marked it,' he said, pointing to a small cross that had been cut into the bark at ground level. He looked measuringly at the tree and swiftly clambered up into the foliage. There was the sound of flapping above and he re-appeared a minute or two later, carrying a couple of large plump pigeons. It might have been understandable if they had been unfledged young, but these were fully adult. It was like a conjuring trick.

'How on earth did you manage that?' I asked, astounded.

Dave was always delightfully willing to share the secrets of his skills with anyone who seemed interested, although usually they were none the wiser after his explanation.

'What you do,' explained Dave, 'is go round the wood in early summer and look for pigeon nests. When you find one, you just climb up to it and tie a bit of fishing line to the leg of one of the squabs. Then you thread it through the bottom of the nest and tie it to a branch underneath. It's simple really. The bird can't fly away and the parents will keep feeding it until it leaves the nest, which it can't do. So it just gets fatter and fatter until you feel like a pigeon for supper and you go and pick it up.'

'Coo!' I said, overwhelmed by the simple efficiency of the scheme.

'The only thing that's a bit difficult is making sure that you give the bird the right amount of slack. Too much and it will topple out of the nest and hang upside down until it dies, and too little and it won't get enough exercise. I've found that it helps if it can flap its wings properly. It builds up the breast and it doesn't get tough. Hold these, will you?'

I took the two pigeons while Dave shinned up another tree and came down with another one. 'You can't help feeling a bit sorry for the birds,' he continued, after he had neatly wrung the neck of his latest acquisition. 'But I don't suppose it's much worse than being a chicken in a battery cage. At least they have a view to look at.'

'That's true.' I had lived in the country long enough to realize that a tender conscience is a city luxury which has to be discarded once one gets beyond the 30 mph limits.

'It keeps the population of pigeons down, you know.'

'How's that?'

'There's no point in shooting up the nests because the adults just go and start another clutch. But this way they keep on feeding their young in the nests and so don't lay again.'

'I see.' By this time we had eight pigeons and were moving

back through the wood towards the clearing. 'How many birds have you got altogether?'

'I didn't do very many this year. I've got about seventy left.'

'That's not bad.'

'I've had a couple of hundred in other years.'

It was a beautiful scheme. If Dave had reared poultry himself, he would have had to provide them with housing and

feed and they would probably die of disease if they were given a chance. This way, he only needed a few lengths of fishing line and the mother birds fed his stock for nothing and looked after them for him if he went away.

We returned to the clearing. The barbecue was set in an old disc of a harrow that was propped up on some chicken wire over the fire. Kelvin, in charge of the fire, had obviously had some difficulty in getting it lit as there was an old tyre blazing merrily away underneath, wreathing black smoke over the chilled lumps of pheasant above and then on into the sky, filling the surrounding air with the stench of rubber. There was a furious altercation going on between himself and Lindy, in charge of the cooking.

'How the hell am I supposed to cook on top of that?' she demanded.

'If you're afraid of the heat, I can put things on for you.'

'Don't be stupid. It's not the heat I'm worried about, it's the smoke. It's going to make everything taste of burning rubber.'

'Just like your home cooking!' Kelvin retired to the shade of a tree with one of Dennis's personal bottles of whisky, muttering and rubbing his skull, off which one of the frozen pheasants had bounced.

The commander looked over in irritation. 'Instead of doing nothing, Kelvin, it would be a big help if you would take your boat out and catch some fish. I thought you said that's what you were going to do.'

Because the majority of the Establishment of the village had come out for the day, the unprecedented step of buying a fishing permit had been taken. Ivor had decided that it would have been too embarrassing for so many respectable citizens to risk being caught without the necessary authorization.

Kelvin got to his feet and wandered to the shore. 'Who's nicked the boat?' he demanded.

'What are you talking about?' asked the commander, who was concentrating on removing the harrow disc from the fire without burning his fingers so that he could give it a scrub and to get rid of the rubber deposits.

'The boat we came over in. It's not here.'

The commander came the few yards down to the shore, looking up and down the beach. 'It must have drifted off.'

'It can't have done. I tied it up.'

'What did you fasten her to?'

'There was a bit of wood in the water. I tied it to that.'

The commander gave Kelvin a withering look. 'You still have the power to surprise me, Kelvin. Your boat and its anchor are both floating down the lake, over there.' He indicated the craft, which was 100 yards away and about 10 yards out from the shore. 'I suggest you go and retrieve it.'

'I don't see why it has to be me who goes,' objected Kelvin.

'I can think of several reasons why it should be you,' replied the commander. 'For a start, you're the only person who's doing nothing round here. Secondly, it's you who needs the boat to go fishing. And thirdly, you were the pillock who tied the boat to a floating branch!'

'You could go and I could clean that there disc,' said Kelvin.

'The final point is that the boat will eventually drift to the dam wall and over the slipway.'

'Tough,' said Kelvin, laconically.

'It will make it a long walk to get home,' said the commander mildly. 'And, of course, the boat was booked out in your name, so you will be liable for any damage that is caused to it. I must get back to my cooking.' The commander knew when he had delivered a clincher, and returned to his scrubbing without a further glance at Kelvin. The latter stared at the commander's unresponsive back in baffled frustration, uttered a few swear words and plodded off down the shoreline. The commander left his task and called the rest of us over: 'Watch Kelvin. It might be fun.'

We watched Kelvin. It was fun. He reached the point opposite the slowly drifting boat and sat down to take off his shoes and socks. He took a long stick and paddled out into the water. He got about a quarter of the way before the water was lapping at his trousers so he retired to the shore and looked thoughtfully out at the boat. He threw a few stones out beyond it which had no discernible effect except to make the boat rock slightly and cause an ugly splintering sound when he misjudged his throw and one of them landed inside.

He then briefly disappeared into the trees that lined the shore and re-emerged without his trousers and waded out towards it. This time, he reached it. The water was just wetting his knickers when he made a last desperate lunge as a puff of breeze caught the boat and pulled it a few inches beyond his reach. There was a sigh of pleasure from the watchers as he measured his length in the water, then emerged, spluttering, to grab hold of the gunwales and drag it towards the shore. He retrieved his trousers, put them in the boat and paddled back along the edge of the lake, dragging the boat behind him.

'Bit wet, are you, Kelvin?' asked Jimmy.

Kelvin was not at his sunniest. 'Yes, I'm bloody wet. You knew this would happen, didn't you?' he said to the commander accusingly.

'How on earth could I know that you were going to fall over?' replied the commander. 'I have to admit that I did hope you would, and indeed I suspected you might, but I couldn't have known it.'

'You're laughing at me,' said Kelvin.

'Yes, but not out loud,' replied the commander. 'Why don't you go and do some fishing now?'

Kelvin did not feel like doing some fishing. He had a deep aversion to immersing his body in water and felt the need to appropriate one of Dennis's whisky bottles and go to sit under a nearby tree in order to recuperate. He took off his baggy grey underpants and strung them over a bush to dry, draping his nether regions in a towel. As the afternoon wore on, he became extremely drunk. This did not matter too much as everyone else became rather inebriated too, but Kelvin is one of those unfortunate people who become increasingly belligerent the more alcohol he consumes. He tried to pick a fight with Bill over a half-cooked pigeon and, when that failed, fell out with Mary Mowbray on the best way to break in a horse. Since Mary knew her horses better than her own children and Kelvin hadn't been near one since he bought a tractor for the first time and stopped using shires, it was felt to be a little unreasonable.

It was a damn good party and it was past 8pm and the light was beginning to fade when we decided that it was time to wend our way homeward. The midges were out and, after a few bites of the over-the-limit blood that was all that there was available, they were kamikaze-ing into the fire and drowning themselves in beer glasses as they hiccuped their way from target to target. Even the trout that had been skulking in the cool depths during the heat of the day were now splashing about on the surface like dolphins, and the excited voices of the professional fishermen that carried for hundreds of yards across the still surface of the water showed that some were letting themselves in for large bills on their return to the control hut with its set of scales, across which tons of slippery, pellet-fed corpses were weighed each year.

While the rest of us cleared up the debris, Kelvin, who had been wandering round like a Roman senator in his towel toga, retired behind a bush to replace his pants and clothes. He was incapable of doing anything low-key which meant that Mandy, Keith's formidable wife, was called over to pass him his pants from their make-shift line as he had forgotten to take them with him.

'Did you know your pants hummed, Kelvin?' she asked as she picked them up.

'What do you mean "hum"? They were clean this morning and they've just got soaking wet.'

'No, I didn't mean that they were dirty. They are humming, literally.'

The clearer-uppers paused in their work to lock into this bizarre conversation.

'Pants don't hum. They can't hum. Not even Kelvin's,' remarked the commander.

'Well, these do. Come and listen.'

While Kelvin spluttered in indignation from behind his bush, we dropped everything else and went over to form an interested semi-circle round Mandy, ready to be serenaded by Kelvin's knickers.

'I can't hear anything,' said the commander.

Mandy lifted up the pants. 'They've stopped now.' She gave them a little shake. They hummed. 'There. Hear that!'

There was a murmur of appreciation from the pants' audience. Most were simply prepared to appreciate the entertainment but the commander was possessed of a spirit of scientific curiosity.

'How extraordinary! Let's have a look.' Kelvin had sat down behind his bush and was muttering and grumbling to himself that his protests about this violation of his garments had been ignored but, as the commander took his pants from Mandy's unprotesting hand and peered cautiously inside, he was moved to complain out loud again.

'Gimme back my clothes!'

'Shut up, Kelvin,' said the commander casually. 'You know, I can't understand this. There's absolutely nothing there. They seem to be perfectly ordinary underpants.' The pants gave lie to this statement by suddenly increasing the volume of their output before shutting up again. The commander turned them over in his hand. 'The only thing that can possibly explain it is that it is the elastic that is making the noise. It must be expanding or contracting and rubbing against the material. It must be something to do with getting wet.'

'Can I have my pants back now?' asked Kelvin plaintively.

The commander reluctantly handed them over the bush to him and returned to the task of clearing up. There was a sudden scream from behind Kelvin's bush and, as people turned to look, the pants sailed over the top, planed across towards them and landed on the ground.

'How very odd,' remarked the commander as Kelvin hopped about, gathering the towel round his loins, and proceeded to dance on top of the garment before sitting down beside them. 'Are you feeling all right?' he called.

'That was dreadful,' gasped the betowelled one.

'What was dreadful?'

'I was just pulling them up my legs when they started to hum again. I looked down and there was a dirty great hornet crawling out from that double bit of material which fits round the crotch.'

'Oh, I see! It must have hidden there when you put them on the bush to dry. It was obviously disturbed when Mandy picked them up. That makes sense. But there was no reason to dance on the poor thing. Hornets are placid insects and are becoming quite rare.'

Kelvin turned wild-eyed to the commander. 'Bugger the bloody hornet. Think what would have happened if it hadn't crawled out when it did.'

We thought and shuddered.

A hole was dug to bury the remains of the hornet, which Kelvin carefully extricated from his knickers, and the rest of the picnic debris, after which the boats were loaded up. Kelvin was well beyond the responsibilities of command and he was unceremoniously dumped in the stern of one of the craft as we tacked our way back across the breadth of the lake with the oarsmen spending as much time disentangling themselves from the bottom of the vessels after they had missed their strokes and fallen off the benches as actually propelling the boats forward. The evening was made hideous with drunken renderings of *Widecombe Fair*. At one point there was a loud splash and there was some discussion of the size of fish that could have made it. Jimmy had just decided on a shark when Ivor noticed something amiss.

'Where's Kelvin?' he asked. 'I thought he was in the front of our boat.'

The rowers looked round.

'Well, he's certainly not here. He must have gone in the other boat.'

'He must have done, I suppose. But it's funny, because I thought he came with us,' said Dennis.

'I thought so too,' said Jimmy. 'I remember trying to persuade him not to sit on my hand when he first got on board.'

'I'd better make sure he's in the other boat,' said Ivor. He cupped his hand to his mouth. 'Ahoy! Commander, me old sea dog!' The commander's boat was about 30 yards away and he raised a drunken arm in acknowledgement. 'Have you got Kelvin aboard?' There was a flurry of activity in the other vessel as they lifted cushions, peered into baskets and looked under the rowers' benches.

'No!' yelled back the commander. 'You've got him. I saw him trying to give Jimmy a kiss as he got on board.'

'I told you I thought I remembered him,' said Jimmy. 'But he sure as hell ain't here now. Poor Kelvin! He must have drownded.'

There was a moment's silence for Kelvin as we thought of the trout picking at his eyeballs.

'I wonder if Prudence will sell the farm,' mused Bill. 'I might be interested in making her a fair offer for it.'

'I should think she'd want to continue farming it herself,' said Jimmy. 'She's been doing all the work by herself for long enough.'

'That splash!' said Ivor. 'It can't have been a shark at all. It could have been Kelvin falling overboard. Let's go back and take a look.'

'There's no point in that,' replied Bill. 'He'd have gone to the bottom ages ago.'

'No, he wouldn't. It was only a couple of minutes ago.

284

Anyway, if they find they have lost a man overboard on one of the Atlantic liners, they about-face and go steaming back for hours to try and find him. And sometimes they do.'

'That's different,' said Bill. 'This isn't an Atlantic liner.'

'That's true,' acknowledged Ivor, 'but I think we ought to make some sort of an attempt to find him. If we pull him out, we've got Lindy on the other boat. She could probably resurrect him with mouth-to-mouth. So I suggest all the rowers turn round and start going back the way we came.'

With considerable trouble, the oarsmen about faced, rocking the boat dangerously as they did so, and went back the way they had come, trying to recall where they had zigged and where they had zagged. Bill was stationed at the stern, which were now the bows, to keep his eye on the water to watch for any Kelvin-like jetsam floating about.

'I think it would be a bit unfair to expect Lindy to do mouth-to-mouth on Kelvin,' said Bill, picking up the conversation where it had been left off.

'Why?' asked Jimmy. 'Nurses are trained for that sort of thing.'

'I know that,' replied Bill scornfully, 'but can you imagine doing it to Kelvin? Would *you* do it? Think of his false teeth, for a start. If he ever takes them out, I reckon he marinates them in horse piss. I can't think how else he'd manage to get them so yellow.'

'Aye,' said Jimmy, 'I can see what you mean.'

'Keep your eyes on the water, Bill,' said Ivor from the bows of the boat.

'Keep your hair on,' came back the reply. 'I am keeping my eyes on the water. . . . Speaking of hair, have you ever heard of scraggy grey water weed?'

'No,' said Jimmy.

'Half a mo, then.'

While the boat slewed to a halt as the oarsmen dug in their blades, Bill rolled up his sleeves and plunged his arm into the water by the side of the boat. He groped around for a few seconds, his eyes closed in concentration and then brought up his dripping hand. Clutched in it was some hair, attached to the end of which was Kelvin's face. As the face broke surface, the eyes opened with a manic glint in their depths. A fist erupted from the water to the left of the face and narrowly missed Bill's nose. 'Bloody hell!' exclaimed Bill, and smartly let go his grip. The head sank beneath the water again. 'Back off a bit,' he said, and the rowers dug in their oars and pulled the boat a bit further away. The head came up again.

'You bunch of bastards!' it yelled. 'Chuck me overboard and then leave me to drown. I'll teach you!' Kelvin started to thresh the water towards the boat.

Jimmy wailed in fear: 'Be careful! Don't upset the ship. I can't swim.'

'Back off a bit more,' said Bill. The oarsmen needed no encouragement.

'Hit him with an oar,' suggested Jimmy. 'He's in a drunken frenzy. It might quiet him down a bit.'

'I'll get you!' yelled Kelvin. 'I heard that. Trying to hit me with an oar!' He was building up quite a foaming bow wave in front of him.

'Be careful, Kelvin,' said Bill. 'Don't forget you can't swim.'

Kelvin stopped. A stricken look crossed his face. 'Christ! That's right, I can't swim!' He threw up his arms and disappeared beneath the water.

'Thank God for that,' said Jimmy, who was crouching in the bottom of the boat for safety. 'Let's go home.'

'We can't just leave him to drown,' objected Ivor as Kelvin's imploring eyes re-appeared above the surface and he opened his mouth. His words were lost to posterity as the water flowed in and he sank again.

'I don't see why not,' said Bill. 'It's not murder or anything. I'm sure just not rescuing somebody is not against the law.'

'Polluting the reservoir with dead bodies. That'll be against the law. And it's us that has to drink the water from it, remember.'

Kelvin didn't drown, of course. The commander found a rope at the bottom of his boat and threw it across to him, along with an inflatable bed on which Mary Mowbray had sunned herself during the afternoon. Kelvin was towed back, beached near the harbour and left to find his own way home once Lindy had established that alcohol was at the root of his problem rather than straightforward senile dementia. He turned up in the pub the following day and his behaviour of the previous afternoon was never mentioned by anyone again – except when he became drunk, abusive or irritating, which was no more than a couple of times a week.

Chapter Three

THOSE WHO live and work in a rural environment find it difficult to show much enthusiasm when a nature-loving townsman bounds into the pub bearing a wilting weed, even if it is worth innumerable points in his *I-Spy* book. To the discoverer it may be a rare and wondrous thing. But the farmer to whom he is talking has probably been trying to eradicate it from his cornfield for ten years and fails to be infected by the nature buff's excitement. In fact, most environmentalists tend to be as popular in the village pub as a Mormon missionary at a cardinal's conclave.

The resident nature bores in our locality were the communards who tried to practise self-sufficiency, with considerable help from the state, in a decaying country mansion with a few acres attached on the edge of the parish. They believed that anything invented in the past thirty years was a bad thing and that their hens should be allowed to roam free so that they were all eaten by foxes, and that machines and herbicides were anathema which meant that their scraggy crops were soon overwhelmed by nettles and fat-hen.

Only one communard ever made the difficult transition from being one of the weirdos whose doings were a source of amusement and entertainment, to becoming one of the real people in the rest of the parish. Dick had been one of the original members of the commune when it had been a post-Dylan colony of gently balding hippies, still hoping for the triumph of Peace and Love in the cruel world of the eighties. But gradually his contemporaries had fallen by the wayside. One started to sell life insurance; another was picked up in the

Channel sharing a yacht with a ton or two of cannabis with the inevitable consequences; while yet a further couple returned to Streatham, whence he travelled up to the West End every day where he worked as manager of an exclusive fashion salon.

Dick soldiered on, but his cracking point came when the new members of the commune decided to adopt ancestor worship as its established religion. Dick had been a devotee of many obscure gurus in his time but he came from three generations of Wolverhampton hairdressers and, while he was able to respect them, he found it impossible to make the quantum leap across into worshipping them. So Dick decided to leave the commune and rejoin the human race, albeit the rather obscure rootlet of it that flourished in the parish.

He found himself an empty farm cottage to rent and set himself up as a jobbing gardener to the old ex-colonial drunks who liked to look over their roses and delphiniums during warm afternoons when the ice was tinkling in their gin-and-tonics. He came to realize that the world of nature was not the Elysian Fields with man as the asp that spoils it, but a balance of terror with each fox needing 2000 vole-equivalents a year to keep alive. Life in the real countryside with people who had to earn their living from it did not destroy his faith in nature but it allowed him to observe it through the rather jaundiced eyes of the rest of the community.

Dick's knowledge of the wildlife of the area was phenomenal. There were one or two hiccups before he was able to change his beliefs, built up during his years in the commune. For instance, he put himself through considerable angst with some bracken. The farmer across whose hillside it had spread wished to spray it to allow grass to grow in its place to feed his sheep. That was just not on for a recently retired graduate of alternative environmentalism. Dick offered to cut it down instead, without charge (at this stage he still had the state's support), to show his dedication to the cause. The farmer was delighted to let him try. With sickle in hand, Dick worked his way steadily along the side of the hill in the summer sunshine and, by the time he had finished, the bracken was already a foot or more high where he had first cut. So he resigned and watched phlegmatically as the helicopter, hired by the farmer, clattered over and killed the lot in one spray-filled minute.

Dick, a small nut-brown man in his thirties, was always being stopped to be asked questions by tourists wanting to hear an authentic local accent. They would back away, appalled, from the sound of the Black Country that issued forth. It was an understandable mistake because Dick really looked the part of the traditional countryman. He always wore old brown moleskin trousers and brown boots with a spiral of First World War surplus puttees round them and his calves in wet weather. He scorned gumboots as nasty modern inventions. He wore a striped cotton shirt without a collar and braces holding up his trousers. He did not believe in feeling the cold and his only concession to winter was a sleeveless khaki pullover that he donned between November and March.

Dick was a natural person to turn to when the pub suffered its infestation. It started quietly enough. The hostelry was going through one of its more popular phases. The normal cycle of this estabishment was that it should be bought for about £70,000, be tarted up a bit and passed on a year later for £85,000, then get sold again a year or two later for something over £100,000, at which point the buyer would find that the custom attracted would not pay for his bank loans and he would become alcoholic and bankrupt in swift succession, after which the price would slump and the cycle would begin again. It had been recently bought by Helga who was about as different from the usual run of landlords as it was possible to get. She brought an unprecedented touch of glamour to the community. Nobody knew very much about her background or the source of her money and nobody wanted to inquire too closely. In a village where everyone knew everything about everyone else, this was extremely unusual. But Helga seemed to be a creature of exotic fantasy. People were afraid that she might disappear or turn to dust if they found out some mundane truth in her background. We wanted to believe in her like children believe in Tinkerbell.

Helga had the ability to make the most arrogant of the old chauvinists who were the patriarchs of the community roll over like puppies to have their bellies scratched whenever she lifted her finger, and there was great competition between them for her favours. They washed up glasses, manhandled barrels of beer and even chucked out drunks at her slightest whim.

On the day when the infestation started, most of the regulars were present. They were deep in conversation about the price of nitrogen fertilizers while a couple of the more powerful ladies of the parish, Lindy and Mary Mowbray, were discussing the local doctor's seat on a horse. It was a peaceful tourist-free time of the year, just before Easter when the hordes descended.

The locals always drank in the public bar, the lounge bar being exclusively reserved for tourists as a ghetto where they could do all the things they liked, such as playing loud music on the juke box, having sing-songs and wearing shorts and tight scarlet T-shirts so that they could show off their tans and bellies to each other. Normally this bar was closed in winter but Mandy and Keith, a couple of summer swallows that had decided to settle in the area, still retained their urban desire for exotic drinks like rum and passion fruit which could only be supplied from the multi-coloured shelves of the lounge. Keith was present that afternoon, telling the bar about his amazing new plastic honeysuckle that he had just tacked all over the front of his cottage. It had a lot going for it. It bloomed all the year round, did not attract insects and had a small receptacle at the bottom which contained an aerosol can of scent with which he sprayed it whenever he wished to sit out of doors. It even came with extensions so that it could appear to grow from year to year.

Keith wanted a whisky and blackcurrant juice, so Helga had to come out from behind the bar and go through into the lounge, switching on the lights as she went. She had been gone only a couple of minutes when she screamed.

'EEEE! Help! Help!'

There was a delay of a second or two before beer glasses

went flying as there was a concerted rush to reach the lounge first. The commander just led the field and was able to enfold Helga to his manly bosom, his sweater redolent of the horse manure that he had been spreading in order to promote the growth of his mushrooms. With his arms locking her so tightly that Helga appeared in some risk of suffocation, and the rest of the regulars spread in a protective phalanx round her, they looked for the reason for her screams. All appeared quite peaceful. There was a notable absence of rapists and there were no vampires lurking by the silent pinball machine.

'What's wrong?' asked Bill.

Helga pointed a trembling forefinger towards the regiments of fruit-juice bottles. 'There's a spider in there.'

'A spider?' Bill's voice dripped with scornful contempt before he recollected who had done the screaming. 'Oh, a spider! How dreadful for you!'

The commander clutched Helga closer. 'Don't worry, I'll sort it out for you.'

'No, I will,' said Bill. There was a run on the juice bottles as he, Kelvin and Keith all tried to outdo each other in a bit of dragon slaying. The commander was seriously tempted to join them but clearly decided that any kudos he gained from spider slaughter would have to be set against the surrender of his advantage in having current possession of Helga's person.

The others rapidly emptied the shelf of bottles and revealed the spider sitting rather self-consciously outside a small tangled web in the corner.

Keith gave a yell of triumph. 'There it is! Quick! Squash it!' He was hopping from foot to foot in his excitement.

Bill and Kelvin peered at the creature. As native-born countrymen, they always had a careful look before they leapt. 'You squash it, Keith,' said Bill.

'Me?' said Keith uncertainly, taking a closer look at the spider. 'I don't see why I should have to squash it. I found it, so somebody else can kill it. I don't like spiders anyway. I've never seen a spider like that. It's not like the ones I see in the bath. It might be poisonous or something.'

It was a rather unusual-looking spider, quite large as

spiders go, with a shiny black body about the size of a pea.

'Don't be silly,' said the commander confidently. 'You don't get poisonous spiders in this country. Someone get rid of the bloody thing.'

'Oh yes, please,' pleaded Helga. 'Bill, you're so brave. You do it.'

Bill shot her a thoughtful look before leaning forward to extend a horny thumb towards the spider. The creature allowed the thumb to come within about 6 inches of its person before it raised itself on half a dozen or so of its rearward legs and waved the remainder threateningly. Bill hurriedly drew back. 'Bloody hell! I don't fancy that. The bugger looks as though it's going to attack me.'

'Get out of the way, Bill,' ordered Kelvin. 'I'll sort it out.' He picked up a bottle of tomato juice and brought it sharply down on top of the spider. The spider exploded, along with

293

the bottle, and the green gunge that spread out from its abdomen was swamped by a tidal wave of red. As the rest of them looked on in disgust at the mess, Helga unwound herself from the commander and gave Kelvin a smacking kiss. 'You were wonderful,' she said.

'I hope you're going to clear that up,' said the commander. 'It looks like the aftermath of a traffic accident.'

'Sorry about that,' replied Kelvin, blushing to the roots of his straggly grey hair as a result of the kiss. 'I didn't mean the bottle to break.'

'You should have used soda water. Then it wouldn't have mattered if it had broken,' said Bill. 'I hope you're going to pay for the tomato juice.' Both he and the commander were irritated that it had been Kelvin who had been the recipient of the kiss.

'I wouldn't dream of asking you,' said Helga. 'You were so brave.'

'Look!' exclaimed the commander, triumphantly wrapping his arms round the rather startled Helga once more. 'There's another of them by that bottle of whisky.'

This time the hunters had enough sense to grab a bar towel apiece as they moved into the fray, but much of the incentive had gone from the chase as the commander deemed it wise to remove Helga from the scene of danger so that she could pour him a barley wine in the bar next door.

After ten minutes of bangs, crashes and exclamations, the dishevelled butchers re-joined us. Kelvin and Bill had each accounted for another spider – Bill with his bare hand, which put him above his companion in the courageous spider-killing league – but they had to admit that several more had given them the slip under the bar counter and down a hole made by the pipes that led from the beer pumps into the cellar.

Helga was a full blown arachniphobe. She insisted that they seal up the lounge bar with strips of blanket and newspaper tacked round the doors, and she was adamant that nobody was going to be allowed down into the cellars until the spider infestation was over.

The following lunchtime, the expert arrived. Dick had been

sent for in order to give his considered verdict on the beasts and the best method of eradication. He would have been willing to come merely to satisfy his curiosity as to the species of spider, but he had also been promised a fee of a couple of pints of cloudy real ale, complete with bits and pieces in suspension.

Most of the regulars turned out to watch Dick at work. He parked his bicycle outside the pub and ducked in through the stone-lintelled door. The door provided one of the strongest indications of the hostelry's claim to be approaching a thousand years old. The building was thatched, but so were dozens of others. Its beams had ancient adze marks sculpted along their length, but they could be scarcely older than Tudor. However, the door was not only well under 6 feet high to give all the necessary access to the midgets who went before us, but the stone lintel had a perceptible hollow in it where centuries of skulls had made contact with shattering effect. Winnie, the professional village eccentric who had been burnt as a witch during one of her previous incarnations, used to clutch at her heart whenever she came through the door, complaining that the weight of people's pain down the centuries had created an atmospheric blackspot that was bound to affect the sensitive.

Dick was not sympathetic to the problem at hand. He made sure that he had his first pint in front of him before he allowed his opinion of the pusillanimity of the regulars to show. 'A plague of spiders! It's ridiculous. Spiders are lovely things to have around. They catch all the flies and their webs sift the dust out of the air. You should think yourself lucky to have them, rather than be frightened by them.'

'That's all very well to say, but Helga doesn't like them and I must say they're pretty nasty spiders,' said Bill.

'Don't be daft,' replied Dick. 'How can they possibly be nasty?'

'One of them threatened Bill,' said Keith.

'How?' demanded Dick.

'Well, it sort of waved its legs at him.'

'That doesn't sound like much of a threat. The Bluebell

Girls go in for leg waving and people don't rush to have them exterminated.' He took a long draught of his pint. 'I suppose I'd better go and have a look at them.'

The commander and Keith carefully removed the strips of carpet from the door to the lounge bar which held the spiders at bay. With Helga keeping well in the background, they went through into the darkened room which reeked powerfully and characteristically of stale beer and tobacco. Keith went over to the window and pulled back the curtains to allow the sun to flood in to the musty lounge. They looked about. There appeared to be a conspicuous lack of spiders.

'I don't seen any spiders,' said Dick. 'What did they look like?'

In the glare of full sun, it was difficult to imagine what all the fuss had been about. Bill, who had traded on his hero status as much as possible over the past twenty-four hours, looked a bit shame-faced. 'They were very unusual-looking spiders. Sort of black and shiny. Very ferocious-looking.'

'Black and shiny?' asked Dick.

'And green,' added Keith.

'They weren't green,' said Kelvin scornfully.

'Their insides were. Don't you remember?'

'I suppose they were. But the colour of their guts is no bloody use as a description.'

'I don't see why not.'

'Of course it isn't. If I was telling someone what you looked like, I'd say you were a bit short and had a scraggy black moustache. I wouldn't say that you had 30 feet of guts inside your belly and that they were purple or green or whatever colour they might be.'

'Is this one of them?' asked Ivor, who had not been part of the great killing the previous day. He was indicating a large plate hanging on the wall which portrayed, in relief, a bunch of jolly smock-clad rustics quaffing ale.

They all went over to see. 'That's one of the little buggers all right,' said Bill, moving in with his horny thumb to flatten it.

Dick caught hold of his arm. 'Don't be in such a hurry.

296

Let's have a look at it first.' He had his look. 'How absolutely fascinating.'

'What's so fascinating about it? It's just a spider,' said Bill.

'Do you know what kind of spider it is?' asked Dick.

'Not really. It's not a money spider. I know what they look like, or I did before I had to get reading glasses, but it's you that's supposed to be the spider expert.'

'I've never seen one quite like this before.' He called out through the door of the lounge. 'Helga, have you been importing anything from America recently?'

Helga stuck a wary head round the door. 'What sort of thing?' she asked suspiciously.

'I don't know. Whatever one does import from America. Baseballs. Indian bonnets. Cadillacs. That sort of thing.'

'I can't think of anything. Why?'

'Because I think that's an American spider.'

'Don't be silly,' said Bill, scornfully. 'An American spider indeed! It took a package holiday into Heathrow, I suppose, and then came down here with a caravan.'

'It could have come over in something else. Odd insects are always turning up inside cargoes of bananas and things like that.'

'You don't see many ships unloading bananas outside this pub.'

'Well, I don't know how it got here, but I think it's a black widow. And they can be deadly.'

The commander was the first to react. He flashed between Dick and Kelvin and had Helga in his arms before she had time to gather her breath for the scream that set the tankards tinkling behind the bar and made the spider scurry for the protection of the web which it had built between the kneecaps of two of the ale quaffers.

Nobody else was hanging about either. The commander had to move Helga sharply aside to prevent her being trampled to death as Bill and Kelvin thundered through the door and out of the lounge. Keith chose a different method. He gave a squeak of dismay and scurried beneath one of the tables in the lounge.

The commander, trained to retain his control during emergencies, was first to gather his wits enough to speak. 'For heaven's sake, Dick, what are you talking about? Poisonous spiders, indeed!'

Dick strolled carefully through into the public bar. 'I may be wrong. But I've never seen a spider like that before and I saw a programme on BBC2 about black widows and it looks just like they did. Black and shiny. About the size of a pea. I think there's supposed to be a red hour-glass shape on their bellies as well. But I'm not sure.' He looked back over his shoulder. 'By the way, Keith, if you're trying to escape from spiders under there, you ought to know that they do prefer to hide in dark places.'

'What do you mean?' asked Keith, suspiciously poking his nose out from under the table.

'I mean that you're more likely to find a spider lurking under the table than you would be almost anywhere else in the room.'

Keith erupted from beneath the table like a Scottish lock forward who had just found the ball at his feet in the middle of the scrum under the English posts at Twickenham. In his enthusiasm he carried the table with him, but it was brushed off his shoulders by the frame of the door and fell violently to the ground, breaking into several pieces.

'You stupid berk!' said Ivor. 'Look what you've gone and done.'

'Sorry,' said Keith, moving towards the door of the pub. 'If you'll excuse me, I think I'll go and warn Mandy.'

'Warn her about what?'

'That there are poisonous spiders in the neighbourhood,' he said over his shoulder as he hurried through the front door.

'At least one good thing may come out of this,' commented Kelvin, 'if it drives that blasted Mandy out of the village.'

Mandy was one of the only people in the community who was scathingly rude to Kelvin to his face. The rest of us contented ourselves with being scathingly rude about him behind his back.

'About these spiders,' said Dick, and the rest of those present snapped back to attention. 'I am not absolutely certain that they are what I think they are, but I don't think we ought to take any risks, just in case.'

'Quite right, darling,' said Helga fervently.

Dick acknowledged her agreement with a courteous nod. 'I think that we ought to call in the council who are best equipped to deal with this sort of thing.'

'They may be quite good at cockroaches, but I doubt if they would have had very much experience of black widow spiders,' remarked the commander.

'You're quite right,' agreed Dick, 'but at least they're geared up to handle this sort of problem and they ought to have the experts on hand who could at least give us a certain identification. I mean, we may be panicking for nothing.'

'But that means bringing in Bert,' said Kelvin.

'That's right.'

'What's the point of that?'

'At least pests are his job.'

Bert was the council rat catcher and he had made the parish his own. It had taken him nearly a decade to get all the farmers and land owners round about to allow him on to their premises on search-and-destroy missions without any warning needing to be given. He hounded the local rats with gun, gas and poison. We were the testing ground where he tried out all the esoteric methods of slaughter that his rat-hating brain could dream up before unleashing them in the rest of the county. Kelvin had entered his barn a few months earlier and had touched a trip wire that had set off a flash camera in his face. It had nearly given him a heart attack and had not warmed him to Bert who had a theory that a species of monster rat lived in the chaos of Kelvin's farm which should be photographed before he committed genocide.

Dick was given the pub telephone to summon skilled aid while the others, under the direction of the commander and Helga, once more re-sealed the lounge bar before departing about their various businesses.

'I'd like to be put through to the pest officer, please,' Dick said, after explaining who he was and where he was calling from.

'I'm afraid he's out. Can I take a message?'

'Yes, I'd be grateful if he could come out as soon as possible.'

'What'y'got then? Rats? Killer bees?'

'No, spiders.'

'Spiders! Is that all? You can't have Bert out for spiders. Spiders aren't pests. All you have to do is put a glass over the top of them and slip a bit of cardboard underneath and then empty them out of doors.'

'They're not ordinary spiders. I've never seen any quite like them before. I think they're poisonous.'

'Poisonous! Coo! They're not those great big hairy ones like you get in the horror movies?'

300

'No. They're the sneaky little black jobs.'

'Like the ones you get in your bath? They're not poisonous. Anyway, you don't get poisonous spiders down here. Bert's never been called out to poisonous spiders|before.'

'Well, he has been now.'

'Oh, all right. I'll pass the message on to him. Spiders, indeed!'

The evening's drinking session was a subdued affair. Kelvin was there, wearing gumboots with his trousers tucked inside to make sure that no spiders should crawl up his trouser leg and bite him. There was even a sprinkling of irregulars: people like Malcolm Jarrett who taught in an education college 20 miles away.

Word of the black widows had got out and fear stalked the deserted streets to an extent not seen since a rather nosy tourist, who had gone round most of the village shops, had been suspected of being a VAT inspector. There was a bit of desultory talk about the falling price of calves and the harvest prospects and a little speculation on whether Michael Green and Mary Webber might be having an affair and whether or not their respective spouses knew about it. Kelvin, self-styled village godfather, brought up the subject on everyone's mind. He had obviously been doing some thinking.

'What are we going to do about these here bugs? That's what I'd like to know.'

'I think we can safely leave it to the ratman, tomorrow, Kelvin,' replied the commander.

'I don't think that's good enough. All our loved ones are at risk. Quite apart from ourselves. Think what would happen if one of those beasts came in here and started|biting.'

'The dog it was that died,' murmured Malcolm Jarrett.

'What's that?' asked Kelvin sharply.

'Just a line from Goldsmith,' replied Malcolm.

Kelvin had a profound contempt for anything he could not taste, touch, see or spend and education came high on his list of life's unnecessary fripperies, so he ignored the interruption and continued, 'I think we ought to take precautions.'

'What sort of precautions?' asked the commander.

301

'This is an emergency, so I think it's only right that we should activate the emergency committee.'

'That's a dreadful idea,' said Dennis hurriedly. Dennis described himself as a gentleman farmer, which meant that he did as little work as possible, keeping only a few bullocks, and drank an enormous quantity of whisky, for the·supply of which he relied on his wife's substantial private income.

'Why?' asked Kelvin. 'It's an emergency, isn't it?'

'Yes, but it's not the sort of emergency that the emergency committee was trained to handle.'

This was a very sensitive area. The committee had originally been set up to protect the village in the event of nuclear attack. It had become apparent during a series of exercises, when annoying little men from County Hall had tried to tell the doughty volunteers what to do, that there was no possible way to protect the village in the event of nuclear attack and that the emergency volunteer system was just an excuse for a lot of grown men to play boy scouts. The committee had resigned *en masse* and had allowed Kelvin, a Cromwell guiltless of his country's blood if ever there was one, to take the whole thing over and ask some of his more Neanderthal cronies to join him. Dennis had suggested that they should change the name of the organization to the Klan and that Kelvin should be called the Grand Dragon, which had quite appealed to him, but headquarters had refused to agree to it.

Kelvin's strategy in the event of war was to impound all the foodstuff in the community and lock it up in the church hall while he stood guard with a shotgun to shoot anyone who tried to take anything. This had led to a secret meeting of the parish council and the appointment of Gerald Mowbray, a farmer of stout thews and a direct if simple mind, to shoot Kelvin as soon as the Russians dropped the bomb to prevent him doing any damage.

'The emergency volunteers are trained for anything,' said Kelvin. He looked round the pub for some of his lieutenants, but there were none present.

'You would need to get the approval of the parish council

302

before the volunteers could be activated,' said Ivor.

'Not necessarily. In the event of breakdown of the normal democratic process, I am empowered to take over.' Kelvin's desire to wield power was greater than that of any politician and he saw potential emergencies everywhere.

'I'm sure that's true,' agreed the commander, 'but I don't think that the democratic process is in danger of breaking down just at the moment. After all, there is quite a difference between a large quantity of megatons being dropped on our heads and a few spiders wandering about in the lounge bar.'

'It's just a matter of degree,' argued Kelvin. 'Nobody could deny that poisonous insects could constitute an emergency.'

'That's a big word, Kelvin,' remarked Lindy. 'And spiders aren't insects.'

'Constitute? It means—'

'Isn't that a spider on your leg, Kelvin?' interrupted Ivor.

It wasn't. It was only a speck of cow dung. But it was enough to drive all thoughts of power from Kelvin's skull and send him hurriedly out of the pub as soon as he had finished his pint and established that there was nobody else who looked willing to buy him another.

The jungle drums in the village muttered and grumbled all night and a great killing took place. By morning the streets were littered with the corpses of a great multitude of spiders, slaughtered in a great pogrom by the fear-driven populace. The Great Spirit above took note of the event and sullen clouds built up above the village and the sky wept.

Bert came splashing into the village in his minivan at about noon the following day and went straight to the pub where he was met by Dick and the rest of the curious. Helga had left the premises at closing time to move in with a neighbour and was not going to return until the all-clear had been given.

Bert was a familiar figure in the parish owing to the frequency of his ratting excursions. He was about forty and astonishingly good-looking with dark Latin-lover features which attracted most of the damsels on the farms into darkened hay barns to hold his poison for him. He only scored with real country girls who had sufficiently strong and experienced stomachs to cope with the miasma of sewers that impregnated his person and his van, thanks to the many subterranean expeditions he undertook in pursuit of his normal quarry.

Bert entered the pub, the dull thud of his skull on the lintel bringing a certain phlegmatic satisfaction to those present. He spent a couple of minutes on his knees, moaning and rubbing his head before he recovered sufficiently to come over to the bar. He looked at Dick in surprise. 'You're not involved in this business, are you?'

'Yes.'

'Poisonous spiders? I was sure that it must have been some daft old biddy who'd found one in her bath. You're not serious are you?'

'Go and have a look.'

'Look where?' he asked, peering round the bar.

'Oh, sorry. They're in the lounge. It's all sealed up to stop them spreading.'

'I see. Well, they're not going to be going anywhere very far. I might as well have a drink first, now I'm here.' He looked hopefully round the others present, but nobody volunteered to put their hands in their pockets. 'Kelvin?'

'I don't mind if I do,' said Kelvin. 'I'll have a pint.'

Bert looked outraged. 'I'm hoping *you're* going to buy *me* a pint, not the other way round. I've got rid of enough of your rats for you.'

'Sorry,' said Kelvin. 'I don't believe in buying drinks for other people. I'm a Methodist.'

'I heard you use cigarette papers instead of lavatory paper, Kelvin,' said Dick.

There were snorts of laughter from the others while Kelvin's face assumed a glazed look as he tried to work that out. 'What do you mean by that?'

' "Mean" is right,' replied Bert.

'Why don't you look at the spiders first and I'll buy you a drink afterwards,' offered Dick.

Bert looked a bit sulky, but he had no alternative unless he was prepared to buy his own beer. Dick carefully removed the towels and wads of newspaper that had been re-stuffed into the cracks round the lounge door and Bert entered and looked round, observed from the doorway by the locals clutching their pints protectively to their bosoms.

There was one of the spiders sitting in the corner of the bar. It must have been a busy night as there was a thick tangled web to its rear. Bert looked at it ruminatively.

'Now there's a thing,' he said, still thoughtfully rubbing his skull. 'It's a funny-looking little beggar, isn't it?' he continued, turning to Dick who had been the only person brave enough to enter with him into the bar. 'Have you seen one like him before?'

'Only on television.'

'Yes. I heard that it was supposed to be a black widow, but I thought it was just blethers. I mean, I'm always being called out to do something about funny-looking ladybirds because people think they're Colorado beetles. But, you know, I'm not so sure about this.' Bert went over to the work surface and peered down at the spider. 'I ain't seen anything quite like this before. Nasty-looking little bugger, isn't it?' He poked at it with his forefinger and the spider obligingly went through its leg-waving act for him. 'That's called a threat display,' said Bert knowledgeably. 'Aren't many spiders that put on a threat display like that.'

'Why don't you get on with it?' said the commander. Bert was leaning forward and gently blowing at the spider which was working itself into a bit of a temper, judging by the rapid series of press-ups which was its reaction to the breeze. Bert paused and looked round. 'What do you mean, "get on with it"?'

The commander was a bit taken aback. 'You are the exterminator aren't you?'

'That's right,' agreed Bert. The spider took the opportunity of the sudden drop in wind speed to scuttle into its web for shelter.

'Well, exterminate then. Spray the room or whatever, and kill everything in it,' said the commander.

Bert sucked in his breath. 'Can't do that, I'm afraid.'

'Why the hell not? That's what we got you out here for and it is your job, isn't it?'

'That's my job, all right. But I can't go around killing things that are unknown. It could be anything, this beast. A species new to science, in which case it would certainly be protected by law; or, if it's been imported from somewhere else, we have to find the source and make sure that no more come in, particularly if it's a poisonous spider. And I have to admit that it looks a bit suspicious. Anyway, I think I've seen enough here. Dick, I'm about ready for that drink, now.'

Bert returned to the public bar and watched while Dick poured him a pint. The voyeurs clustered round, waiting to find out what he was going to do next. He knocked back a large draught of beer and smacked his lips appreciatively. 'Pity about the weather, isn't it?' he said conversationally.

'Yes. But what are you going to do about the spiders?' asked the commander.

'The spiders? I suppose I ought to get on the telephone and find someone who might know something about them.'

The commander leant over the bar, pulled up the telephone and plumped it down in front of Bert. 'There you are!'

'Let me finish my beer first.'

'Make the phone call, then finish your beer. The sooner these damn insects are out of here, the sooner we can all get back to normal.'

'There ain't no need to worry about a few spiders.'

'Kelvin's gone around telling the village that we've got a plague of black widows. And everyone's in a bit of a flap.'

'Oh. If Kelvin's going round stirring things up, then it does make a bit of a difference.'

'Damn right it does.'

Bert picked up the telephone while the rest of us re-sealed the lounge door.

'It's all sorted out,' he said a few minutes later. 'The Ministry of Agriculture are sending out a couple of entomologists. I told them that I agreed with Dick and that they were probably black widows and they said that they'd be out within a couple of hours. Who's going to buy me another pint?'

The emergency, together with the absence of Helga, provided an opportunity to ignore the normal licensing hours. Percy, our local policeman, looked in and seized the chance to extract drinks from everyone in return for not enforcing the law. The Dunkirk spirit was abroad in the pub although everyone made sure that they stayed down the far end of the bar away from the door to the lounge. A beer barrel ran dry while they waited and Bert, with Dick covering his back with an aerosol can of insecticide, bravely went down into the cellar to change it.

By the time the experts arrived, the gathering had developed into a really good crisis party. The man in charge was pointed towards the spider still sitting peacefully on the

plateful of rustics and he whipped out a little net and neatly popped the creature inside a jar. He was not messing about. He came back into the bar. 'Telephone!' he snapped. It was provided. He dialled through to headquarters. 'It's a black widow all right. I've got a sample and I suggest that we send it up to the Natural History Museum for a definite confirmation. Meanwhile we'll get on with clearing the area.'

It was quite a hairy business. A team descended on the village and pumped noxious chemicals throughout the pub and down into the sewers and made careful inspections of most of the houses round about. More spiders were found in the house immediately next door and the extermination teams moved in, spraying and gassing as they went, in spite of the protests of the elderly occupant who claimed she had never been afraid of spiders in her life and saw no reason to start being afraid of this one. Matters were beginning to look quite

nasty and there was some talk of putting the village under a movement restriction order to prevent the spiders taking over the country.

Then word came back from London. They were not black widows. They were not even poisonous. They belonged, in fact, to a rather obscure species of cave spider that was normally to be found in Cornwall. Although they were not actually protected by law, added the letter, they were extremely interesting and completely harmless and the fact that they had extended their range so far from their original habitat was ecologically fascinating and an arachnicologist would be coming down to investigate the following week. Even Helga agreed that it was a pity they were all dead.

Chapter Four

THE PRECISION of the social hierarchy of the countryside broke down with the Second World War. Before then, everyone knew exactly where they stood, to whom they could be rude and to whom they must tug their forelocks. The squire was at the top of the social tree. Then followed the vicars, rollicking hunting Philistines throughout the nineteenth century, who had left their work to be done by the pale and trembling curates, at least one of whom, legend has it, was defrocked after being found *in flagrante* with a nanny goat. They represented the gentry, and beneath them was the doctor, then the larger farmers, the tradesmen who did not dirty their hands, the tradesmen who did and, finally, the peasants.

That was then. Now the squire was just a farmer like any other. The vicarage had been bought by an antique dealer and the minister of the few souls that were still interested in being ministered to whizzed through the village on Sunday morning in his Fiesta, tossing wafers and communion wine out of the window as he hurried to cover the five churches in five parishes that were his responsibility. The doctor had his practice based a dozen miles away; the skilled tradesmen were down to a few scrub mechanics, the myriad of different shopkeepers were reduced to a handful and only the farmers still soldiered on in the same sort of numbers that had been there before. Even the pub had lost the eight rivals which had formerly competed to satisfy the bucolic thirsts of the village's ancestors.

We had gained one professional – the vet. Our vet was a brave man. The United Kingdom consists of a network of jealously guarded territories. It is not only the birds and animals who fight to maintain their own exclusive patches over which they hunt to feed their young; people do it as well. The solicitors, estate agents and builders mixed happily with each other, sharing the same territory just as robins, blackbirds and tits can share the same garden. However, should another of the same species or profession intrude, then they bristled, fluffed out their feathers at each other and did their best to drive out their rivals, determined to protect their own interests and food supply against those of their opposing colleagues.

Our village and its surrounding farms were part of the veterinary territory of a group practice of half a dozen partners who covered a large chunk of the country. The vets were computerized and hammered round the countryside between calls in a fleet of fast saloons. The senior partner even managed to pass off a light aeroplane as a legitimate business expense, although the only time he had tried to land it in the parish it had caused a herd of cows to stampede into the river. The local livestock was used to the thunderous jets of the RAF skimming down the river, sometimes dropping their under-

carriages in an alarming game of chicken to see if they could touch the water without coming to grief. But when the senior partner decided to visit an urgent calving in response to this buzzer going off in his pocket during an afternoon's spin and came over the trees sounding like a demented chainsaw to land in a field next to the river, the cows rebelled. Their life was supposed to consist of peaceful dreams amid the buttercups while they made milk. A foot- or wheel-borne vet was bad enough. He always seemed either to stick his arm up into their innards in a gross violation of their bodily integrity or else stab them with needles and force a variety of noisome liquids into them. When the bastard turned up like a fixed-wing angel of mercy, it was definitely time to go and jump in the river.

Bernard Bessington-Omerod was a most unusual vet. He first turned up in the area attached to the established practice as a student in search of experience. He was an exception to their normal rule of only taking on females for the practical part of their course. It pleased all the partners to speed round the countryside with pretty young girls by their sides, and it pleased the local garages as their cars were often hitting hedgerows in mid-grope. Bernard was male, if a little precious, and extremely well-bred, having gone to a good school and being rumoured to have titled ancestors. He would have fitted in beautifully to the budgie-and-borzoi belt in SW3 where the rich dowagers would have adored his vague, little-boy charm, but out in the sharp end of the business we were used to a stouter breed of vet: those who could wrestle a yearling bullock into submission whilst holding a syringe in their teeth, or could plunge an arm to shoulder-depth up the arse-hole of a bull to stimulate it to ejaculation, ignoring the terrible tourniquet effect of the mightly bovine sphincter. (Cattle have to have powerful sphincters as efficient as those of the whale: the latter has to keep *out* liquid under pressure, while the average cow has to contain a seething cauldron of substances resembling the aftermath of a vindaloo curry consumed at a backstreet stall in Bombay.)

Bernard was a breath of fresh air in the neighbourhood. As

312

a student, he was not expected to be much of a vet. Few farmers require much of the vet anyway. They know their stock and the ailments to which they are subject as well as any professional, but they need the vet to get access to bottles of antibiotics to pump into them. Therefore Bernard's incompetence did not really matter and he did brighten up normally dull days. He was asked to examine rams that were having difficulty in lambing, milk bulls and inject bunches of young pigs that had been carefully greased beforehand. He could have had a laugh every hour of the day or else beaten the brains out of his tormentors. But he neither laughed nor wept; he just plodded on, accepting the practical jokes with a rather worried expression on his appropriately chinless face and falling, delightfully, into every trap that was set for him. When he went back to university, the farmers were all rather sad to see him go.

Then a brigadier's widow died in her house near the pub. Within a month its cellar containing 3000 empty gin bottles had been cleared and the house bought by Bernard, who stuck a brass plate on the door announcing that B. Bessington-Omerod, MRCVS, was open for business. It was courage beyond the call of duty to trespass so openly on the territory of such a powerful bunch of professionals as the local vets and they soon began a campaign to drive him out. They went round their customers casting aspersions on his competence. He would have been asked to join them, they said, after he had graduated had he not been so piss useless. The farmers found many of the vets that they sent round piss useless already, so that charge carried little weight. They even put pressure on the drug dealers. Anyone who supplied Bernard would lose their business. That did not work very well either, since there were plenty of shady characters who could supply anything from the boot of their car from streptomycin to sten guns and so he did not go short of the necessary equipment.

Bernard found that a substantial proportion of the local farmers were prepared to give him a try. It was nothing to do with the charm of his baby-blue eyes, but a matter of hard finance. The other vets with their virtual monopoly were ruthless in collecting unpaid bills, sending out their Sierra-driving commandoes on the first day of the month to dun any of their clients who were late in paying. This was deeply resented. Ordinary businessmen do not like paying bills and farmers are extraordinarily tight-fisted businessmen, particularly where the vet is concerned. Vet bills were traditionally paid, partially paid at least, once a year after harvest or after the sale of the year's crop of lambs. If prices were poor, the vet was lucky if they settled at all.

Bernard either understood this system or was too well-bred or chicken-hearted to go and ask farmers for money. It was not long before the group vets discovered that they had lost their really bad payers and the unprofitable tail end of their list and so they began to warm to the existence of Bernard. Our parish contained a high proportion of poor payers – farmers who saw no reason why they should pay a vet's bill unless the patient fully recovered – but Frank Mattock, who considered himself to be a bit of an agricultural whizz kid, was mortified when the aviating senior partner suggested that he might consider switching his allegiance to Bernard. The fact that he had owed £1000 for eighteen months was no reason to remove him from their list.

Bernard had private means, otherwise he would have starved, but even so he was awarded the almost unique privilege of being allowed tick in the pub which was right next door to the house he had bought. Helga's tender heart had ached for him when he staggered in at opening time, hair awry, chinless chin trembling with emotion and eyes filled with horror at the dreadful veterinary experiences he had had to undergo in the agricultural underworld that was now his sphere of operation. He fell in at the deep end on his first day, being summoned to visit a difficult calving by Gilbert Clattermole.

Gilbert Clattermole was one of the old school. In our part of the country, that meant a very old school indeed. He was a true peasant, about forty-five, going bald, illiterate, dirty, social-security numberless and unknown to the Inland

Revenue. It was believed that a tax inspector had unearthed the fact of his existence about a decade earlier and had gone to visit him. At the end of the afternoon, the inspector had left, but not before he had torn up Gilbert's newly created file to ensure that no other member of the Revenue should ever have to meet him again. One of the lesser difficulties that the inspector would have encountered was that Gilbert believed in neither bank accounts nor record keeping. In fact, it was doubtful if more than a couple of hundred pounds went through his hands in any given year, since almost all his dealings with outsiders were done by barter.

Gilbert called up Bernard on his newly installed telephone. (He had it for two months until British Telecom took it away again when they realized that Gilbert was under the impression that telephone calls were free once the device was in place.) 'It's Bessie,' he had announced. 'She's calving and I can't sweeten it out.' There were many strange ways of persuading cows to yield up their calves. Frank's favourite method was to affix a rope from the calf to his tractor tow bar and pull. That was the juggernaut school of calving which could result in bits of the calf or the cow becoming detached from the main body with consequent deleterious effects. Gilbert believed in the efficacy of placing a heaped teaspoon of demerara or white sugar by the cow's vulva. This was supposed to be irresistibly attractive to the calf, which would fight to get clear of its mother, while the type of sugar determined its sex: white for a bull and brown for a heifer.

It had been very exciting for Bernard: his first client/patient on his first day. He had donned his green surgeon's outfit, just like they wore in hospitals in American TV serials, which was unused and pristine, as were his instruments and his bottles of antibiotics – a virgin vet without a splatter of dung anywhere on his person. It was unfortunate that Gilbert was the first customer. It should have been someone like Frank Mattock where he would have visited his patient in the immaculate holding pen off the milking parlour which Frank scoured down with a pressure hose twice a day after each milking and then sprayed with disinfectant. If one did not mind the risk of carbolic poisoning, one could eat one's dinner off the pen floor. Certainly no bacteria could survive.

It wasn't like that at Gilbert's, however. Had he ever given the matter any thought, he would have been of the opinion that if God had meant stock to be free of germs, he would have blessed them with a disinfectant gland to add measured doses to their dung. Gilbert's farmyard had not been mucked out for years. Due to the scarcity of livestock on his farm – he didn't want money, so there was no reason to give himself work – the couple of feet of dung that raised the ground level of his yard above that of the surrounding countryside, had decayed to a pleasantly friable and sweet-smelling humus, but the number of tiny little beasties that lived and copulated there would have led to a prosecution being taken out against him by the RSPCA, had an Inspector ever stuck a dung fork into it.

Bernard drove down the lane, biting his lip in anxiety as the bottom of his new car crunched on the ground while it dipped and swayed its way through the potholes that were home for some storm-tossed tadpoles. He parked in front of the house and Gilbert came out to greet him, pulling his braces up over his shoulders as he passed through the door. The curtains of the Clattermole living room were always drawn, for he and his wife began watching television at 11am after he had done his morning chores and stayed in front of it until the national anthem came on around midnight. His wife was almost unknown locally since she rarely visited the village. On the rare occasions that she came out of their house, she looked like some nervous cave animal as her eyes blinked suspiciously at the hard bright world that existed beyond the safe insulation of her living-room curtains.

Gilbert led the way across his farmyard towards a dark stable doorway, framed by nettles which thrived on the rich compost in which they were rooted. It lay in the centre of a long barn, half of which had been the original farmhouse before Gilbert's father had put up the current prefabricated dwelling before the war. Now the loft of the barn and the first floor of the house had been knocked through to store hay and straw and the two small rooms in which generations of little

316

Clattermoles had been reared were homes for chickens and calves. The calving cow was in the original barn and Bernard had to adjust his eyes to the darkness of the interior before following Gilbert's tracks up the mountain of ancient dung that filled it to waist|height, in order to reach the cow.

She was tethered in one of the old milking stalls with her head held down so that it nearly touched the ground. The chain was cemented into the wall at the correct height but the dung had built up so much that it was now barely a foot off the surface. The first thing that Bernard did was to untie her so that she could stand up properly. He looked worriedly at her back end. She had the swollen vulva of a calving cow, but there was no evidence of an offspring and only the scattering of white sugar to show that she had been straining. She was a beef animal – a Hereford/Friesian cross – so Gilbert wanted a bull.

'Er,' said Bernard, as the cow rolled her eyes at him while he rustled and crackled in his new green waterproof gown, 'would you please get me a bucket of warm water and some soap, please?'

'She wants a calf, not a bath,' said Gilbert.

'It's for me. I want to wash my arm before I introduce it and the soap acts as a lubricant.'

Grumbling, Gilbert went off on his errand while Bernard and his first patient continued to eye each other uncertainly. It would have been difficult to decide which of them was the more nervous about the coming encounter; in fact it was probably Bernard, for his patient was a Clattermole cow and Clattermole stock had to be very near death before Gilbert called in veterinary help. They saw vets so rarely that they did not associate strangers in funny clothes with the outrages that make vets so unpopular amongst all right-thinking livestock.

Bernard stuck his arm up the back end of the cow to sort out the tangle of limbs inside and began to pull. The cow had obviously been straining for some time and so Bernard needed to apply a lot of soap to lubricate the calf's passage to the outside world. He also had to tie ropes to the animal's legs, once they had emerged, to give him a better pull. Throwing his soul into the business, he looped the rope round his back to give himself greater leverage and, as Gilbert looked gravely on, the cow ran around the pen a couple of times, bouncing Bernard through the dung behind her. It was very old dung, so Bernard did not suffer unduly and, after picking himself up, he eventually managed to extract the calf. He was administering some brisk slaps to its flank to clear mucus from its lungs and encourage it to breathe when Gilbert spoke.

'Well done. That's not a bad calf. If it's all right by you, there's another thing I'd like you to take a look at.'

'I'd be delighted to,' replied Bernard, on his knees by the calf. 'What is it?'

He looked over his shoulder and was extremely alarmed to see Gilbert taking his braces off his shoulders and pulling down his trousers. Apart from his lack of chin, Bernard was a good-looking young man, in an inbred sort of way, but he had not been given the wind up like this since he had been approached by a prefect in a school lavatory when he was fifteen. As Gilbert began to pull down his incongruous underpants – cotton with pictures of Mickey Mouse on them – Bernard checked to ensure that his all-enveloping green suit was still securely fastened at the back and tried to decide how best to deal with the situation. Gilbert was his first and, so far, only client so he had to tread cautiously. He backed carefully to the wall, leaving the calf to the rough tongue of its mother.

'Mr Clattermole, I'm very sorry, but I don't do that sort of thing.'

Gilbert paused with his pants halfway down towards the top of his dung-encrusted bedroom slippers and his trousers.

'Course you do. You're a vet, aren't you? The last vet seemed to thoroughly enjoy himself. He said it was a pleasure to do it with a man rather than with animals.' Gilbert finished removing Mickey Mouse from the area of his loins and turned to display his ample and hairy backside to Bernard.

Bernard felt his forehead break out into a thin film of sweat. He had known that the countryside had been likely to be rather raunchier than his protected upbringing had prepared him for, in spite of five years at Eton, but this experience made

it look as though it could plumb depths beyond his most gruesome imaginings.

'What would your wife think, Mr Clattermole?' asked Bernard wildly.

'My wife? It was her idea to ask the vet in the first place. She thought it was silly to travel 20 miles for it when I was paying for him to come out already.' Gilbert looked sourly over his shoulder at Bernard. 'I suppose you can add it to your bill but the last vet said it was a pleasure.'

First customer or not, Bernard could feel himself beginning to lose his cool. 'Mr Clattermole, I really must insist that you pull up your trousers. For heaven's sake, we're in a cowshed!'

'That's what's worrying you, is it? We can go into the house. Do it in the bedroom if you like.'

'Mr Clattermole!' exclaimed Bernard weakly. Perhaps Belgravia would have been a better idea.

'I've been sitting in a bucket of cold tea for a week and that helped a bit,' continued Gilbert.

This *non sequitur* registered on the periphery of Bernard's brain as it was thrashing around feverishly for a diplomatic way out of the situation. Perhaps he could throw himself on the calf and pretend it was dying? It might distract its owner. Already Bernard knew that the prospect of losing money was the average farmer's deepest concern – next to the chance of making money. 'Tea?' said his tongue, puzzled.

'Like bunches of grapes,' droned Gilbert.

'Bunches of grapes?' What possible further horrors were about to be asked of him? He began to edge towards the door, pausing only to pick up his bag of instruments. He had left his calving cords tied to the infant's front legs, but Gilbert was between him and the calf. Gilbert suddenly noticed that he was trying to sidle away.

'Where do you think you're going?' he demanded.

'I've got another call to make,' replied Bernard, clutching his instruments to his bosom.

'But what about my piles?'

'Your piles? What are you talking about?'

'Yes, my bloody piles! What do you think I was talking about?'

'Piles!' shouted Bernard, a great wave of relief washing over him. 'You've got haemorrhoids!'

'Of course I've got bloody piles. What do you think I pulled my trousers down for? You're a vet. You should be able to do something for them.' Gilbert came out of his worries for long enough to register Bernard's relief. 'What's up with you? You look as though you've just heard that your mother-in-law isn't coming to stay after all.'

'Nothing, nothing at all,' replied Bernard innocently.

'About my piles, then,' continued Gilbert.

320

'I'm sorry,' broke in Bernard. 'Unlike your last vet, I know nothing whatsoever about piles. If I were you, I'd go and see your doctor, or keep sitting in cold tea.'

'You really think it does any good?'

'It can't do much harm as long as you don't drink it and, if you'll excuse me, I have another call to make. And if I give you any further advice, I'm afraid I shall have to add it to your bill.'

'That doesn't matter,' came the reply. 'I never pay the vet's bill anyway.'

It was not surprising that Bernard felt rather jaundiced with the world at the end of his first day and, by the end of his second, he had stopped asking for half-pints of shandy at the pub and was grimly knocking back the barley wines. By the end of his first week the worm had turned, and when he came into the pub at lunchtime on Saturday he was still spluttering with indignation.

He had received a telephone call at 3am from the Loosemires. Every community has its problem family and ours was the Loosemires. Bernard was too new an arrival in the village to have known about them. Father Loosemire was the postman and village peeping Tom. Nobody worried too much about him as he liked to peep only at Mrs Shapcott, who found it rather flattering. He had been peeping at her for decades and the longer it went on the more flattered she became. Even Mr Shapcott was rather touched when he still kept coming every Friday night after Mrs Shapcott had passed the twin milestones of sixty years and 16 stone. The loser in the deal was Mrs Loosemire who had to accommodate her husband when he returned from his Friday nocturnal excursions in a lather of lust, babbling about mountains of yielding flesh the colour of a 5p stamp. As a result there was a whole litter of little Loosemires, though now not so little, growing up surly, uncommunicative and wont to do the rounds of the neighbouring village discos on a Friday evening, looking for youths from the neighbouring towns with whom they would pick fights.

The Loosemires' phone call to Bernard had been to report

the state of their cat. It had been Jason Loosemire, nineteen and recently out of borstal, who had rung.

'Here, are you the vet? Took your bloody time in answering, didn't you?'

'It is three in the morning,' replied Bernard.

'So what? I've got an emergency. You must come out right away.'

'Yes,' replied Bernard, wondering, through his haze of sleep, whether he dare charge double time. 'What's the problem?'

'It's our cat. Its back legs have gone stiff.'

'At 3am?' queried Bernard.

'Yes. What's the time got to do with it?' asked Loosemire belligerently.

'Well, it's just that stiff legs are probably due to something like a touch of rheumatism and are not likely to constitute an emergency.'

'We think it's an emergency and the cat sure as hell thinks it's an emergency. It doesn't seem to be able to walk.'

'It would be a lot cheaper for you if you just put it in its basket for the night and brought it round here in the morning.'

'I'm telling you, it's an emergency. I think you ought to come out right away.'

Bernard sighed. 'All right. Where do you live?'

They lived about 2 miles out of the village, and Bernard grimly fought to extract comprehensible directions involving winding lanes and signposts that had been obscured by ivy. He then dressed, took his car out of the garage and set off. He didn't have much difficulty in finding his destination. In the countryside, life tends to shut down well before midnight and a house with lights blazing out across the fields could only have been the one he was looking for, although he made several abortive forays off the main road before he discovered that the lane that took him to it started off in the wrong direction.

When he finally drew up outside the house, he saw that most of the windows were open. Loud rock music was blaring out into the night. Still feeling rather dopey with sleep, he got out of his car and knocked at the door. He knocked for about five minutes until he was forced to pick up a stone and batter on the wooden panel; judging by the dents in the door and the white paint adhering to his selected rock, he had not been the first to use it for the purpose. The door opened. The opener, a man in his early twenties, was clearly drunk and had an aggressively punk female hanging on his arm.. The effect of her appearance, however, was softened by her eyes which were country-placid rather than street-wise.

'Yeah?' said the man.

'Er. . . Jason Loosemire?' asked Bernard.

'Who wants to know?'

'I do,' replied Bernard.

'I know that. But who the hell are you? You're not the fuzz, are you?' He looked at Bernard. 'No, you're not the fuzz. The fuzz don't look like you.' His girlfriend broke into giggles.

'I'm not the fuzz. I'm the vet. Mr Loosemire telephoned me about a cat.'

'Did he now? Hang on a second. I'll go and get him.' He turned from the door and disappeared down the passage towards the source of the rock music, leaving his girlfriend vacantly surveying Bernard, her mouth rhythmically chewing gum.

'Stop leering at the poor bugger, Bernadette,' ordered a slightly younger though just as drunk version of the first man, pushing the punk back from the doorway. 'Took your bloody time about coming out, didn't you?' he said to Bernard.

'You only called me fifteen minutes ago.'

'Fifteen minutes! I told you it was a bloody emergency. It doesn't take you fifteen minutes to come a couple of miles.'

'It does if you start counting when you're still in your pyjamas in bed. May I see the patient? Then I can go home again.'

'Sure. Come in.' Bernard allowed himself to be led through to the kitchen. The house was a typical 1930s barrack-style council house built in the days when the authorities had begun to accept the need to supply public housing for the poor but saw no reason why it should be either comfortable or well designed. It had been a Loosemire home since it had been put up and the council had long given up replacing plaster that had been kicked off walls or ceilings when feet had poked through them while stolen goods were being hidden. It was, therefore, a peculiarly charmless dwelling. In each of the four corners of the room blared an enormous speaker, and the water in the plastic bowl in which Father Loosemire was bathing his feet was trembling as the sound vibration rocked the house to its foundations.

Bernard smiled weakly at Father Loosemire. He recognized him as the deliverer of letters, although he was rather surprised to see him up. Postmen, in his experience, had to go to bed early as they had to get up early.

'Where's the cat?' he bellowed at Jason.

Jason cupped his hand to his ear and shook his head.

Bernard raised his voice to a maniacal scream: 'Where's the cat?'

This time Jason did not even appear to notice that he was talking as he had gone over to a cupboard and was pouring himself out a glass of beer.

Bernard felt his temper begin to fray at the edges. He moved over to the machine that squatted at the centre of its web of speakers and pressed a button. There was instant and total silence.

'Thank Christ for that!' said Father Loosemire.

'What the hell do you think you're doing?' demanded Jason, turning from his cupboard. 'I was enjoying that.'

'Where's the cat?' repeated Bernard.

'Over by the sink,' replied Jason, as he moved towards the record player.

'And keep that bloody noise off until I've examined it,' continued Bernard. 'How the hell am I expected to hear anything through my stethoscope? The cat's probably had its auditory centres destroyed and may well be suffering from further brain damage.'

He moved towards the sink. The cat, a rather moth-eaten tabby, was lying on the draining board. Bernard found that he did not need to utilize his many years of expensive training in order to make a diagnosis, nor did he need to use his stethoscope. The cat was dead.

'Is this the cat?' he asked.

'That's right,' replied Jason. 'Its back legs have gone all stiff and I don't think it looks at all well.'

'It's suffering from rigor mortis.'

'Is that serious?' asked Jason. Much as on the occasion a few days earlier when he had been trapped in the barn with an apparently sex-crazed Clattermole, Bernard was torn between laughter and tears. His ability to make up his mind which of the two paths to follow was not rendered any easier by the fact that it was 3am and he wanted his bed.

'You could say that it was serious. It only occurs several hours after death.'

'Is it suffering?'

'I said it's dead,' replied Bernard shortly.

'Dead? You mean you can't cure it?'

'The last living creature to be cured in the same condition as that cat was Lazarus. That was 2000 years ago and it was a miracle.'

'It wasn't dead when I telephoned you.'

'I'm afraid it must have been.'

'It was not. If you had come a bit quicker, it would have been all right.'

Bernard felt like bursting into the famous Monty Python sketch, substituting 'cat' for 'parrot': it's dead, deceased, a late cat, gone across the great divide, paid its penny to Charon, been harvested by the grim reaper. 'Your cat is as dead as a doornail. All its nine lives were used up by, I would think, about 8pm this evening.'

'Oh. What did it die of?'

'If you want me to find that out, I would need to do a post mortem which would not affect my prognosis on the animal one whit and would cost you more money.'

'More money! What do you mean "more money"? You're not going to try to charge for doing nothing at all?'

Bernard began to experience a buzzing in his ears the like of which he had not felt since taking part in a boxing match at school. His opponent had struck him on his nose and had subsequently regretted his temerity when Bernard had waded in and half-murdered him in his ensuing rage.

'Look, Mr Loosemire. You have called me out in the middle of the night to make use of my professional services. The fact that my diagnosis could have been given by a bloody moron, provided he had not been drunk, does not alter those facts and my bill will be fully in accord with the time of day and the circumstances.'

Bernadette had slunk into the room to find out why the music had stopped and was listening casually to the altercation from her position leaning against the doorpost. Jason appealed to her.

'Here, listen to that. He's saying that I'm drunk!'

'Well you are, aren't you?' answered Bernadette unhelpfully. 'Drunk as a skunk. Gary said that the bleeding animal was dead, but you still had to go and phone for the vet.'

'I wasn't sure, was I? I didn't think it looked dead. Just a bit stiff.'

'You're a right bloody berk, Jason Loosemire.'

'So I was wrong. But he's got no right to go and send me a bill for doing nothing.'

'Yeah. That does seem a bit stiff.'

'Yeah. Look, mate – '

'I am not your mate,' said Bernard. 'My name is Bessington-Omerod.'

'You poor old bleeder. I bet your first name is Cecil,' said Bernadette.

'No, actually. It's Bernard,' said Bernard.

'Look, Bernie,' said Jason, 'why not just have a little drink and we'll forget about the bill?'

Bernard would not be moved. There was a principle at stake. His other clients watched with gradually increasing respect as he doggedly fought for his bill to be paid over the ensuing weeks. It went through two reminders, a solicitor's letter, a summons and a county court judgment which joined the sheaf of other writs outstanding against the Loosemires.

The conclusion was a tit-for-tat when Gary Loosemire thoughtlessly did some work on Bernard's car and was told to whistle for his money. Although Gary was the wrong Loosemire, the considered opinion of the village was that justice had been done. Some of Bernard's other customers were sufficiently impressed to start paying their bills. In spite of his effete exterior, he had shown himself to be a vet who was not to be trifled with. Not too much, anyway.

Chapter Five

IN SPITE of the desires of ninety per cent of those who lived in and around the village, all sorts of things seemed to conspire to make it a tourist attraction. To most of the inhabitants, tourists were nothing more than a nuisance. Their coaches, caravans, cars and bodies clogged everything up and slowed everything down when their swarming season came round. The cafe, those who took in bed and breakfasters and the various shops found profit in them, but they were very much in the minority.

On sunny summer days, the village could have been posing for its calendar photograph. There was the vivid green backdrop behind the houses of the tree-covered hillsides. There were the neat thatched houses with their colourful cottage gardens. There was the river, its clear bubbling water spanned by its medieval bridge, and, right at the top of the village, there was the church with its humped graveyard that was a mass of crocuses and daffodils in spring. All that lifted the community from this ghastly cliché of English country life was its people. They did not go round in smocks, chewing grass and knuckling their foreheads at the sophisticated urbanites who came out to visit, but ripped them off, or tried to run them down in their cars and managed to behave towards them as if they were members of a lower race of mankind – which, of course, they were. By definition a tourist both exploits the places that he visits and is exploited by them.

Over the years, villagers had been doing what they could to discourage the tourists by uglifying the community. Many of the thatched cottages had been re-roofed. Those that had been

bought by the affluent retired had been covered in slate or tiles, while those who still needed to earn the meagre country living on the farms and in the shops put on corrugated iron which soon turned red with rust under the ceaseless showers that came down from the moorland above us. There had even been a rash of modern bungalows erected on the approaches to the bridge in an attempt to de-prettify the village, but nothing worked. Nature still conspired to make the area beautiful, in spite of the best endeavours of the populace.

One example of the uncaring way that Nature treated the wishes of the villagers was to be found in the ducks that lived on the river. They had a fluctuating population but, over the course of the year, there averaged about thirty individual birds which lived on the 200-yard stretch of the river as it ran through the village. They were a horrible, mongrel crew consisting of a basis of mallard with dashes of Indian Runner, Khaki Campbell and Aylesbury thrown in. These birds had evolved purely in response to the tourists. In the same way that various birds and animals are supposed to be able to foretell the hardness of the winter or the fineness of the summer by their behaviour, so could these ducks foretell the number of tourists that were going to be coming for the season. The first clutches of eggs would hatch just before the Easter weekend when the visitors would first arrive, and the number of ducklings that wandered about was always shrewdly matched to the quantity of feed that the tourists would supply.

If these creatures had stayed on the river or on its banks and waited for the tourists to come to them, they would have been less obtrusive. But they did not. They harried visitors like the child beggars of Calcutta, demanding crumbs, cakes and sandwiches while the visitors, not realizing the ruthless way in which they were being exploited, found them sweet and stuffed their greedy beaks with goodies.

It was painfully obvious to the beholder that the ducks looked on their young only as useful accessories in their search for food, for the lack of maternal care shown to the offspring was lamentable. Ducks would sneak up to each other's broods and drown them if they should appear to attract more food than their own; drakes would kill their young when they encountered them; and there was a fatal flaw in the use of the leat above the weir as a ducks' nursery. It was fairly fast-flowing and had several waterfalls upon it where the old mill wheels used to be. Any unwary duckling that allowed itself to be distracted by a piece of succulent bread or weed from the task of paddling continuously, in order to keep its place in the family convoy, would find itself swept away over the mill races and totally unable to re-make contact with its siblings. Such refugees ended up eventually in the main river where they would wander round for an hour or two or three, peeping piteously, before falling prey to a passing drake, heron or crow, or else be swept way down the river to the badlands to the east, from where no riverbound traveller returned.

Reluctantly, but inevitably, the villagers found themselves drawn into the fate of these ducklings. Most people were connected with farming or actually were farmers; the one cardinal agricultural crime is waste and these ducklings represented waste in its most heinous form. Potential meals – crisp sizzling skin, tender breast marinated with orange – were, for the want of a month or two's basic care, being squandered on the broad, uncaring face of the river. Then there was another reason for the locals' interest which was never admitted to: there can be nothing in nature, except possibly a young koala bear, that is so skilfully designed to appeal to the tender recesses of the human heart as a duckling. Writers from Beatrix Potter to Hans Christian Andersen have known and exploited this fact. At the beginning of the duckling season, one would see hard-bitten characters like Bill or Kelvin leaning over the edge of the wall that bordered the leat, looking down with concern at some separated youngster and, if they thought that nobody was looking, they would bend down and sweep it into captivity in their cap. They would then croon at the fluffy little bundle of yellow or speckled feathers – the colour dependent on the degree of miscegenation that its parents had been up to – with its tiny duckling beak that opened to peep trustingly up at its captor and saviour.

There was always the problem of what to do with the ducklings once they had been rescued, as it was often impossible to identify the particular family from which they had come. One year, Dick announced that he wanted as many ducklings as possible. He had moved from the commune into an ex-gamekeeper's cottage on the top of a hill just outside the village and was hard at work turning himself into a real countryman, earning his living from a bit of contracting round the local farms, a bit of tree felling and a bit of poaching as well as his gardening.

Dick was building himself up some kind of a smallholding in his back garden. He had a few hens wandering about, some goats which he used to milk and a young red deer hind which he had rescued when its mother had been shot on a poaching escapade. It was a fairly silly collection of creatures with a whiff of the commune about it, but Dick was a recognized local eccentric and he could be forgiven his aberrations.

The back garden of the pub tended to be the local collection point for rescued ducklings and, when a few had been gathered in, they were taken up to Dick's house or else he came down to pick them up. One Saturday, when the current number of refugees had built up to six, Helga and Lindy decided to take them up to Dick during the course of the afternoon, as much to have a look at Dick's house as to get rid of the ducklings.

Dick lived in a tiny example of stockbroker Tudor at the end of a rough track in the midst of a conifer forest. He rented it from a local farmer, but rarely had to pay. Many of the farmer's previous tenants had been the hard country boyos who could become extremely violent when they had taken drink and Dick, as gentle as a lamb, profited by this. His landlord had once tried to put up the rent of a previous tenant at 10pm one Saturday evening and the response had given him such a fright that he rarely could screw up his courage to go to collect his money when it was due. Dick did not mind. He pottered happily about his tiny estate and probably never even noticed that his rent was months behind. He was out the back of his house, fiddling with his bicycle, when the ladies arrived with their goodies.

Dick thanked Lindy and Helga prettily for the ducks and asked them in for a cup of tea – an invitation that was accepted with alacrity, since entry into his house was the main purpose of the expedition. The interior of the house was a reflection of the man. It fitted Dick like a well-worn overcoat. A few female refugees from the commune, their minds destroyed by irrational philosophies and drugs, would come and live with him for a week or a month, but they never stayed long enough to make any impression upon its contrived disorder before drifting off again to seek some purpose to their dreary lives. The kitchen was piled high with dirty crocks, sprinkled with a scattering of pheasant feathers – although the opening of the shooting season was still some months away.

Dick ushered them into his sitting room. It had a brown carpet and a small wood-burning stove in the fireplace. There was a bookcase containing volumes on birds, beasts and flowers, while the wall creaked under the weight of a couple of dozen sets of antlers which tended to be the local symbol of virility. People scoured the moors during spring in search of cast antlers and, together with those given out by the hunt for services rendered, they were highly prized possessions to be mounted and preserved or traded and sold for surprisingly large sums of money. There were skins of foxes, deer and goats scattered over the floor and the chairs, and in one window sat a stuffed tawny owl. It was a horribly masculine establishment and the women perched uneasily in their seats to the accompaniment of sounds of shifting crockery from the kitchen as Dick sifted through the debris for a supply of cups.

'Do you think it was a good idea that we stayed?' whispered Lindy from a sofa placed in front of the window. 'Judging by the mess, we may pick up some nasty disease.' As a nurse, Lindy was particularly conscious of such things.

'I should think it would be all right, although I had expected that Dick's house would be filled with Buddhas rather than dead animals,' replied Helga.

'We'll probably pick up fleas at least,' continued Lindy gloomily. Dick had a large black, flea-ridden Alsatian that he kept chained up outside when he was present and released when he went out so that it could guard his property. It was a locally notorious animal since, if you visited his house, it would come bounding over and jump on you. If you were not ready for it, or were not strongly built, it would knock you off your feet and proceed to do its best to kill you through drowning you with huge slaps of its great pink tongue.

Dick came bustling back through, bearing three large mugs of brown liquid. 'I assumed you all take sugar,' he said cheerfully.

'Sometimes,' replied Lindy, as she took one of the mugs and

gave it a cautious sip. 'I do quite like tea with my sugar, though.'

'It'll give you extra energy,' replied Dick.

There was a short pause while Helga and Lindy wondered what to say next. Dick was a silent man by nature and neither Helga nor Lindy were used to social gatherings without small talk.

'It's a very interesting room,' said Helga politely. 'You've got some fine sets of antlers.' Helga could not have cared less about antlers, but as landlady of the pub she had learned something of her customers' interests.

'Are you interested in deer?' asked Dick.

'Well, yes,' replied Helga cautiously.

'I've got a little present for you, then,' said Dick.

'A present? Oh, how very sweet of you.' Helga had probably, since puberty, been the recipient of presents from men with whom she was barely acquainted and she had learned to accept them gracefully as her due. Dick went to a drawer and removed a small furry object and passed it over.

'Dick! You didn't buy that at the knickerware party did you?' asked Lindy.

'Certainly not,' he replied as he handed it over. 'I made it myself. It's a purse.'

'How nice!' said Helga, turning it over and putting her hand inside. 'Thank you very much. You made it from the skin of a deer? It's beautifully soft inside. It's absolutely lovely, isn't it, Lindy?'

Lindy took it from her and stroked it. 'There doesn't seem to be a seam. How did you stick it together?'

'I didn't need to. It's a purse.'

'Yes, I know that. You said so already, but what part of the deer is it made from?'

'A purse. A stag's purse. Its scrotum.'

Lindy knew what a scrotum was and delicately placed the object on the arm of her chair before changing the subject.

'What exactly are you going to do with the ducks? You're not going to rear them to sell their eggs are you? Duck eggs can be very dangerous if the birds do not live in scrupulously clean conditions. Salmonella, you know. I might have something to say about it if you tried to do it from here.'

'Don't you worry. I'm not going to be selling any eggs.'

'Good.'

Helga suddenly let out a little scream. 'Your owl! It blinked!'

Lindy turned to the window where the bird was sitting on a branch about 18 inches away from her. 'Don't be silly. It's stuffed.' The owl suddenly opened its beak and clicked it several times. 'Good heavens! It's alive!' She hastily moved to the other end of the sofa, away from the bird. 'What the hell's a thing like that doing here?'

'That's Twit,' said Dick proudly. 'He's a owl.'

'Yes, I can see that,' replied Lindy testily.

'I've had him for coming up for a year now. He's very affectionate.' Dick moved his hand towards the owl and started to stroke its breast feathers. The owl clicked several more times, fluffed up its feathers and sank its beak into Dick's finger. Dick gave it a buffet with his free hand and the owl hissed at him. 'Bastard thing,' he said, sucking his finger. 'It must be hungry.'

Lindy withdrew to another chair, out of range of the clicking beak and away from the purse. 'Where did you get it?'

'I was chopping down a tree last season and there was a nest in it. One of the chicks was killed straight away and Twit had a broken wing. It's mended now but he doesn't seem too keen on flying away. I climbed up a tree with him the other day and dropped him, but he just fell to the ground like a dead chicken. He's been in a bad mood ever since.'

'Poor little thing,' cooed Helga, which earned her a look as poisonous as only an owl could deliver and another ill-tempered bout of beak clicking. 'Is little diddums hungry?'

'What do you feed it on?' asked Lindy. 'I don't suppose a packet of birdseed would get you very far.'

'No. Owls eat meat. I used to get a supply of dead day-old pheasant chicks from the rearer down the road, but his birds have got beyond that stage now, so I have to scrabble around a bit. But those ducklings you brought up will do very nicely.'

Helga looked horrified. 'You can't mean that you intend to feed those dear little babies to that foul creature, do you?'

'Of course. That's what I want them for. They're just about the perfect size. I'll show you.' Dick left for the kitchen and returned with the pathetic remains of a duckling. 'Incidentally, I don't need them to be alive like the lot you just brought. Twit prefers them to have been dead for a day or two so that they're getting nice and gamy, and I can always stick them in the deep freeze. So I don't mind if you bring them up dead.'

Before the horrified eyes of the two women, he tossed the duckling to Twit who deftly fielded it and made a gallant attempt to swallow it whole. He got stuck just before he completed his meal, which left him with a couple of small web-footed legs sticking out on either side of his beak. For some reason it looked quite extraordinarily obscene.

Lindy was appalled. 'I think that's one of the most revolting sights I've ever seen.'

Even Dick seemed rather shaken by the macabre spectacle. 'He normally manages it in one gulp,' he said. 'It was quite a large duckling,' he added apologetically, clicking his fingers at Twit who managed another gulp which left merely the feet dangling out. It did not really improve the way he looked. 'I think it's time we were going,' said Lindy, rising to her feet.

'Yes,' agreed Helga. 'How many ducklings has your owl eaten?'

'Dunno, really. Must be about thirty, I suppose. You've been bringing them up quite regularly over the past few weeks.'

'About those ducklings we just brought in. Do you think we could have them back?' said Lindy.

'What for?'

'Well, I thought I might rear them,' said Lindy.

'What did you bring them up here for, then?'

'We didn't know you were feeding them to that bird. If we'd known that, they might as well have stayed in the river and died there.'

'But Twit's putting them to good use.'

'I'm sure he is, but it's not quite what we thought was happening to them.'

'If that's what you want,' said Dick, who obviously failed to understand what the fuss was about. They went outside to the shed where he had put the ducklings when Lindy and Helga arrived. The door of the shed was open and there were no ducklings to be seen – only a rather guilty-looking black Alsatian at the limit of its chain, thumping its tail ingratiatingly as they approached.

'Bad dog,' said Dick unconvincingly. 'It looks as though we're too late.'

'So I see,' said Lindy. There was a certain frost in the air as they said their goodbyes.

Kelvin, Bill and all the others who spent their time rescuing ducklings did not quite know how to react to the information that the women had uncovered. They were all hard-nosed countrymen who took a certain pride in the ruthless way in which they sent much-loved cows for slaughter or sent a shiver of horror up the spine of any visiting tourist when they despatched a chicken with a casual and much-practised flick of the wrist. Dick was behaving absolutely in the true rural tradition and yet, like any lily-livered townsman, they found the idea of their carefully harvested ducklings being fed to an owl extremely difficult to cope with.

There was a debate in progress in the pub as to what the foundlings' future should be, when Ivor came in. He had been fishing in the river downstream of the village and, as well as a selection of tiny trout, he had caught a duckling. It was pounced on by the newly established protectionists of this species who had thrown all dignity and caution to the winds. Kelvin and Bill broke into gruesome baby talk when he dumped it on the bar.

' 'Oo's a dear little ducky-wucky, then?' crooned Kelvin as he leant over the unfortunate bird which took one look at his bristly grey whiskers and blackened, ill-fitting false teeth, gave a squeak of terror and dived off the edge of the bar. Kelvin tried to catch it in a palm so calloused that a cut had to be half an inch deep before it would draw blood, and, instead of duck, caught hold of a strand of fishing line which left the bird dangling upside down by its legs. 'What's this, then?' he demanded accusingly, as he held it up for all to see.

'Put the poor little bugger down, Kelvin,' ordered Bill and the duckling was deposited back on the bar where it lay on its back and looked sorry for itself.

'I told you I caught it when I was out fishing,' said Ivor apologetically. 'I made a cast and this creature just swam straight into my line and got itself in a most frightful tangle. I did not catch it with the hook so it ought to be all right.'

The duckling was spread out over the bar while a circle of faces peered down at it.

'He's a bit funny-looking,' said Bill. 'I don't think he's very well. He's big, mind you.'

The various bastardized genes that filled the cells of our duck population seemed to have come together to produce a rather odd little specimen. It was yellow below and mottled above and looked a bit larger than most.

Jimmy leaned over to have a look. He was a little bit blind and his vision was further obscured by the rolling bank of smoke issuing from the cigarette that was always stuck to his bottom lip. The duckling coughed as his miasma swept over it. 'I think he might turn out to be one of those Russian jobs.'

'A muscovy?' said Kelvin. There was some dismay in his voice. We had one pair of them on the river and they were the least popular individuals among the duck population. They showed even less respect for human kind than the other ducks and, being twice the size of the mallards, produced turds of twice the dimensions, twice the slipperiness, twice the odour and, it appeared, at twice the frequency. 'Ah well, I don't suppose any of us can help who our parents are. Helga! Have you got a pair of scissors?'

With Bill and Ivor helping to hold the patient still, Kelvin, breathing heavily through his mouth, began to snip away the fishing line which swathed the duckling. His first snip removed a patch of down about the size of a ha'penny and his second neatly cut off one of the bird's toenails.

'For heaven's sake! How many pints have you drunk?' asked Bill, as the next snip nearly removed his finger. 'You're going to chop the little bugger in half next.'

'It's not that I've been drinking, it's just that I haven't got my specs on,' said Kelvin.

'Well, put them on then, you silly old fool.'

'I haven't got them with me.' Since Kelvin could barely read anything except the fatstock prices which only appeared in his paper once a week, he rarely bothered to carry his glasses round with him.

'How about looking through a glass of beer? It should work as a magnifier,' suggested the commander.

'Not in this pub, it won't,' retorted Bill. 'I haven't been

served a clear pint of beer for the last three landlords.'

The duck seemed to have understood the threat that it was under as it began to struggle in a rather hopeless fashion.

'Shall we give it a bit of brandy to calm it down?' asked Bill.

'No, just hold it tight.' Bill and Dennis each had hold of a wing, while Ivor and the commander held on to the legs. By more luck than judgement, Kelvin managed to snip through a vital strand on the fishing line and the duckling's bonds fell away. The liberator sat proudly back. 'There!'

'What are we going to do with it now?' asked Bill.

'Isn't it sweet?' said Helga. 'Let's call it Donald.'

'Why don't you raise it here?' suggested Ivor.

'Here?' said Helga.

'Yes. Once it grew up, you could always eat it, I suppose.'

'That's what I'd suggest,' said the commander. 'If you were too squeamish yourself, you could always serve it in the restaurant.' The pub had long had the custom of selling deep-frozen, microwaved rubbish to tourists who were not capable of recognizing or appreciating good food, but Helga was doubtful.

'We never do duck,' she said. 'Chicken in the basket is very popular and scampi, but I don't think there would be much of a demand for duck.'

Bill and Kelvin had been listening with growing discomfort.

'You couldn't eat this little duckie,' said Bill. 'We've just saved its life.'

'Don't worry. Nobody's going to eat this little duckie. We're going to wait until it's a big duckie,' replied the commander cruelly. He stroked the head of the duck. 'Isn't that right, little fellow?'

'Peep,' said the duck, as it closed its eyes appreciatively.

'There's no room for sentiment when it comes to rearing livestock,' continued the commander, pompously parroting the lectures he had been given when he first came into the community. 'Life in the countryside is a hard taskmaster for man and beast alike and each depends on and exploits the other.'

340

'That's quite true,' said Kelvin. 'But you can't really mean that you'd eat this little chap.'

'Just watch me,' replied the commander, cheerfully. 'However, if you were to buy me a few drinks, I would consider changing my mind.' He did not need to consider it.

The duck was installed in the garden behind the pub and fed on rejected scampi and anything else that it could scavenge. It was given the free run of the pub, spending much of its time sitting in the bread oven to the side of the huge open fireplace, demanding crisps from the customers, and it began to grow.

It kept on growing until it turned out not to be a duck at all, but a goose, a Canada goose. By the time it was half-grown, it was testing the limits of its power. The other web-footed denizens of the locality would beg for hand-outs from the tourists. The goose would wake in the morning, decide what it wanted to eat for breakfast and then go for a gentle constitutional round the village. If it found a tourist or even a local eating anything, it would waddle up for a look and, if it approved, it would grab it. If one dared to object, the creature would raise itself to its full height, hiss and flap its wings and, if the objection continued to be made, it would start pecking.

It behaved equally badly in the pub. It shat on the floor, which was not quite so appalling as it sounds since the carpet in the public bar was encrusted with the offerings of generations of agricultural gumboots; a little extra from the bowels of the goose was neither here nor there. But it also shat on the bar and sometimes even on the pub cat.

Sentimentality was all very well, but there were limits to what the pub's customers would tolerate and Donald, as this brute was firmly labelled, would have speedily been despatched to join its ancestors because of its revolting behaviour had it not had one supreme cardinal virtue. It did not seem to like anyone very much: it attacked dogs, children, women, cows, cars and ducks with complete impartiality, but what saved it was that it was always willing to drop whatever it was doing to assault Kelvin. It grew up to hate Kelvin with a deep implacable loathing. This was not apparent during the creature's goslinghood, when Kelvin would scoop the bird up from whichever corner of the pub in which it was trying to hide and carry it over to the bar to scratch and tickle it with a finger that must have felt like a dibble, all the while uttering a tuneless, mindless crooning. Initially the bird was too small to make any objections to this, but as it grew it began to peck at his finger with all the understandable malice that it could muster and this Kelvin interpreted as a sign of spirit. As it continued to grow, it would run at Kelvin, hissing and flapping its wings, which Kelvin managed to decide were signs of affection.

Even this manifestation of extreme shrewdness when it came to character judgement was insufficient to maintain Donald's reputation. His popularity rapidly drained away when he began to assault and beat up the local dogs which most people were more attached to than their children. He even had the temerity to brave the wrath of Mandy by visiting the garden of her gnome-ridden cottage to uproot all the plastic flowers, shit on the shubunkin in her tiny pool and upturn a pot of pink paint, with which she had been touching up the window frames, all over the patio. A petition was raised to propose the bird's liquidation and even Kelvin was moved to consider it when it came across his van parked in the street and proceeded to rip off its windscreen wipers and defecate copiously all over the bonnet. Percy swore that it had nearly taken off his hand when he had tried to interrupt this act of wanton vandalism and he pored over the books that he had once studied, in a vain attempt to pass his sergeant's exam, to find out whether a goose could be charged with assaulting a police officer in the course of his duty. Part of the trouble was that Donald was owned by nobody which meant that nobody took responsibility for his behaviour or could be sued for any damage that he caused.

Then Donald became a hero. One bright and sunny afternoon he was sitting outside the butcher's shop begging for bits of offal and bones which the butcher, showing an appropriate sense of humour, tried to ensure came from ducks if he could not find a goose, when three small boys on bicycles

came along the street past the post office. There were plenty of witnesses around to see what happened next. One of the reasons that Donald found this a satisfactory vantage point was that it commanded a right-angled corner, which meant that Kelvin could be seen well in advance from whichever direction he approached and an attack could be prepared. The streets were narrow at this point – in fact they were narrow everywhere – and lined with thatched cottages and multi-coloured tourists meandering slowly between the church and the bridge which crossed the river at the bottom of the village.

The small boys were locals and, like all the locals, cousins, uncles, nephews of each other, products of the incestuous pavan that had whiled away the pre-television evenings for several centuries. Donald unfolded himself from the butcher's doorstep as they swooped down the road towards him, much faster than was safe under the circumstances. He waited until they were 20 yards from the corner before making his move. He launched himself into the air with a mighty hiss and flap of wings, and crunched into the leading cyclist just as he came to the junction. The impact knocked the boy off his bike, bringing down the second rider while the third just managed to stop.

As Donald grabbed his victim by the throat with his beak and began to disembowel him with his scrabbling feet, the second part of the drama had got under way. The village had no mains gas and so a large lorry turned up once a week loaded with three layers of gas cylinders to power the heaters and cookers of all those who were rich enough to afford to buy and use them. Victor was unloading them and Victor was not the smartest person in the community. He decided that it would be easier to unload the cylinders from the bottom with the obvious result – obvious to everyone but himself – that the greater part of the load was deprived of support and came cascading into the road making a noise like every cutlery factory in nineteenth-century Sheffield being picked up and shaken at the same time. If the small boys had been still astride their mounts and travelling, they would have been pulped. As it was, only Donald was in the way, gallantly shielding the body of the boy with his own. Donald was missed by the big cylinders that looked like blue dustbins, but was caught amidships by a small one. He was not a quitter. With the dreadful cacophany of a hundred cyiinders cascading all over the road, bringing the dead snorting out of their coffins in the churchyard under the impression that the Lord had decided on a last timpano instead of a trump. Donald, one wing trailing in the gutter, turned on the offending cylinder and proceeded to give it a drubbing. Victory his, he fainted gracefully on the pavement.

It was generally agreed that Donald had saved the life of the three boys. He hadn't been trying to beat them up. He had been trying to interpose his body between them and disaster. It was an example of selfless courage that was rare in humans, let alone in geese. He was a hero and carried his broken wing, which had been plastered by Bernard, proudly round the village, beating up cats, assaulting old ladies and generally behaving like his old self.

It was very sad when the commander ran him down in his car, just a day or two after Donald had broken into his rabbit house and caused around twenty of his does to die of heart failure. A terrible tragedy, it was, and the local paper gave him an obituary. Kelvin wanted Percy to prosecute the commander for dangerous driving, but it was not to be. Donald is still with us, stuffed, above the fireplace in the pub. Dick did the stuffing, and even if Donald's neck does sag a bit and even if he was extremely smelly for a couple of months, everyone agrees that he's much nicer how he is than how he was. Even Kelvin has come round to it at last: he gives him a stroke whenever he goes into the bar and Donald doesn't seem to mind a bit.

Chapter Six

THE COMMANDER was not a practical man. What skills he possessed were cerebral rather than manual. He could play a reasonable game of chess, had once completed the *Daily Telegraph* crossword on the day of publication and could say 'good morning' in at least a hundred languages, almost emptying the pub when he had proved it. However, when it came actually to turning theory into practice, he was not so good, which made it all the more unfortunate that he should have chosen to supplement his pension during his retirement by running a market garden.

He had tried other things as well. He had bred quail, but a fox had got in and killed them all. He had tried chinchillas, but had found them so pretty that they had ended up in the house as pets instead of being turned into fur coats. He had even tried to sell life insurance and had been so impressed by his training that he had bought enormous policies for himself and his wife but had subsequently resigned when he discovered that his earnings, gleaned from the cynical farmers who had cut their teeth on their first insurance salesman when the commander had been still doing PT at Dartmouth, amounted to rather less than the premium that he had to pay for his own policies. He was currently into rabbits and was discovering that their enthusiasm for premature death would put a lemming to shame.

His wife, Elfrieda, was the daughter of an admiral. She would never have claimed to be all that smart. The traditional admiral's daughter is supposed to single out the brightest young officers to whom to hitch her wagon. But Elfrieda had taken on the commander who had grimly struggled up the promotional ladder until he finally became irretrievably stuck when he had driven his boat into an American merchantman. Elfrieda looked a bit like a friendly camel and usually wore an air of pained resignation when she went to chivy her husband out of the pub at closing time, or to placate the greengrocer who had found rather more slug than lettuce when he had bought from her the meagre surplus left by the pigeons and the commander's own marauding pigs. Local opinion had long respected Elfrieda as a good worker, but she had never made much of an impact on the community – not until her husband made an unexpected impact on her.

It all began when the commander found himself a gatepost. He had strung up an electric fence to keep his bald Jersey cow, his pigs and his two sheep apart from his cabbages and had then found he needed a gate so that he could wheel his barrows between the two enclosures without being bitten by the fence. He had discovered the iron axle of an old farm wagon in a hedge and decided to use it as a gatepost. It was about 8 feet long and 3 inches in diameter and was a splendid lane-combing, even if there was the probability that it would short out his entire system.

George Loosemire, father of the afore-mentioned delinquent family, was the village's informant on the circumstances of Elfrieda's metamorphosis. He had been passing in his post office van and had stopped to watch the episode. Elfrieda had been detailed to prop up the post while the commander stood on a step ladder and prepared to wield the first mighty blow that would drive it a couple of yards into the soil. He raised the hammer, his moustache glinting as its nicotine-stained white hairs caught the sun, and then swept it down with the grace of a fishmonger splashing down a large cod on a slab. The hammer caught the top of the post a glancing blow and continued down to strike Elfrieda on the back of her head. She let go the post and sank to her knees. The post sagged against the steps and brought them and the commander down into some redcurrant bushes. George had been entranced. He had left his van and come into the cabbage patch so that he would

miss nothing. It was quite a few seconds before the commander had recovered sufficiently to begin to splutter.

'You clumsy idiot! Why let the thing go? If you had to let it go, you might have made sure that it was going to fall the other way. You might have killed me!'

As he slowly extricated himself from the bush, the commander became aware that answer came there none. Elfrieda was sitting back on her heels with a silly expression on her face clutching the back of her head. The commander clicked his tongue in annoyance. 'Come on, old girl. I hardly touched you.' He picked up the mallet and wiped the head absently with his hand. There was blood on it. He started. 'Good grief! I say, are you all right?'

She wasn't. George volunteered his van and they whipped her off to the local doctor where they were shown straight into the surgery.

'Hmm. Whatever happened to you?' asked the doctor. Elfrieda was still wearing her fixed and stupid expression and the commander had to answer for her.

'We were putting in a gatepost and my sledgehammer slipped.'

'Hmm. Nasty crack it must have been. Broke the skin. I don't think there's a fracture, but I would recommend taking her to the hospital for an X-ray to make sure.'

348

'I see. Thank you, doctor.' The commander helped Elfrieda to her feet and turned to leave the room.

'By the way,' said the doctor. 'It was jolly bad luck, but it's your own fault. You really ought to use an axe or a meat cleaver next time. If you're going to do the job, you might as well do it properly.'

'Er. . .yes. Thank you, doctor.'

The commander and George took Elfrieda the dozen or so miles to the casualty department of the local hosital where she was X-rayed. A young Asian doctor examined the plates. 'No, there doesn't seem to be anything broken, although I would recommend a day or two in bed in case of concussion. You ought to try shooting her, or use a knife next time.'

'I beg your pardon?' said the commander icily.

'A sledgehammer is dangerous. You might easily hurt yourself. Hit yourself on the knee or something.'

'How dare you insinuate such a thing!'

The doctor patted the commander consolingly on the shoulder.

'I know how disappointed you must feel. Better luck next time.'

'Really!' exclaimed the commander, outraged.

It was a fortnight before he stopped being the butt of such merciless jokes. Bill even passed him some paraquat in the pub with a nod and a wink, saying that he knew how difficult it was to get hold of the stuff if one was not a proper farmer.

Elfrieda seemed in no great hurry to recover from her injury. The commander was quite worried about her. Not only did she show little enthusiasm for spreading the 10 tons of horse manure that he bought from the hunt, but she also took to reading strange magazines: *Spare Rib* and the *Spectator*, according to Maud at the post office. She was as silent as ever when she visited the pub, but she cut off most of her hair and took to wearing granny spectacles. And then she disappeared.

The pub noticed.

'You've managed it this time, commander. Well done,' said Bill.

'As long as you did not stick her in my slot in the churchyard,' added Jimmy.

'Where's she gone then, commander?' questioned Kelvin.

'She's just gone up to stay near Newbury for a few days.'

'Gone to Greenham Common?' asked Dennis with a laugh.

'As a matter of fact, she has,' replied the commander stiffly.

There was a short silence.

'Good God!' exclaimed Ivor.

'Good for her,' said Malcolm Jarrett, who had the *Guardian* delivered each morning.

'What do you mean by that?' blared out Kelvin, whose daughter read out the leader column of the *Sun* to him over breakfast. 'Those women are nothing but scum, tying up police time and going against what most people want anyway.' Kelvin, as well as looking forward to nuclear war when he was officially empowered to take over command of the village, was more right-wing than a barracuda and had all the *tendresse* of a drake mallard towards females.

'Are you calling my wife "scum"?' bristled the commander.

Kevin realized that his remark might have been construed as fairly rude. 'I wasn't talking about your Elfrieda. I meant those women that you see on the television, all dirty and making Indian war whoops.'

'Those women, as you call them, at least have the guts to turn their lives upside down in order to fight for something in which they believe,' replied the commander, showing what power love can bring to bear on the most unlikely characters, even *Daily Telegraph* readers.

Ivor and Dennis shot him a look of sympathetic understanding.

'Why exactly has she gone to Greenham?' asked Ivor. 'I never thought she'd be that way inclined. She always struck me as such a solid sensible woman.'

The commander spread out his hands in resignation. 'Search me. She'd never mentioned nuclear bombs before in her life. She even wanted me to work on a nuclear submarine once. But she dressed up in her potato-picking jeans and took the car and was off. She didn't even leave me anything in the

350

oven. I don't know what's come over her. She's been behaving very oddly since she hit her head on my sledgehammer.'

'Yes, it does take some women that way,' said Dennis.

'What else has she been doing?' asked Bill. This was raw gossip, straight from the horse's mouth, so to speak, and thus more precious than rubies. It was only devalued by being delivered in front of an audience, thus immediately becoming part of the common currency.

'Well, she didn't do a wash last week. When I asked her for a shirt, she told me to look up the instructions in the washing-machine book. And she said that I was a bit of an old bore the other day. For some reason, that was even worse than being called a bore or an old bore. "A bit of an old bore" seemed to be sort of wet as well as boring.'

'How old is Elfrieda?' asked Dennis.

'She must be forty-eight, I suppose. It just goes to show how dangerous a crack on the head can be.'

'I wouldn't worry, old chap,' reassured Dennis. 'I don't think it's anything to do with that. I think it's probably the change of life.'

'What the hell is that supposed to mean?' asked Kelvin. His wife had scurried gratefully off to Abraham's bosom when she had been in her thirties, so it was understandable that Kelvin, not being a reader of women's magazines, had not come across the expression.

'It comes when a woman reaches a certain stage of her life and her hormonal balance changes,' said Dennis.

'Sort of like an identity crisis?' asked Kelvin.

'Well, yes. It often does involve an identity crisis. I wouldn't have thought you would know about that sort of thing.' Dennis was rather surprised. Crises of identity are one of the luxuries of the twentieth century and Kelvin's knowledge of modern human psychology could have been written on the head of a pin.

'Prudence bottle-reared a lamb a couple of years ago and it thought it was a dog. I had to get the vet out to it and he said that it was probably suffering from an identity crisis.'

Elfrieda spent a week up at Greenham. To the commander's mortification she was arrested for obstruction, which led to an extraordinary meeting of the committee of the local Conservative branch, of which she was a member, where it was agreed that she would not be asked to renew her subscription nor would she be invited to the wine and cheese party at which our MP was to be present. Elfrieda was totally oblivious to this pointed snub. She was embarking on a new life. When she came home, she ignored the commander's plaintive request that she cook him some dinner and went to visit the communards instead.

As mentioned earlier, the communards dwelt a mile or two outside the village in an enormous decaying mansion where they lived out an alternative lifestyle. To most of the villagers, who looked on their antics with a bemused but tolerant eye, all they seemed to have in common was a shared love of squalor and soya-bean cutlets. There were about a dozen adults currently in residence, with roughly the same number of children, and neither parents nor offspring seemed entirely sure who belonged to whom. The communards lived quite nicely on the proceeds of the social security cheques that wafted through their letterbox and were able to prevent even the remotest possibility of being asked to take a job by giving their occupations as astrologer, ley-line researcher or meditative therapist, none of which was much in demand at the local job centre.

Elfrieda had to wait a while before she got to speak to them because they were having a meeting with their sex therapist. This was a weekly event since the stress of living as sexually free agents led to all sorts of bourgeois emotions like jealousy and insecurity which they had thought they had left behind them in Esher and Neasden and all the other places whence they had come. The centre of the commune lay in the kitchen, which had a great deal in common with the ordinary farmhouse kitchen of a century earlier. There was an enormous old black iron cooking range over which were hung various clumps of drying herbs, most of which were legal. The floor was covered with flagstones, and what would otherwise have been an echoingly empty chamber, not unlike an old main-line railway-station public urinal, was dominated by 30 feet of kitchen table, cluttered with pots of home-made chutneys and jams and with a couple of dozen rickety chairs gleaned in batches of four from the local auction rooms lining its sides.

Elfrieda pushed her way through the front door and entered this kitchen, avoiding the old sitting room which lay at the front of the house and from which much wailing and passionate sobbing showed that everyone was having a wonderful time revealing their innermost fears and anxieties to the therapist. One wall of the kitchen was covered with notices advertising weekend courses in massage, alternative technologies and the politics of lesbianism. There were batches of magazines applicable to the lifestyle of the commune and with these Elfrieda occupied herself until the weekly purgative session should be completed. At intervals small and dirty-faced children would peer at her round the door or come into the kitchen and make unpleasantly precocious remarks about her age and the consequent deleterious effect of it upon her shape. One even told her that she looked like a llama which she absently corrected to camel.

The meeting in the next room ended with a burst of clapping which followed one of the members of the commune recalling his first significant sexual experience when his mother had lifted his penis as she had been changing his nappy. Then the communards came exuberantly through into the kitchen. This was the first time that Elfrieda had actually been inside the house, although she had attended the annual barbecue which was held in the stableyard at the back. The communards paused suspiciously when they saw her. Elfrieda, in spite of her short hair and specs, still looked like an ex-naval officer's wife. They were used to free spirits as visitors whose dog-like acceptance of every idea and belief that was put forward was only equalled by the equally doggy odour when one was downwind of them. Elfrieda looked as if she paid taxes.

Their visitor was equally uneasy. She had had no trouble in

associating with strangers at Greenham, but these were familiar strangers who had her pigeon-holed in a particular slot. Moreover, she did not know them individually. Nobody in the community did except for Dick who had once been in their midst. The communards all looked much the same, wearing similar drab clothes, and when they appeared in public one tended to look at their dirty toes poking out of their sandals or at their chests in an attempt to ascertain their sex: one did not look at their faces and, consequently, they were as indistinguishable from each other as traffic wardens.

'Oh hullo,' said one communard. He wore a straggly beard.

'I do hope that you don't mind me bursting in like this,' said Elfrieda, 'but the front door was wide open and I did not want to interrupt your meeting. You seemed to be having such fun.'

Communards do not have fun. It was something that Elfrieda ought to have known and it showed her essential naivety to have said what she did. Fun is frivolous and alternative livers take themselves desperately seriously.

The communard frowned in disapproval. 'We were exploring our unconscious.'

'How very interesting,' said Elfrieda politely. 'I was wondering if you would like to join the CND.'

'What?'

'I suppose I was a little abrupt,' said Elfrieda with a small laugh which sounded like the sand shifting under a camel's hoof. 'But I've just come back from Greenham Common and it struck me that there was no branch of the Campaign for Nuclear Disarmament in the village and that somebody ought to start one up.'

The communards looked at Elfrieda with rather more interest than before. 'You've been to Greenham?' asked one of them incredulously. Elfrieda did not fit into the popular conception of a Greenham woman but one would have hoped that the communards would have been above such prejudices.

'Yes.'

'Gosh!' Communards liked to think about things and even think about doing things, but they very rarely actually did

354

things. They all looked at Elfrieda with wary respect.

'Well?' demanded Elfrieda. 'Will you join?'

The communards looked at each other uneasily. 'How many members have you got already?' asked one of them, who was already wearing a CND badge.

'None.'

'So it's not a very big group, then?'

'Not at the moment. But there's no reason why it shouldn't become one. After all, Christianity started off with only one man.'

'Yeah. That's right. So it did.'

'So will you join, then?'

The communards continued to shift uneasily from foot to foot. 'We don't really believe in joining things.'

'But you do believe in nuclear disarmament?'

'Oh, sure. And the banning of nuclear power and going back to a simpler way of life.'

'So if I organize a meeting or a demonstration, you might be willing to come to it?'

The communards looked at each other again. They did not seem to think individually, but by osmosis. What one knew or did not know seemed to be shared with all the others without the need for speech. If such a gift could have been shared by statesmen or scientists rather than communards, the human race would transform its condition almost overnight.

'Yeah,' was the eventual reply from the CND badge wearer who seemed to be the leader in this matter.

Elfrieda had to be satisfied with that. As part of her new lifestyle, she had bought herself a racing bicycle with which to travel round the neighbourhood. It was not the safest way of getting about, for she had not used a bike for at least three decades and, on the intricate cat's cradle of lanes that meandered from farm to farm, the ideal mode of transport would have been a tank with a permanently wailing siren to warn other vehicles of one's approach round the blind corners and to provide adequate protection when one met the inevitable deaf, drunk, retired colonel in a Land Rover coming in the opposite direction. Elfrieda rode home from the commune, climbing a hedge once to avoid a milk tanker and spending much of the rest of the time pushing the bicycle up the hills which, in the local vernacular, steepified considerably as one reached the village. Once home, she looked round for her husband, but he had made himself scarce rather than face her.

The commander was occupying his usual stool in the pub that evening, drowning his confusion as to what was going on in his personal life with barley wine. One could tell a great deal about the commander's emotional state by the condition of his moustache. He was a heavy smoker and used a petrol-powered lighter which erupted in a volcano of fire that covered its casing and sometimes dripped on to the floor when he cranked it into action. When times were tough he drank more, and when he drank more he singed his moustache with his fireball. During one crisis it was not only his moustache that had suffered; while his right eyebrow was its normal bushy white self, his left was reduced to a short brown stubble.

The commander was an object of sympathy, although a rather isolated figure. People talked to him about cars, the weather, crops and politics, but tiptoed round the subject that was known to be obsessing him. There was a fear that Elfrieda's rebellion or emancipation might be contagious, and wives, like children, should be seen and not heard.

Kelvin had the commander engaged in a careful conversation about his chances in this year's horticultural show when Elfrieda came into the pub, putting a stop to the small talk. As always when the door squeaked open, everyone inside turned to look in unison, rather like a Wimbledon tennis crowd. The commander appeared pathetically pleased when he saw who it was. Usually she came up to the pub in the middle of the evening when her experience had taught her that her husband would have drunk enough. Since the accident, however, she had not put in one appearance but let the commander fend for himself against the demon drink, which had meant that he became Helga's responsibility at closing time and it was up to her to organize a party to carry him through the village and pour him on to the carpet in his hall. Perhaps this visit augured that Elfrieda was getting back to normal, although it was noted that there was a gleam of intelligence in her eye which was not part of her pre-sledgehammer look. Her dress had changed as well. Before she had been flattened by the bolt from the briny, she had gone in for twinsets and pearls; now she wore loose kaftans and headscarfs, while her feet were usually shod in a pair of old tennis shoes. The squire had informed Percy the policeman that he had seen a strange woman going into their house when he had first spotted her in her new rigout.

Elfrieda acknowledged the uneasy greetings from the resident fauna with a vague smile and ploughed her way through to her husband's side to engage him in earnest conversation. There was some relief that she appeared to be taking on her old responsibilities once more, especially when the commander began to become agitated at the prospect of being torn away from his booze and shook his head

vehemently when she seemed to be suggesting it. Kelvin decided to try to talk to her and went over. In her old pre-head-banged days, she had appeared to find Kelvin rather quaint and he had managed to extract the odd drink out of her, but not today. She left her husband and moved towards the door and, as Kelvin approached, she looked him straight in the eye and swept past him without a word. Kelvin shrugged and turned to the commander instead.

'What was all that about?' he asked.

'She came to tell me that I had to join in the march tomorrow.'

'What march?' asked Kelvin.

'How should I know?' said the commander, hurling his arms apart to show the extent of his ignorance and teetering dangerously on his bar stool.

'Don't be absurd,' replied Kelvin. 'Of course you should know. She wouldn't tell you to join in something if she didn't say what it was.'

'That's perfectly true, come to think on it.'

'Well?' demanded Kelvin impatiently.

The commander had his eyes closed. 'Don't rush me. I'm thinking on it.' There was a pause. 'Oh yes, I've got it. She's organizing a CND march through the village tomorrow.'

'CND?' asked Kelvin, wrinkling his brow.

Dennis rolled his eyes at such ignorance. 'Campaign for Nuclear Disarmament,' he explained patiently.

'That's right. She's got a bunch of people from the commune coming along and the Jarretts and they're marching through the village to the church hall where the vicar is going to make a little speech and then they'll start up a CND branch. She wanted me to join in because they haven't got many of the ordinary people of the village coming along.' The commander shut up and looked smugly about him. He hadn't thought that he was in a state to make such a long speech and impart so much information.

'And are you going?' asked Dennis.

'I don't see why not. It may pacify her and make her do a bit of work round the house again. And it might be quite fun as long as the communards don't have anything catching.'

Kelvin was aghast. 'She can't do one of those marches in the village.'

'I think she's going to,' replied the commander.

'But I'm head of the emergency volunteers,' said Kelvin.

Dennis looked at him doubtfully. 'Isn't that a *non sequitur?*'

'No, it's a Dubonnet and blackcurrant. It makes a change from beer.'

'No, I mean what have the volunteers got to do with the CND? You surely don't think she wants to take over your job,' said Dennis.

' 'Course she couldn't take over my job,' replied Kelvin. 'She's a woman. But it's downright unpatriotic to want to get rid of our bombs. And anyone who joins the march is a traitor.'

'That's a bit strong, Kelvin,' protested the commander mildly. 'Unilateral disarmament may be considered by many to be unwise but disarmament itself, if the Russians get rid of theirs as well, is in all our interests.'

'Of course, that's a bit different. I mean if the Russians said they would get rid of theirs as well, then we could just pretend to get rid of ours and blow them to bits.'

'I'm not sure that that is the point,' murmured Dennis.

'Anyway, if people like Elfrieda get their way and we get rid of all our weapons, then all the work I've done to prepare fertilizer bags full of soil to put round my cattle sheds and making our cellar into a bomb shelter will have been for nothing. If there's no war, then there would be no point in having the emergency volunteers. And all that money that we've been spending on submarines and missiles and things like that will have been wasted.'

'I see what you mean,' said Dennis thoughtfully.

The commander was not going to allow Kelvin to get depressed. 'Come on, Kelvin. It won't be that bad. If Elfrieda's lot got their way and we did disarm, then the Russians could do as you suggested and drop their own bomb on us quite safely. So you'd still get to use your shelter and everything else.'

359

Kelvin was not to be mollified. If Elfrieda was going to organize a demo in the village, he was going to organize a counter-demo. He had had a red telephone extension installed in his cellar, which he referred to as his command line, and he sped home to muster his troops for the coming conflict.

The morrow dawned bright and clear. The village had never had a demo before, so there was considerable interest in what was to come. It might have been wiser had the commander biffed his wife in the autumn rather than late spring, because that would have meant that she would have organized a winter demo, when there would not have been any tourists around, rather than a summer one.

The pub was full at lunchtime. Word had got round the neighbourhood that there was to be some excitement that afternoon and the surrounding countryside had emptied as everyone came in to make sure that they did not miss any of the fun. Ninety per cent of the locals were either self-employed or retired so pleased themselves whether they worked or not. Most entertainment took the form of whist drives and slide lectures that were announced beforehand in the local papers; this was a genuine spontaneous happening.

It was all due to begin at 2pm down at the bridge, according to the commander who had come into the pub for some Dutch courage before the march got under way. He had just started on his third barley wine and was beginning to feel more calm in his mind when the pub door opened, letting in a stream of sunshine, Kelvin and Gary Loosemire.

Kelvin looked ferocious. He was wearing his wellies, since they were the closest thing he had to jackboots, and dark glasses and carried a walkie-talkie radio. Master Loosemire followed in his rear in similar garb. Kelvin strode over to the commander and stood beside him with his legs slightly apart and his hands behind his back. He was carrying a swagger stick with which he was tapping his gumboot.

'What's the procedure, then?' he asked briskly.

The commander looked at him suspiciously. 'I'm not sure that I ought to tell you,' he said. 'After all, you are the enemy.'

'If you don't tell me, I'll make you join the volunteers.'

'Don't be silly. I'd refuse. After all, I've already resigned once. I'll tell you if you buy me a drink.'

'Agreed,' said Kelvin without hesitation. 'Well?'

'I'll have the drink first,' said the commander.

'Don't you trust me?' asked Kelvin indignantly.

'Certainly not. I'll have a large scotch.'

'You're joking. I'm not going to buy you a large scotch. You can have a barley wine like you always do. I'm not going to have you in this demonstration inflamed with alcohol.'

Kelvin invested in a barley wine amid total silence from the rest of the customers who had been struck dumb by the sight of him buying a drink for someone else. The commander took a large draught and smacked his lips. A freebie always tastes nicer than anything one has had to pay for oneself.

'Right. Elfrieda has told me to report to the bridge at 2pm and then we're going to march up to the church hall and hold a meeting. Everyone is asked to come. I don't honestly know what you'll be able to do.'

'We will counter-demonstrate,' replied Kelvin stoutly.

'How?'

'Well, like they do on the telly. Picketing and that,' said Kelvin rather uncertainly.

'Throw stones and yell?' asked Dennis.

'I'm not so sure about throwing stones, but we might yell a bit.'

'If you yell at me, I'll certainly yell back at you,' said the commander. 'You'll have to be jolly quick about it, though, because it won't take all that long to get to the hall. It's only a couple of hundred yards.'

We enjoyed a desultory conversation about the prospects of the skittle team in a forthcoming match against the Rose and Crown in the neighbouring village during the half-hour before the demo was due to start. Then Kelvin rousted out the commander and they went down to the bridge to begin the business of the afternoon. Most of the rest of us went along to watch.

It may have been a mistake to have the start at the bridge as it was crowded with milling tourists. A couple of coaches had just vomited forth their loads which were wandering aimlessly around in the road as they waited for a leader to emerge from their ranks who would pioneer the route to the souvenir shop and the ice-creams. Elfrieda was there, together with the vicar and the Jarretts, but there was no sign of the expected demo-fodder from the commune.

Kelvin's turn-out was rather better. The squire had brought along a couple of his shooting cronies and there was a whole gaggle of Loosemires, all of whom were members of the emergency volunteers. After the bomb, when the telephone lines had been knocked out, Kelvin was going to communicate with his troops and the outside world by CB radio, and this was the attraction of the organization to the Loosemires. Their radios allowed them to talk to each other when they were on poaching expeditions. Since most of their poaching took place on the squire's shoots, the two groups were standing a few icy yards apart, eyeing each other with dislike. They both greeted Kelvin's arrival with relief. So did the vicar.

'My dear Mr Morchard,' he gushed, 'I'm so glad that you have decided to join us. It's so important that the leaders of our community are seen to be concerned about the prospects of atomic warfare.'

Kelvin was delighted that his importance should be recognized, particularly in front of the squire. 'I feel that it's my duty, Vicar,' he said with a simple but modest smile.

'He's in charge of a counter-demonstration, Vicar,' interrupted the commander. This was not news to the Jarretts or Elfrieda, but it certainly was to the vicar.

'I don't quite understand,' he said in some bewilderment.

Elfrieda explained. 'That lot,' she said, indicating the squire and the rest of the volunteers, 'think that the bomb is a good thing and they have come along to harass us. Don' worry, though. We have the right on our side.'

'I was thinking, Elfrieda,' said Kelvin, 'that it might be a good idea if you marched up to the church hall and then came back down to the bridge and marched up again so as to spin i out a bit. Otherwise it will be a bit short.'

'Yes,' she agreed, 'that seems quite a good idea. Are all your people here?'

'I think so,' said Kelvin, looking round at them. 'But you seem a bit light.'

'I'm hoping that there might be a few more.'

'We could always ask some of these people,' said the squire, indicating the Loosemires, 'to join up with Elfrieda's lot just to pad them out a bit.'

'That's a good idea,' said Kelvin.

'Here, wait a minute,' said Jason. 'I'm against these damn socialists. I'm not marching with them.'

'You'll do what you're bloody well told,' retorted Kelvin, 'if you want to stay in the volunteers and keep your radio.'

There were rebellious mutterings from the underlings and they went over to sit on the bridge parapet with the customers from the pub while the leadership continued to discuss matters of procedure in the forthcoming event.

'What exactly are you going to do, Elfrieda?' asked Kelvin.

'Walk through the village shouting, "Ban the Bomb," I suppose.'

'What do you think we should do?'

'I haven't really thought about it. Let's see.' Elfrieda thought a bit. 'It would probably be best if you marched behind us shouting, "Keep the bomb." '

Kelvin considered this, as did the commander and the squire, the chief lieutenants. 'I think we should walk in front,' he said.

'That would be silly. It's you who are counter-demonstrating against us. It would look as if it was the other way round if you were in front.'

'Darling,' interrupted the commander, 'I'm quite willing to walk by your side, but I'll feel an awful fool if I have to shout slogans.'

'I quite agree,' said the squire. 'No gentleman goes around shouting in the street. It's just not done.'

This was a serious rebellion, and the whole march would have been aborted before it had got under way if the police had not intervened. Percy was the police. He spent his summer sunbathing behind his car in remote parts of the moor with his shirt off and, on cloudy days, he went bird watching instead. Despite his being unaccustomed to any kind of dramatic occurrence, it was clear to him that this gathering of the village establishment needed investigation.

Percy was a stout man in his fifties and he pondered his way across the bridge towards them. He touched his cap as he came up. 'Afternoon,' he said, looking around hopefully for enlightenment as to what was going on. Nothing was forthcoming. 'Is anything the matter?'

'No, nothing is the matter,' said the commander eventually. 'We're just trying to settle details of this march through the village.'

'March? What march? Nobody told me about any march.'

After her experiences at Greenham, Elfrieda was ill-disposed to representatives of the Establishment. 'We're about to have a march against the bomb, but I don't see that it is any of your business,' she said.

Percy had heard about her little accident with the sledge-hammer and its unfortunate consequences and he was prepared to give her some latitude because of her condition, but he was not going to accept a trouble maker.

'It is my business. Marching and demonstrating is against the law unless you have the permission of the chief constable. And you haven't got his permission, otherwise I would have heard about it. So I'm afraid I must ask you to move along.'

Percy had to be professionally schizophrenic. With visiting tourists, he was said to be thoroughly policemanlike, right down to accepting into safe keeping fivers and tenners which had been 'found' by erring motorists. When it came to dealing with the locals, it was rather different. Percy was considered to be a cross between a gamekeeper, translator of government forms, odd-job man and receiver of complaints about one's neighbours. The last thing expected of him was that he should order locals about. The squire, the commander and Kelvin looked at him in surprise. Elfrieda, however, had recently had some experience of police in this sort of situation.

'You cannot interfere with the democratic rights of citizens to protest against the fascist policies of the state,' she announced.

'Er . . . quite,' agreed her husband.

'I'm sorry,' responded Percy, 'you have every right to protest, but you need the permission of the chief constable first. Anyway, if you ask me, it's a bit bloody daft to have a march here. What the hell's the point of it?'

'We're showing the people that there is an alternative to the horror and absurdity of nuclear weapons.'

'That's right,' agreed Kelvin, 'and we're showing them that they're a damn good thing.'

'Why don't you just write a letter to the *Gazette*?'

'But we're going to have a meeting in the church hall to found a peace branch in the village.'

'You'd get a lot more people turning up if you wrote a letter.'

'Well, we're going to do it this way,' said Elfrieda obstinately.

'No, you're not,' said Percy.

'Yes, we are.'

'If you do, I'll arrest you.'

From all the spectators except the Loosemires, there was a murmur of astonishment. We had seen policemen going about arresting people in television series and read about it in thrillers, but Percy was not a real policeman. He was the man who grew stunted onions which were always defeated by those of the commander or Jimmy for the Onion Shield at the horticultural show.

The squire cleared his throat. 'Excuse me, Constable.'

Everyone else called him Percy, but the squire was conscious of his position and felt it incumbent upon himself to retain the old standards.

So did Percy. He touched his cap. 'Afternoon, Squire.'

'Good afternoon, Constable. Don't you think that this fuss is a bit unnecessary?'

'I quite agree. But the law is the law and my job is to enforce it.'

'What about closing time, then?' said Kelvin. The pub closed when the last customer was shovelled out the door when Helga wanted to go to bed. It was the custom that Percy did not have to pay for his drinks should he still be in the bar after 11pm.

'That's different,' said Percy, refusing to be ruffled.

'Why?' demanded Kelvin.

'Because I say it is,' replied Percy, with magnificent and uncharacteristic confidence.

'Are you saying that this march can only proceed with the permission of the chief constable?' asked the squire.

'That's right, Sir.'

'In that case, I'll have a word with him.'

The squire swiftly moved towards the communal telephone box on the other side of the street. Percy, highly alarmed, pattered after him, accompanied by raucous noises from the Loosemires. Percy used to clatter but his feet had been giving him a hard time recently and he was wearing tennis shoes which his wife had dyed black. The square slammed the door behind him, leaving Percy hopping from one foot to the other outside. A tide of spectators crossed over to form a circle round them. Percy was trying to force open the door of the box, but the squire was holding it firmly shut. Not being a chicken, Percy was unable to run round in a circle clucking, but he was badly in need of some form of displacement activity. The spectators were spilling off the pavement on to the road and so he began to chivy at their edges. Nobody, not even he, took his efforts seriously, but it gave him an occupation while the squire made contact with his supreme commander.

The squire poked his head round the door. 'Henry would like a word with you, Constable.'

Percy turned white. The Loosemires jeered. 'Go on, Percy. Go and speak to Henry. There's a good boy.'

Percy rounded on them. 'Shut up, you lot.' He straightened his tie and marched towards the receiver which the squire was holding out to him through the door of the telephone box. He took it in a hand which had a distinct tremor and went inside closing the door firmly behind him. The crowd pressed against the glass but, maddeningly, the conversation was inaudible.

'We might as well get going, then,' said Elfrieda.

'It might be best if we waited for Percy, dear,' replied her husband. 'Now that he's involved, it might look a bit more . . . er . . . professional if he's walking beside us. I mean, when you see any marches on the news, there are always policemen walking along beside them.'

'You're quite right,' said Elfrieda. 'We'll wait.'

The commander almost blushed. It was the first time that he had been right in the eyes of his wife since he had hit her over the head.

Percy came out of the kiosk and strolled across the road trying to look like the majestic guardian of the law that he was not. 'This is all most irregular,' he said. 'As I told the chief constable, it's just not good enough to have verbal permission. I have to have it in writing at least seven days before the event takes place.'

'You mean that you're still going to try to stop us marching?' asked Kelvin.

'I didn't say that,' said Percy hastily, giving the squire a nervous look in case he made a beeline back across the road to the telephone. 'All I said is that you are supposed to give me at least a week's notice.'

'Why?' asked Elfrieda.

'Why?' repeated Percy. 'It's obvious, isn't it? So that we have time to draft in police reinforcements for crowd and traffic control and that sort of thing. There might be clashes between rival groups and we have to be prepared to prevent civil disorder by keeping the two sides apart. One of those big demonstrations like they have in London would be more than one man could control.'

'You're not going to try to keep us apart?' asked Kelvin.

'That's my job,' replied Percy, with the simple air of a man who knows his duty.

'But we want to march together.'

'Well, you can't. You might riot. The chief constable said that it was up to me as the man on the spot to decide how best to handle the situation and I say you can't march together.'

'You're not being very helpful,' said the commander mildly.

'It's your own fault. You shouldn't have gone ahead and organized something like this without letting me know about it in advance. It doesn't make me look too good and I'm going to get blown up when my inspector finds out that I've been chatting on the telephone to the chief. Anyway, I wish you'd hurry up and get going. My wife has got freshly made scones for tea and I don't want to hang around here all day.'

'All right, all right,' said Elfrieda and, with her husband by her side, and the massed ranks of her supporters – all five of them – following behind, she began to lead the procession on its way. Afterwards came Percy and, a couple of yards behind him, Kelvin and his men. There was one more anti than there was pro and so Lindy was prevailed upon to come out of the crowd to join the protesters. Elfrieda raised her arm like a US 7th Cavalry captain leading his troopers out of the fort for a dangerous patrol amid the Apaches, and the village's first political demonstration and counter-demonstration were under way.

'Ban cruise missiles!' yelled Elfrieda as she cleared the car park at the head of the procession and entered the street.

'Shh, you're embarrassing me,' muttered the commander as the tourists turned to look with the blank, bovine gaze with which all tourists view the world around them.

Elfrieda's reply was drowned by the stentorian tones of Kelvin.

'Support the Independent British Nuclear Deterrent!' he bellowed.

Elfrieda flung her arm in the air. 'Stop!' The procession stopped. She left her place at its head and walked back to Kelvin. 'If you must shout something out, at least make sure it's accurate,' she said.

'What's wrong with that?' replied Kelvin, rather hurt. 'It's not easy to say "Independent British Nuclear Deterrent". I thought I had said it rather well.'

'I don't deny the quality of your diction. But cruise missiles are under American control.'

'Oh,' replied Kelvin, somewhat deflated. 'Does that matter?'

The squire came to his aid. 'He didn't mention anything about missiles. He could have been referring to submarines or bombers. All he's saying is that he supports the British deterrent.'

'Yeah. That's right,' agreed Kelvin.

'This demonstration is against cruise missiles,' said Elfrieda.

'So you say,' replied Kelvin. 'Your demonstration may be against cruise missiles. But that doesn't mean that ours has to be.'

'I'm not suggesting that it has to be against them. We disagree. But if you're holding a counter-march it ought to counter us, not talk about something totally different.'

'Why?'

'Why? Well, it's silly. You might as well walk behind us shouting "Votes for women" or "Keep Britain tidy".'

Kelvin thought about that for a few seconds. 'Why should we shout "Votes for women"?' It took incomers years to learn to appreciate and cope with the remarkable literalness of the locals' manner of thought. Elfrieda had lived in the village for only a few years and still tended to forget that natives thought with the logical simplicity of computers.

'For heaven's sake! I'm not suggesting you should. All I'm saying is that if you have to tag along behind us, at least be relevant. Otherwise go away and have your own demonstration.'

Kelvin was miffed. 'If you're not going to appreciate us, we'll bloody well do just that.' He turned round to his troops. 'Come on, lads. We'll go back to the car park and wait for this lot to get well away and then we'll have our own march.'

Percy was not going to put up with that. 'You will bloody well do nothing of the sort. The chief constable said it was up to me to maintain order and I can't be in two places at once. If you want to march, you march behind Elfrieda.' He turned to higher authority for help. 'Squire, you tell him.'

The squire was not playing. 'It's nothing to do with me, Constable. In this situation, I just take orders from my superior officer.'

'And that's me,' said Kelvin.

Percy sighed heavily. 'Kelvin, your tractor hasn't got a licence. The MOT has run out. It's got a bald front tyre. You've got ragwort rampant in one of your fields. You've got an unlicensed dog. You leave the public highway in a muddy and dangerous condition every time you drive your cows across it and I'm sure the water authority would like to know that it was you who released all that slurry into the river a couple of weeks ago. So I suggest you march along behind me nice and peaceably. And quietly. If you don't shout anything, then Elfrieda won't either. Isn't that right, Elfrieda?'

'I'm sorry, but I can't agree to police dictates like that.'

'Yes, you can,' interrupted the commander. 'If you shout anything out, you're on your own. Me and the vicar will leave

370

you to march by yourself. Isn't that right, Vicar?' That was right by the vicar.

With that incipient rebellion quashed, Elfrieda took her place at the head of the procession once again and it moved out from the car park on to the road and began the long march to victory. It became apparent quite quickly that there was a problem. Without the freedom to shout, the demonstration did not look much like a demonstration. There were at least one hundred tourists in the village – two coachloads and a stiffening of car travellers – and all they saw were a dozen or so people rather foolishly walking on the road instead of the pavement and another bunch, the pub customers, walking behind them. They did look a bit odd; none of them, for example, was sucking an ice-cream or wearing nylon shorts and, instead of the discreet day-glo reds, blues and yellows that the tourists favoured, they wore browns, greens and the muted colours of the countryside. The whole procession was forced to skip on to the pavement when a luxury busload of Germans fanfared its way up the street before coming to a stop as a small horse and its young rider, obviously hot favourites for the Thelwell class in the gymkhana the following week, skittered in fright in front of it.

'This is not working very well,' said Elfrieda, dissatisfied, as they stood on the pavement in the great shadow cast by the side of the bus as it throbbed impatiently, waiting for the obstruction in front of it to clear so that it could move on and envelop the pedestrians in clouds of black smoke from its exhaust. 'Kelvin!' she had to shout to make herself heard above the engine of the coach, 'come here!'

Kelvin shouldered his way through the tourists and his followers who were hemmed in by the bus. 'What we need are banners. If we held up banners as we marched, then there would be no doubts as to what we represented.'

'Where are we going to get banners from, Elfrieda?'

'Where do all these posters come from that advertise the flower show and the jumble sales?'

'You buy the blanks from the post office and fill in the words yourself.'

371

'Let's do it, then,' said Elfrieda crisply.

The procession moved quickly across the street, Percy kindly holding up his hand in front of the traffic which was not going anywhere since the pony had decided that it was more fun to practise its pirouettes in front of the bus than to risk squeezing between it and the parked cars that lined the other side of the street. There were a couple of tourists already in the post office, buying stamps to stick on their postcards, but they were easily swept aside.

'Posters, please, Maud,' demanded Elfrieda.

'That'll be £1.60, please,' said the shopkeeper, handing over the goods.

'Give her the money, dear,' said Elfrieda to her husband.

'I don't see why I should,' objected the commander. 'This business is not my idea so I don't see why I should have to pay.'

'I haven't got my handbag with me,' said Elfrieda patiently.

'You pay then, Kelvin.'

'I'm not paying for anything,' said Kelvin hurriedly.

'If you don't pay, I won't give you any of the posters,' warned Elfrieda.

'Maud, you'll let me charge a packet of posters, won't you?' asked Kelvin confidently. Maud was part of his mafia. Established villagers were either the Montagues of Kelvin, or the Capulets of Bill, although there was some blurring where an individual was equally related to both of them. Maud was only Bill's second cousin, whereas she was twice a cousin of Kelvin and the sister of his late wife.

'No,' said Maud.

'Go on. I'll be able to reclaim the money from the government or the Ministry of Defence. After all, we're doing their job for them, demonstrating against a demonstration.'

'No,' repeated Maud.

Percy intervened at this point. 'Maud, do us a favour, love. Give them the sodding posters, otherwise this business is going to take all day.'

Maud softened, giving Percy a smile. She was quite fond of

him as he generated a good deal of business for her by chasing up out-of-date licences for TVs and cars. 'No,' she said.

Percy sighed and pulled out his wallet. 'Okay, but give me a receipt, please, although I've no idea how I'll get the money back.'

The demonstrators looked on with satisfaction as Maud counted out his change. 'Has anyone got a felt pen?' asked Elfrieda.

Percy sighed again and purchased four of them. The demonstrators shooed out the tourists who were beginning to back up into the street in their quest for stamps, spread the blank sheets of paper over the floor and began to fill in their slogans.

The antis had it easy: 'Ban the bomb', 'Ban Cruise missiles' and 'Send Maggie on a Cruise' they wrote, and filled out the rest with some rather uncertainly drawn CND symbols. Kelvin went into a huddle with the squire and they conferred for some time before they came over to see how the opposition was doing.

'I was wondering if you had any ideas about what we should put on our posters,' said Kelvin hesitantly to Elfrieda.

'You know, Kelvin, you've really got a blasted nerve. You not only muck up my march, but you expect me to help muck it up for you.'

'If it wasn't for me, you wouldn't have a bloody march. There wouldn't be anyone here.'

'Do you know, that's a very good point,' said the squire. 'If we go home and leave Elfrieda by herself, we'll have won.'

'You wouldn't!' cried Elfrieda in horror.

'Why not?' said the squire, looking smug.

'I'll tell you why not,' said Kelvin. 'Because I'm enjoying myself. That's why not.'

'And because I've spent £2.20,' agreed Percy, 'and if you cancel the march, I won't have a chance in hell of getting my money back. Anyway the chief constable is now expecting a march and there'll be hell to pay if we don't give him one. So you keep your law-abiding ideas to yourself, Squire, if you don't mind.'

With the squire crushed, Kelvin and Elfrieda put their collective minds to the problem of the right slogans.

'Nuke the Russkies?' suggested Kelvin.

'It's a bit crude,' replied Elfrieda critically. 'What was it that you were shouting earlier on?'

'Support the British Independent Nuclear Deterrent?'

'That's right. How about that?'

'I thought you didn't approve of that.'

'Oh, nor I did, but I don't suppose it really matters.'

Kelvin started to write. He got halfway through before he started to worry. 'How do you spell "deterrent"?'

'One "t" and two "rs".'

'And is it "ant" or "ent"?'

' "Ent".'

He continued to write, breathing heavily through his mouth as he concentrated. 'There isn't enough room to get it all in.'

'Well, use the back too.'

It took Kelvin a long time as calligraphy was not his forte, and to speed things up everyone lent a hand. It was an odd selection that he ended up with: 'We want the bomb', 'The bomb puts the 'B' in Britain'. There was some discussion about 'Maggie deserves her Cruise' but it was felt that there was some ambiguity about it. His own said 'Support the British' on the front and 'Independent Nuclear Deterrent' on the back.

Eventually all was done and the procession vacated the post office and returned to the street. It was one of the disadvantages of the village that once the traffic stopped it tended to stay stopped. A large vehicle in the centre or on the bridge faced by another large vehicle meant that one of them would have to reverse extremely quickly before traffic built up behind it. This left a problem for Percy. One of his main duties was to keep the local arteries from furring up but, as we all know, once they had done so, it was a virtual impossibility for anything except time to flush them out. He took a swift look outside the door of the post office and dived back inside.

'Can I use your back door, Maud?'

'What's wrong? Has the traffic seized up again?'

'I'm afraid so. It looks like a bad one, too.'

Elfrieda was not going to allow this. 'Percy! What do you think you're up to? I'm not letting you sneak off somewhere. Your job is to escort our demonstration and make sure that there's no trouble.'

'You wanted rid of me a few minutes ago.'

'I know, but I reckon a policeman adds a certain *gravitas* to something like this.'

'If I go out there, it won't be to escort you. I'll be sorting out cars from now until supper time. There's no easy way of doing that job.'

'You mean no easy way of skiving,' said Kelvin.

'That's right. So I've found that it's a lot easier if I just make myself scarce when it gets like this. That bus is driven by a foreigner too and I've found that it is bad enough trying to get them to drive on the right side of the road but bloody nearly impossible to get them to manage it going backwards. So I'm nipping out Maud's back door and going home for my tea. It's—'

'—Scones and clotted cream. I know, you told us,' finished Elfrieda.

'So bye-bye, then. Enjoy yourselves.' He nipped behind the counter and was gone along a route that he had obviously travelled many times before, behind the pub and across a couple of garden fences before cutting beneath the bridge, well out of sight of the passing populace and back up to the policeman's cottage to his cream tea.

Elfrieda sighed. 'Right. I suppose it's time we got on with it.'

The protesters got under way once again. There were plenty of tourists on the pavements, but the road was clear the 50 or so yards between the busload of tourists and the hay wagon. Many tourists stopped to watch as Elfrieda lined up her marchers on the roadway.

'Ho Ho Ho Chi Minh!' she shouted, right in the faces of a couple of startled Americans who must have wondered if they had ventured into a time warp.

The commander cracked. 'Right!' he said. 'That's it. I warned you that if you started shouting then I was off. Take this damn poster!' He thrust one of the posters – 'Ban the bum', it said with a surprisingly good image of Reagan on it – into Elfrieda's hands and stalked off down the street, past the German bus, ignoring his wife's despairing cry to come back. He was warmly received back into the bosom of the pub customers who were idling their time away a little further down the pavement, waiting for something interesting to happen. One of them had thoughtfully brought along a bottle of barley wine, the commander's favourite tipple, and he gratefully poured it down his throat, turning his back on the political event. Elfrieda's procession was in danger of haemorrhaging away. Without Percy and the commander, it had lost twenty per cent of its available strength and the bulk of Kelvin's supporters, the Loosemires, were only hanging on by a thread.

Elfrieda had learned something about organization in the past week or two. Only herself and Kelvin were fully committed to their causes and so they amalgamated. Elfrieda stayed at the front to lead and Kelvin remained at the back to prevent anyone else making a break for it. During the confusion as they sorted themselves out, the squire managed to abandon the leaking ship by slipping back into the post office, ostensibly to check on Christmas posting dates for sending smoked salmon to some relation in New Zealand.

Elfrieda's troubles were far from over. She had just remustered the few protesters that remained and was inspecting the banners that were unfurled, ensuring that those held by her supporters masked, as far as possible, those held by Kelvin's, when Jimmy came tacking down the street towards her, carving a wide path through the tourists whom he ignored as he would a flock of sheep that were blocking his way. Jimmy had bandy legs, giving him a rolling gait which pitched him violently to starboard at every second pace when he would thrust out a knobbly blackthorn stick which stopped him falling into the road. If there was anyone in the way of the stick, that was their bad luck.

Jimmy pulled his limbs into a stationary position as he came towards Elfrieda and surveyed her little group. He had not been in the pub over the past few days since his rheumatics had been playing him up and he had therefore not been aware of the demonstration. He had also been quaffing large quantities of elderflower wine at home, and it showed. His mood had not been improved when he had heard that there was a busload of Germans in the village: he had come to have a look to ensure that Martin Bormann was not on board.

'What's all this, then?' he asked suspiciously.

'We're demonstrating,' replied Elfrieda, with a certain degree of satisfaction, since Jimmy was the first member of the general public to enquire and there was very little point in demonstrating if nobody knew that one was doing so.

'What are you demonstrating?' asked Jimmy.

Elfrieda thought about that for a few seconds. 'It's not what we're demonstrating. It's why we're demonstrating.'

It was Jimmy's turn to think. 'I went to a demonstration the other day. It was run by the Ministry of Agriculture and they

377

were demonstrating sheep dip. Sheep dip was the what, and the why, I suppose, was that it was their job.'

'Ah, but that was a different sort of demonstration. This is a sort of parade. We're against the Cruise missiles.'

'Is that right?' asked Jimmy. He looked at the odd assortment of folk behind her. 'And what's Cruise missiles?'

'They're a new way of delivering nuclear bombs.'

Jimmy shook his head. 'That's terrible, isn't it? Them bloody Russians will get up to anything. All the same, I don't see much point in walking through the village waving bits of paper in the air. You'd have more chance if you wrote to our MP and told him that we ought to have some ourselves. You'd think the bloody Americans would have a few. They're always piss useless when it comes to the crunch.'

'But that's the whole point, Jimmy,' said Elfrieda patiently. 'It's not the Russians who have the missiles. It's the Americans and they've stationed them in this country.'

Jimmy looked disgusted. 'They're threatening us with them? I always knew those bloody Yanks were not to be trusted. They want our women and they always have done.'

Elfrieda, had she been of a lesser breed, might have considered giving up at this point, but she was a graduate of Greenham and there can be few tougher training schools in the world. 'You don't understand, Jimmy. The Americans are threatening the Russians with these missiles. They are part of the NATO deterrent.'

'You mean that they're our missiles?'

'Well, not exactly ours. The Americans control them.'

'But they're not aimed at us, they're aimed at the Russians?'

'They're certainly supposed to be used against the Russians in the event of war.'

Jimmy chewed this information over before deciding that it called for some action. 'In that case, you're a disgrace to your country. Excuse me, ladies.' Jimmy must have been drinking rather more than usual, for he proceeded to step round Elfrieda and Lindy and wade into the male demonstrators behind them. He got in one blow against Kelvin but Jason Loosemire ducked, causing him to overbalance and fall down on the pavement.

It was bad luck on Elfrieda. By the time she and Lindy had got him to his feet and brushed him down, her fellow demonstrators had disappeared, abandoning their posters all over the road. Even Kelvin had given up in disgust in the face of the busload of Germans who had disembarked with their cameras clicking like typewriters to preserve this authentic slice of English rural behaviour. With the tourists following a wary 20 yards behind her, Elfrieda picked up one of her posters and trailed up to the church hall on her own for the meeting, but the door was locked. It was not her day.

She managed to achieve something out of the debacle, however. The commander was stricken with guilt and, at the next meeting of the parish council, he proposed that the village be declared a nuclear-free zone. It was carried, with Kelvin providing the sole dissenting vote.

Chapter Seven

ARTHUR MEE, in his monumental work *King's England*, described our parish as being 'remote and lost in the high moorland'. Daniel Defoe had journeyed nearby a couple of centuries earlier and had contented himself with a sour remark about the poverty of the land through which he had travelled. Before that, Celia Fiennes had considered the locals to be dirty and ill-mannered. About the only thing of interest that had ever occurred in the parish was the advent, during the nineteenth century, of a coach with a crest on the door which had deposited a young lady in the latter stages of pregnancy at the village inn. She and her child had both died in labour and still lay in the churchyard. The funeral had been paid for from a store of sovereigns found in her room after her death and her name had never been discovered. The legend, still mulled over when there was nothing more current to gossip about, held that part of the crest had been a ducal coronet.

In many ways, the village still seemed to be out on a limb. It lay at the junction of three parliamentary constituencies. The neighbouring parish was in the next county. We paid rates to two separate water boards and were ruled by a district council whose headquarters lay in a city an hour's drive away instead of in the town where everyone did their shopping and whose newspaper reported on the doings of the local hunts and the winners of whist drives and trophies at the horti-cultural show.

Because nobody bought the newspaper in which official events were reported, information, sometimes quite important official information, tended to pass us by. The commander was first to come across a rather critical example of this. It was about 4pm on a fine Thursday afternoon. Elfrieda was away for a couple of days at a seminar on the international role of women in nuclear disarmament. The commander now approved of her new interest, mainly because, at 4pm on a fine summer's day with her out of the way, it allowed him to snooze in front of the Test match with the curtains in his sitting room drawn instead of feeling obliged to slave away amid his cabbages and courgettes to keep the bank manager at bay.

Then there was a knock at the door. The commander's first thought was to slip through the French windows and out to the vegetables so that he would not be caught *in flagrante lethargo* by whoever was calling. He gave himself a quick lecture about being a man entitled to do as he pleased and how, in his retirement, he need no longer concern himself about what other people thought of him before padding to answer the door in his slippers. On the threshold was a small man in his fifties wearing a shiny suit and carrying a briefcase. He smiled apologetically at the commander who smiled politely back. It is very difficult to prevent this normal human reaction even if, as in this case, the commander had a nasty suspicion that the knocker might be an insurance salesman, if not a disguised Jehovah's Witness.

'Are you the man of the house?' asked his caller.

'If you must put it that way,' replied the commander. 'What can I do for you?'

'Do you have a television?'

'Ah!' said the commander, comprehension dawning. 'It's another collapse. Both Botham and Lamb are out.' The commander looked at his caller sympathetically. He must be a very dedicated afficionado to knock at the doors of strangers to find out the cricket score.

'So you have a set?'

'Yes, I've just said so. Would you like to come in and watch for a bit?'

'Thank you very much.'

The commander led his strange guest through into the living room where, in the gloom, burbled Messrs Laker and Benaud who were forced to shout to compete against the snores and farts from the commander's geriatric basset hound which lay on a stinking bean bag in a corner.

'Do you watch television regularly?' asked the caller.

'Well, fairly regularly. Not usually at this time of day, though. My wife's away,' explained the commander.

'May I see your television licence, please?'

The commander's blood turned to ice in his veins. That has got to be one of the most dreaded sentences of our age, comparable to 'I forgot to post the coupon' or, in earlier days,

382

'It looks like the plague' or 'Say now shibboleth'. 'Why?' he prevaricated.

'My name is Mr Harbottle. I am from the Post Office and we are checking licences in this area. It was announced in the local paper a couple of weeks ago.'

'Which paper?'

'The *Courier*.'

'Everyone round here takes the *Gazette*,' said the commander.

'Is that so? Well, we have no record of a licence being issued at this address so I would like to see it, please.'

'Ah!' replied the commander. 'You won't have a record because we've only recently moved in.'

'That would explain it then,' Mr Harbottle continued to look expectantly at the commander, who walked briskly out of the room towards the front door.

'If there's nothing else, I'll show you out. The match is at a critical stage.'

His visitor did not move. 'May I see your licence, please?' he repeated.

The commander was fighting a losing engagement in face of the mindless tenacity of a dedicated bureaucrat, but he had had not achieved rank in the service that still revered the memory of Nelson by retreating in the face of any enemy, even if the odds were overwhelming. '

'I've a nasty feeling it may have got lost in the move,' said the commander optimistically.

'I see,' said Mr Harbottle. 'When did this move take place?'

'Only a year or two ago.' The commander was not so much skating on thin ice as trying to walk on water.

'The licence is issued annually.'

'Oh, is it? My wife must have renewed it, then. It must be in her desk somewhere. Hang on a second.'

Elfrieda's desk, unfortunately, was in the same room as the television. The commander shuffled through the papers in the drawers and pigeon holes, hoping for a miracle in that one of them might turn into the required document.

'It doesn't seem to be there,' observed Mr Harbottle

politely. 'I don't think you have got a current television licence, have you?'

The commander changed his tactics. 'I don't see why I should need one. The reception here is lousy.'

This was quite true. The signal had to travel many miles and it was often exhausted by the time it came to trickle down the sides of the hills that surrounded the village, often achieving little more than snowstorms and wavy lines on local sets.

'That's as may be,' said Mr Harbottle. 'This does not obviate the necessity of ensuring compliance with the Wireless Telegraphy Act of 1949.'

'What?'

'You still need a licence.'

The commander swivelled his gun turret, probing for a weak spot. 'I see no reason to pay for the sort of pap they put on these days. Apart from the cricket, there hasn't been anything worth watching since they took off *The Magic Roundabout*.'

'I sympathize with your point of view. My wife insists on watching *Dallas* and *Dynasty*.'

'How dreadful for you!'

Mr Harbottle gave a little shudder but recalled himself to his duty. 'However, I am an employee of the Post Office and not the BBC and you still need a licence. I am afraid I am going to have to report you and it will be up to my superiors whether they take the matter any further.'

The commander came into the pub that evening in a lather of concern. He was not the only person who had been visited. Ivor had been out making hay and had found a note from Mr Harbottle in his letterbox promising a return visit. He had been round most of the village and Kelvin had actually been forced to deny on his doorstep that he owned a TV set, claiming that the aerial had been installed as a perch for the housemartins that nested along the front of his house. The whole pub was behaving like a herd of zebras when a lion is in the vicinity, honking and whinnying in alarm and restlessly shifting about. After some heated discussion, there was a run on the post office the following day led by the commander, and Maud took enough to finance at least one episode of *The Sky at Night*.

For almost everyone, it was just a seven-hour wonder, a brief flurry of excitement that squalled its way through the even tenor of our ways before receding rapidly into the recesses of memory – nasty, but short. It became much more interesting a few weeks later when the commander received his summons through the mail. There was nothing that the village enjoyed more than a disaster happening to someone else. Frank Mattock drove everyone potty when he kept winning competitions, but the commander's popularity rose considerably when it was realized that he would be going before the courts. There was a heady whiff of doom, shame and disgrace emanating from him that allowed the rest of us to feel pleasantly secure and superior.

It was Kelvin, with his inimitable lack of subtlety, who expressed the general feeling of the community. 'You won't be able to go to America, you know, Commander.'

The commander looked up from his drink. 'Why ever not?'

'Because you'll have a criminal record,' replied Kelvin with relish. 'They're very particular about that sort of thing over there. They don't let riff-raff into their country.'

'Don't be silly. Not having a TV licence is like a parking offence. They don't mind about that sort of thing.'

'It's not quite the same thing as a parking offence,' said Bill. 'One's a footling bit of nonsense and the other . . . well, there's the intention to defraud.'

'Nonsense!' said the commander.

'I reckon it is. You've been watching things on TV which the rest of us have to pay for. It costs money to put things on the TV, you know. All those widows and orphans who pay their licence have been letting you watch it for free. You've been stealing from widows and orphans and that's a serious business.'

'That's right,' agreed Kelvin. 'Come to think on it, I'm an orphan, so I suppose you've been stealing from me.'

'For heaven's sake!' said the commander. 'I don't want to go to America. Anyway you're a fine one to talk, Kelvin, because you haven't got a licence yourself.'

'But they didn't catch me, did they?' crowed Kelvin.

The commander could normally stand up for himself, but he was oppressed by his forthcoming humilation. 'It's not bloody fair that they should pick on me. You know, they couldn't even get the date right on the summons. I think that that Mr Harbottle tricked me into letting him into the house. I've a good mind to fight the whole thing.'

'You hadn't got a licence, so you're guilty and there's no point in whingeing about it. You'll have to take your punishment like a man. I think they can fine you up to £400. And your shame will be reported in the paper.' Kelvin was really enjoying himself.

'Jesus!' said the commander despairingly.

'What do you mean, they got the wrong date on the summons?' asked Helga from across the bar.

'They dated the summons the day that Harbottle came out and put yesterday's date in the space where they should have put the other.'

There was a silence while everyone tried to work out what the commander was trying to say. Helga got there first. 'You mean they are summonsing you to appear for not having a TV licence the day before yesterday?'

'That's what it says.'

'But you bought a licence a month ago.'

'Yes.'

'But don't you see? You're not guilty then.'

Kelvin, in mid-sip, was seized by a violent coughing fit. His fellow drinkers looked at him with interest as he doubled over, spluttering beer on to the floor. He straightened and mopped his face with a large khaki handkerchief. 'What do you mean "not guilty"?' he said weakly. ' 'Course he's guilty. He didn't have a licence and he was nicked.'

'That's true, but it looks as though they may have charged him with the wrong thing. They're accusing him of not having a licence when he had one.'

'Well, I think it'll be a bloody scandal if he gets away with it.'

There were quite a few people of Kelvin's opinion. After all, where lies the pleasure in attending a hanging if the victim gets a reprieve on the scaffold? In spite of this, half a dozen went along to see the commander have his day in court, just on the off-chance that he might receive his come-uppance. He had taken the trouble to consult his solicitor and had been advised to hold his peace for as long as possible, because the further the prosecution got into his case, the less simple it would be for them to correct what was a minor clerical error.

The villagers filed into the benches at the back of the courtroom before the start of business. The commander looked most peculiar since he had put on a suit for the occasion and a white shirt which had been carefully ironed by Elfrieda before she had left to attend her consciousness-raising class.

The usher suddenly said, 'All rise,' and we scrambled to our feet as the three magistrates filed on to their platform and sat down.

'Christ!' muttered the commander. One could understand

why. The bench was occupied by a stout woman in her late forties who had stood as the Ecology Party candidate at the last general election, an extremely small and very old man with a bad cold, and the squire.

The last was a bit of a shock. At intervals news percolated round the community that the squire was in receipt of certain semi-hereditary honours: high sheriffdoms, deputy lieutenancies, council membership of the Country Landowners Association and as an adornment at the top of various local charities. It was alarming, however, to find a man of his calibre in a position of real power over the destiny of others, particularly since he was in the midst of one of his periodic attacks of gout, during which his outlook on the world was extremely malevolent.

It took Kelvin a minute or two to realize the identity of the third magistrate as he had been admiring a large-busted female solicitor near the front of the court. Then he clicked. 'Look who's there. It's the squire.' He waved his arms, shouting 'Yoo-hoo!' across the room.

The commander was not happy. 'For heaven's sake, behave, Kelvin!' he hissed. 'It's all very well for you, but I am dependent on the goodwill of that lot to the tune of £400.'

Kelvin was indignant. 'That's the squire up there. What's wrong with saying hullo to him? He's a friend of mine.' The commander had learned to whisper, but Kelvin had not.

'Silence in court,' said an official.

'It's all right,' replied Kelvin, nodding at him in a friendly fashion. 'The squire's up there, we know each other.' He turned his attention back to the squire. 'Didn't expect to see you here on a nice haymaking day like this,' he bellowed. 'Going to send the commander to jail, I hope.'

The chairperson looked annoyed, as did the usher who was unused to having his orders treated so lighly. The squire cast an outraged look in our direction and proceeded to erect a large pile of books in front of him which effectively obscured him from our sight. The chairperson found a gavel and thumped the desk. 'I must ask the public to remain silent.'

A black-leather-clad figure on the bench in front of Kelvin, probably up for biting the heads off chickens, turned round.

'Yeah. Shut your face, you silly old berk.'

Kelvin was not prepared to tolerate that. 'Who do you think you're talking to, you cheeky bastard? I'll have you know I used to be a special constable and I'm chairman of our branch of the emergency volunteers.'

'For Christ's sake, Kelvin,' moaned the commander as he slid along the bench to put as much distance between them as possible in order to dissociate himself.

'What's wrong with you?' demanded Kelvin. 'That cheeky sod called me a silly old berk. You heard him.'

The chairperson banged again. 'Sir,' she shouted. Kelvin looked enquiringly at her. 'It is customary, in fact it is compulsory, that those not involved in the business of the court should remain silent.'

'But—' started Kelvin.

'And even if you are involved in the business of the court, you should remain silent until you are spoken to.'

'Well, you are speaking to me,' said Kelvin reasonably.

'Be silent!' said the usher.

'Yeah,' said the leather jacket.

'And that goes for you too!'

'What the hell do you mean?' said the leather jacket angrily. 'I'm on your side.'

'You've never been on the side of anyone but yourself in your life, you damn yob,' flared Kelvin.

The commander was rocking himself backwards and forwards with his hands clasped between his knees. The angrier those on the bench became, the higher he foresaw his fine.

The chairperson banged her gavel once more. 'If there are any further interruptions, I shall clear the court.'

Both the magistrates and the usher glared across at Kelvin, ready to pounce should he open his mouth. It opened but only to let out a gasp as Ivor, sitting next to him, sank his elbow into his mid-riff. Kelvin disappeared from general view behind the leather jacket as he slid to the floor, fighting to get air into his lungs. Ivor put his boot on the back of his neck in order to keep him there for the time being, receiving a look of gratitude from the usher who was in a position to see what he was doing.

The business of the court finally got under way. There were a couple of poachers, both of whom received jail sentences. There was a wife beater who was fined £25 and, judging by the look he gave his missus as he left the dock, he was likely to be making a repeat appearance before too long. A couple of young men were up for pushing broken bottles in each other's face at a disco and they were put into the care of the leather jacket who turned out to be a probation officer. The greatest degree of calumny was reserved for a farmer who diverted a stream through his slurry pit when it needed emptying, and it was his bad luck that he should have been on the receiving end of the chairperson's election address before she fined him £200.

Then came the TV-licence offenders. The commander had slid forward several rows during the breaks between cases and was now well away from Kelvin who had become sulkily silent since Ivor had released him. Consequently only the squire knew of his connection to the earlier disturbances and the squire had been shooting poisonous glances at him and us throughout the morning. The commander, to the bafflement of Mr Harbottle and a solicitor from the Post Office, was the only accused who had turned up to plead not guilty. The rest were represented by a pile of cringing letters, all pleading guilty. The commander was summoned to the dock. He looked extremely impressive – upstanding, white-moustached, besuited and sober – and the chairperson looked benevolently upon his countenance. The old magistrate had dropped a box of paper handkerchiefs on the floor during the chairperson's peroration on the evils of modern agriculture and he appeared to have lost interest in his duties as he scrabbled around trying to recover them. The squire was still in a foul mood. He leaned over and whispered something in the chairperson's ear. She spoke to the commander.

'My colleague has indicated that he knows this defendant and is prepared to step down. Have you any objection to his remaining on the bench?'

The commander considered. It was a tricky decision. Having a friend at court should have been a highly desirable state of affairs but the squire was not in a state of mind in which it would be wise to depend on his benevolence.

'Well?' prompted the chairperson.

'I have no objection, M'Lud.'

The squire snorted in derision, but the chairperson almost simpered. 'It should be "Your Worship". I could feel that "M'Lud" was a little rude. It might at least have been "My Lady".'

Mr Harbottle of the Post Office was looking a bit concerned at this exchange, but the commander scented that he might be on to a good thing. He actually preened his moustache. 'My dear Madam Chairman, or should I say Chairlady, I can assure you that I used the title merely out of respect for your position and abilities. I would not dare to say in open court what my heart tells me that I would like to call you.'

'Jesus wept!' muttered Ivor into the startled silence, broken only by some semi-stifled giggles from the press bench.

The chairperson tittered. 'How very sweet of you—' The squire's snort brought back her sense of occasion. She reluctantly tore her eyes away from the commander. 'Er . . . Mr Macluckie.'

Mr Macluckie was the solicitor for the Post Office. He outlined the damning facts: how the commander had been caught watching television and how, eventually, he had been forced to admit that he had no licence. Mr Harbottle then came to the stand and corroborated all the evidence with the addition that the commander had originally claimed to have a licence. The squire frowned down at such perfidy and even the chairperson looked disapproving. The commander twizzled his moustache to keep his spirits up and refused to take advantage of the opportunity to question the witness. Mr Harbottle sat down and Mr Macluckie summed up the case for the prosecution and sat down with the air of a busy man who did not like to have to waste his time with idiots who defended the indefensible.

The usher addressed the commander. 'You may go into the

witness box and allow yourself to be cross-examined, or you may make a sworn statement from the witness box which would carry less weight, or you may speak from where you are which will carry least weight of all. Which do you wish to do?'

The commander looked vaguely round. 'I think I might as well stay where I am. It looks perfectly all right.'

'Very well. You may say what you wish.'

The commander put his hand in his pocket and fumbled round.

'Ah!' he said, pulling out his TV licence. 'Here we are. That fellow [indicating Mr Harbottle] said I hadn't got a licence. But I've got one here.'

There was a slight frisson from the Post Office. The chairperson leaned forward. 'You are not charged with not having a licence, Commander, but for not having a licence on 14 May.'

This was the commander's moment. 'With the greatest possible respect, Your Worships, it states on my indictment that I have been summonsed for not having a licence last week. It says nothing about 14 May.'

Consternation! Everyone examined their papers and the Post Office went into a huddle while the bench sent for and examined the commander's licence. The chairperson had the suspicion of a smile on her lips, but the squire did not appear to be amused. The old man was still retrieving tissues and had a respectable pile of them on his lap.

Mr Macluckie jumped to his feet. 'Your Worships, it appears that there may have been a clerical error, I would be grateful if you would allow us to correct it.'

'I'm very sorry, Mr Macluckie, but I'm afraid that you should have asked to change the date before the case was heard. You are too late now.'

'In that case, may we issue a fresh summons?'

There was a whispered discussion between the chairperson and the squire. It was closer to an argument and it was clear to those waiting for the result that the squire was losing, particularly after the chairperson had dug the old man in the ribs and startled him into an animated series of nods which went on like those of a toy dog in the back window of a car. She made her pronouncement. 'The defendant is found to be not guilty and he cannot be tried twice for the same offence, Mr Macluckie.'

And that was that.

The commander threw a celebration party a couple of nights later. He had been expecting to be found guilty and fined, so had cut down on his drinking and sold a consignment of radishes in order to amass £100 to go towards it. The money was aching to be squandered. Elfrieda wanted to donate the money to *Spare Rib* but the commander won through without too much diffiulty as she was quite fond of a party as well. They placed the television, in whose honour the party was being held, in the centre of the living room, surrounding it with chairs and arranged for the antiquated record player to have a good supply of Gilbert and Sullivan while a couple of barrels of beer were brought in from the pub. The commander declared open house and all flocked to do him homage. Even Kelvin said he had thought all along that he deserved to get off.

It was not a bad party. Mandy came down from her bijou cottage further up the village, having decked out her husband Keith for the occasion in a neat two-piece suit which contrasted ill with the professional drinking sweaters of everyone else. She took him back home early, however, which allowed him to return *sans* jacket after she had gone to bed. He was supposed to be working on the 'painting by numbers' portrait of a kitten that Mandy wished to give their teenage son for his birthday – she had refused his request for a year's subscription to *Mayfair*.

The squire turned up late and left early. Judging by his behaviour when he was there, it was hard to understand why he had bothered to come at all. He may have thought it his duty. He greeted Elfrieda and wandered over to the alcohol.

'Pretty disgraceful business that, Commander,' was his initial gambit as he watched his host milk a barrel on his behalf.

'You mean the way Kelvin behaved? Yes, I'm sorry about that. You must have found it embarrassing. I know I did.'

'I didn't just mean that. I've never believed that nonsense about better a hundred guilty going free rather than one innocent being punished, or whatever it is. I thought you deserved a bloody great fine and I hope you don't mind me saying so to your face.' The commander turned rather red about the gills as the squire continued, 'Mind you, even if you did mind me saying so, I'd still say it. I don't expect gentlemen to come before the court for that sort of thing. Lied to that little man from the Post Office too, didn't you? Friend of mine was once up for shooting a poacher. That's the sort of thing a chap could understand.'

The commander was doubly annoyed because he could see the truth in what the squire was saying. 'Look, I was charged with an offence and found not guilty.'

'Oh, quite. But both you and I know you didn't deserve to get off. Barrack-room lawyer's trick. It was that stupid woman who let you get away with it. I feel it's up to people of our kind to set an example to everyone else and we deserve to be heavily penalized when we don't. Wouldn't you agree?'

'No,' said the commander. 'I think everyone should be equal in the eyes of the law.'

'I still think you ought to be ashamed of yourself, letting the side down and all that.'

'Look, you don't have to come here to drink my beer and insult me.'

'I don't mean to be offensive. But you'd better make jolly sure that you aren't up before me again for stealing from the collection plate or anything. I'd make sure you wouldn't get away with it again. The law's not to be mocked with impunity, you know.'

'If there are people like you to administer it, how is it possible not to mock it?' snapped the commander.

This discussion had attracted an interested circle of spectators who were feeding on the raw emotions on display. The commander had been known to get cross before but it was rare to see the squire bandying insults. He had been known to

go around kicking disobedient gun dogs and there were certain words like 'Scargill' and 'Benn' that were always guaranteed to produce an interesting reaction but, to the villagers, he was normally the epitome of old-fashioned courtesy. It was not part of his code to argue in front of his social inferiors. He was not a snob, but he would normally no more behave like this than he would say 'dog' rather than 'hound'. His gout had much to answer for.

Ivor, ever the diplomat, stepped in. 'Shall we change the subject? It's all over, after all.'

'As long as I receive an apology,' said the commander stiffly.

'I'm damned if you'll get an apology from me, I'm only sorry we had this conversation in your own house. If you'll excuse me.' The squire turned round and left the room.

There was a buzz of interested conversation after he had left. Many had been disappointed that the commander had not been found guilty, but this was almost as good.

Ten minutes later, to everyone's surprise, the squire returned, looking even more agitated than when he had gone out.

'What do you want?' said the commander.

'It's my car. I can't get it going.'

'What a shame! You can always walk home. It won't take you more than fifteen minutes.'

'Look, I'm sorry about what I said earlier on. I take it back. I wouldn't really have wanted to see you go to jail.'

'That's nice to know anyway. What do you want? A push? Or a lift?'

'I'm blocking the entrance to your yard, I'm afraid. I don't think anyone else can get out.'

'Let's go and have a look.'

Many of the guests followed them out. Before the commander and Elfrieda had bought their house, it had been owned by a retired farmer from 'up country' – in his case it meant from the flat cornlands about 20 miles east. He had made sufficient of a pile when he sold his farm to have had delusions of gentility and had converted the barns into up-to-date stables to house his hunters and had concreted the old yard. The yard was currently used to store the dismantled greenhouses and sheds that the commander found irresistible at sales. At its exit on to the road, two tall pillars had been erected, each capped by a stone ball about a foot in diameter. The squire, for some obscure reason, had decided to reverse out of the yard and, his vision obscured by a dog grille to which were clipped gun racks, had failed to negotiate the narrow space between the two pillars. He had brushed the left-hand one and brought down the stone ball on to the bonnet of his estate car.

'Oh dear,' said Ivor. 'How on earth did you manage that?'

'I don't quite know. I wasn't really concentrating and sort of went squint. The car won't start. I think it's quite serious.'

'Ho-ho,' said the commander.

'Ha-ha,' agreed Elfrieda, who had not appreciated the squire's handling of her mate.

'It's not a joke,' said the squire.

396

'Tee-hee,' said the commander, pulling out a handkerchief and wiping tears from his eyes.

'Honestly!' said the squire.

The commander was in no condition to be useful and he went back into the house to recover from what was beginning to look dangerously like hysteria. Kelvin and several others heaved the bits of ball off the car and put them out of the way, returning to inspect the damage. With some difficulty the buckled bonnet was prised open and a torch was found in order to examine the interior.

'It's smashed your distributor,' said Ivor. 'You won't be going anywhere until you get another cap for it. The bonnet's not in too great shape either.'

'I'm perfectly capable of seeing that!' snapped the squire. 'I only just touched that pillar. That damn ball must have been just balancing on top, waiting for any breeze to come along and blow it off. Criminally negligent to have something in that condition. Someone could easily have been killed.'

Kelvin stiffened in excitement. 'Criminally negligent, squire? That sounds as though it might be against the law.'

'Oh, do shut up, Kelvin!' said Lindy. 'We've had enough trouble for one night.'

'It's our duty to uphold the law,' said Kelvin virtuously.

'You're absolutely right, Kelvin. I've a damn good mind to report it to the police,' said the squire.

'I'm sure Percy would take it very seriously. Criminal negligence and all that. Especially with you being a magistrate. You might even end up trying the case.'

'So I might,' said the squire brightening.

'Why not let's push your car out of the way and come in and have another drink, Squire. I can run you home later,' said Ivor.

'That could be construed wrongly, you know,' said Kelvin. 'Taking favours from accused persons. That was the beginning of the end for Bobby Moore, you know.'

'What *are* you talking about?' asked Ivor.

'It was Bobby Moore, wasn't it? That bloke who had his head chopped off in a film on telly the other night?'

'Sir Thomas More, you mean.'

'That's the bloke. Anyway, he first got into trouble for accepting a cup from a woman who was supposed to be coming up before him.'

'That's quite true,' said the squire. 'I saw that film too. Perhaps I ought to leave now.'

Lindy had had enough of this. 'Kelvin, do shut up. You're just trying to make trouble.'

'It's nothing to do with you, Lindy,' said Kelvin.

Lindy turned to Ivor. 'Do you know whereabouts Kelvin had a carbuncle a few months back?'

Before Ivor had time to translate the gleam of interest in his eyes into words, Kelvin broke in. 'All right, all right. I'll hold my peace.'

'Thank you, Kelvin,' she replied sweetly. She took control and ordered the voyeurs to push the car out of the way before ushering the squire back into the party. She then led him over to the commander. 'It's time you two made up,' she said briskly.

The commander had regained control of himself. He had

enjoyed the sight of the squashed motor car so much that he was quite happy to make friends again. Lindy left them to it, which was a pity as it gave Kelvin the opportunity to play Iago once more.

'Hope you didn't take offence, Commander,' said the squire a little stiffly.

'Not at all. Elfrieda has moods like this sometimes. She calls it pre-menstrual tension. Come to think on it, she's been much better lately.'

'Something to do with being over fifty, dear. You're a bit of a freak if you have PMT at my age,' said Elfrieda.

'I can assure you that I do not suffer from PMT,' said the squire, who did not know what it was but suspected that it was something female and terrible. 'My gout has been playing up a bit. Marcia says I'm hell to live with.'

Kelvin was hovering at the squire's elbow. 'Aye, it's a terrible thing, gout. Adam Pennyfeather, he that died forty years ago, used to suffer from gout. Said it was like having a carthorse standing on his toe. He was a drunkard, of course.'

One was never quite sure whether or not there was a *double entendre* in many of Kelvin's utterances. Ivor played the accordion which Kelvin had once described, with wistful sincerity, as being as beautiful as the sound of a litter of new-born piglets. The squire remained silent while he tried to work out if he had just been insulted, so Kelvin continued to make innocent conversation. 'You were lucky out there, Commander. The squire reckons he could have had you for having that there stone in a dangerous condition.'

'What do you mean?' asked the commander.

'Criminal negligence, that's what he reckoned it was.'

'Really? Well at least you were wise enough not to make a fool of yourself on that one, Squire.'

'Quite,' said the squire.

'Fool of himself?' said Kelvin, working away busily. 'If what the squire says is right, that stone was just hanging there by a thread, waiting to crush some kiddie walking past.'

'Balls!' scoffed the commander. 'It took a bloody great

Volvo ramming into it, driven by a fool who wasn't looking where he was going to bring it down.'

Kelvin sighed with pleasure.

'Good God, you're a shit, Kelvin,' said Elfrieda.

'I'm not a fool. Nor did I ram the pillar. I merely scraped it,' said the squire testily.

'Of course, of course. A couple of hundredweight of solid rock cemented into a saucer leapt like a fairy on to your car when it saw you coming.' The commander had begun to chortle again.

The squire, to the satisfaction of Kelvin, was reddening up. 'I said it then and I'll say it again now. It was criminal negligence. If I took the matter any further, you wouldn't worm your way out of it a second time.' He waggled his finger under the commander's nose. 'Oh no you wouldn't. I'd make jolly sure that there were no slip-ups this time. The least I intend to do is sue you for the damage you did to my motor car. You'll be hearing from my solicitors. Kelvin, I'd be grateful if you could take me home now.'

'Hang on, Squire. The party's not over. There's plenty of beer left in the barrel.' But he was speaking to the squire's fast-disappearing back. In the latter's childhood, underlings had always done as he asked and he had not quite grown out of the habit of expecting it always to be so. 'Oh hell, I suppose I'd better take the silly old bugger home.'

The commander looked after them with narrowed eyes. Elfrieda glanced at him with concern. 'Oh dear,' she said, 'I haven't seen anyone look so cross since I pinched a policeman's bottom up at Greenham.'

The commander poured some more beer, forgot the squire and got on with the party.

The manor was little more than half a mile away from the commander's farm. Neither household was particularly quick off the mark, but their opening salvos would have crossed each other on their way to their respective targets. The squire used more sophisticated weaponry. Through the commander's letterbox came a letter from a firm of London solicitors which informed him that their client intended to sue for damage to his motor car caused by the commander's negligence unless reparation for the damage was speedily made.

The commander was more direct. He had merely sent the squire a postcard telling him that, since he had broken the stone ball, he was expected to replace it. There was a quote of £175 for the manufacture and installation of a suitable ball which was available for inspection. The commander felt himself so secure in his position that he did not react with the outrage that might have been expected to the communication from the squire's legal advisers. He took a postcard from Elfrieda's desk with a large CND symbol on the front, which he knew would annoy, and sent it to the squire. He pointed out that nobody else over the three years he had been in the village had hit the post, that he could produce witnesses who could say that the squire had been drinking and who had heard him say that he was not paying attention when he had bashed into the pillar and that he, the commander, would start getting nasty unless his stone was replaced forthwith. It produced the desired reaction.

Postcards through the mail served a specific purpose in the community. They were used to mobilize public opinion on the sender's behalf. Ordinary complaints and gossip were overt but both Maud and Father Loosemire, the postie, read the messages on the cards and the information they gleaned from them had more impact since it was supposed to be confidential. When one used a postcard, one always had to be aware of one's wider public – a bit like a cabinet minister writing his private diaries. The commander's postcard yielded a more direct benefit. Father Loosemire told his son Jason about it; Jason was currently supplementing his social security payments by working as a builder and went straight round to see the squire with the upshot that he arrived on the commander's doorstep the following day.

The commander was a Wodehouse fan and he called his pig the Empress after that owned by Lord Emsworth. He also liked to contemplate it and scratch it. He had recently discovered that, if he scratched its belly rather than its back, the pig would stop whatever it was doing and fall on its side, grunting with delight. This gave him a feeling of great power as well as exciting his scientific curiosity. He had succeeded in making the Empress lie down in a bed of nettles and in a bramble bush and he was working on his latest experiment. He was absorbed in carefully placing some pigmeal on a small patch of concrete which had been sown with broken bricks. Jason came, stood and pondered.

'Afternoon, Commander,' he said eventually.

The commander had been so interested in his task that he had not noticed Jason's approach. Jason had been stealing pheasants for fifteen of his twenty years and stealthy movements had become second nature. The commander jumped. 'Oh, hullo. I didn't see you coming.' He looked a little guilty.

'If you don't mind me asking, what exactly are you doing?' queried Jason.

'We . . . I'm carrying out an experiment.'

'Oh, I see. An experiment.' Jason was an old-fashioned country lad in that he had truanted all his school days and was scarcely literate. Experiments were things that educated people did, like reading books and keeping money in banks instead of in the tea caddy. All such behaviour was incomprehensible and therefore not worth bothering with. 'I've been told by the squire to replace your stone ball.'

'Really?' The commander was a bit annoyed. 'He might have bloody well told me that he was admitting liability.'

'I don't know about that, but it means he admits it was his fault. I'm to send my bill to him.'

'I'm glad to hear it. But I think it would have been better if he had let me organize the repair and sent the bill on to him afterwards. I've had somebody quote already and I would have liked to have chosen him to do the job.'

'Yeah, I thought you might, so I went to the squire and offered to do it for £150. If you don't make waves, there's £50 in it for you.'

'How dare you!' exclaimed the commander, his honour impugned.

'All right, I'll make it £60, if you sign my bill to say you're satisfied with the job.'

'£60! How on earth can you afford to give me £60 out of it?'

Jason shuffled in apparent embarrassment. 'You won't tell, will you?'

'Tell what?'

'Tell what I'm going to tell you.'

The commander worked it out after a few seconds' pause. 'No, all right. I promise not to tell.'

Jason looked smug. 'I know where there's the spitting image of that ball and I reckon I can get hold of it.'

'You're not suggesting that you're going to steal someone else's ball?'

'Did I say that?' demanded Jason, trying to look offended. 'Don't worry, it'll never be missed.'

'I certainly do not intend to condone theft.'

'There's £60 in it. All you've got to do is sign the bill. I'll say on it that I made the bloody ball myself and that'll let everyone off the hook if there's any comeback.'

'I know absolutely nothing about it,' said the commander.

' 'Course you don't,' replied Jason encouragingly.

The commander stood up and squared his shoulders. 'Right. Just so long as that's understood. When will you finish?'

'It's already done, my son.' Jason liked to watch television programmes like *Minder* and *The Professionals*. 'I've just finished.'

'You might have bloody well checked with me first.'

'You weren't around.'

'Yes I was. I was out here. It can't have taken long.'

'It didn't. I had the ball already, you see. Come and have a look and then you can sign that I've done it and we can get our money off the squire.'

'Even if I do get £60, I'm not signing anything unless it's a good job,' warned the commander as he followed Jason round the side of the house.

They crossed the courtyard and halted beneath the pillar and the commander looked up and scrutinized the ball.

'See?' said Jason. 'It's a bloody fine bit of work. It matches the other ball perfectly.'

The commander was grudgingly forced to agree. 'Hmm. It's not bad. The colour's a bit funny.'

'A month or two of weather will soon put that right. I've got the bill here. Will you sign?'

'I suppose so.' The commander got out his reading glasses and carefully perused the document. It needed careful perusal since Jason had been its author. 'Loosemire has only one "m",' said the commander, mentioning the most important flaw that he could see. He took the proffered pen from Jason and signed as instructed, adding 'in full and final settlement'. 'Thank you very much, Jason.'

'Quite all right, Commander. I'll get your money to you just as soon as the squire settles.'

Jason paid his money and, as the squire's gout improved, he and the commander made friends once again. It would have been the end of the matter, too, had not the pigeons decided to move into the commander's lettuces. He bought a .22 air rifle and spent all hours of the day in makeshift hides waiting to ambush them as they arrived to steal his produce. The birds obviously thought him some kind of nut and found it safer to move in after he had retired to the house for his meals, having first disentangled himself from his camouflage of strawberry netting intertwined with grass.

Then one morning he was awakened by one of the offending birds cooing at him. He crawled to his bedroom window with his air rifle and, ignoring Elfrieda's protests, slid open the sash and shot at it. There were several things that did not work out as the commander intended. First of all, his target was a perfectly innocuous collared dove. That did not matter too much, since the commander missed it. What was unfortunate was that the bird had been cooing from the new ball. The commander's shot struck this perch fair and square and, to the palpitating horror of both the bird and the commander, the ball exploded with a loud report and sagged down on the top of the pillar.

The squire found it all a great joke. The commander had

signed the bill for the replacement of the damaged ball and it
was his own fault if he had failed to observe that Jason had
stuck up a plastic football that he had painted grey. The
commander recalled his £60 and how he had been led to
believe that he was profiting from stolen goods, and swallowed
his indignation as best he could. Jason himself was unavailable
for comment since he was in police custody answering
questions on sheep rustling. The squire dismissed the charge
the following week. They had been very small sheep, he
explained to the surprised court, and there had not been very
many of them.

Chapter Eight

ALTHOUGH THE manor was still there, gently decaying through successive centuries of summer heat and winter frost, it was no longer the economic powerhouse of the parish. The days when most of the village depended for its living on the largesse that emanated from the capricious and bottomless pockets of the big house, in domestic service, as tradesmen and as workers on the land supplying its various needs, had vanished. The cunning which had enabled the squire's ancestors to back the right side in 1688 and thus establish a dynasty, had been bred out of his descendants over the years. While the ancestral brains had been lost, the ancestral beauty had remained until the Great War which had enabled the amiable grand- and great-grandfathers of the current squire to ensnare heiresses and keep them in the manner to which they had grown accustomed, but even this talent had disappeared with the squire's father. He had married the daughter of a bishop, a financial disaster, and his son, the present incumbent, had also married for love.

Now the squire had only the mouldering manor and a few hundred acres of wood and scrub in place of the few thousand that he had inherited. Several of the canny yokels whose ancestors had depended on the manor for their existence could now have bought him out, but the villagers preserved the fiction that the manor was the fountainhead of the community. The squire was still the monarch, albeit the constitutional monarch, of the horticultural society, the parochial church council and the committee which, for twelve years, had been trying to raise the funds necessary to build a village hall.

The squire and his wife had four children. The eldest worked for a merchant bank in London, another was in the army, the third had married a farm in Gloucestershire, showing that not all the ancestral skills had been dissipated, and the fourth was a daughter called Caroline. She had attended the village primary school before being packed off to Benenden, from where she had returned during the holidays to ride furiously in gymkhanas and learn the simplistic ways of rural love from some of the lusty local youths. She passed on this knowledge to a whole generation of stammering graduates of *Penthouse* and single-sex public schools on the county circuit of hunt balls when she would lead them out into the rose garden to taste wonders that they had only dreamed about. Many dim, horsy wives later had reason to thank her, but they never knew it.

Caroline was a lovely, warm-hearted girl and the village was sorry to lose her when she found a job with a little art gallery just off Bond Street. But her mother proudly showed her photograph round the village when she appeared in glossy magazines as a guest at a wedding, talking to dukes and earls or at the grand London charity balls. She still sometimes came down to the village at weekends and gently rebuffed those of her old friends, most now laden with the responsibilities of wives, small children and the need to pay the rent, who considered that their early tuition in the art of love had left them with life-long rights to give her revision.

Then her photograph appeared as the frontispiece of *Country Life*. Caroline was engaged to the heir of a bart. He was not only the heir of a bart, according to the squire's wife, but he was loaded as well: oodles of boodle which manifested itself in Porsches, helicopter trips, fast motorbikes and a pop group all of his own, with himself on drums, which played at smart dances within a hundred-mile radius of London and turned out records which were bought by all his friends and were played at the fashionable discotheques.

The quality of being extraordinarily rich is still surprisingly common among the British aristocracy. What is much rarer is the ability to spend it with enjoyment. The aristocracy have been cowed by a century of terror of the fiscal tumbrils and by the concept of *noblesse* having to *oblige*. Few are aware that the great mass of the proletariat could no longer care less about them and that there is nothing, save their own lack of imagination, to prevent them coming out of the financial closet to join the pop stars and vulgarly successful entrepreneurs.

The wedding was to be an extravaganza. There was a problem with the size of the village church into which it was impossible to shoehorn more than a couple of hundred people. This did not matter at the funerals of some of the old hunting farmers which always had a good turn-out. The service, conducted by the frozen-faced anti-bloodsports vicar inside the church, was a far less successful and appropriate affair than the alternative mourning amongst the gravestones in the churchyard outside where his cronies sat and pulled on their whisky flasks while discussing the antics of the departed on the hunting field. For the wedding, it was decided that the church should be filled by the country grandees in their Edwardian morning suits redolent with the odour of mothballs which would be exhumed for the occasion, whilst the godless metropolitan social butterflies, amid whom the happy couple had passed the previous few years, would have to be content with attending the reception which was to be held in a huge marquee on the manor lawn.

It was looked forward to as the largest and most spectacular social event held in the village for the past half-century, particularly when it was learned that a brace of minor royals had been invited. This was discovered by Maud at the post office who had vetted the addresses on the envelopes after the squire's wife had put the invitations into the pillar box. There was a careful social gradation at functions like this. People like Ivor and Dennis who farmed and spoke proper were invited. The commander spoke proper and sort of farmed, but he had not been in the village long enough to be asked. Others, such as Kelvin and Bill farmed, much more successfully than the squire, Ivor or Dennis but, although they could trace their local ancestry back through the centuries and into the Tudor mists, they spoke with the local accent and would not expect to be asked.

Originally the social divide had been a matter of class; now it was cultural. None of those not on the invitation list, save possibly the commander who had been trained to prostrate himself before more senior officers, considered those invited of higher class than themselves. But they no more expected to be asked than they would expect the squire to come to a whist drive in aid of the skittle team or turn up in the room behind the pub where, on a Saturday night, an organist played such ditties as *Home Sweet Home* and *Widecombe Fair* for everyone to join in. In the same way a maharajah might have met a duke: both men might like each other and respect each other but neither really envied the other. Deep down they both knew that the other was their inferior and could hardly be expected to observe their shibboleths.

As the wedding grew closer, it began to generate business. Because of the distance from 'town', guests were quartered in country houses for miles around, but a gaggle of what Caroline referred to as 'Hooray Henrys', who included the best man and the ushers, were booked into the fishing hotel that lay a mile or so downstream of the village. Mick was asked to tender for the supply of champagne and Caroline neatly press-ganged many of her old swains into acting as waiters and ferried them all in to the nearest dress-hire shop so that they could all be kitted out. Percy, the local policeman, became insufferably self-important. He was in charge of security for the royals. He had not actually been officially notified as to their attendance, but Maud had carefully checked the replies to the invitations, had asked the squire's wife about the one with the pretty coat of arms on the back of the envelope and passed the resultant information on to Percy and everyone else who came into the post office.

One way and another, a substantial proportion of the villagers were involved in the wedding; those who were not included the hard core of people who spent most of their time in the pub. But they did not want to be left out entirely. The knowledge that there were Hooray Henrys to be found in the

409

hotel the night before the festivities gave them sufficient incentive to leave their regular habitat to go down to take in a slice of the action there. The regulars were not entirely sure what a Hooray Henry was and were most interested in finding out. Bernard, the new vet, came along, as well as Dennis – Bernard because he had very nearly become a Hooray Henry himself, and Dennis because he suspected that he may well have been one during his youth. They were to be our experts in case there was difficulty with identification.

Although the hotel lay only just beyond the parish boundary, it had nothing in common with the village or its way of life. It was a great, grey Victorian structure, inside which time did not appear to have moved since the 1930s. Immense stuffed trout, the like of which had not been seen in the river in living memory, clung to the walls between hunting prints and gloomy oil paintings of highland cattle hunching themselves to withstand the onslaught of rainstorms sweeping down the side of the mountain to overwhelm the glen in which they stand. Most of the furniture was antique and the tables in the lounge were scattered with issues of the *Field* and old bound copies of *Punch*. The clientele matched. It is said that one can go into any country pub and shout 'Major' and someone will answer. But this was not a pub, it was a sporting hotel, and here one could shout 'General' or 'Admiral' and be sure that some bent old man would turn his frosty eye towards you to check whether you wanted him or the other general at the next table.

During the day these ancient warriors would spread themselves along the various beats of the river which were owned by the hotel, cast a few shaky flies at the water and then retire to the shade of the conveniently placed willows along the bank to sup their flasks of whisky well out of the way of their wives who stayed behind to gossip about who did what to whom in Gib. or Ootacamund in 1932. In the evening they tottered home with, if they were lucky, a couple of sardine-sized trout apiece, for dinner, more whisky and bed.

The establishment was presided over by Julian Shaw, an exceedingly precious ex-interior decorator who had inherited it from an aunt. He was a very good host to his own specialized type of guest. He called the warhorses 'Sir' and flirted with their wives who were all old enough to describe him as 'such a gay young man' without the thought of a *double entendre* in their heads.

The hotel had a slightly uneasy relationship with the village. Julian was an entirely urban animal who played a part very successfully to woo his guests, but he found it hard to cope with raw rurality. The sight of an early-morning rabbit defecating on the immaculate lawn that lay in front of the hotel made him shudder with disgust and he had had to leave a pre-Christmas drinks party given by Ivor shortly after he had taken over the hotel when Kelvin had held the rest of us spellbound with his description of a particularly difficult calving of a couple of twins which had called for mouth-to-

mouth resuscitation. Although Julian was invariably polite to the locals, he did not put himself out to make them welcome. His aunt had tolerated a crude, sawdust-carpeted public bar behind the hotel, known as 'the Snuggery', which was reached by going past the dustbins and through a small alley that throbbed in unison with the ancient coal-fired central-heating boiler, but Julian had closed it down and now used it as an annex to house young men who were there to learn the hotelier's profession. It had now been re-christened 'the Buggery', which may or may not have been unfair.

Julian was understandably rather alarmed to see a group of yokels come steaming in to the lobby of the hotel and pause, looking hopefully round them. He abandoned a querulous old dowager who was complaining at the reception desk about the temperature of her hot-water bottle when she woke up in the early hours of the morning and failed to get back to sleep.

'Er . . . hullo, Kelvin, Commander. What can I do for you?'

'Hello, young Julian,' replied Kelvin. 'We just thought it was time that we had a drink in your lounge bar for a change. We can't show favouritism, you know, and someone pointed out that we give too much of our custom to the pub in the village and that we ought to spread our money around a bit.'

The others glanced at Kelvin with approval. Julian's opinion of the rough trade was well known, but it would have been difficult to react churlishly and kick out someone who had his interests so clearly at heart. Julian himself looked as if he might be tempted to try the difficult thing but Kelvin flashed the best that he could muster in the way of a friendly grin. This consisted of parting his lips to display his false teeth. Kelvin's bottom plate was anchored to the blackened remnants of his own teeth which stood out like the spars of an ancient wreck from a sand bar. Julian reared away in alarm, but Kelvin was used to this type of reaction to his friendly grins and, no doubt, interpreted it as a start of delight.

'Er . . .' faltered Julian, his winsome charm momentarily deserting him.

'Young man!' boomed the dowager by the desk impatiently. Julian rolled his eyes unto the wood-panelled ceiling and returned to the reception desk. Kelvin and the rest of us clumped across the worn Persian carpets into the bar, our antennae twitching for any evidence of a Hooray Henry.

There was one other guest present, an old man crooning over a large gin and a springer spaniel that lay at his feet. Judging by the immensity of his white handlebar moustache, he was a retired air-marshal. Behind the bar was Patrick, one of the many youngish men in the parish who did a bit of this and a bit of that in order to earn a crust. They would do anything as long as it did not interfere with their hunting and as long as it came in cash so that it would not jeopardize their social security payments. Like almost everyone in the area, he was related to both Kelvin and Bill and stopped reading the racing pages of his paper to greet us warmly.

'Get your dirty paws out of there!' he said as Kelvin and Bill stuck their fists straight into the two bowls of peanuts that lay on the bar, removing half the contents of each. 'Does Mr Shaw know you're here? We're expecting to be rather busy later on.'

'I know,' said Kelvin. 'That's *why* we're here.'

Before Patrick could pursue that fox, the door to the bar opened and a couple of tall men in their twenties wearing dinner jackets came in. They looked rather alike, although one had dark hair and the other had blond.

Kelvin stiffened. 'Are those Hooray Henrys?' he asked in a hoarse whisper.

Dennis looked them carefully over. 'They could well be,' he admitted, as they came up to the bar alongside us and stood politely as Patrick filled our order. Kelvin and Bill examined them critically and openly. It takes a great deal to pierce the skin of a Hooray Henry and make him uncomfortable but the combined stare of those two would have wiped the smile off the face of the Mona Lisa and made her wonder if her slip might be showing. The Henrys began to shoot nervous glances at their neighbours. One of them – the dark one – smiled placatingly.

'Good evening,' he said. His smile was very sweet.

'Christ!' breathed Kelvin, a man unused to the social graces, 'I think the man's a bloody poofter like Julian.'

The commander frowned at Kelvin to shut him up. 'Good evening. Lovely weather we're having, isn't it?'

'Yes. Jolly hot. Could do with a spot of rain.'

'What the hell are those two going on about the weather for?' whispered Kelvin to Dennis.

'They're being polite. Good manners are the oil of social intercourse.'

'Not in public, I hope. I never knew that Hooray Henrys did that sort of thing,' said Kelvin.

'I'm not sure that I quite understand,' said Dennis puzzled.

'Social intercourse,' muttered Kelvin darkly from behind the hand that he was holding over his mouth so that he could not be overheard by anyone less than half a mile away.

The Hooray| Henry, if that's what he was, and the commander were still labouring away trying to ignore the ripples among the rest of the bar customers that their innocuous little conversation was creating. It was difficult, and the blond one turned directly to Bill.

'Pretty country round here, don't you think?' he said.

Bill did not think it was pretty. He had lived in it all his life and it was just home but, for politeness's sake, he was willing to grapple with this unusual concept.

'Some of it, I suppose. A lot of the moorland is rubbish but there are one or two decent farms. Is your name Henry?'

'No. Roy, actually.'

'Are you here for the wedding?'

'Yes. Do you know Caroline's parents?'

' 'Course I do. He's the squire, isn't he? Patrick here knew Caroline well, once upon a time. He's my wife's cousin's son. Where do you come from?'

One could see Roy delicately toying with the word 'knew', wondering if it could mean what he thought it could mean.

'Come from? Oh, we farm in Yorkshire.' If he had been brought up in the country, he probably knew about 'knowing'.

'Farm do you? What sort of farming?'

'A little bit of this and that. You know the sort of thing.'

'How many acres?'

'I think it's about 5000.' This brought about a startled

414

hush. Our region was too remote from the centres of power ever to have attracted the great magnates seeking to establish their dynasties by buying up vast tracts of the countryside. Our farmers were the yeomen of England, each with a hundred or so acres passed down through the generations and hardly a tenant amongst them. There was only one land owner within 50 miles who owned an estate of comparable size.

Kelvin was first to break the thoughtful silence. 'Do you do beef?'

'I think so.'

'I've got some really good pedigree Devons that I might be willing to sell.'

Bill nearly spat his beer out on to the bar. Kelvin *had* had some pedigree Devons which he had bought nearly ten years before, but their pedigree had been greatly diluted as a result of incursions by a randy little Hereford bull belonging to the dairy farmer next door. Roy, the dark Henry, was spared the necessity of responding to Kelvin's kind offer by the arrival of another half-dozen dinner-jacketed aristocrats. Patrick had topped up all our glasses, and so we retired to the far end to observe. There were lots of people living in the neighbourhood who had been born with plums in their mouths – with three thriving hunts within a dozen miles it was unavoidable – but this lot seemed to have spat out their plums and replaced them with melons. Another one came through the door and emitted a noise.

'What did he say?' whispered Bill to Kelvin.

'He said "Air, hair, lair," I think,' replied Kelvin, 'but I can't think why.' He nudged the commander. 'What's he talking about?'

'Shh,' said the commander. 'It's just the way he speaks. He said, "Oh, hullo." '

Kelvin was entranced. 'Go on,' he said incredulously. 'Did he really?'

'Yes, he really did.'

'Air, hair, lair. I must remember that.' Kelvin had rolling West Country 'rs' and it did not come out of his mouth with

415

quite the same purity of diction as it had from the mouth of the Henry, but Kelvin loved it. He rumbled away contentedly, practising this new language, at idle moments during the rest of the evening.

The Henrys were not hanging about. When they went to the bar to order a whisky or a gin, it was not the normal gnat's pee-sized measure that was poured into their glasses, but Patrick handed full bottles across and he didn't even take any money for them. It was all put down on the slate. Over the course of the next hour, they became more and more loud and more and more melonic in their vowel sounds. The air-marshal eventually decided he had had enough. He rose to his feet, waited for a lull in their conversation, let out a snort of contempt that would have been appropriate from a shire mare being propositioned by a Shetland stallion and stalked out of the room, his spaniel skulking after him. The Henrys appeared oblivious, but we were nearer the door and we could hear him bollocking Julian who was at the reception desk outside. His voice was a growled protest while Julian could be heard verbally washing his hands like an obsequious Edwardian grocer's assistant. After pacifying the guest, Julian came through to the lounge bar to see what all the fuss was about. He looked distastefully at the group of locals, saucer-eyed at the amount of spirits that the Henrys were consuming and went up to Patrick.

'Have they got going yet?'

'I think they're just warming up, Julian.'

'I wish they'd bloody well get a move on. I'm going to start losing guests soon.'

'Get a move on doing what, Julian?' asked Kelvin with interest.

'Get a move on running up a decent bill,' replied Julian. There was a crash from the corner as one of the Henrys overbalanced on his chair and fell to the ground. 'Aha!' cried mine host and he rushed over, full of apologies, to help him back to an upright position. He returned to the bar. 'That's a bit more like it, Patrick. Stick down £20 damages.'

'But the chair's not broken.'

'That silly sod is too drunk to notice so shove it down.'

'You're running a bloody clip joint,' exclaimed the commander.

'You don't have to be here. In fact, I wouldn't object if you weren't here at all,' snapped Julian nastily.

'You watch your tongue, Julian,' warned Kelvin.

'In my own establishment, I can do precisely as I please.'

'And I own the field next door and I am about due to spread some chicken shit.' It was believed that the only reason that Kelvin still kept chickens was in order to be able to make this threat to people who displeased him.

'If you bloody well dared, Kelvin, I'd have the law on you.'

'A fat lot of good that would do you when Percy wants to do some pigeon shooting on my land this year,' countered Kelvin smugly.

One of the Henrys approached the bar, placing a tumblerful of whisky on its top. He was awfully polite and awfully drunk.

'Excuse me,' he said.

'Yes sir?' said Julian, wiping the frown from his face as he turned from Kelvin to a rich customer.

'I do hope you'll forgive me, but those glasses up there . . .' He paused.

'Which glasses?' asked Julian helpfully. The Henry was swaying on his feet, so Julian shooed the commander from his stool and placed it carefully beneath the Henry who subsided gratefully back on to it. He pointed his arm towards the ceiling.

'Those up there in that rack thing.' We followed his gesture.

'Above the bar!' exclaimed Kelvin in the tone of one who has just guessed the object in a difficult game of I-spy-with-my-little-eye.

'That's right!' said the Henry with delight. Along the full length of the bar were a couple of strips of wood between which was suspended a long line of wine glasses which were held there by their bases. We all looked at them.

'They're certainly very interesting,' said Julian politely. 'But what about them?'

417

The Henry stood up from his stool. 'I do hope you will forgive me, but this is something that I have always wanted to do.' He reached up to the glass at the far end and, with a look of solemn concentration on his face he took hold of its bowl and pushed it along the rack. The principle was much the same as that employed by engine drivers when they shunt wagons: the whole line of glasses moved along and one at the other end fell off. Bill, still retaining his stool, carefully moved it aside as the glasses began to patter down from the roof. Alerted by the sound, the air-marshal put his head round the door to investigate and stayed, spell-bound, to watch.

418

There must have been nearly a hundred glasses hanging from the rack and, to begin with, they did not give up their lives easily. As the Henry pushed, they grated together and overlapped at their bases. A couple even expired prematurely as their bowls shattered under the pressure imposed on them by their neighbours. By the time twenty per cent of them were on the floor, the line began to move faster and they plopped down from their launch points with a precision and regularity that would have inspired Isaac Newton to carve his niche in history decades before he did, had he not been forced to wait for the revelation beneath his apple tree.

For those of us who would not be involved in clearing up the mess or having to make good this glassy genocide, it was a deeply moving experience. As the majestic procession continued to shuffle along the rack to cascade to its destruction in a glitter of climactic splinters, the Henry's audience was entranced. So was the Henry. There was a dreamy look on his face as if he were listening to the orchestra starting up for the opening dance at his very first Queen Charlotte's Ball.

The last glass toppled lazily down from the rack and the Henry took down his arm, carefully picked up his whisky and took a small sip. There was complete silence in the room although, from the lobby behind the air-marshal, whose red face and bulging eyeballs spoke of an unquiet spirit within, there were hoots and nasal brays as the gerontocracy of the British armed forces sought to establish whether the sound of all that breaking glass meant that the enemy were coming through the windows at them.

Kelvin was first to break the hallowed silence. 'By heck. That was lovely. You know what that reminded me of? It was like when you go into a well-cropped sheep pasture in the autumn with your plough and it cuts its way neatly through the turf. There's something so right about it.'

'Or the look of an even bunch of store cattle,' Bill contributed.

'Or cleanly killing a really difficult pheasant,' said Dennis. 'It's the simple pleasure of seeing a job well done.'

The Henry was coming out of his trance. He reached inside

his pocket and brought out a cheque book, looking at Julian. 'How much do I owe you?'

Julian looked gloomily down at the wreckage. 'It'll take some clearing up and there must have been not far short of a hundred glasses there. They alone must have been worth £50.'

'Bring me a dustpan and a brush and I'll clear it up,' said Kelvin. 'It doesn't seem fair that you should be the only one to pay, because we all enjoyed it.'

'That's awfully kind of you,' said the Henry, looking enormously gratified.

'Think nothing of it,' replied Kelvin, crunching across the glass shards on the carpet and putting his arm round the Henry's shoulder. 'Do you often do things in that sort of line?'

'Well, yes, I do sometimes. I always feel that one shouldn't plan them ahead. For some reason, if they are spontaneous, they always seem to be much more fun. A couple of weeks ago I pushed an apricot and meringue flan into someone's face.'

'Marvellous!' breathed Kelvin.

'Shall I put the broken glasses on your bill, Sir?' asked Julian.

'Yes, do that,' said the Henry dismissively. He turned back to Kelvin. 'Why don't you all come over and join us for a drink and then have dinner with us?'

'I don't mind if I do,' Kelvin replied, dumping his half-pint tankard and deftly swiping the one remaining spirit glass off the bar before following him across to the others.

Julian looked sourly after him. 'So much for Kelvin's desire to sweep up the mess.'

The air-marshal, now that the danger of being injured by flying glass had passed, stepped cautiously through the doorway and into the room. 'You, Sir!'

Julian looked round rather wearily. 'Me, Sir?'

'Yes, you, Sir! What the Hades do you mean by allowing that sort of behaviour?'

'I'm very sorry if it upset you, Sir!'

'Upset me? Of course it upset me, and the old girl's in a terrible state out there.'

420

'I do apologize, Sir, and I'm extremely sorry that your wife is distressed.'

'Wife? What are you talking about, man?'

The customer was always right, of course, but Julian had to make a perceptible effort to contain himself and respond in an adequately obsequious fashion. 'I do apologize,' he said again, 'but I thought you said that your wife was in a bit of a state.'

'The dog, you fool, the dog. Bugger the wife!'

'I'd prefer not to, Sir.'

Julian received a sharp kick on the ankle from the commander and made a big effort to pull himself together. 'Once again, Sir, I am most extremely awfully sorry about the incident.'

The air-marshal snorted. 'It's quite disgraceful. This used to be a decent hotel but you seem to be cramming it with peasants and hooligans.'

The peasants were not going to lie down beneath that one. Bill stirred. 'Now look'ee here, Mister . . .'

Julian was not going to allow half-pint buyers to give any lip to his bed-buying customers. 'Shut up!' he said savagely out of the corner of his mouth. Bill looked outraged and opened his mouth again, but Julian had someone on whom he felt he could relieve his feelings: 'Shut your bloody mouth.' Bill did but the air-marshal didn't.

'How dare you talk to that man like that! You should be ashamed of yourself. You're a disgrace to your trade and if you think I am going to stay here a moment longer, you are mistaken.' The air-marshal was being extremely loud in his disapproval and he had even penetrated the miasma of booze and bonhomie round the Henrys who were passing ribald comments about the noise he was making. Julian looked down at the floor, considered the mass of splinters that were being ground into the carpet and thought briefly about the air-marshal's point before deciding that a man sometimes had to do what a man had to do, even if he had to do it to a paying customer.

'That suits me fine,' he said curtly. 'I shall make out your bill and you can be on your way.'

The air-marshal turned even redder. 'What? You're throwing me out? You horrid little poo-puncher!'

Julian may have worn rather colourful sweaters; in fact he was currently wearing a pink, chunky-knit cardigan which had a cord sewn round the neck ending in two large pom-poms dangling just below his waist, but even he was not accustomed to that type of description. The Henrys, too, thought it a little strong. There were rhubarb noises from their corner, amid which phrases like 'I say!' and 'Steady on!' were discernible. The locals just sat and marvelled, although their brains were clicking as they filed away the expression for retrieval during the long winter evenings in the pub where it could be mulled over, savoured and discussed amid the company of their peers.

If one is slightly out of the norm in one's sexual predelictions and one is prepared to come out of the closet to face the world, few of the words of man hold terrors. The concept which was embodied in the insult may have been shocking to some but, presumably, it was part of Julian's life. At any rate, he could handle himself. He rose to his feet and approached the air-marshal.

'You are not a gentleman, Sir.' The effect was devastating. It was not so much the words used as his cardigan. He had been sitting on one of the pom-poms and, when he got to his feet, it remained wedged between his legs. As he stretched to his full height in order to add dignity to his pronouncement, the cord stretched as well. The pom-pom catapulted free and struck the air-marshal on the chest. He let out a hoarse cry of horror at the sight of this circular pink object erupting from the vicinity of Julian's loins and sat heavily down on the floor. There was just time for the commander to murmur 'Oh dear' before he gave tongue again. This time it was a scream.

'What's wrong with him?' asked Bill, looking dispassionately down at the air marshal.

'He's just sat down on all the glass,' replied the commander.

'Shit!' said Julian and suddenly became the hotelier once more, kneeling down beside the stricken warrior. 'Are you all right, Sir?'

The warrior waved his arms at him. 'Get them away from me!' Julian looked puzzled.

'I think he means the pom-poms,' said Bill.

'I'm so sorry, Sir,' said Julian, gathering his pom-poms which had been dangling rudely above the air-marshal's face and stuffing them inside the cardigan. 'Are you all right?'

'Of course I'm not all right, you bloody fool. I've cut my arse to ribbons.'

'Turn over and let me have a look,' said Julian solicitously.

'If you think I'm presenting my posterior like a blasted baboon to someone like you, you're mistaken. Call a doctor, immediately.'

'I could call the doctor, but he won't come out,' said Julian. 'He never does when it's good gardening weather.'

'Call an ambulance, then.'

'It takes forty-five minutes to come.'

'This is unbelievable! I got better attention when I was shot down over Berlin.'

'There's a vet here.'

'He'll do. Tell him to hurry up before I bleed to death.'

Julian beckoned Bernard out of the crowd. 'For Christ's sake, do the best you can,' he whispered. 'If this bastard doesn't sue, there'll be a few quid in it for you.'

'And if he does sue?'

'That's the ticket, lad,' said Bill approvingly. He took a benevolent interest in the progressive loss of innocence that Bernard had undergone since his arrival in the community.

'What do you mean?' asked Julian. The air-marshal began to groan.

'If he does sue, how much will you give me?'

'A tenner?'

'A tenner a stitch.'

'But how many stitches will he need?'

'I won't know until I turn him over.' He came forward and looked down at the air-marshal who was still lying flat on the ground. 'Good evening, Sir.'

'He always is a polite lad,' said Bill approvingly.

423

'Would you mind turning over so that I can look at your . . . er . . . wounds?'

'I'm not a bloody Indian fakir, you fool,' replied the injured man. 'If I turn over, I'll chop my front side to bits as well.'

'Oh, yes,' said Bernard. 'Julian, can we carry this gentleman to his room where I can examine him more easily?'

Patrick came out from behind the bar and, with the help of Bill and Ivor, the air-marshal was carefully lifted up and carried out into the lobby, his backside gently dripping blood on to the carpet as they went. Julian then firmly closed the bar door in the accusing faces of the other guests.

'I reckon this will set the hotel back ten years,' he said bitterly. 'Once word gets around about what has happened, all the old goats will go and stay somewhere else.' He walked round to the other side of the bar. 'I'm going to get drunk.'

'That's what I call a damn good idea,' said the commander. 'I'll have a barley wine.'

The locals and the Henrys joined forces in response to the obvious disapproval of the other hotel guests. The Henry party was originally for a dozen but there were now eight locals too, so Julian went through to the kitchen to order extra food and more place settings in the dining room. He then temporarily abdicated his position at the helm of the hotel to Patrick. Patrick had enough sense to delay the serving of the bachelor dinner until as many of the other guests as possible had cleared from the dining room. It worked in one way, but it also gave those in the bar considerable time to fill themselves with strong drink. By the time Patrick summoned them through, the locals, including Julian, had caught up with the Henrys, and one look at them as they entered the dining room drove out the few lingering diners faster than a fire alarm.

It was a good meal. The Henrys were in full cry, subjecting waiters and waitresses to a barrage of bread rolls whenever they entered the dining room. After a few tentative lobs, Kelvin, Bill and most of the other locals were bouncing their rolls off the kitchen door and the skulls of the staff with all the aplomb of heirs to an earldom.

The staff gave almost as good as they got. Julian's young

men from the Buggery may have found the hailstorm
intimidating, but the waitresses were stout-hearted country
girls who were only too delighted to return the missiles
launched by their Uncles Bill and Kelvin and Cousin Ivor.
Julian was a little twitchy about this. His bread rolls were
extremely high-class, which meant that they were as hard as
bricks. It was not injury to his employees that concerned him
but damage to the room. The dining room was the archi-
tectural high point of the hotel as half of it had been a
Victorian conservatory. Across the centre of the room was a
line of arches, beyond which both the roof and the walls were
glazed, so that diners could look out over the floodlit lawn
stretching down to the river.

It was nearly midnight before the meal ended. Julian was as
pissed as anyone else, although he retained sufficient control
to mark down in his little book stains on the carpet from

spilled wine and a broken French window which one Henry was forced to kick open on his way to relieve himself on the flowerbed.

Then the glass-smashing Henry suggested a midnight swim in the river. It was thought to be an excellent idea. The entire group piled into the hotel's minibus and weaved an erratic course to the pool about half a mile up from the hotel where most of the villagers washed the dust of the day's work from themselves on hot, lazy afternoons. Those over forty did not actually swim but sat on the bank in the moonlight with Julian, who had brought along a couple of bottles of whisky to keep the party well lubricated. The summer night was full of horrid shapes and shrieks and sights unholy, the chief of which was Kelvin who got a bit over-excited and removed his teeth so that he could go round biting the pimply naked buttocks of the Henrys without becoming too intimately involved.

We returned to the hotel along the deserted lanes. Locals knew that post-midnight driving was dangerous and, if sober oneself, it was politic to park by the verge and abandon one's own car if another set of headlights came into view, gleaming on the telephone wires. Percy had made his position clear a few weeks after he had come to the village and seen the amount of drinking that went on. He was willing to chase drunks if that was what the public wanted, but they would have to live with the consequence that most of them would be deprived of their licences within a few months. His advice to the minority who were sober after closing time was that they keep off the road. The van came to a juddering halt in front of the hotel and its passengers disembarked to stand around trying to remember whether they were supposed to be staying at the hotel or if they had homes to go to. There was a shriek from Julian.

'Look at my bloody lawn!'

We looked at his bloody lawn.

'What about it?' asked Kelvin, gazing rather blearily across it. The floodlights were still on, no doubt ticking up like a taxi meter inside Julian's little book.

'There's a bloody great furrow across it! No there isn't. Look! There are two bloody great furrows across it.'

'Oh yes, so there are. I wonder how that happened?' mused the commander.

Julian was virtually frothing at the mouth. The froth might have been worth collecting and bottling to be sold as blanched advocaat, for it must have been seventy per cent proof. 'It's obvious, isn't it? Some drunken bastard has driven across it. It's ruined.' He turned to his guests. 'I bet it was one of you lot.'

The Henrys clutched each other for support and formed a defensive circle like a wagon train under Indian attack in face of Julian's venom. 'It was all right when I went out for a piss before we went swimming,' said the pissing Henry. 'I remember thinking what a superb croquet lawn it would make.'

'That's quite true,' said Kelvin, nodding owlishly.

'You would have been too drunk to notice,' snapped Julian.

'I don't mean the furrows. I mean the croquet lawn.'

'Oh, I see.'

'It must have been done by someone when we were out,' said a Henry.

'Of course!' cried Julian. 'Let's find out who's come back late.'

'Or went out late,' added the Henry. There was one member of staff still up – one of the younger cooks, who was sitting disconsolately in the hall. His blue eyes lit up as he saw Julian burst through the door.

'Julian! I thought you were never coming back,' he said. 'I thought you must have been drowned.'

'Don't be silly, Simon.'

'I'm not being silly. You said we'd have some time together this evening. And look what's happened. It's two o'clock in the morning. You just don't care any more.'

Everyone else started to make tactfully loud conversation just outside the front door while Julian sorted out his domestic arrangements. About five minutes later he came out again. 'I can't understand it. According to Simon, nobody has been in or out since we left.'

'That's not so difficult to understand,' said the commander. 'I've been thinking about it and it's obvious, isn't it? It must have been the minibus we were in that messed up the lawn. We were all so drunk that nobody noticed.'

'That's it!' said Julian in a state of great excitement. 'It was us. Who was driving?'

'Well, I was on the way there—' began the commander.

'You bastard!' exclaimed Julian. 'I might have known it would be you.'

'But I can't have gone over the lawn because the van was parked halfway down the drive and the tyre tracks come right up here. It must have been done on the retun journey just now.'

'Oh, I see. Well, who drove on the way back?' asked Julian.

'I don't remember,' said the commander.

The guests and the locals were beginning to mill around in the same disjointed, headless-chicken fashion which can be observed in the few Glaswegian pedestrians who are abroad on 1 January. Julian called them to order. Rage had burned up most of the alcohol in his bloodstream. 'Who was driving the minibus on the way back? Kelvin?'

'It wasn't me,' replied Kelvin hurriedly. 'I can remember sitting in the back, trying to get my teeth back in.'

'And I was lying on the floor,' said a Henry.

'And it wasn't me, because I was sitting in the passenger seat at the front,' said Ivor.

Julian spun on his heel towards him. 'Aha! If you were sitting in the passenger seat, you must have seen who was driving. Who was it?' Ivor shut his eyes in an effort to remember and Bill put out a supporting hand as he moved dangerously out of the perpendicular. He opened them again.

'I can't recall.'

'Of course you bloody can. You're just not trying,' said Julian in frustration. 'Think, man. Did you talk to him?'

Ivor shut his eyes again. 'I don't think I talked to him. Hang on a minute. Of course! He was singing!'

'Singing! What?' demanded Julian.

Ivor thought again and his face crumpled in disappointment. 'I don't know. I knew the tune, but I couldn't understand the words. They were foreign. It was all about psychologists. In German. Freud and Jung and something. It was that tune that the children always play on their recorders at the carol service.'

'Psychologists? Freud?' Julian looked baffled for a few seconds as he thought. Then his face cleared. 'Of course! *Freude, schöner Gotterfunken*,' he sang. 'Beethoven's Ninth!'

'That's it!' said Ivor.

'Right! Now we're getting somewhere. Who knows Beethoven's Ninth?' He received blank looks from everyone. 'Come on: *Freude, schöner Gotterfunken, Tochter aus Elysium*! Someone must know it.'

Kelvin broke the ensuing silence by clearing his throat.

'Yes, Kelvin?' said Julian.

'It occurs to me,' said Kelvin, 'that you are probably the only person who knows it.'

'Well, yes, I do know it. But so what?'

'Then it stands to reason that you were sitting beside Ivor and that it must have been you that was driving and it was you that ran over the lawn.'

'Oh, come off it,' said Julian, a bit uncertainly. 'I would have remembered.'

'And there's another thing,' continued Kelvin implacably, 'you've been holding the van's ignition keys in your hand for the last half-hour.'

It was game, set and match to Kelvin and everyone went to bed.

Julian reckoned later that, in spite of hitting the Henrys for well over £1000, he lost on the weekend. It was the air-marshal's fault. He did not sue, but probably cost Julian more through lost bookings than he would have succeeded in winning in damages. Julian even had to write off the Henrys' breakfast bill.

The morning after the night before, Julian had laid on the most expensive breakfast he could devise. It was to be his last opportunity of wresting any money from their capacious wallets. Kelvin and Ivor had failed to make it home the night before and they, as pale and delicate as the Henrys, had been rousted out of their temporary accommodation in the resident's lounge by the staff. There was a large circular table laid out in the glassed portion of the dining room on which Julian had laid out the whole works from kedgeree through champagne and kippers, kidneys, figs, porridge and all items in the hotel's deep freeze that may not have had the legs to stagger on for very much longer. There was a whole platter of tiny trout. The fact that those for whom it was intended were incapable of doing more than trickle into the room to sip delicately at glasses of grapefruit juice, nurse their blinding hangovers and dread the responsibilities, the noise and the need for polite conversation that lay before them as ushers at the wedding, was immaterial to him in his search for profit. They came in, one by one, to sit in silence trying to ignore the thunder of the bluebottles, trapped under the glass of the dining-room roof.

The air-marshal had been nursing his injuries in his bedroom since his accident the night before. Bernard had sprayed his bottom with purple veterinary Terramycin from an aerosol can, bandaged it and advised him to stay in bed for a day or two to give it a chance to heal. To keep him away from the telephone and his solicitor, Julian had sent a couple of bottles of gin up to his bedroom and the air-marshal had spent a sleepless night finishing them to ensure that he could demand some more in the morning.

What goes in must come out, and the air-marshal no longer had the capacity of bladder that he had enjoyed in his youth. Because of this, he had developed the custom of carrying his own chamber pot with him wherever he went. This saved him from the need to tramp the corridors of strange houses and hotels in search of a bathroom during the still watches of the night. His habit was to empty the utensil the following morning.

So far, so good. But the air-marshal had cut his bum and had drunk the best part of two bottles of gin, so he did not feel like walking all the way to the bathroom when it came to pass that his pot was due to be emptied. Circumstances were building up with the remorseless precision of a Shakespearean tragedy.

In the dining room, life was beginning to stir. The room had filled up with the other guests, silent save for the clicking of false teeth as they chomped their way through bacon and eggs and the rustle as they turned the pages of *The Times* and the *Daily Telegraph*. Even the Henrys were beginning to realize that it was possible to function, provided that they did not move their heads too quickly, and started to pick over the trout and nibble tentatively at the kidneys. It was Kelvin who provided the catalyst for their revival. He was not sure whether he would be asked to pay for his breakfast or if Julian would slap it all on the Henrys' bill. He did know, however, that he would not be asked for more than his tithe. No hangover could prevent him from eating, given his awareness that the food might be free, or at least reduced in cost the more he ate. The sight of him sturdily ploughing through as many different dishes as possible, secure in the knowledge that Prudence was doing the morning agricultural chores, inspired the others to action. Conversation even broke out.

'What time are you on duty?' asked Ivor.

'I think we're all meant to be meeting somewhere for lunch, but I'm not sure where,' replied the Henry to whom this remark was addressed. 'Are you coming?'

'He is, but I'm not,' replied Kelvin. 'They didn't invite me.'

'Oh, what a shame!' said the Henry. He really did seem rather sorry, which showed how little he knew Kelvin.

'A wedding like that is not for the likes of me,' said Kelvin, helping himself to a kipper and putting a poached egg on top of it. There was a silver bowl full of roses in the centre of the table and Kelvin looked as if he might start on that, once he'd cleared the rest of the table. The other Henrys were beginning to realize the danger and were taking kedgeree and bacon while there was still some left.

'Oh, you really must come. It'll be such fun and I'm sure nobody will mind. Nobody would notice you in the crush at the reception, anyway.'

Kelvin seemed mildly interested in the idea so Ivor

hurriedly broke in. 'I think Kelvin would be noticed. It would be awfully rude to go without an invitation, and anyway Kelvin hasn't got any clothes.'

'I've got the suit that I wore to the Loosemire wedding last year,' said Kelvin indignantly.

'You need a morning coat,' said Ivor. 'A tail coat.'

'What does a tail coat look like?' asked Kelvin.

Most of the Henrys had already put on their striped trousers. One had on his waistcoat and jacket too and he put down his coffee cup and stood up to rotate for Kelvin's benefit.

The air-marshal was a traditionalist. He did not like waste and the precious nitrogen in his pot was far better spread on the flowerbed beneath his window, he felt, than poured away down the sewers. He did not believe in investing in a modern chamber pot, even if such things existed; he preferred a pretty antique one with flowers all over it. A Victorian pot might inculcate the Victorian virtues that made the Empire. But the pot was in much the same condition as the Empire and the air-marshal had never really bothered to look out of his window to admire the view. Up in his room, the air-marshal had crawled over to the window and hung out his pot. He rotated it so that its contents would void themselves into the flowerbed beneath. As his wrist started to turn, incalculable forces were unleashed upon the join between the handle and the main body of the utensil and they parted. It was not the fault of the century-dead potter, but of the quality of the glue that the air-marshal had used a couple of years previously to join the two together.

The defenestration of the pot as well as the contents was accidental, but the air-marshal's lack of reconnaissance beforehand was criminally negligent. The combination of booze and bottom must have clouded his judgement. The flowerbed was not there at all. Instead, the pot met the glass roof of the dining room and plunged through in a blizzard of splinters, losing scarcely any of its momentum. It retained its physical integrity until it struck the silver rose bowl in the midst of the pre-nuptial breakfast, whereupon it exploded. The roses leapt out of the bowl to escape, falling amid the kippers and kidneys, but they were overwhelmed by a shower of flowery fragments of pottery and a great, golden sunburst of processed gin which spread outward, dissipating in quantity and in speed of progress to break feebly against the extremities of the room. Barely a breakfaster escaped from at least part of the fall-out, while the wedding guests endured its full force.

The gerontocrats reacted first. With hoots and bellows of rage and dismay, they rose from their tables and vacated the dining room. Reaction was slower from the wedding party. The Henry who had been standing up had had his back to the table at the moment of impact and was not fully aware of the nature of the disaster. He turned and sat down as the first of the Henrys picked up his napkin, delicately re-folded it inside out and began to mop his face.

Kelvin expressed the mood of the moment. With urine

dripping from his chin, he surveyed the devastated table. 'Thank God there was a cover on the kedgeree. That'll keep us going until they bring some more food.'

Kelvin made the wedding. Julian unearthed a trunk of ancient tail coats and trousers in the attic of the hotel which had been part of the uniform of the hotel staff fifty years earlier and these were handed out to the wedding guests whose own garments had blotted up most of the explosion. There was one set that fitted Kelvin and he was smuggled into the church by the ushers. He even achieved fame. Three months later the festivities featured in the society section of one of the glossies. There was a picture of a group of guests, taken after the service beneath the Virginia-creeper-clad clock tower of the church as the bells rang out in celebration. Princess Peter Grimescu and the Hon. Michael Berkeley-Howard were in animated conversation with each other, while a third figure leered at the photographer over the princess's shoulder. Somebody had tried to touch up his teeth and airbrush out some of his spiky grey hair, but it was not necessary to read the caption to identify him. Mr Kelvin Morchard went out and bought eighty copies of the magazine.